PRA[illegible]

"[illegible] of history in Jefferson Bass's impressive new novel. . . . In addition to being a riveting mystery with an intricately emotional conclusion, *Bones of Betrayal* bears witness to the past with great respect for the long shadow it casts."

Washington Post on *Bones of Betrayal*

"This novel shines with its sophisticated and subtle humor, and the decency of its characters. . . . Jefferson Bass is my new favorite crime writer."

Nancy Sapir on *Flesh and Bone*

"The story is razor sharp . . . with a nice mixture of mystery and horror. Fans of forensic fiction will want to add this author to their list of favorites."

Booklist on *The Devil's Bones*

"The Sherlock Holmes for bones has arrived. . . . A priv[illegible] world of a grou[illegible]

Katherine Ramsland, a[illegible] *of C.S.I.* [illegible]

"Religion and science collide, with results both thought-provoking and eminently plausible as the book races toward its unexpected (and highly original!) resolution."

BookPage on *The Inquisitor's Key*

"Entertaining . . . fascinating forensics. . . . Readers . . . will take to Dr. Bill, a hero with a big heart who isn't afraid to tackle complicated issues."

Publishers Weekly on *Flesh and Bone*

"This series . . . just keeps getting better. [*Bones of Betrayal*] features both the most compelling story and the best portrayal yet of Brockton, who has completed the transition from fictional representation of coauthor Bass to fully realized protagonist."

Booklist on *Bones of Betrayal*

"*Bones of Betrayal* has more than its share of twists, turns, and red herrings. . . . Wartime Oak Ridge proves nearly as atmospheric a crime scene as Sam Spade's San Francisco or Philip Marlowe's L.A."

Wilmington Star News on *Bones of Betrayal*

"A superb mystery novel—well-plotted, filled with memorable characters, based on accurate forensic science and written with more flair and literary sensibility than anything by John Grisham. The novel, in fact, is in Cornwell's league, high praise indeed."

Houston Chronicle on *Carved in Bone*

Books by Jefferson Bass

Fiction

Cut to the Bone
The Inquisitor's Key
The Bone Yard
The Bone Thief
Bones of Betrayal
The Devil's Bones
Flesh and Bone
Carved in Bone

Nonfiction

Beyond the Body Farm
Death's Acre

JEFFERSON BASS

CUT TO THE BONE

A BODY FARM NOVEL

HARPER

An Imprint of HarperCollins*Publishers*

HARPER

An Imprint of Harper Collins*Publishers*
195 Broadway
New York, New York 10007

ISBN 978-0-06-226231-8

First Harper premium printing: July 2014
First William Morrow hardcover printing: October 2013

Printed in the United States of America

Visit Harper paperbacks on the World Wide Web at
www.harpercollins.com

10 9 8 7 6 5 4 3 2 1

**To our loyal and encouraging readers,
who've made these last ten years—and
these first ten books—such a pleasure**

And this is the forbidden truth, the unspeakable taboo—that evil is not always repellent but frequently attractive; that it has the power to make of us not simply victims, as nature and accident do, but active accomplices.

—Joyce Carol Oates

PROLOGUE

SOME WOUNDS HEAL QUICKLY, the scars vanishing, or at least fading to thin white lines over the years. Some assaults are too grave, though; some things can never be set right, never be made whole or healthy again, no matter how many seasons pass.

In this regard, wounded mountains are like wounded beings. Cut them deeply—slice off their tops or carve open their flanks—and the disfigurement is beyond healing.

So it was with Frozen Head Mountain, in the foothills of the Cumberland Mountains of East Tennessee. In the early 1960s, Frozen Head's northern slope—thickly forested with hardwoods and hemlocks—was blasted and bulldozed away by wildcat strip miners to expose a thick vein of soft, sulfurous coal. Geologists called it the Big Mary vein, and for three years, Big Mary was illegally carved up, carted away, and fed into the insatiable maw of Bull Run Steam Plant, forty mountainous miles south. Then Big Mary's vein ran dry, and the miners and their machines—their dredges and draglines and stubby, hulking haul trucks—departed as abruptly as they'd appeared.

They left behind a mutilated mountainside, naked and exposed, its rocky bones battered by the sun and the rain, the heat and the cold. After every rain, a witch's brew of acids and heavy metals seeped from the ravaged slope, blighting the soil and streams in its path.

And yet; and yet. Nature is persistent and insistent. Years after the wildcatters moved on, kudzu vines began slithering into the shale, latching onto bits of windblown soil and leaves. Scrubby trees—black locust and Virginia pine—slowly followed, clawing tenuous toeholds in the rubble. A stunted sham of a forest returned, one instinctively shunned by birds and deer and even humans of right spirit.

And so it was the perfect place to conceal a body.

Like the mountain, the corpse was partially reclaimed by the persistence and insistence of Nature. A year passed, or perhaps two or three or five. One spring afternoon, a seedpod on a nearby black locust tree split open, and half a dozen dark, papery seeds wafted away on a warm mountain breeze. Five of the six seeds drifted and sifted into deep crevices in the shale. The sixth spun and swirled and settled into a neat oval recess: the vacant eye orbit of a now-bare skull. By summer the seed had germinated, sending pale tendrils of root threading down through fissures in bone and rock. One day a female paper wasp—a queen with no court yet—lighted on the skull, tiptoed inside, and began to build her small papery palace. And so was formed an odd ecosystem, an improbable peaceable kingdom: wasp colony, flowering tree, crumbling corpse.

The world contains a multitude of postmortem microcosms. Many remain forever undiscovered. But all leave some mark, some indelible stain, upon the world; upon the collective soul of mankind.

Some—a handful—give rise to reclamation or redemption.

PART 1

In the Beginning

And the earth was without form, and void; and darkness was upon the face of the deep.

—Genesis 1:2

Now the serpent was more subtle than any beast of the field which the Lord God had made.

—Genesis 3:1

SEPTEMBER 1992

CHAPTER 1

Brockton

TUGGING THE BATTERED STEEL door of the office tight against the frame—the only way to align the lock—I gave the key a quick, wiggling twist. Just as the dead bolt thunked into place, the phone on the other side of the door began to ring. Shaking my head, I removed the key and turned toward the stairwell. "It's Labor Day," I called over my shoulder, as if the caller could hear me. "It's a holiday. I'm not here."

But the phone nagged me, scolding and contradicting me, as if to say, *Oh, but you are.* I wavered, turning back toward the door, the key still in my hand. Just as I was about to give in, the phone fell silent. "Thank you," I said and turned away again. Before I had time to take even one step, the phone resumed ringing. Somebody else was laboring on Labor Day, and whoever it was, they were damned determined to reach me.

"All right, all *right,*" I muttered, hurrying to unlock the bolt and fling open the door. "Hold your horses." Leaning across the mounds of mail, memos, and other bureaucratic detritus that had accumulated over the course of the summer, I snatched up the receiver. "Anthropology Department," I snapped. The phone cord snagged a stack of envelopes, setting off an avalanche, which I tried—and failed—to stop. I'd been without a secretary since May; a new one was scheduled to start soon, but meanwhile, I wasn't just the department's chairman; I was also its receptionist, mail sorter, and answering service, and I was lousy at all of those tasks. The envelopes hit the floor and fanned out beneath the desk. "Crap," I muttered, then, "Sorry. Hello? Anthropology Department."

"Good mornin', sir," drawled a country-boy voice that sounded familiar. "This is Sheriff Jim Cotterell, up in Morgan County." The voice *was* familiar; I'd worked with Cotterell on a murder case two years before, a few months after moving to Knoxville and the University of Tennessee. "I'm trying to reach Dr. Brockton."

"You've got him," I said, my annoyance evaporating. "How are you, Sheriff?"

"Oh, hey there, Doc. I'm hangin' in; hangin' in. Didn't know this was your direct line."

"We've got the phone system programmed," I deadpanned. "It puts VIP callers straight through to the boss. What can I do for you, Sheriff?"

"We got another live one for you, Doc. I mean, another dead one." He chuckled at the joke, one I'd heard a hundred times in a decade of forensic fieldwork. "Some fella was up on Frozen Head Mountain yesterday, fossil hunting—that's what he says, leastwise—and he found some bones at a ol' strip mine up there."

I felt a familiar surge of adrenaline—it happened every time a new forensic case came in—and I was glad I'd turned back to answer the phone. "Are the bones still where he found them?"

"Still there. I reckon he knew better'n to mess with 'em—that, or he didn't want to stink up his jeep. And you've got me and my deputies trained to leave things alone till you show up and do your thing."

"I wish my students paid me as much mind, Sheriff. Have you seen the bones? You sure they're human?"

"I ain't seen 'em myself. They're kindly hard to get to. But my chief deputy seen 'em yesterday evening. Him and Meffert—you remember Meffert? TBI agent?—both says it's human. Small, maybe a woman or a kid, but human for sure."

"Meffert? You mean Bubba Hardknot?" Just saying the man's name—his two names, rather—made me smile. The Tennessee Bureau of Investigation agent assigned to Morgan County had a mouthful of a name—Wellington Harrison Meffert II—that made him sound like a member of Parliament. His nickname, on the other hand—"Bubba Hardknot"—sounded like something from a hillbilly comic strip. The names spanned a wide spectrum, and Meffert himself seemed to, also: I'd found him to be intelligent and quick-witted, but affable and respectful among good old boys like Sheriff Cotterell. "Bubba's a good man," I said. "If he says it's human, I reckon it is."

"Me and Bubba, we figured there weren't no point calling you out last night," Cotterell drawled on. "Tough to find your way up that mountain in the damn daylight, let alone pitch dark. Besides, whoever it is, they ain't any deader today'n what they was last night."

"Good point, Sheriff." I smiled, tucking away his observation for my own possible future use. "Couldn't've said it better myself." I checked my watch. "It's eight fifteen now. How's about we—my assistant and I—meet you at the courthouse around nine forty-five?"

"Bubba and me'll be right here waitin', Doc. 'Preciate you."

TYLER WAINWRIGHT, MY graduate assistant, was deep in thought—figuratively and subterraneanly deep—and didn't even glance up when I burst through the basement door and into the bone lab.

Most of the Anthropology Department's quarters—our classrooms, faculty offices, and graduate-student cubbyholes—were strung along one side of a long, curving hallway, which ran beneath the grandstands of Neyland Stadium, the University of Tennessee's massive temple to Southeastern Conference football. The osteology laboratory lay two flights below, deep beneath the stadium's lowest stands. The department's running joke was that if Anthropology was housed in the stadium's bowels, the bone lab was in the descending colon. The lab's left side—where a row of windows was tucked just above a retaining wall, offering a scenic view of steel girders and concrete footers—was occupied by rows of gray, government-surplus metal tables, their tops cluttered with trays of bones. A dozen gooseneck magnifying lamps peered down at the bones, their saucer-sized lenses haloed by fluorescent tubes. The lab's cavelike right side was crammed with shelving units—row upon row of racks marching back into the sloping darkness, laden with thousands of cardboard boxes, containing nearly a million bones. The skeletons were those of Arikara Indians who had lived and died two centuries before; my students and I had rescued them from rising river reservoirs in the Great Plains. Now they resided here in this makeshift mausoleum, a postmortem Indian reservation beneath America's third-largest football stadium.

Tyler laid down the bone he'd been scrutinizing and picked up another, still not glancing up as the steel door slammed shut behind me. "Hey, Dr. B," he said as the reverberations died away. "Let me guess. We've got a case."

"How'd you know?" I asked.

"*A*," he said, "it's a holiday, which means nobody's here but me and you and a bunch of dead Indians. *B*, any time the door bangs open hard enough to make the stadium shake, it's because you're really pumped. *C*, you only get really pumped when UT scores a touchdown or somebody calls with a case. And *D*, there's no game today. *Ergo*, you're about to haul me out to a death scene."

"Impressive powers of deduction," I said. "I *knew* there was a reason I made you my graduate assistant."

"Really? You picked me for my powers of deduction?" He pushed back from the lab table, revealing a shallow tray containing dozens of pubic bones, each numbered in indelible black ink. "I thought you picked me because I work like a dog for next to nothing."

"See?" I said. "You just hit the deductive nail on the noggin again." I studied his face. "You don't sound all that excited. Something wrong?"

"Gee, let's see," he said. "My girlfriend's just moved four hundred miles away, to Memphis and to med school; I've blown off two Labor Day cookouts so I can finally make some progress on my thesis research; and now we're headed off to God knows where, to spend the day soaking up the sun and the stench, so I can spend tonight and tomorrow sweating over the steam kettle and scrubbing bones. What could possibly be wrong?"

"How long's Roxanne been gone?"

"A week," he said.

"And how long does medical school last?"

"Four years. Not counting internship and residency."

"Oh boy," I said. "I can tell you're gonna be a joy to be around."

THE BIG CLOCK atop the Morgan County Courthouse read 9:05 when Tyler and I arrived in Wartburg and parked. "*Damn*, we made good time," I marveled. "Forty minutes? Usually takes an hour to get here from Knoxville."

Tyler glanced at his watch. "Sorry to burst your bubble, but it's actually nine thirty-seven. I'm guessing that's one of those clocks that's right twice a day."

"Come to think of it," I recalled, "seems like it was nine oh five two years ago, too, when I was here on another case."

The stuck clock seemed right at home atop the Morgan County Courthouse, a square, two-story brick structure built back in 1904, back when Wartburg still hoped for a prosperous future. The building's boxy lines were broken by four pyramid-topped towers—one at each corner—and by a graceful white belfry and cupola rising from the building's center. Each side of the cupola—north, south, east, and west—proudly displayed a six-foot dial where time stood still. I suspected that it wasn't just eternally 9:05 in Wartburg; I suspected that it was also, in many respects, still 1904 here. Sheriff James Cotterell, who stood leaning against the fender of the Ford Bronco parked behind the courthouse, would certainly have looked at home perched on a buckboard wagon, or marching in a Civil War regiment. Special Agent Meffert, on the other hand—one foot propped on the bumper—was a different matter. I could picture Meffert wearing a Civil War uniform, too, I realized, but Bubba's eyes somehow had a 1992 knowingness to them; a look that—Civil War uniform notwithstanding—would have branded Bubba as a modern-day reenactor, not a true time traveler.

I made the briefest and most perfunctory of introductions: "Sheriff Cotterell, Agent Meffert, this is my assistant, Tyler Wainwright"—and then Tyler and I followed the lawmen out of town and up a winding mountain highway, parking on the shoulder at a narrow turnoff. There, we transferred our field kit into the back of the sheriff's Bronco, a four-wheel-drive vehicle with enough ground clearance to pass unimpeded over a knee-high tree stump. The road to the strip mine was far too rough for my UT truck, Cotterell had assured me, and Meffert had agreed. Once we turned off the winding blacktop and into the pair of ruts leading up to the mine, I realized how right they'd been: I saw it with my jouncing eyes, and felt it in my rattling bones.

Cotterell and Meffert rode up front; Tyler and I sat in the back like prisoners, behind a wire-mesh screen, as the Bronco lurched up the mountain. "Last time I had a ride this rough," Tyler shouted over the whine of the transmission and the screech of clawing branches, "I was on the mechanical bull at Desperado's, three sheets to the wind. I hung on for twenty seconds, then went flying, ass over teakettle. Puked in midair—a comet with a tail of vomit."

"If you need to puke now, son," Cotterell hollered back, "give me a heads-up. You ain't got no window cranks nor door handles back there."

"I'm all right," Tyler assured him. "Only had two beers for breakfast today." He was probably joking, but given how morose he seemed over his girlfriend's move to Memphis, he might have been telling the truth.

Eventually the Bronco bucked to a stop beside a high, ragged wall of stone, and the four of us staggered out of the vehicle. The shattered surface beneath our feet might have been the surface of the moon, if not for the kudzu vines and scrubby trees. "Watch your step there, Doc," Cotterell warned over his shoulder as he and Meffert led us toward the looming wall. The warning was absurdly unnecessary—not because the footing was good, but because it was so spectacularly bad. The jagged shale debris left behind by the strip-mining ranged from brick-sized chunks to sofa-sized slabs.

"I'm glad y'all are leading the way," I told the backs of the lumbering lawmen.

"Be hard to find on your own," said the sheriff.

"True, but not what I meant," I replied. "I figure if anybody's going to get snakebit, it'll be the guy walking in front. Or maybe the second guy, if the snake's slow on the draw."

"Maybe," conceded Meffert. "Or maybe the two crazy fools sticking their hands down in the rocks, rooting for bones."

"Dang, Bubba," I said, wincing at the image he'd conjured. "*That'll* teach me to be a smart-ass."

"Man," muttered Tyler after a hundred slow yards. "Every step here is a broken ankle waiting to happen." The gear he was lugging—a big plastic bin containing two cameras, paper evidence bags, latex gloves, trowels and tweezers, clipboards and forms—couldn't have made it easy to see his footing or keep his balance. The trees were too sparse and scrubby to serve as props or handholds; about all they were good for was to obscure the footing and impede progress.

"Bubba," I huffed, "you came out with the guy that found the bones?"

"Yup," Meffert puffed. The TBI agent appeared to be carrying an extra twenty pounds or so around his middle.

"He said he was hunting fossils," I went on. "You believe him?"

"Seemed believable. Name's Ro-*chelle*. Some kind of engineer at the bomb factory in Oak Ridge. Environmental engineer. Maybe that's why he likes poking around old mines. Fossils plus acid runoff—a twofer for a guy like that, I guess. There's damn good fossils right around the bones. You'll see in just a minute." He paused to take a deeper breath and reach into a hip pocket. "Yeah, I believe him," he repeated, mopping his head and neck with a bandanna. "He came into the sheriff's office and then brought us all the way back up here. No reason to do that, except to help, far as I can see. Hell, that shot his Sunday right there."

"You never know," I said. "Sometimes a killer will actually initiate contact with the police. Insert himself in the investigation."

"Return to the scene," grunted the sheriff.

"Sometimes more than that, even," I said. "An FBI profiler I worked with a few years back told me about a California killer who spent a lot of time hanging out in a cop bar, making friends, talking about cases. Ed Kemper—'Big Ed'—was the guy's name. When Big Ed finally confessed to a string of murders and dismemberments, his cop buddies thought he was joking."

Meffert shrugged. "This Rochelle guy seemed okay," he said. "He's got a high-level security clearance, for whatever that's worth. But like you say, you never know."

Fifty yards ahead, I saw yellow-and-black crime-scene tape draped around an oval of scrubby foliage and rugged shale. "Did somebody actually stay out here overnight to secure the scene?" I asked.

Cotterell made a guttural, grunting sound, which I gradually realized was a laugh. "*Secure* the *scene?* Secure it from *who*, Doc?"

MEFFERT WAS RIGHT about the fossils. Just outside the uneven perimeter of crime-scene tape lay a flagstone-sized slab of black shale, imprinted with a lacelike tracery of ancient leaves. Beside it, angling through the rubble, was a stone rod the length of a baseball bat. Its shape and symmetry made it stand out against the random raggedness of the other rocks, and I stooped for a closer look. Diamond-shaped dimples, thousands of them, dotted the entire surface of the shaft. "I'll be damned," I said to Tyler. "Look at that. A lepidodendron."

"A what?" Tyler set down the bin and squatted beside me. "Butterfly fossil?"

I nudged it with my toe, and it shifted slightly. "Close, but no cigar. Your Latin's rusty."

He snorted. "My Latin's nonexistent."

"Butterflies are Lepidoptera—'scaly wings.' This is a lepidodendron—'scaly tree'—a stalk from a giant tree fern. Ferns a hundred feet tall. Carboniferous period. That plant is three hundred million years old if it's a day."

Tyler grasped the exposed end of the fossil and gently tugged and twisted, extricating it in a succession of rasping clinks. He sighted along its length, studying the intricate geometry of the diamond-shaped pattern. "You sure this is a scaly stem? Not a scaly snake?"

"Those scales are leaf scars," I said. "Also called leaf cushions. But they do look like reptile scales, for sure. Actually, circus sideshows used to exhibit these as fossilized snakes. You're a born huckster, Tyler." I stood up, scanning the ground ahead and catching a telltale flash of grayish white: weathered bone. "But enough with the paleo lesson. We've got work to do. Let's start with pictures." Tyler laid the fossil aside and opened the equipment bin.

A few years before—when I'd first started working with the police on murder cases—a detective at the Kansas Bureau of Investigation had taught me a crucial forensic lesson: You can never have too many crime-scene photos, because working a crime scene requires dismantling it; *destroying* it. The KBI agent's approach to crime-scene photography sounded like something straight from Bonnie and Clyde's bank-robbery playbook: "Shoot your way in, and shoot your way out"—start with wide shots, then get closer and closer, eventually reversing the process as you're finishing up and leaving the scene. Tyler had been quick to master the technique, and even before we stepped across the tape at the strip mine, he had the camera up and the shutter clicking. It wasn't unusual for Tyler or me—sometimes both of us—to come home with a hundred 35-millimeter slides from a death scene, ranging from curbside shots of a house to frame-filling close-ups of a .45-caliber exit wound.

As Tyler shot his way in, so did I, though I was shooting with my eyes and my brain rather than a camera. The pelvis: *female*, I could tell at a glance; *subadult; probably adolescent*. The size: *small—five feet, plus or minus.* As I zoomed in on the skull, I reached out to pluck a seedling that was growing beside it and obscuring my view. As I tugged, though, the skull shifted—bone grating against rock—and I froze. "I'll be damned," I said, for the second time in minutes. The seedling, I realized, wasn't growing *beside* the skull; it was growing *from* the skull—from the left eye orbit, in fact—something I'd never seen before. Wriggling my fingers gently beneath the skull, I cradled it, then lifted and twisted, tugging tendrils of root from the rocky crevices below. The seedling was a foot tall, the fronds of tiny oval leaves reminding me of a fern. As I held it up, with Tyler snapping photographs and the sheriff and TBI agent looking on, I felt as if I were displaying a bizarrely potted houseplant. "Bubba," I said, nodding toward the bin, "would you mind opening one of those evidence bags for me?" Meffert scrambled to comply, unfolding the paper bag and setting it on the most level patch of rubble he could find.

Leaning down, I set the skull inside the bag.

"You gonna just leave that tree in it?" asked Meffert.

"For now," I said, bending the seedling so I could tuck it completely into the bag. "When we get back to UT, I'll take it over to a botanist—a guy I know in the Forestry Department—and get him to slice it open, count the growth rings. However many rings he finds, we'll know she's been here at least that many years."

"Huh," Meffert grunted, nodding. Suddenly he added, "*Watch* it!"

Just as he spoke, I felt a sharp pain on my wrist. I

looked down in time to see a wasp pumping the last of its venom into the narrow band of skin between the top of my glove and the bottom of my sleeve. "Dam*na*tion," I muttered, flattening the wasp with a hard slap. "Where the hell did *that* come from?"

"Yonder comes another one," Meffert said, "right out of the evidence bag." Sure enough, at that moment a second wasp emerged from the open bag and made a beeline for my wrist, drawn by the "danger" pheromones the first one had given off. Meffert's hand darted downward, and by the time I realized what he was doing, he had caught and crushed the wasp in midair, barehanded. "Sumbitches must be nesting in that skull," he said. I was dubious, but not for long; two more wasps emerged from the bag, both of them deftly dispatched by Meffert. We watched and waited, but the attack seemed to be over.

"You're quick, Bubba," I said, rubbing my wrist. "You that fast on the draw with a gun?"

He smiled. "Nobody's ever give me a reason to find out."

"Well, watch my back, if you don't mind."

I resumed my inspection of the postcranial skeleton, scanning the bones from neck to feet. "Y'all were right about the size," I said. "Just guessing, I'd say right around five feet. And female," I added, bending low over the flare of the hip bones. "And young."

"How young?" asked Cotterell.

I hedged. "Be easier to tell once we get the bones back to the lab and finish cleaning 'em up. But I'm guessing teenager."

"Any chance this is just some old Indian skeleton?" the sheriff asked hopefully. "Make our job a hell of a lot easier if she was."

"Sorry, Sheriff," I said. "She's definitely modern."

Meffert chuckled. "Isn't that what you said about that dead guy over near Nashville a couple years ago? The one turned out to be a Civil War soldier?"

"Well, she's lying on top of all this shale," I pointed out. "If she's not modern, this must be the world's oldest strip mine." I said it with a smile, but the smile was forced, and it was contradicted by the deep crimson my face had turned at the reminder of the Civil War soldier.

"Don't take it so hard, Doc," Meffert added. "You only missed it by a hunnerd-something years."

"Too bad that soldier didn't have a tree growing outta *his* head," the sheriff added. "Big ol' pecan tree, with a historical marker on it? You'da got it right for sure."

Meffert grinned. So did I, my teeth clenched behind drawn lips.

WE RODE IN silence down the winding mountain blacktop toward Wartburg. Tyler was absorbed in the fossil he'd brought back, his fingers tracing the intricate diamond patterning as if he were blind, examining it by touch alone.

For my part, I was brooding about the parting shots by the TBI agent and the sheriff. They'd been joking, good-naturedly, no doubt, but the conversation had stung, even worse than the wasp, and the sting took me back, in my mind, to the event they were dredging up. Just after my move to Knoxville, I'd been called to a rural county in Middle Tennessee, where a decomposing body had been found in a shallow grave behind a house. The remains were in fairly good shape, as rotting bodies go—pink tissue still clung to the bones—and I'd estimated that the man had died about a year before. In fact, we later learned, the dead man was Col. William Shy, a Civil War soldier killed in the Battle of Nashville in 1864.

In hindsight, there were logical reasons I'd missed the time-since-death mark so widely. Colonel Shy had been embalmed, and until modern-day grave robbers had looted the grave—looking for relics—the body had been sealed in an airtight cast-iron coffin, which had kept bugs and bacteria at bay. But those explanations sounded more like excuses than I liked. They also provided precious little comfort in court, I'd learned, again and again: Hostile defense attorneys in contemporary criminal cases took great delight in bringing up Colonel Shy, rubbing my nose in my blunder as a way of undermining my testimony against their clients.

Colonel Shy wasn't the only case where I'd been derailed by difficulty in determining time since death. Another murder case—a case I'd consulted on shortly before my move to Knoxville—still haunted me. A suspect in the case had been seen with the victim two weeks before the body had been found—the last known sighting of the victim—and the investigator and prosecutor pressed me hard: Could I testify, with certainty, that the murder had occurred then? "No," I'd been forced to admit, "not with any scientific confidence." As a result, the suspect had gone free.

Hoping to fill the gaps in my knowledge—determined to avoid such frustrations and humiliations in the future—I had combed through stacks of scientific journals, seeking data on decomposition. But apart from a few musty articles about insect carcasses—dead bugs found in bodies exhumed from old cemeteries—I'd found virtually nothing. Nothing recent, at any rate, though I had come across a fascinating handbook written by a death investigator in China centuries before, in 1247 A.D.—a research gap of more than seven centuries. The good news was, I wasn't the only forensic anthropologist who was flying by the seat of his pants when estimating time since death. The bad news was, *every* forensic anthropologist was flying by the seat of his pants.

The *interesting* news, I realized now, as Tyler and I reached the base of the mountain, and the road's hairpin curves gave way to a long, flat straightaway, was that the field was wide open. Time since death—understanding the processes and the timing of postmortem decomposition—was fertile ground for research.

The sun was low in the sky, a quarter moon high overhead, when Tyler and I passed through Wartburg's town square on our way back to Knoxville. As I glanced up at the courthouse belfry, still pondering ways to unlock the secrets of time since death, I found myself surrounded by markers and measures of time: A frozen clock. A fossilized town. An ancient fern. The bones of a girl who would never reach adulthood.

A girl for whom time had stopped, sometime after wildcat miners had ravaged a mountainside; sometime before a papery seed had wafted from a tree, and a wasp queen had begun building her papery palace in the dark.

CHAPTER 2

Satterfield

SATTERFIELD OPENED THE DOOR and reached into the wire-mesh hutch. Grasping the soft, loose skin just behind the ears, he raised the animal slightly, then cupped a hand beneath the chest and lifted it out of the hutch. The rabbit was young and small—scarcely larger than the palm of Satterfield's hand—and its large, luminous eyes dominated its face, in the way of all baby mammals. The eyes flitted back and forth, and the animal trembled.

Satterfield crossed the room to a second enclosure, also made of wire mesh. This one was sturdier and larger—as big as a baby's playpen, though only half as high—and its floor was covered with sandy earth, flat rocks, and good-sized pieces of driftwood. The enclosure was split down the middle by a removable panel of wire mesh, inserted through a narrow slit in the top. Cupping the rabbit to his chest, Satterfield stooped to unlatch the door in the top, then set the animal inside. It sat, motionless except for the tremor. On the other side of the divider, the other side of the cage, Satterfield glimpsed a trace of movement, slow at first, then more rapid: a slender, bifurcated black ribbon of tongue sliding in and out of a mouth, flicking as it sampled the new scent in the air.

The snake—a fer-de-lance that Satterfield had paid a thousand dollars to have imported from Costa Rica—measured four feet long and three inches thick; its broad back was saddled, from neck to tail, by bold, black-and-tan diamonds. The head—a flat-topped triangle with thin black stripes running from the eyes to the back of the jaws—was nearly as broad as Satterfield's hand.

Satterfield had kept snakes for most of his life, but the fer-de-lance was different from others he'd had. It was fearless, irritable, and aggressive, and that was on its mellow days. Most snakes in the present situation would've sat tight, studying the rabbit for a while, maybe even waiting for it to lower its guard, perhaps even wander foolishly toward the jaws of death. The fer-de-lance, though, after a few more confirmatory flicks of the tongue, slid slowly but confidently toward the rabbit. The rabbit emitted a squeal and then leaped away, huddling in the corner of the cage. The snake slithered along the divider, its head reared, its tongue flicking through open squares in the wire mesh one by one as it drew closer.

Driven by some ancient, embedded survival instinct, the rabbit began lunging against the walls and roof of wire. After a few moments, Satterfield threaded a hand through the opening, managing to corner the creature and extract it from the cage.

He cradled it against his chest as it panted, its small heart fluttering as fast as a hummingbird's.

Once the rabbit had stopped quaking, he lowered it into the cage again, both hands gripping tightly as it began to squirm and struggle. The snake had not moved, and when Satterfield released the rabbit—this time setting it practically against the divider—the triangular head darted forward, striking the mesh with enough force to make the cage shudder. Again the rabbit began battering itself against the corner and top of the cage, as the snake's head, too, lashed against the screen with primitive force and ruthless frustration. After a few moments Satterfield retrieved the rabbit once more. He'd had a rat die swiftly of fright in just such circumstances on a prior occasion, and he did not want a repeat of that premature disappointment.

By the time Satterfield had performed the ritual half a dozen times—insertion and extraction, insertion and extraction—the rabbit's quaking was constant, even when it was cradled against his chest; any time Satterfield made the slightest movement toward the cage, the creature began to struggle. Satterfield experimented, extending the rabbit toward the cage and then pulling it away several times without actually putting it inside. The creature was now crazed with terror, all sense of safety having been systematically destroyed. Its breathing was ragged and shallow, and the flicker of the heartbeat felt weaker now, less regular against Satterfield's palm. The rabbit was clearly approaching exhaustion.

Satterfield, too, was reaching a turning point: He could feel the faint but familiar beginnings of boredom setting in. Leaning down again, he set the shivering rabbit in the cage, and this time he latched the door above it. Then, gripping the protruding handle of the divider screen, he slid the panel upward through the narrow slit, removing it from the cage and setting it aside. All the while, he kept his gaze fixed on the two animals.

The snake's head swayed slightly toward the rabbit, almost imperceptibly, as if it expected the wire screen to materialize out of thin air. When it did not—when the snake's reptilian brain sensed that no obstacles blocked the path to its prey—it drew its body into a muscular S, the raised head remaining motionless as the body drew up behind it. It held that serpentine shape for only a moment, then, in the blink of an eye, it straightened and shot forward, its jaws gaping and its fangs snapping down from the roof of the mouth.

Two seconds after the bite, the rabbit was convulsing; ten seconds later, the convulsions gave way to small twitches; another half minute and it lay motionless, its eyes already going glassy in death.

By the time the snake stretched its jaws around the rabbit's head and began choking down the dead animal—its girth as big as the snake's—Satterfield had already walked away. The feeding was utterly uninteresting to him, and even the death itself had been only mildly entertaining. No, it was the prelude to death—the surges and spikes of terror he'd learned to orchestrate: *that* was what he found addicting. Exciting. Arousing, even.

CHAPTER 3

Brockton

PEERING OUT THE GRIMY windows of my office on the second floor of Stadium Hall, gazing through the thicket of steel girders and concrete ramps, I glimpsed the emerald waters of the Tennessee River spooling past downtown Knoxville and the university. Most of the hundred-yard distance between the stadium and the river was covered in asphalt—parking lots and the four lanes of Neyland Drive—and the pavement shimmered in the late-summer afternoon, creating the illusion that the river itself might begin to boil at any moment. The Anthropology Annex, where I needed to go, was a small, freestanding building fifty sweltering yards away.

When I opened the door and stepped outside, exchanging the stadium's cool, dark corridors for the sun-soaked outdoors, I felt as if I'd entered a blast furnace. Behind me, bricks radiated the pent-up heat like an oven; ahead, the asphalt lay like a sea of lava, and as I swam across through the heat and humidity, my clothes grew wet with sweat, my shirt plastering itself to my back.

A half-dozen rusting air conditioners jutted from the corrugated metal walls of the Annex, their compressors chugging full blast—*full steam*, I caught myself thinking ironically as I tugged open the balky steel door and stepped inside. The air conditioners did manage to lower the humidity a few notches, but they hadn't made much headway against the heat, and none at all against the smell.

The Anthropology Department's main quarters—built by bricking in the wedge of space beneath Neyland Stadium's grandstands, decades before—weren't exactly prime real estate; far from it. But Stadium Hall was palatial compared with the Annex. In winter the Annex was an icebox, rattling in the wind; in summer, it was a solar oven, its metal panels creaking and popping in the heat. And no matter the season, it stank inside, for the Annex was where we did the dirty work of processing human remains: simmering and scrubbing; separating flesh from bone; removing life's lingering vestiges.

One corner of the processing room was taken up by an industrial-sized sink, which was flanked on one side by an immense steam-jacketed kettle—a cauldron big enough to simmer an entire skeleton—and on the other by a wide counter that ran the length of the wall. The counter was covered with blue surgical pads to absorb moisture from damp, freshly scrubbed bones, and when I entered, Tyler was laying out the last of the bones we'd brought back from the strip mine, neatly arranging them in anatomical order.

Normally I began my forensic examinations at the skull, but in this case—a case where the questions of age and sex seemed to converge, to entwine, in a pivotal way—I found my eyes drawn first to the pelvis, which confirmed what I'd thought in the field: female, beyond a doubt. The hip bones flared widely, giving them the distinctive shape that always reminded me of elephant ears; the sciatic notches—openings at the base of the sit bones where major nerves emerged from the lower spine—were broad, unlike the narrow notches of a male pelvis; and the pubic bone curved outward and down to create a concavity in her belly and birth canal, making room for babies that this particular female would never have.

But if her pelvis said "woman," her mouth whispered a different, sadder word to me: "child." If she had lived to be my age, the ripe old age of thirty-seven, her maxillary sutures—the seams in the roof of her mouth—would have begun smoothing out and filling in, eventually becoming nearly invisible. But the maxillary sutures in the skull I cradled upside down in my hand were rough and bumpy, the bones barely beginning to fuse. In fact, if I hadn't known from years of study that the bones were slowly joining, I might have concluded that something had struck the hard palate at its center, creating a cruciform pattern of cracks. But it was her life, not her palate, that had shattered.

Tyler studied my face as I studied the dead girl's skull. "How old you think she is?"

"Not old enough," I said. "Fourteen; fifteen, tops. But maybe only twelve or thirteen."

He frowned and shook his head—not in disagreement, but in dismay. "That's what I figured, too, but I was hoping you'd tell me I was wrong."

"Any skeletal trauma?"

"A couple healed fractures in the arms," he said. "One in the left humerus, the other in the right radius, about three inches above the wrist. And two ribs. But nothing perimortem. Nothing *I* could see, anyhow. Maybe you'll spot something I've missed."

I pored over every bone twice—with my eyes and with my fingertips—in search of a fresh, unhealed fracture, or the ragged nick of a knife blade, or a telltale smear of lead from a passing bullet—but there was nothing to be found. Finally, circling back to the skull once more, I shone a flashlight through the foramen magnum and peered inside the cranial vault, in case there was a fracture on the inner surface that might have ruptured one of the meningeal arteries, the arteries carrying blood to the brain. "I'm not seeing anything, either," I said. "Doesn't mean she wasn't killed. Just means that any injuries she had were soft-tissue trauma." I took a final look into the cranial vault. "Oh, hey, did you find a wasp nest in here?"

He reached up and plucked a small gray object from the narrow shelf above the counter, then dropped it into my palm. A dozen or so hollow, hexagonal cells made of dry, papery pulp, it weighed almost nothing. "It's a little crunched on the sides, from the forceps," he said. "Getting it out through the foramen magnum was like trying to pull a ship out of a bottle."

"Any more wasps on board?"

He shook his head. "Nah, I think ol' Bubba Ray Peckerwood done got 'em all."

"Careful," I cautioned. "If you slip up and call him Peckerwood to his face, Special Agent Meffert might just feel obliged to open up a can of whup-ass on you."

"Ha—let him try," said Tyler. "I'll lay some yoga on him. He'll never even know what hit him."

"What," I scoffed, "you're gonna meditate him into submission?" Tyler was a recent and enthusiastic convert to yoga, for reasons I didn't fully grasp. "Weren't you an athlete—a real athlete—once upon a time? Weight lifting or shot putting or some such? One of those manly sports dominated by hulking women from East Germany?"

"Hammer throw," he said. "The ultimate test of strength and coordination. But by the way, there *is* no East Germany. The wall came down three years ago, in '89, remember? 'Mr. Gorbachev, tear down this wall?' Ronald Reagan's finest moment. You're showing your age, Dr. B."

Summoning up my reediest old-man voice, I piped, "Back when I was a boy . . ."

"Yeah, yeah," he said. "Save it for the undergrads, Gramps."

Was he just kidding, or was there a slight edge in his voice? Worse, was there a kernel of truth in his jab? Was I fossilizing even before I turned forty?

Time was much on my mind these days. Time since death was foremost in my thoughts. But time *before* death—my time; my sense of urgency about creating a research program to fill the gaps in my knowledge—that, too, was tugging at the sleeve of my mind.

"HANG ON A second, Doc, I'm fixin' to put you on speakerphone," drawled Sheriff Cotterell. I had swum back across the sweltering sea of asphalt to the stadium just in time to catch the call. "Bubba Hardknot's a-settin' right here with me, and I know he'll want to hear whatever you got to say."

I heard a click, then a hollow, echoing sound, as if the phone had been lowered down a well. "Hey, Doc," Meffert's voice boomed, from deep in the depths. "Whatcha got for us?"

"Not much, I'm afraid," I admitted. "I'll send you both a written report in the next couple days, but here's the bottom line. No skeletal trauma, so the bones can't tell us how she died. All they can tell us is a little about who she was. White female; stature between five foot one and five foot three; age thirteen to fifteen. I estimated the age by looking at the pelvis, the teeth, the epiphyses of the long bones and clavicles, the—"

"Excuse me, Doc," Meffert interrupted, "the *what*-ih-sees?"

"Epiphyses," I repeated. "The ends of the bones. In subadults—children and adolescents—the ends of the long bones haven't yet fused to the shafts; they're connected by cartilage, at what's called the growth plates. That's how the arms and legs can grow so much when kids hit puberty. Toward the end of puberty, the epiphyses fuse, and the long bones don't get any longer; you don't get any taller. This girl's epiphyses weren't fully fused yet, so she hadn't quite finished growing. She had her second molars—her twelve-year molars—so she was probably at least that old. And her pelvic structure had started getting wider, so we know she'd entered puberty. But her hips were still getting wider, so she wasn't out of it yet."

"How can you tell *that*?" asked Cotterell.

"Good question, Sheriff. There's actually an epiphysis on the outer edge of each hip bone, too—it's called the iliac crest, and all through puberty, the iliac crest is connected to the ilium—the wide bone of the hip—by cartilage. It's another growth plate. Somewhere around age sixteen or eighteen, the iliac crest fuses. After that, the hips don't get any wider."

I heard a rumbling growl, which even over the speakerphone I recognized as Sheriff Cotterell's laugh. "Doc," he chuckled, "you ain't never seen my wife."

"Let me rephrase that," I said. "After that, the *bones* of the hips don't get any wider."

"What else you got?" said Meffert. "You hear back from your buddy in Forestry?"

"I did. That little black locust seedling was two years old. So she's been dead at least that long."

"And no *more'n* how long?" asked the sheriff.

"I don't know," I admitted. "Nothing in the bones to tell us. When did that wildcat mine shut down?"

"Twenty-two years ago," said Meffert. "In 1970."

"Then she died somewhere between two years ago and twenty-two years ago," I said.

"Twenty years? That's as close as we can nail it?"

The frustration in the sheriff's voice was crystal clear, even though he was forty miles away.

"I'm afraid so, Sheriff. I wish I had more for you, but I don't. We need better tools and techniques for determining time since death."

"Got *that* right," he said. I was glad he and Meffert weren't there to see my face redden once more.

CHAPTER 4

Satterfield

HE PICKED UP THE sheaf of pages and tamped their bottom edges on the kitchen table to align them, then turned the stack sideways and repeated the maneuver to even up the sides. Once the sheets were in perfect alignment, he inserted them into the three-hole punch and swung the lever down slowly. Closing his eyes to concentrate, he savored the slight variations in resistance as the steel posts punched through the five single-spaced pages, sheet by sheet by sheet.

A loose-leaf binder, already half filled, lay open on the table in front of Satterfield. Popping open the gleaming chrome rings, he threaded the freshly punched pages onto the stack, then clicked the rings shut and began rereading the text, twirling a pink Hi-Liter with the thumb, index finger, and middle finger of his left hand as he read. When he came to the description of the cut marks, he uncapped the marker and highlighted the passage: "The bones were severed with a curved tool of unknown type, the cutting edge having a curved shape approximated by the arc of a circle 3.5 inches in diameter."

A yellow legal pad and a mechanical pencil lay beside the binder. Setting down the marker, Satterfield picked up the pencil and drew a curved line on the pad, then—doubting the accuracy of the drawing—he pushed back from the table and went to one of the kitchen drawers. Rummaging in the drawer, he found a metal tape measure and extended the tape to 3.5 inches. Next he opened the cabinet containing glassware and held the tape across the mouths of various vessels until he found one—a coffee mug—whose diameter fit the description in the forensic report. Setting the mug on the legal pad, he ran the mechanical pencil one-third of the way around the base, then set the mug aside and inspected the neat arc he had traced. The shape puzzled him. Trying to imagine the head of an ax or a hatchet behind the curve he'd traced, he frowned; the arc was too steep to fit either of those tools. Besides, he suspected that both of those implements—certainly a hatchet—lacked the weight required to cut cleanly through bone in a single stroke. Rereading the highlighted passage, he concluded that he'd interpreted the text correctly and had drawn the curve accurately. That meant he simply needed to do more research. Tearing the perforated page from the yellow pad, he folded and tucked it into his pocket. Then, closing the binder, he returned it to its hiding place—the cold-air return of the ventilation ductwork—along with the box of stolen files, the mother lode of material he'd begun to build his plans around. Fitting the slotted grille neatly over the mouth of the duct, he flipped the latches to lock it into place.

He checked his watch. Home Depot would be closing in an hour, but Satterfield figured an hour was plenty of time. It wouldn't take him long to find just the right tool for the job, if Home Depot had it. Satterfield was a man who believed in having the right tool for the job, whether the job was cutting up a corpse or eviscerating an adversary.

FROWNING, HE HUNG the ax back on its pegs—the blade was too tall, the arc of the edge too shallow—and continued down the aisle. Next he picked up a maul, a wood-splitting tool whose wedge-shaped head was like a cross between an ax and a sledgehammer. The tool's heft was good, promising to strike with tremendous force, but again, the cutting edge lacked the curvature he was seeking. Satterfield took the sketch from his pocket and compared it with the edge of the maul. *Could I file it down?* he wondered. *Reshape it? Probably not*, he decided. *It'd take forever, even with a bench grinder.* He was mildly disappointed, but he was also intrigued; the puzzle—the quest—was challenging and invigorating, and solving it would be hugely satisfying: it would redouble his adversary's frustration, and underscore Satterfield's superior intellect.

"Help you, hon?" The question caught Satterfield by surprise. He looked over his shoulder at the questioner, a middle-aged woman in an orange Home Depot apron. Stoop-shouldered and beaten-down looking, she fell somewhere on the spectrum between mousy and hard-bitten. She clearly had never been pretty, and now her face was drooping and folding in on itself, as if she were already losing teeth. He caught a whiff of stale cigarette smoke coming from her, which explained her leathery skin and ashen hue. Satterfield found her not merely unappealing but actively repellent, not that he was shopping for anything but a tool here anyhow.

"No thanks. Just looking." He turned back toward the display, folding the sketch and replacing it in his pocket, then drifted back toward the axes.

"Gotcha some trees need cuttin'?" she persisted. *Christ*, he thought, *is she working on commission? Trying for Employee of the Month?* "We got chain saws, too, next aisle over."

"No trees," he said flatly. He glanced over his shoulder again—she was still there—and then he slowly turned to face her. "No *trees*," he repeated, cocking his head slightly, as if something about the word itself suddenly struck him. With a slight smile he added, "Just . . . *limbs*."

"*Oh*, you're *prunin'*. How thick are the limbs?"

"Not very," he said. His eyes drifted from her face to her shoulder and then down her arm, and he reached out and took hold of her left wrist, encircling it completely with his thumb and middle finger. Startled, she yanked her arm, but he had a firm grip. She opened her mouth to protest—maybe even to yell—but he bore down hard, pressing his thumb into the bony side of her wrist, and all she could do was gasp now, her eyes darting in panic, the way the rabbit's had. "Not thick at all," he said, smiling, raising her arm for a closer look. "Probably about like this. Maybe not quite so skinny." He turned her forearm this way and that, examining it from various angles, still bearing down on the bone. Finally he let off, though her wrist remained firmly in his grip. "What do you recommend?"

She cleared her throat. "Well, if you're just cutting branches," she said, her voice strained and trembling, "a lopper might be what you want." She pointed her free hand toward the wall at the end of the aisle. Satterfield noticed that the hand was quaking; he liked that. He raised his eyes to study her face—her eyes downcast, her posture cringing, like a chained dog about to be beaten—and then he glanced in the direction she was pointing. When he saw the assortment of long-handled pruning tools there, he released her and walked wordlessly to the wall. The woman scuttled away, rubbing her wrist, keeping a wary watch over her shoulder.

Satterfield took one of the tools from the wall and spread the handles, causing the metal jaws to gape; then, as he squeezed the handles, the jaws clamped shut. The cutting blade looked powerful and wickedly sharp, but the edge was all wrong—straight as a ruler—and he frowned and hung the tool back on the wall. He was turning to go when he noticed that there was more than one type of lopper. The one he'd inspected and rejected was an "anvil lopper," according to the shelf tag. Satterfield puzzled over the name for a moment, then noticed that the cutting blade—the straight, sharp-edged blade that wouldn't serve his purpose—closed against a lower jaw that was broad and flat, like a small steel chopping block. *Like a little anvil*, he realized. Hanging beside the anvil lopper, though, was another lopper—with a different name, a different design, and a different cutting action. This one was a "bypass lopper," and it cut scissor fashion—the edges of the two blades sliding past one another as the handles were squeezed together. The blades weren't straight like scissor blades, he noticed, with growing excitement. The tool's lower jaw was blunt edged and concave, to encircle and support a branch from beneath as the upper jaw—the sharp-edged, steeply curved, convex upper jaw—sliced into the limb from above.

The bypass lopper came in three sizes. The biggest had handles as long as Satterfield's arm; in addition, the jaws incorporated a cam to compound the handles' leverage, multiply their force. Satterfield took the tool down from its pegs and opened and closed the handles a few times. He nodded approvingly at the metallic friction he felt; at the precision and power with which the edges slid past one another.

A selection of rakes and hoes hung on the wall a few feet away, and Satterfield walked toward them, the lopper in one hand, swaying beside his right leg. The handles of the rakes were about an inch in diameter: about the thickness of his thumb, he noticed when he held up a hand to compare. Taking a step backward, he spread the handles of the lopper wide and fitted the jaws around the wooden shaft of a rake. He closed the handles slowly, feeling for resistance—just as he'd done earlier, with the hole punch—as the concave jaw hugged the wood and the sharp edge began to bite into the layers of grain. Once the edges were well seated, he gave a smooth squeeze. The rake's handle snapped with a dry pop, the amputated portion clattering to the floor as a razor-thin smile etched Satterfield's face.

He took a step to his right. The hoes had heavier-duty handles: hickory, by the look of it, and nearly twice as thick as the rake handles. Satterfield opened the handles wide and worked the jaws around one of the handles. The blade cut easily at first, but the going got tougher fast, the steel handles of the lopper bending under the strain as he bore down. Just as Satterfield feared the handles might buckle, the hoe's shaft snapped. The cut piece clattered on the concrete floor with a resonant, musical note, like the ring of a baseball bat colliding with a fastball. Satterfield bent and picked up the severed piece, studying the cross section closely. The cut was clean, but when he held the wood so that the ceiling lights raked across the end at a low angle, he could discern the cut marks, a myriad of ridges and valleys etched in the wood as the jaws had bitten through it. The marks were steeply curved, approximating "the arc of a circle 3.5 inches in diameter."

Pocketing the piece of wood, Satterfield headed for the front of the store to check out. On the way home, he'd stop at Kroger, whose meat department sold big beef bones for soup, or for dogs. More tests were needed, but so far he had a good feeling about the bypass lopper.

He found a checkout lane with no line, and slid the tool across the stainless-steel counter. The young man working the register said, "Is that it for you today?"

"Only thing I need," said Satterfield, but then

he added, "Whoa, wait, I take that back. One more thing." He backtracked two steps, to the end cap at the entrance to the checkout lane, and snagged a fat, striated roll of shrink-wrapped silver-gray tape. He stood it on edge and rolled it toward the scanner as if it were a thick slice from a bowling ball. With a broad smile and a worldly wink, Satterfield said, "A man can never have too much duct tape, can he, now?"

CHAPTER 5

Brockton

TYLER SHOOK SWEAT FROM his face, like a wet dog, spattering the ashen ankles of the corpse he and I were carrying toward the pig barn. "Hang on a second," he said.

I stopped. "You need to set him down, Mr. Yoga Super-Athlete?"

"Naw. I just need to get the sweat and sunscreen out of my eyes." He shrugged his shoulders and craned his head from side to side, rubbing his face on the sleeves of his T-shirt—like a dog pawing at itchy eyes. The movement made the sagging body sway from side to side, like a guy sleeping in a hammock, except there was no hammock. And the sleeping guy wasn't ever going to wake up. "Okay, that's better."

As we resumed walking, I heard a familiar buzzing. A small squadron of blowflies materialized and began circling the corpse.

"Amazing," said Tyler. "Those guys can smell death a mile away. Hell, you don't even have to kick the bucket—just swing your toe *toward* the bucket—and *bzzt,* they're all over you." He grimaced and sputtered, spitting out a fly that had strayed into his mouth. "*Hey,* you little bugger, get out of there. I'm not *quite* dead yet."

"Maybe your personal hygiene isn't what it ought to be," I said. I mostly meant it as a joke, but at the moment, Tyler was trailing a fairly pungent cloud of aroma. For that matter, I probably was, too. "Speaking of flies, though, we need to talk about your thesis project." I'd been poring through the Chinese forensic handbook the night before—it had been my bedtime reading, much to the dismay of Kathleen, to whom I'd read several graphic passages aloud—and during my sleep, something in the thirteenth-century book had clicked, connecting somehow with the wasp nest and tree seedling we'd found in the skull from the strip mine.

"What do flies have to do with my thesis? I'm making good progress, by the way. Honest. That's why I was in the bone lab on Labor Day—looking at a bunch more pubic bones."

"I know," I said. "I saw the tray of bones. But I've been thinking."

"Crap," he muttered. "I hate it when you think."

"What? Why?"

"Because whenever you start thinking, I end up with more work," he said, glancing over his shoulder as he backpedaled toward the barn. Wafting toward us through the open door came the unmistakable smell of death, mingled with another powerful stench. Tyler disappeared as he backed into the darkness. "*Christ*, this place stinks," came his voice from within, floating on the fumes.

I suspected Tyler was stalling, trying to distract me from the thesis discussion. But he was right about the stench; in fact, if anything, he was understating things. Over the course of several decades, countless litters of pigs had been farrowed and nursed in this barn, and every pig—sows and piglets alike—had left a legacy of stink. As the state's only land-grant university, UT still had a strong agricultural college, but in recent decades the school's working farms had been scaled back in favor of a more academic orientation for Ag majors. By 1992, the university was largely out of the farming business, with the exception of a few cornfields along the river and a small dairy farm adjoining the hospital.

We laid the body down in one of the empty stalls, the ground soft and slippery underfoot from decades of pig droppings and a half-dozen decomposing corpses donated to me by medical examiners so that I could begin building a teaching collection of modern, known skeletons.

The barn was windowless, but shafts of sunlight angled through gaps in the plank siding. Dust motes drifted and danced in the shafts of light. The blowflies—a dozen or more by now—appeared and disappeared in strobing succession as they traversed the slivers of light.

"Funny thing," Tyler mused. "I don't mind the smell of the decomp so much; it's the pig shit I can't stand."

"Anyhow," I resumed, "I've been thinking about

your thesis, and I think you need a different research project."

"*What?* I've spent weeks—months—looking at pubic bones. I've looked at hundreds of pubic bones. Maybe a *thousand* pubic bones."

"But wouldn't you rather do something important?"

"You said the pubic-bone study was important, Dr. B."

"It is. But not as important as this."

"As what? Never mind—I don't want to know."

"*Everybody* studies pubic bones," I said. "I'm talking about seminal research, Tyler."

"You want me to research *semen*? I'm supposed to write a thesis about spunk?"

"Don't be so literal. Or so argumentative. This research will be unique. Original. A pioneering contribution."

"*Dammit!*" He swatted the back of his neck.

"You need to quit killing the flies, Tyler," I said.

"Why?"

"Because they're your new best friends. The stars of your new thesis project."

"What new thesis project? You keep dropping these veiled hints," he grumbled. "Veiled threats. Just spit it out, Dr. B."

"The first detailed study of insect activity in human corpses," I said. "Our first step toward basing time-since-death estimates on scientific data. One blowfly at a time."

"Let me get this straight. You're saying you want me to spend even more quality time out here, crawling around in pig shit?"

"Gathering data," I said. "Advancing the cause of science."

"And in your new vision, how much more time do I spend out here advancing the cause of science? How many data trips a day? This is a long damn way from the bone lab." He had a point there, I had to admit. "Any chance you could get me a transporter beam, so I don't spend four hours a day shuttling back and forth from campus?"

"I'll figure something out," I said, hoping it would prove true. My flash of nocturnal inspiration hadn't extended to anything so mundane as transportation logistics.

In the darkness a few feet away, I heard the sound of one hand clapping—Tyler's hand clapping against a fly on the back of his neck. Perhaps he had not yet fully grasped the brilliance of my new research plan. But he would. What choice, after all, did an indentured academic servant have?

CHAPTER 6

Crystal

CRYSTAL HEARD THE GROAN of the semi's brakes close behind her, then the popping and skittering of gravel pinched by the edges of the tires, as a massive cab—no trailer—drew alongside her and stopped, the big pistons of the diesel knocking in its iron heart. The brakes hissed, causing her to jump. The truck was a long-hooded Peterbilt, which loomed over her like a locomotive; its small, divided windshield was shaded by a metal visor, jutting and ominous; the sleeper compartment, grafted behind the cab, looked half the size of Crystal's house trailer.

Crystal took two more steps forward, into a band of shadow, to avoid being blinded by the sun as she looked up at the driver. The shadow, she realized, was cast by the Baptist Church's giant cross, and for the first time in hundreds of comings and goings past it, Crystal was glad the cross was there, dispensing a bit of shade along with its monumental dose of disapproval.

The cross, the shade, and Crystal were thirty

miles northwest of Knoxville, atop Jellico Mountain. Just beyond the point where I–75 finished its long, slanting climb up the mountain's flank and leveled out, a handful of buildings clustered at Exit 141: a blue-roofed Comfort Inn; a Pilot truck stop; Redeemer Primitive Baptist Church; and—last but not least—Crystal's place of employment, XXX Adult World. Adult World was the seamiest and the flashiest of the exit's buildings: a neon-emblazoned establishment surmounted by a pair of billboards and ringed by a gravel lot capable of accommodating half a hundred tractor-trailer rigs at a time. For efficiency's sake, Adult World ought to have shared a parking lot with the Pilot truck stop, since truckers constituted most of Adult World's clientele—and since women like Crystal spent a lot of time shuttling back and forth between the two businesses. But irony had trumped efficiency in this case: The truck stop lay on the opposite side of the interstate, and Adult World instead sat cheek by jowl—or haunch to haunch—with Redeemer Primitive Baptist, a corrugated metal building whose five-story cross did double duty, inspiring multitudes of passing motorists while simultaneously rebuking Adult World's lusty customers and fallen women.

"DIDN'T MEAN TO scare you." The voice floated down from the cab toward Crystal. "You want a ride?"

She looked up, over her right shoulder, shading her eyes against the glare of the slanting morning sun. All she saw were wraparound shades, the brim of a cap, chiseled cheeks, and a stubbly jaw leaning out the driver's window. "I don't care to walk," she said. "I'm just going over yonder to the truck stop. Thanks anyhow."

"You fixing to get some breakfast? Come on, I'll buy." He took off the sunglasses so she could see his eyes. He was looking at her face, not her tits. She appreciated that, though she knew he'd already had plenty of time to check her out as he pulled up behind her and then drew even. Hell, he'd probably seen her naked not more than twenty minutes before, dancing on the peep-show stage.

She noticed a chrome silhouette of a nude woman on the truck's mud flaps, as well as a bumper sticker on the sleeper cab, just below the door handle: *I ❤ LOT LIZARDS.* She had mixed feelings about the sticker. On the one hand, it meant he was willing to pay for sex. On the other hand, it showed that he considered the truck-stop prostitutes he bought it from—"lot lizards," in trucker slang—to be less than human.

Crystal's head was pounding and she was seriously pissed off; she'd worked all night for seventeen dollars in tips, and that bastard Bobby T had given her an "attitude adjustment"—a one-week suspension—for sassing a customer who'd looked and groped but never did tip. She'd wanted to sass Bobby T, too—to say, "Hey, man, *you* try dancing bare-assed all night for a bunch of fat guys with BO and grabby hands, see how chirpy *you* feel." But she'd bitten it back, because this was her second attitude adjustment, and she knew Bobby T had a strict three-strikes-and-you're-out policy. "They's plenty other crack-whores to take your place in here, princess," he'd told the last girl he sent packing. Sad truth was, he was right. Seventeen bucks wouldn't go far, but zero bucks went nowhere. And the night before last had been all right, thirty-something in tips, plus two quick twenty-dollar blow jobs in the parking lot out back. "Sorry; what?" she said, realizing that the trucker had said something to her and was waiting for an answer.

"I said business looked kinda slow in there." She shrugged by way of a noncommittal acknowledgment. "Wondering if you might like to make a little extra on the side."

On the side, hell, she thought. *On my ass, you mean.* But what she said was, "Might. Depends on what you're lookin' for. And what you're offering." Careful not to say what she'd do, and careful not to ask outright about the money. She'd never heard of an undercover cop driving a semi, but you couldn't be too careful.

"The no-frills, good old-fashioned way, forty bucks," he said. "Take me around the world, I could go sixty. Show me something I've never seen before, might be worth a hundred."

She didn't much like feeling pressured, but she definitely liked the prospect of making a hundred first thing in the morning. Maybe he'd even spring for a room in the Comfort Inn, which would give her a chance to shower and nap before traipsing home to the trailer. "Well then," she said. "All aboard, I reckon."

He grinned down at her. "That's the ticket. Come on around. You need help getting up?"

"Nah, I can manage. I've done it once or twice before."

"Ha. I bet you have, babycakes. I bet you have."

She walked around the long, looming prow of the truck, the top of the hood a foot higher than her head, the windshield blocked from view by the mammoth engine. When she got to the side, the passenger door swung open for her. Planting her left foot on the thigh-high step, she grabbed the chrome bar running up the side of the cab and swung her right leg up to the floorboard, almost as if she were climbing onto a horse.

"Oh yeah, I'd say you've done this once or twice," he said, grinning.

He was younger than most truck drivers. Better looking, too—good muscles, no gut. Well, that would change soon enough, if he ate and drank and sat on his ass all the time, like every other truck driver she'd ever known. Once she was in, he eased out the clutch and the truck rumbled forward. "Name's Jake. As in 'jake brakes.' What's yours?"

"Crystal," she said. It wasn't her real name—or at least, it didn't used to be—but maybe by now she'd turned into Crystal. Didn't matter anyhow. Plus she was pretty sure his name wasn't really Jake.

"Crystal. Pretty. So how's about we work up a little more appetite before breakfast, Crystal?"

She was already starving, but she figured she'd best reel him in while she had him on the hook. "Whatever you want. You're in the driver's seat."

He smiled, putting the shades back on. The truck rumbled up to the stop sign where Old Kentucky Road intersected I-75. He turned left, toward the underpass and the Pilot, but then he cut the wheel to the right, turning onto the interstate's northbound on-ramp instead of heading for the truck stop.

"Hey," she said, turning in her seat. "What the hell you doing?"

"Just finding us a little privacy," he said. "You know Exit 144? Three miles up the road? There's a nice little pull-off there where nobody'll bother us."

She thought about opening the door and jumping out onto the ramp, but the truck had already picked up a fair amount of speed, and she didn't think she could do it without hurting herself pretty bad. She sat back in the seat, her nerves jangling, magnifying every jolt as the truck shuddered over seams and patches in the pavement. Her anxiety lessened a bit when he put on his turn signal and downshifted to take the exit.

"Stinking Creek Road," he said. "Reckon how come they give it such an ugly name?"

"I reckon it don't smell too good," she said. He probably wanted her to say something more clever or funny, but she was feeling hungry and nervous, not entertaining.

"Down near Chattanooga, there's a stream called Suck Creek. Suck Creek Mountain, too. I'd hate to have to tell people I lived on Suck Creek Mountain." She didn't say anything. After a moment he added, "Up in Virginia, I–66 crosses Dismal Hollow Road. That'd be a bad address, too."

Halfway down the ramp, on the left, they passed a long shed with a Quonset-hut roof. He braked and turned onto the gravel, crossing the far end of the structure. The shed was completely open on the end, and inside she saw an immense mound of salt—the highway department's stockpile for the coming winter, she supposed. The four-mile grade on Jellico Mountain was a nightmare when it snowed; the lanes were in the shadow of the mountain for most of the day, so stuff was slow to melt. *Take a hell of a lot more'n you to thaw that damn mountain*, she thought, as if the salt could hear what she was thinking.

Just past the end of the shed, he spun the wheel again, tucking in behind the building so the truck was screened from view. "See?" he said. "Close, but quiet. If it don't come a blizzard in the next hour, won't nobody bother us here." He smiled at his joke. "Aw, relax, darlin'. You changing your mind? Hell, I'll take you back to the Pilot right now and still buy you breakfast, if you want to call off the deal. I'd be disappointed—who wouldn't be, a good-looking woman like you?—but I'm a big boy. I reckon I'd get over it. In a year or two." He grinned and winked.

She shook her head. "Not changing my mind. I just need to . . . switch gears, I guess," she said. "My boss was giving me a hard time back there."

"You want something to take the edge off? Sip of Jack Daniel's? A little reefer?"

She felt a glimmer of what passed for hope these days. "You gonna smoke?" By way of answering, he took a fat joint and a lighter from the pocket of his denim shirt. He lit it and then handed it over so she could take a hit. She took a long drag and held it; when she exhaled, she seemed to be letting go of not just the smoke but also the stress of the night, the meanness of Bobby T, and the flash of panic she'd felt when the truck had taken the on-ramp instead of ducking under the freeway to the Pilot.

"That looks like just what the doctor ordered," he said, and she was thinking he was right. Long as she didn't forget to collect the money, being stoned would make it easier to zone out while he did his business. A good buzz might even help her think of something kinky enough to score the extra forty.

She was feeling pretty good by the time he helped her down from the cab and up into the sleeper. He gave her a hand as she stepped onto the bottom rung of the ladder, then boosted her up the rest of the way by cupping her ass in both palms and pushing, with a little squeeze for good measure.

The inside of the sleeper was like a cave; the compartment had two windows, but both were covered with blackout shades. "Here, let me turn on a light so you can see," he said, switching on a dim dome light.

The sleeper contained a double-sized mattress along one wall, a galley kitchen in one corner, and a shower in the other corner. "Hell's bells," she said, toppling backward onto the mattress, "this is nicer'n where I *live*." She spread her arms wide and swung them up and down, like wings. "I ain't never been in a sleeper this big."

He smiled. "I don't expect you ever will be again, angel," he said.

CHAPTER 7

Tyler

TYLER LOCKED THE BONE lab behind him and hustled out the stadium's lower door. He'd parked his truck right by the door—a prime spot, except for the fact that it was illegal. *Just for two minutes*, he'd told himself; just long enough to drop off the strip-mine girl's bones, which he'd carefully boxed after photographing and measuring them. But the two minutes had turned to ten, then thirty. He scanned the windshield, didn't see a ticket. *Whew*, he thought. *That's lucky.* Then he saw the figure on the far side of the truck. It was a man, standing on the running board, cupping his hands against the driver's window so he could peer inside. "*Hey!*" Tyler yelled reflexively, wondering whether he was about to plead with a traffic cop or punch out a thief. The man straightened; the man was . . . his *boss*. "Hey," he repeated, still feeling trespassed against; puzzled, too. "Uh, what's up, Dr. B?"

"I was just looking to see how many miles you've got on this thing."

"Last time I looked, the odometer was showing ninety-nine thousand eight hundred and change," Tyler said. Dr. B lifted one eyebrow—his trademark expression of skepticism. The man was no fool. "I thought you had a meeting with the dean today," Tyler went on, uneasy about Brockton's interest in the truck—interest that seemed not just intense, but somehow invested. "You said you were gonna ask him for some land closer to campus."

"I do, but he was running late. I'm headed there now."

Tyler pointed at the glossy dress shoes trespassing on his running board. "You should be wearing yesterday's boots to the meeting," he said, "not that fancy footwear. Grind a little pig shit into the dean's carpet, so he knows what it's like for us out here."

"Good idea, Tyler. Antagonize the boss—always a great strategy when you're asking for a raise or a favor. You're wasting your gifts in anthropology. You'd make a hell of an ambassador." Dr. B stepped down from the running board but lingered by the truck, looking thoughtful. "Automatic or stick?"

"Stick, course. Three on the tree." The term was archaic—slang for a three-speed gearshift on the steering column, the prehistoric predecessor to four-on-the-floor and five-speed manual transmissions—but Brockton was plenty old enough to know what it meant. "You couldn't *pay* me to drive an automatic."

"See, *that's* what I'm talking about," said Dr. B.

"Huh?"

"Oh, nothing. I'm just having an argument with Kathleen and Jeff."

"Your son?"

"He just got his driver's license, and he's badgered us into helping him buy a car. Me, I didn't have a car till I was out of college, but that's a different argument, and I've already lost. Anyhow, Jeff and Kathleen are dead set on an automatic. But I say he needs to know how to drive a stick shift. What if he needs to drive somebody else's car in an emergency, and the car's a stick shift?"

"Uh, right," said Tyler. "Or what if a meteorite shower wipes out every automatic-transmission factory on the entire *planet*?" Brockton frowned, unhappy to have his point undercut, and Tyler figured he'd better throw his boss a conciliatory bone. "But it *is* a useful skill. Especially if he's gonna travel overseas—hard to rent anything *but* a stick, most places. Just the opposite of how it is here." Dr. B nodded. "Main thing, though—and maybe he'd listen to this—is that you've got so much more *control* with a manual. *I* want to be the one that decides when to shift. Automatics drive me crazy, especially on hills."

"Exactly," said Brockton. "All that downshifting and upshifting, every five seconds? Don't get me started." He ran his eyes over the truck again. "Tell me, what year is this?"

"Unless I'm mistaken, this is 1992."

"Ha ha. Not the *calendar*, smart-ass—the *truck*. What year is the *truck*?"

"It's a 1950."

"Amazing. You'd never know. How long you had it?"

"Me, only a couple years. But it's been in the family from the get-go."

"No kidding? Since 1950?"

"October '49, actually. My granddaddy walked into the showroom, pocketful of cash from his corn crop, and drove it home. Drove it for the next twenty years, then gave it to my dad. Dad had it for twenty, too, but some of those, it gathered dust in a shed behind the house."

Dr. B appraised the truck again. "*How* many miles you say it's got?"

"I didn't. I said it *shows* ninety-nine thousand and some. True, far as it goes." He hoped the conversation was over, but his boss waited expectantly. "The *whole* truth would take another digit—another *one* on the left side of those numbers."

"A *hundred* ninety-nine thousand?"

"Yeah. Back in 1950, Detroit took it for granted a car wouldn't make it past ninety-nine thousand, nine hundred ninety-nine point nine. If by some miracle it *did*, all those nines rolled over—"

"Sure," Brockton interrupted, "to zeros, all of 'em. Back to the beginning. Clean slate. Fresh start."

Rebirth, or at least the illusion of it, long as you looked only at the numbers—not at holes in floorboards, or rusted-out fenders, or cracking, chalky paint, or rotted upholstery and shredded headliner.

Tyler had been a kindergartner the last time the Chevy's odometer had racked up so many nines, but he remembered the event with Kodachrome vividness.

IT WAS A *summer Sunday afternoon, after church and after dinner, everyone stuffed and sleepy and still in their hot polyester church clothes. The truck was what his* *dad drove to work, or to the lumberyard or the dump or to Sears to get new appliances; everything else happened in the Oldsmobile Vista Cruiser, the big station wagon with the skylight windows. But that Sunday, the four of them piled into the sweltering, musty cab—no air conditioner, of course; the seat belts long since lost in the gap between the seat cushion and seat back. His parents perched on either side of the broad bench seat, with Tyler sandwiched between them, his baby sister, Anne Marie, age two, on his mom's lap. They'd driven the thirty miles from Knoxville to Lenoir City, to the white farmhouse on River Road where Gran and Pop-Pop lived. The whole way down, his father's gaze was glued to the odometer, and he nearly ran off the road—not once but twice, the second time provoking a gasp and a sharp "Wesley" from his mother. As they turned off River Road and crunched to a stop in the gravel driveway, his father tapped the instrument panel. "Look at that," he'd said, "ninety-nine thousand, nine hundred and ninety-eight point two. Perfect. Plenty of margin." He'd then commenced to honking, laying on the horn for what seemed like forever, until Gran and Pop-Pop emerged at last, looking nappish and puzzled and maybe not all that thrilled at the surprise visit.*

"What are y'all doing here?" Gran had said, then her cheeks turned red. "I mean, in that old thing? That bucket of bolts should have gone to the junkyard years ago." Her flustered expression brightened when Tyler's mom handed Anne Marie to her.

"Bucket of bolts? Are you referring to this marvelous machine, Mama? This paragon of mechanical perfection?" Tyler's father had acted indignant, but even at five, Tyler could tell he was teasing, and he giggled.

"Mama dear, we have come all the way from Knoxville to take you two for an old-fashioned Sunday drive. Get in. You'll like it." Tyler's mom reclaimed Anne Marie momentarily, and Gran clambered into the cab, still looking baffled. Pop-Pop resisted, insisting he should ride in the back so Tyler's mom wouldn't have to.

"Are you kidding?" she'd said, handing Anne Marie into the cab, back to Gran. "I love riding in the back of a pickup. Makes me feel like a kid again." She fiddled with the latch, and the tailgate fell open with a screech and a bang. "Tyler and I will be happy as hound dogs back here," she said, boosting him up onto the tailgate. Tyler could scarcely believe his good fortune. Never—never—had he been allowed to ride in the back of the truck. "It's a death trap," his mom would invariably say, any time his dad suggested that maybe, just this once, it might be okay.

With another screech and a bang and a sly wink at Tyler, his dad slammed the tailgate and got behind the wheel once more. Tyler's mom settled them in the front corners of the bed, frowning at the dirt and the rust. "Now you sit still and hold on tight," she said, and Tyler nodded eagerly.

Driving far more slowly than usual, Tyler's dad pulled out of the driveway and headed farther out River Road, along a stretch that ran straight and flat between fields of dark, glossy corn. After a couple of miles, he eased the truck to a stop, right there in the road, and cut the engine. Then he shifted into neutral, pulled the emergency brake, opened the driver's door, and got out. "Come on around her and take the wheel, Daddy," he'd said to Pop-Pop. "Ease off that brake and let her coast when I give you the word." Then, walking to the back of the truck, he'd opened the tailgate and helped his son and his wife hop down. Motioning her toward the truck's right rear corner, he'd placed Tyler behind the center of the tailgate, then stationed himself at the left rear corner. "Ready, Daddy?"

"What on God's green earth are y'all doing?" squawked Gran.

"The odometer's fixin' to turn over, Mama," he'd hollered. "One hundred thousand *miles! Daddy, let that brake off so we can push this fine machine into its second lifetime."*

"Lord help, you people are nuts," Gran laughed.

The road must have had a slight downgrade—either that, or the universe joined in the celebration—because the truck rolled easily, and soon the three of them were running just to keep from losing touch with it. As they ran, Tyler's dad began to sing. "Swing low . . . sweet chariot . . . comin' for to carry me home." His strong, clear voice rolled out across the fields.

"Swi-ing low," his mom chimed in, "sweet cha-ri-o-ot . . . comin' for to carry me home."

"Here it comes, here it comes!" shouted Pop-Pop. "Point eight . . . Point nine . . . Zero!" His shout was joined by the truck's wildly honking horn—a trumpeting horn, a jubilant horn; a horn the Angel Gabriel himself would have been proud to blow, if only the Almighty had allowed him to turn in his angel wings and trade up to a 1950 Chevy half-ton: a bug-eyed, bona fide miracle of American engineering and mass production.

Fifteen years later, when Tyler graduated from college, his dad had surprised him by giving him the truck—but the truck as Tyler had never known it: a glorious, ground-up restoration of the truck, with gleaming new paint, leather interior, seat belts, and a stem-to-stern mechanical rebuild that rendered the rings, valves, and gearbox as tight as they'd been the day Pop-Pop had driven it out of the showroom. It was not so much a restoration as a reincarnation: as if everything else—everything but the odometer—had rolled over to zeros this time around.

"SORRY; WHAT'D YOU say, Dr. B?" Tyler blinked, somewhat surprised to find himself in 1992, standing at the base of the stadium, his boss staring at him, bringing him back to the present—back from the sweet childhood memory to the grim realities of death and decay and unrelenting demands.

"I said, what would you think of selling it?"

"Selling what? The *truck*?" Tyler looked at Dr. B, who cocked his head, waiting. "You mean to *you*?" Dr. B nodded. "What, for your son?" Another nod. Tyler was startled by the question; no, more than startled, he was stunned and unmoored. Unhappy, too. He stared at the truck, as if it had suddenly coalesced out of thin air; as if it were some . . . alien . . . *thing*, rather than a steadfast fixture of his entire existence. Was Brockton trying to take over his whole damned life?

Finally he spoke, choosing his words carefully. "*This?* For a teenage driver? You gotta be kidding. No air bags, no shoulder harnesses, no impact protection. Hell, if he hit something head-on, the steering column would go right through his chest, like a spear. This thing is a *death* trap."

Dr. B smiled slightly, looking . . . what? Wistful? "I don't blame you," he said. "I'd hang on to it, too, if I were you. Twenty years from now, you'll be giving it to *your* son."

Tyler hoped the subject of selling the truck was closed, but—knowing Dr. B—knew it would come up again. "Maybe not," he said. Brockton looked hopeful for a moment, until Tyler added, "Maybe I'll be giving it to my daughter."

CHAPTER 8

Satterfield

THE WAND AND HOSE of the pressure washer twitched and swayed in the air like a living creature—*like a cobra,* Satterfield thought—as the water hissed against the long hood of the Peterbilt. Bright red water sheeted down the side of the truck's cab, a visual echo of the blood spilled inside the sleeper so recently. Fanning the seething spray back and forth in the morning sunlight, creating airy rainbows and red puddles, Satterfield envisioned the pressure washer's long, thin nozzle as a magic wand. "Abracadabra," he murmured, liking the feel of the word in his mouth, liking the sense of power he felt as a sorcerer. "Presto change-o, red to blue-o." As if in response to the spell he was casting, the Peterbilt was transformed, wand wave by wand wave, the red truck dissolving and melting—molting—to reveal its inner self, its true colors: gunmetal blue, with a fringe of orange flames edging the back of the sleeper.

He'd been watching the news—on television and

in the newspapers—but he'd seen nothing about the woman's body being found. Apparently nobody even missed her yet, as there'd been no reports of a search, either.

He'd be in Birmingham by sundown tonight, and back in Knoxville by morning, his tracks fully covered. The fuel tanks still had a hundred gallons of diesel in them—at six miles a gallon, more than enough to make the trip—and he was ready to roll, as soon as he washed off the last of the paint.

Satterfield felt confident that no one had seen the woman get into the truck; I–75 ran right alongside Adult World, true, but the truck's cab would have hidden her from the view of the motorists whizzing past. Remarkable, really, how oblivious most people were as they went about their daily business and their little lives. Still, it never hurt to be careful, and if—*if*—someone eventually came forward to say they'd seen a woman—a trashy, slutty-looking excuse for a woman—climbing into a tractor-trailer cab, the police would start looking for a truck that was red. *Water-soluble paint*, he thought. *Brilliant. Long as there's no rain in the forecast.*

After he'd made two meticulous circuits with the pressure washer, perching on a stepladder to reach the roof of the cab, the water sheeting off was crystal clear, and only traces of red remained in the puddles and cracks around the concrete pad and drain. "Abracadabra," Satterfield said again, giving the pressure-washer wand a final flourish before releasing the trigger.

Some things wash away easier than others, he thought.

"BOY, YOU DROP *them britches and bend over that bed, and I don't mean in a minute." His stepfather's voice was low but menacing, and Satterfield knew better than to protest. "How long you been spying through that peephole? How many times before?"*

"None." The boy's voice quavered. He wasn't good at lying, and he already knew what was coming. A hand gripped his neck and hinged him forward onto the bed. "I wasn't spying," he pleaded. "I heard noises. I thought somebody was hurt. I was just looking to see if somebody needed help."

"Somebody's fixin' to need help, all right," the man snarled, unbuckling his belt and yanking it through the loops with seething, snapping sounds. He'd gotten home less than thirty minutes before, his arrival announced by the hiss of the Peterbilt's air brakes, and he still smelled of the road—a week of diesel fuel and sweat and stale cigarettes and greasy truck-stop food—topped off now with whiskey and something muskier. Satterfield heard the air hiss as the leather strap swung overhead and then down, gaining momentum as it descended. It struck the mattress with enough force to shake the bed. "Don't you lie to me, boy. That peephole ain't nothin' new. You been spyin' on us a long time, ain't you? Watchin' us in the bed?"

"No, sir," Satterfield whined. "Never." The belt swung again, and again the bed shook, but this time the belt struck the boy's buttocks, not the mattress, and he shrieked and began to sob. A few more blows, and suddenly the mattress grew warm and wet against him as his bladder let go from pain and fear.

His stepfather paused, bending over the whimpering boy, and sniffed the air. "Boy, did you just piss yourself?" His free hand slid roughly beneath the boy's belly. "By

God, you did. Twelve years old, and still pissing yourself. You little sissy-boy. You little piece of dog shit. You nasty little faggot." A pause. "You know what happens to nasty little faggots? I'm fixin' to show you."

Satterfield heard the belt clatter to the floor, then heard his stepfather unzipping his jeans, then felt a searing pain. It took the boy two days to begin to recover.

A week later, the Peterbilt had hissed to a stop in the driveway once more, and the man and woman had disappeared into the bedroom and locked the door, and the sound of their groans had drawn Satterfield again to the peephole.

The peephole that his stepfather had made no effort to patch.

SATTERFIELD STUDIED THE sunset through the passenger side of the Peterbilt's windshield—the sky going red-orange and turquoise behind the silhouette of Birmingham's blocky Civic Center and the I–59 viaduct—as he waited to hear the verdict from the asshole sitting in the driver's seat.

"Drives okay," said the asshole finally, but his tone was skeptical, as if what he really meant was "Drives like a piece of shit."

The asshole—a beer-bellied, dumb-shit redneck of a prospective buyer—slouched behind the wheel, his hand rubbing the gearshift knob as if the truck were already his. They were just back from a twenty-mile test drive out I–59, which skirted downtown Birmingham on miles of elevated roadway, and they now sat idling beside the Sheraton and the Civic Center. To their left, traffic overhead rumbled and clattered across the viaduct's expansion joints; to their right, the blank end wall of the high-rise hotel echoed every clatter a quarter of a second later, as if, in some parallel universe, identical cars and trucks were rumbling and clattering along an identical viaduct, in almost-but-not-quite-perfect sync.

Satterfield wasn't staying at the Sheraton. He'd said he was, when he'd arranged the meeting with the asshole, but the moment the deal was sealed and the asshole was gone, Satterfield would jog beneath the roaring roadway to the Greyhound station, six blocks south, huddled beneath the forty-story BellSouth building. The next bus for Knoxville was scheduled to leave in less than an hour, and Satterfield was growing impatient with the slow-talking, slow-witted buyer.

"If it's so damned good, how come you're so hot to sell it?"

Satterfield shook his head, his eyes downcast. *Don't you even think about backing out on me*, he thought. "It's my wife," he said sadly. "She's sick. Real sick—breast cancer. Doctor says she's got three months. Six, at the most." He heaved a deep sigh, loud enough to be heard over the traffic and the clatter of the truck's idling pistons. "We've got a lot of hospital bills. Got a four-year-old, too, that I got to raise on my own pretty soon." He turned to look at the guy now, his eyes full of ginned-up sorrow and anger, daring the asshole to do anything but sympathize and cough up the cash. "*That's* how come."

The asshole nodded slightly, working the tip of his tongue into the crevice between two top teeth, digging for the bit of food that Satterfield had noticed was caught there. "Hmm," the guy grunted, "too bad." Satterfield felt a flash of fury at the lukewarm response. So what, if his tale of familial woe was totally fabricated, his tragic characters spun out of thin air? This guy had no way of knowing that. *I got a dying wife and a motherless kid on my hands, and all you got to say is "too bad"? You coldhearted, little-dicked son of a bitch.* "And you brought the title?"

"Got it right here," Satterfield said, opening the glove compartment and removing a fat folder. "Maintenance records, too." He handed the folder across, and the guy riffled through it, glancing at the receipts. "I haven't put many miles on it this past year. Not since she got sick."

The guy pulled out the title and studied the name on it. It was Satterfield's stepfather's name; it was the name Satterfield would sign, assuming the guy ever shut up and paid up. "And the title's clean? No liens?"

"Abso-fuckin'-*lutely* clean," Satterfield snapped. "I gave you the damn VIN number. Didn't you check it? I told you to."

"Yeah, I checked it. Came back clean. Just askin'. Just makin' sure." His tongue began rooting around in his teeth again, fishing for more scraps—*Why's he stalling?* wondered Satterfield, and then he realized, *Ah, here it comes.* "Thirty thousand, that's a lot of cash," the guy said. He chewed his lip and shook his head, looking pained—like he really wanted the truck after all but just couldn't quite scrape up the asking price.

"Thirty's a damn sight less than forty," snapped Satterfield. "This truck's worth forty, easy, and you know it. If you want it, you put thirty thousand dollars cash money in my hand right now. If you don't want it, get your ass out of my truck and quit wasting my time." *Don't you dare fuck with me, fat-ass*, the voice in his head hissed. *I will gut you like a big-bellied hog.*

"Easy, hoss," said the guy. "I want it. But I'm a working man, and that kind of cash don't grow on trees." He waited, apparently still hoping Satterfield might cut him a break on the price. Finally, when Satterfield didn't budge, he reached into an inner pocket of his jacket and brought out a fat manila envelope, as thick as a brick, the top of the envelope wrapped around the money and rubber-banded. Satterfield had already spotted the rectangle hanging heavy inside the coat; he'd considered killing the guy while they were out on the test drive—snagging the cash and dumping his body somewhere on the way back to Knoxville, maybe in Little River Canyon, up toward Chattanooga—but that seemed risky, given that the guy's wife was waiting for him at a McDonald's around the corner. No, better to take the money, let the guy drive away, and stay as far under the radar as possible. The truck could tie him to his *dead* stepfather, if *that* body was ever found, and it could tie him to the stripper he'd dumped in the ravine. The truck needed selling. Besides, the money would be useful; he could live for a year—two, if he had to—on the thirty grand plus the monthly infusions of cash his mother's Social Security checks provided.

Satterfield took the envelope in his left hand, reaching into the glove compartment again with his right, this time feeling for his straight razor. Flipping open the blade, he slid the tip lightly across the rubber band to slice it, then laid the razor on his right leg, still open. He pulled the stack of currency—also rubber-banded—from the envelope and riffled through one corner of the stack, as if the bills were a deck of cards. The number *50* fluttered past many times, jerking and shimmying in small movements, like an animated drawing in a child's flip-book. He tugged one of the fifties free and tucked it into his shirt pocket—he'd be paying cash for his bus ticket, so there'd be no paper trail leading from Birmingham—then tucked the rest between his thighs. He took a pen from his shirt pocket. "Okay, then. Hand me that title and I'll sign it over."

"Don't you want to count it?"

Satterfield looked at him coolly, holding the stare long enough to make the guy squirm. "Some reason I *need* to count it?"

Even by the last light of the sunset and the first flickers of the streetlamps, he could see the guy flush. *Is he insulted, because he wouldn't dream of shorting me? Or is he worried, because he actually did?* "No reason, hoss. It's all there."

"Good." Satterfield picked up the straight razor and angled it toward the light spilling through the driver's window, sighting along the edge of the blade, inspecting it for nicks. He glanced up from the blade and smiled. "Be a real shame if I had to come back to settle up."

CHAPTER 9

Brockton

TYLER AND I WERE thirty miles northwest of Knoxville on I–75, the sun beginning to sink as we began to climb Jellico Mountain. An hour before, I'd gotten a call from the sheriff of Campbell County—"Sheriff Grainger," he'd said on the phone, without giving his first name—asking if I could come recover a body from a creek bed. "It's in pretty rough shape," he'd said. "The TBI agent up here says this is just your kind of thing."

"The TBI agent up there wouldn't happen to be named Meffert, would he? Bubba Hardknot?"

"Sure is," Sheriff Grainger had answered. "He covers Campbell, Morgan, and Scott Counties."

"Lucky him," I'd said, then realized the remark might sound offensive. "That's a lot of ground to cover." All three counties were mountainous and sparsely populated; coal rich but dollar poor. "Bubba be at the scene?"

"On his way over from Oneida right now. Reckon he'll be along directly."

"We'll get there as quick as we can, Sheriff."

"LOOK AT THAT," I said, pointing out the right side of the windshield. "Nature's flying buttresses."

"Huh?" Tyler followed the direction of my point. "Oh," he said. "Yeah. Gotcha."

"That's *it*?" I shook my head. "A miracle of nature, and the best you can manage is 'Gotcha'?" We were halfway up Jellico Mountain on a crisp, clear afternoon in late September; a hundred yards to the east of the interstate, a series of massive stone pillars—as plumb and parallel as stonemasons could have set them—jutted from the mountainside, each pillar rearing a hundred feet high against the reds and golds of the turning leaves. "Tyler, you have no poetry in your soul."

"I've got no lunch in my belly, either," he grumbled, "and it's three o'clock. Hard to hear poetry over the growling of my stomach."

"Not my fault you didn't eat at noon," I pointed out.

"It's not? Wasn't it you who told me to finish grading those exams by two?" He did have a point there. "Besides, we've passed a dozen fast-food places since we left UT."

"Yeah, but the sheriff called thirty seconds after you finished grading," I said. "And we don't have a lot of daylight left." I glanced again at the sun, already nearing the ridgeline. "A couple hours, tops, now that the days are getting short." I did feel bad about dragging him to a death scene unfed, though. "Look in the glove compartment," I told him. "I think there's a Snickers bar in there somewhere."

He pushed the button; the door popped open and a box of surgical gloves launched itself at him, latex fingers twitching in midair. Tyler rooted through the recess. "Papers. Registration, insurance, maintenance records, owner's manual," he itemized. "No Snickers."

"Keep digging," I said. "I could swear there's one in there."

"Oh," he said after a moment. "Yeah. Down here in the Jurassic stratum, I think I've discovered a fossilized candy bar." He fished out a Snickers, the wrapper rumpled and misshapen, and peeled it open. Inside was a cylinder of graying chocolate, misshapen from numerous cycles of melting and resolidifying. Tyler eyed it with distaste. "Oh, did I say *candy bar*? I meant *coprolite*." I had to admit, the lumpy extrusion *did* look remarkably like fossilized poop. He chomped down on it and wrestled a chunk free. "Mmm," he mumbled sarcastically. "Tasty." He took another bite.

The traffic was crawling. The right lane was slowed by a flatbed trailer hauling a bulldozer up the mountain; I had no idea what a bulldozer's top speed was, but I suspected it couldn't be much slower than the snail's pace at which the truck was transporting it. In the left lane, cars were bunched up behind a coal truck, which was creeping past the bulldozer at what appeared to be half a mile an hour faster.

"Wish they'd warned us about the rolling roadblock," Tyler mumbled through the caramel. "We could've zipped in and out of that Hardee's back at Lake City without losing any time. Forensic anthropology, NASCAR style."

"If you want to jump out and run back, go for it," I said. "You could probably catch up with me by the top of the mountain." He grunted and popped the last lump of the Snickers into his mouth.

Just as we crept over the lip of the mountain, the coal truck eased into the right lane, allowing the long line of cars to begin passing. As we drew nearer, I noticed both trucks turn and lumber down an exit ramp. "Nice," Tyler fumed at the coal truck. "Cause a bottleneck for dozens of cars, just so you can get to the exit two seconds ahead of the bulldozer."

"No point getting mad," I said. "Doesn't get us there any faster, and it sure doesn't hurt the truck driver. Just makes you feel worse. Don't they teach you that kind of stuff in yoga? *Ommmm* and all that?"

Tyler turned and stared at me. "Where was that laid-back vibe two hours ago, Mr. Mellow, when you were flogging me to get those papers graded?"

"That's different," I pointed out. "Those trucks aren't in my power. You, on the other hand . . ." I didn't need to finish the sentence; Tyler knew better than anyone that "graduate assistantship" was synonymous with "indentured servitude."

He tapped his window and pointed. "Classy," he said. I looked out and saw the coal truck and the bulldozer-hauler both turning into the parking lot of a garish, neon-lit store—XXX Adult World—advertising books, videos, novelties, and *Live Girls, Girls, Girls*. "Also classy," he said, now pointing to a corrugated metal building that was overshadowed by a gargantuan corrugated cross. "Not exactly Saint Peter's, is it?"

"Not exactly," I agreed. "But I suspect the Vatican's art and architecture budget was a little bigger than these folks'." Tyler grunted, glancing down at the directions the sheriff had given me.

A mile or so later, Tyler pointed to a road sign. "That's our exit," he said. "Stinking Creek Road. One mile." I passed another lumbering coal truck, then signaled and eased into the right lane, just in time to catch the exit. "Left onto Stinking Creek."

As we coasted down the ramp, Tyler leaned forward and looked out my window. "I'd like to build a house like that someday," he said.

I glanced to the left, and then at the outside mirror. "What, a house filled with rock salt?"

"No, a house made from a Quonset hut. Actually, a house made from *two* Quonset huts, crossing in the middle, like a big plus sign. Like a cathedral, with a nave and a transept. Earth sheltered, for natural insulation; walls of glass at all four ends; a big skylight above the intersection, for plenty of natural light."

"So," I said, making a left at the bottom of the ramp, "the floor plan of a cathedral, the elegance of a drainage culvert? Classy. How does Roxanne feel about the idea of living in a burrow?" He frowned, which might have meant that he hadn't asked, or might have meant that he had, and that she wasn't wild about the idea.

Just then we rounded a curve and nearly rear-ended a Campbell County sheriff's cruiser, which was parked at the edge of the pavement with its rear end angling into the road. In front of it was another cruiser and, ahead of that, an unmarked black sedan—Meffert's TBI-issued Crown Victoria. Just beyond the Crown Vic was a bridge spanning a narrow gorge—a gorge carved, I assumed, by Stinking Creek. Midway across the bridge, a figure I recognized as Meffert leaned over the railing, looking down.

I tucked the pickup behind the cruisers, trying to feel for the margins of the shoulder through the tires. Tyler opened his door and looked down, frowning. "What's the matter?" I asked. "Did I not leave enough room?"

"Plenty of room. For a mountain goat."

The door of the nearer cruiser opened and a uniformed officer got out. "He's here," I heard him saying into the mic of his two-way radio, the coils of the cord stretched to their limit. "Just pulled up." He released the mic, which the cord yanked from his hand, and closed the door. "Dr. Brockton?"

"That's me." I extended my hand, walking toward him.

"Sheriff Grainger." He took a few steps toward me, and we shook hands midway between the two vehicles—a tiny patch of neutral ground. I'd never had any territorial squabbles with law-enforcement officers—any "whose-jurisdiction-is-bigger contests," as Tyler called such things—but it never hurt to observe a few unwritten rules of courtesy and common sense. Meet in the middle, as equals; don't kowtow to the cops, but don't rub their noses in your Ph.D., either.

I introduced Tyler, and then Sheriff Grainger led us toward the bridge. A steady breeze was funneling up the narrow valley of Stinking Creek, spooling across the roadway and humming up the ridge. The temperature was dropping along with the sinking sun, and I was grateful for the sweatshirt I'd added beneath the windbreaker. I sniffed the air and caught the nutty smells of autumn leaves, fall acorns, and a faint, acrid scent that might have been sulfur from the creek. I didn't pick up any trace of decomp in the air, but unless the two dozen buzzards overhead were badly mistaken, it was there; definitely there. Some of the birds wheeled above the ravine; others hovered, surfing the wind that rippled up the ridge.

Just as we reached the bridge, a shotgun boomed, loud and near. I dropped to a crouch beside the Crown Vic, and Tyler scuttled into the gap behind it. The sheriff laughed. "Sorry, Doc," he said. "That's just Aikins, shooing off the buzzards." He pointed skyward, and I looked up just in time to see the last of the birds hightailing it over the ridgeline. "I should've warned you about that. *My* bad."

"No harm done," I said, rising from my crouch. "Y'all sure know how to keep a fellow on his toes. Tyler, you okay?"

"Hoo-*eee*," Tyler said, rising and dusting himself off. "Love the adrenaline rush. Hate wettin' my pants."

The sheriff turned and yelled toward the far end of the bridge. "Hey. *Aikins!* Next time you tell us before you do that."

"Sorry, Sheriff," came a voice from the shadows across the ravine.

"He's a good boy," the sheriff muttered, "but not a whole lot upstairs. Come on out on the bridge, and I'll show you where she is. You can figure out the best way to get her out."

He turned and walked toward the bridge, then

onto the span. Twenty feet across, just short of the midpoint where Meffert stood, a loop of crime-scene tape hung from the concrete rail. I followed the sheriff, my heart still thudding and my skin prickling from the shotgun blast. Below, I heard the churning of the creek as I walked along the right-hand side of the bridge, peering over the waist-high rail. The creek was fifteen or twenty feet below, a narrow torrent of tumbling water, edged and obstructed by ledges and boulders, by hemlocks and rhododendron. When I reached the yellow tape, I saw why it was there: A wide smear of dark brown covered the top of the rail, and several drips ran partway down the side. In the creek bed below, a few feet downstream from the bridge, lay the body of a woman—or, rather, what had once *been* a woman. She lay just above the waterline, on the right-hand bank. She was lying, undressed and in several pieces, near a jumble of blood-soaked fabric that was wedged between rocks at the water's edge.

Tyler joined me at the rail; Meffert stood slightly behind us, not speaking, allowing us to take in the scene on our own. "Tell me what you see, Tyler," I said. It was my favorite teaching technique—like taking medical students on hospital rounds, but instead of sick patients and puzzling diseases, my rounds revolved around stinking bodies or bare bones.

"What I see is a lot of work getting her up out of there," he began. I waited, knowing that after mouthing off—partly to stall for time, but also to take the edge off the grim work that lay ahead—Tyler would begin to wheel and spiral in, a forensic version of the buzzard spiral that the deputy's shotgun blast had interrupted. "Looks like she was dismembered," he said slowly. "Her limbs appear severed, not gnawed off." I'd already come to the same conclusion. I also felt sure she'd been dismembered before she was dumped into the creek bed, not after. Tyler glanced down at the rail. "There was lots of blood," he said, "but there's not as much on the rail as it looks like."

"Explain," I encouraged.

"It didn't *pool* up here at all." I nodded, impressed by how much detail he was noting and interpreting intelligently. Tyler had worked a dozen death scenes with me by now, and he seemed to soak up knowledge the way gauze soaks up blood. He pointed, tracing the margins of the big bloodstain without quite touching it. "And see how the edges are feathered, rather than sharply defined? So it's mostly just a smear, but a smear from a big, wide area." He squatted down, studying the few drips there were, and then dropped to all fours, his face just inches from the pavement. I smiled, having a pretty good idea what he'd spotted. "There's a little spatter down here," he said, "the drops diverging from the rail. Means she landed on the rail pretty hard. I'd say she fell a ways—maybe a couple feet—before she hit the rail and then tumbled on over the side."

Meffert stepped closer, unable to hold back any longer, and squatted down for a look. "Huh," he said. "I missed those spatters. You got better eyes than I do, young man." He straightened up with a lurch and a grunt. "Better knees, too."

Tyler squinted down at the remains in the streambed. "Female torso, probably adult, but the soft tissue's too far gone to tell," he said. "We can narrow down the age once we get a good look at the bones." He paused and considered before adding, "That's about all I've got so far."

"That's about all there is to get from here," I said. "Sheriff, you weren't exaggerating—it's a mess, all right."

"Wish the mess had been a couple miles farther north," the sheriff replied.

"Why?"

Meffert answered my question. "That'd make it Kentucky's mess, not Tennessee's."

I was turning away from the railing when something tugged at the sleeve of my awareness—something I hadn't even realized I'd seen. I turned back, scanning the concrete.

"What is it?" asked Tyler.

"Not sure," I said. "Something caught my eye. I thought so, anyhow. But maybe I was wrong. Maybe it was . . . " Just then I saw it, on the inside of the concrete rail, an arm's length beyond the end of the blood smear. The tiniest flash of light, like a droplet of dew glinting. It was a small fleck of paint—red paint—glinting in the afternoon sun. "I might be wrong," I said, "but I'm guessing there's a truck out there somewhere that's got a little ding in the edge of one door." I guesstimated the height of the railing. "About thirty-two inches off the ground. Too high for a car door, I'd say."

"I've got a tape measure in the car," said Meffert. "I can measure it. And I'll scrape that paint off and get it to the TBI lab. See if they can find a match."

"Well, shit," said the sheriff. "If it's a trucker, could be from anywhere in the country. We get thousands of 'em passing through here on I–75 ever' damn day."

I nodded sympathetically. "Hard to know even where to start looking." I turned to Tyler. "We'd better get on down there. We've got an hour of daylight, at best."

"We can get you some work lights if we need to," Sheriff Grainger said. "The highway department garage ain't far away."

I shook my head. "Even with good lights, it's just not the same," I said. "You always miss something. If we can't finish up by dark, I'd rather come back in the morning."

Sheriff Grainger shrugged. "Whatever you want, Doc." He pointed at the trees lining the nearer side of the gorge. "We went ahead and rigged you a rope down through that notch in the bluff. You said y'all have a litter in your truck?"

"We do." I studied the bluff. Even the notch—a narrow gap in the rock face, threaded by a thin yellow strand—was almost vertical. "Probably best to lower the litter from here on the bridge. Bag the remains and whatever else we find, lash everything to the litter, and hoist it back up."

"That's how I figured it, too," he said. "We've got more rope. We'll rig you two hauling lines and lower the litter, while y'all start on down."

"How about you tie our gear on the litter and lower it down? Lot easier to shinny down that rope if we don't have our hands full."

The sheriff saluted and called the deputy over.

Tyler was already halfway back to the truck. I caught up with him as he was laying the litter crosswise on the tailgate. He looked up. "What all you want to take, Dr. B?"

"Both cameras. Body bag, ID tags, a few biohazard bags, box of rubber gloves," I said. I tucked a pair of leather work gloves into a pocket of my jeans and stuffed a pair into one of Tyler's pockets, too. "To prevent rope burn," I said, then, "hmm. Two flashlights and two headlamps, just in case the time gets away from us. Oh, and the hoe."

"The hoe?" Tyler looked puzzled. "Nothing but rocks and water down there. What for?"

"You never know," I said. "I was a Boy Scout. Our motto—"

"I know, I know," he interrupted wearily, probably because he'd heard me say it a thousand times. "*Be Prepared.*"

We met the sheriff and Meffert at the end of the bridge and handed them the litter and tools—everything except the hoe, which I wanted to carry with me. Tyler shook his head, as if I were crazy; when the two officers looked quizzically at me, I simply smiled. Deputy Aikins pointed. "See that big ol' hemlock right yonder?" I looked, then nodded. "Rope's tied to that. Just foller it down. Bring you right to that ledge where she's at."

"Either one of you touch anything down there?"

"Nossir, not me," said Aikins. "Ain't been down there."

"None of us have," said Meffert. "We figured we'd leave the dirty work for y'all."

The deputy chortled. "Got *that* right," he said.

Tyler and I wriggled into coveralls—one-piece jumpsuits made of heavy canvas, the sort worn by mechanics and highway crews—which we wore to keep contamination off our clothes. The temperature was dropping as the afternoon waned, and the extra layer of warmth felt good. Moving fast, we scrambled down the steep shoulder and into the woods at the edge of the ravine. A hemlock, its trunk a full two feet thick, grew from a cleft in the rock bluff, curving outward above the stream to claim as much sunlight for itself as possible. Tied snugly around the trunk was a thin rope of yellow polypropylene. Tyler eyed the knot dubiously. "You think that'll hold?"

I took a look. "Sure," I said. "That's a figure eight on a bight. I recognize that—"

"Yeah, yeah, from your merit badge in knot craft. So it's got the Woodchuck Seal of Approval, right?"

"Hey, don't be dissing the Scouts," I said. "The knot's fine; the rope's the problem. I've seen a lot of ski ropes break, and that's basically what this is—polypropylene ski rope. Probably snap if you put more than a couple hundred pounds on it. But long as we're not both hanging from it at the same time, it ought to be okay." I eyed him; Tyler was an inch taller than I was, but skinnier. "How much you weigh?"

"One sixty," he said, his eyes zeroing in on my waistline. "You?"

"One seventy."

"Okay then," he said. "Heft before beauty. Think helium-filled thoughts."

Backing up to the notch in the bluff, I spiraled

the rope around my left forearm to create a bit of friction and then clamped my fist around it. Then, with my right hand, I pulled the rope snugly around my butt, gripping it with my right hand at waist level. The skinny plastic rope was lousy for climbing, but I hypothesized—and hoped—that I'd get enough braking power from the combined friction of both hands, the spiral around my forearm, and the detour around my rear end. Leaning back slightly, I tested my theory. The thin rope bit into my forearm and the backs of my thighs, but it didn't slip through my hands. "Not great," I said, as much to myself as to Tyler, "but it'll do. Stick that hoe under my left arm, would you?"

"Why don't you just chuck it down there?"

"And chip that edge I spent an hour sharpening? No way. Besides, I want it with me. Call me crazy."

"Crazy," he said, but he brought me the tool. I raised my left elbow, as if it were a chicken's wing, and he tucked the handle into my armpit, the blade flat against my chest. Still leaning away from the tree, the handle of the hoe jutting into the ravine, I stepped backward and down, into the crevice, and began my descent. The bluff wasn't high—only about twenty feet—and the notch offered plenty of footholds, so I made it down with no trouble, despite the awkwardness of the hoe.

Just as I stepped onto the ledge at the base of the bluff, I heard a sound that sent a shock wave of fear coursing through me. It was a dry, hollow buzz: the buzz of a rattlesnake. I froze, trying to pinpoint the source. It didn't take long. The snake—a big timber rattler, its body as thick as my wrist—was eighteen inches from my right foot. Head up, tail vibrating, the snake was coiled to strike. The rock ledge was catching the last of the afternoon sun, and the snake had been basking in the warmth—possibly the last real warmth for months. No wonder it was mad about the disturbance. Its eyes, I noticed, looked cloudy—a sign it was about to shed its skin. The good news was, that meant its vision was impaired; the bad news was, rattlesnakes get more aggressive when they can't see well, so the snake might launch a preemptive first strike.

Moving with excruciating slowness, I relaxed my right hand, lowering the loop of rope with what I hoped was enough subtlety to escape notice. Then I eased the hand up and across my chest, grasping the blade and sliding the hoe upward from beneath my left arm. The snake buzzed steadily, its head motionless except for the tongue sliding in and out, in and out, as it sampled and resampled my scent. My scent was changing fast, I suspected, with the flash flood of sweat, adrenaline, and whatever other chemicals were triggered by terror. *Fearomones*, I thought. When the hoe was halfway out from under my arm, I inched my right hand down the metal neck to the midpoint of the shaft, and then eased my left hand onto the thicker wood near the end.

Twenty feet above me, Tyler's footsteps crunched on leaves and twigs as he approached the edge of the bluff. "Dr. B?" he called. "You down yet?" I dared not answer. "Dr. B? Are you okay?" I hoped his voice might persuade the snake to crawl away, or at least distract it enough to allow *me* to move. No such luck—it remained poised, and it continued to buzz its warning. "Shit," I heard Tyler mutter, and then, loudly, "Hang on, Dr. B, I'm coming down. Don't worry!"

Suddenly I felt my left arm jerk wildly as the rope—still spiraled around my forearm—was yanked from above. Pulled off balance, I stumbled, and the snake hurled itself at my leg. In desperation I swung the hoe, knowing I was too late, too wild with my panicked swing. But to my astonishment, the snake's head stopped in midair, as if it had hit a pane of glass, then the body dropped to the ground. The edge of the blade, I saw, had sliced halfway through the snake's lunging body, pinning the creature to the ground, its jaws snapping an inch from my shin. Pressing down on the handle, I stepped away; then—when I was safely out of reach—I raised the hoe and brought it down on the neck, severing the head.

"Doc?" It was Sheriff Grainger on the bridge. I looked up and nearly fainted: Aikins had the 12-gauge at his shoulder, and the barrel appeared to be pointing straight down. Straight down at me.

"Jesus, Deputy, don't shoot," I shouted, and the sheriff pushed the barrel of the gun to one side, then pried it from the deputy's grip.

"Don't shoot, *don't shoot*," yelled Tyler, his voice high and strained. "Dr. B? *Dr. B?* Are you all right? What the *hell* is going on?"

"I'm all right," I said weakly, twisting my arm free of the rope. "I'm fine. Come on down."

Sixty seconds later, Tyler was on the ground. "Why didn't you answer me before? Why was he pointing a gun at you? What was all that racket you were making down here?"

Wordlessly I nodded in the direction of the snake. The mangled body was still writhing and thrashing, the spinal nerves continuing to send impulses to the muscles, even though the brain had been disconnected. When Tyler saw the snake, he jumped back as though he'd been bitten, then gasped, "God *damn*, I hate snakes. *Hate* 'em."

"I know," I said. "That's why I didn't tell you what the hoe was for."

"How'd you know this thing would be lying in ambush?"

"Didn't know. Just knew to be prepared. Knew this is the kind of rocky habitat they like, and this is the kind of weather that brings 'em out."

"You keep using the plural," he said, his face ashen. "*They* and *them*. Those pronouns are making me really nervous."

"I was just talking about snakes in general," I assured him. "The same way I might hold up one human skull but use the word 'humans.'" I resisted the urge to tell him that in the fall rattlesnakes sometimes converge in dens by the dozens or even the hundreds. If the sight of a single dying snake could spook Tyler so much, I hated to think how he'd react to the notion of scores of writhing vipers; serpentine spaghetti.

I clapped him on the shoulder. "Come on, we've got work to do now. Plenty of time for post-traumatic stress later."

THE WOMAN—DEFINITELY a woman—lay facedown, the skull misshapen, probably fractured by the fall. The arms and legs had tumbled free of the body and lay at odd, unnatural angles, the knees and elbows bent. The soft tissue of the extremities was largely gone, as were some of the finger and toe bones. Gnaw marks on the remaining bones of the hands and feet, as well as on the distal ends of the long bones, suggested that canine scavengers—coyotes, probably—had been sharing the remains with the buzzards.

We took a series of photos—both of us shooting, in the interest of speed. "Okay, good enough," I said. "Let's get her tagged and bagged." Normally we'd have spent more time observing and interpreting the scene, but time was a luxury we didn't have in the fading light of the mountain ravine. Tyler unfolded and unzipped the heavy, rubberized fabric of the body bag, and together we worked the big C-shaped opening underneath the torso. As we did, maggots—some of them as small as rice grains, some a half-inch long—wriggled from the corpse and dropped into the crevices between rocks. A thought struck me. "Before you put her in to simmer," I said, "find the five biggest maggots and put 'em in alcohol."

"Uh, okay. How come?"

"The biggest ones must've been the first to hatch," I told him. "Next donated body we get, we document how long it takes the maggots to reach this size. Presto—we know how long this woman's been dead."

"So, when you say, 'we document' . . ."

"I mean *you* document," I clarified. "But we both learn something. We start learning to read the bugs like a time-since-death stopwatch. Timing is everything." He nodded thoughtfully.

Once the torso was inside, we tucked in the limbs as well, then slid the bag onto the litter. Tyler began zipping it shut, sliding the zipper across the bottom, up one side, and across the top.

"Don't close it all the way just yet," I said. "We might find a few bones from the hands and feet in the crevices."

"You want to reach your hand down into snakeland, you go right ahead," said Tyler. "I'll start in on this pile of clothes and stuff." He unfolded a biohazard bag, then began tugging the tangle of fabric from the crevices in the rock. "Looks like some bloody sheets," he narrated, as I peered down into nooks and crannies beneath the spots where the hands and feet had lain. "Tennis shoes. Bra. Panties. T-shirt. Blue jeans." He had just finished extricating the blue jeans from the tangle when he gave a low whistle. "Holy shit," he said, holding up the jeans, "look at this, Dr. B." I was puzzled at first—the jeans had wider legs than any pants I'd ever seen. Had the woman been morbidly obese? Then I realized what I was seeing: a single layer of fabric, as if one of the seams in each leg had been left unsewn. But that wasn't the explanation. The explanation was, the legs of the pants had been sliced open, from top to bottom, up the front of each leg. The pants had been removed by cutting them off.

I took a closer look, and suddenly my blood ran cold. The cut edges of the jeans were stained, for their entire length, with blood. Whoever had cut the jeans off hadn't done it the way I'd have expected—hadn't put the blade inside the legs of the pants and then sliced up and out, away from the skin. The jeans had been cut from the outside, by bearing down on the blade and slicing inward. The killer had used the victim herself as a cutting board.

WE LOADED THE litter by the last of the daylight, pausing to put on the headlamps we would need for the climb out of the gorge. We had laid the body bag on first, then the biohazard bag containing the shoes and blood-soaked clothing, all of it cut. Last came another biohazard bag, this one containing a blood-soaked sheet and mattress pad. I lashed the bags tightly in place, so that nothing would spill if the litter tipped or even flipped as the officers hoisted it. When I was sure everything was secure, I slid the handle of the hoe beneath the lashings.

Tyler turned to look at me, his headlamp bright enough to be blinding even in the twilight. I held up a hand to shield my eyes, and he angled the headlamp down to lessen the glare. "You're sending the hoe up? Are you sure that's a good idea?"

"Look who's become a believer in the value of the hoe," I said.

"Hey, if you'd told me why you wanted it in the first place, I'd have believed you," he said.

"If I'd told you why I wanted it in the first place, there wouldn't have been a second place—you'd have stayed up on the bridge," I countered. "Or locked yourself in the truck."

"Could be. But now that I've seen the light, I

think we should hang on to the hoe till we're out of the woods. Figuratively and literally."

"Can't. We need both hands free to climb. Besides, the snakes are probably holed up for the night by now." I didn't actually know if that was true, but I wanted to reassure Tyler. And myself.

I looked up at the pale line of the bridge, where Meffert, Sheriff Grainger, and Deputy Aikins were silhouetted against the pewter sky. "Okay," I called. "Take up the slack. Easy does it." I stepped away from the litter as the lines twitched and grew taut and the litter slowly ascended. Ascended, but not into heaven.

Tyler struggled up the rope first, and I followed. We met the sheriff and Meffert on the bridge, where the litter now lay, and we each took a corner and carried it to the truck in silence. For reasons I couldn't have explained—because I didn't fully understand them—the procession had a solemn, almost sacred feel to it, as if we were pallbearers at a funeral. Which, in a way, we were, because this was almost certain to be the most attention and dignity that would attend this woman's death.

THE FUEL WARNING light blinked on just as Tyler and I turned off Stinking Creek Road onto the ramp for I–75 South. "Crap," I muttered. "We need gas."

"I think there's a Pilot station—maybe a truck stop?—at the next exit. Just before we start down the mountain."

"Yup," I said. "You want to grab some food there?"

"Not really. Last time we ate at a place like that, I got really sick. Remember those chili dogs in

Ooltewah? Woof. They tasted bad going down, and worse coming up. I've had bait shyness about truck-stop food ever since."

"I didn't realize your digestive system was so delicate," I said. "You sure you've picked the right career path?"

"Hey, I don't mind the bodies and the bugs. It's just the snakes and the gut-bombs I hate."

"Duly noted. I think there's a Cracker Barrel just down the mountain, at LaFollette. Think you can handle that?"

"Cracker Barrel? Are you kidding?" He made exaggerated smacking sounds. "I could eat there every day. The merchandise is tacky, and the biscuits aren't what they ought to be, but the food's great."

The Pilot truck stop, with its giant glowing sign of yellow, red, and black, loomed out of the darkness two minutes later. The fuel-pump islands were surrounded by a sea of asphalt, much of it occupied by tractor-trailer rigs that seemed settled in for the night. Many of the cabs were curtained off, but the trucks' running lights remained on, and the air thrummed with a chorus of diesel engines and auxiliary generators, running to keep refrigerated trailers cool and sleeper cabs warm.

As we threaded our way through the rows of parked rigs, I glimpsed a pair of legs—pale, bare, female legs—clambering down from one of the cabs. When she emerged from the narrow gap between two trucks, I was stunned to see that she was naked from the waist down, except for a pair of high-heeled shoes. As she crossed the asphalt to the opposite row of trucks, she tugged at the hem of her shirt, pulling it down enough to cover—or nearly cover—her rear end.

"Jesus," said Tyler. "Looks like you can get more than chili dogs and indigestion here."

"Sure does," I agreed, wondering what sort of desperation would induce a woman to have sex with multiple strangers every night in a truck-stop parking lot. "Looks like you could definitely get diseased here, too." I thought of the remains in the back of the truck. "Or maybe dead."

The woman rapped on the cab of a truck that was practically outlined in amber running lights. The door opened, and she climbed up. As she did, the hem of her garment crept up her flanks, as if the very fabric had somehow been programmed by some efficiency expert to shave every possible second and excise every scrap of humanity from the transaction about to be executed.

THE BIG SCOREBOARD-STYLE clock on the *Knoxville News Sentinel* building read 9:57 P.M.—three minutes shy of my usual bedtime—by the time Tyler and I reached the city and took the exit for Neyland Drive. It was past Tyler's bedtime already, if his slumped posture and rumbling snores were any indication. I slowed down, savoring the view on the final mile of the drive. The riverfront stretch of Neyland Drive was pretty by daylight, but it was beautiful by night. The lights of the Gay Street and Henley Street Bridges pooled and smeared in the water, like an Impressionist painting of Paris streets after an evening rain.

Neyland Stadium loomed dark and hulking as I

threaded the truck down the narrow service lane around its perimeter. Weaving between concrete columns and steel girders to the base of the mammoth oval, I tucked the truck into the narrow dead end of asphalt beside the osteology lab. “Tyler, we’re here,” I said. He didn’t answer, so I shook his elbow, causing him to bolt upright and look around, wild-eyed and disoriented. “We’re here,” I repeated.

“Okay,” he mumbled. “Be right there.” He rubbed his eyes and shook his head. “Wow,” he said, sounding slightly more cogent. “I was really out.” He massaged his neck and rolled his head from side to side to work out the kinks. “You want me to start processing the remains now?”

“Nah. Go home. She’s locked in the back.” I thought of the line the Morgan County sheriff had used a few weeks before. “She won’t be any deader in the morning than she is now. But *you* might be, if you don’t get some sleep.”

“Thanks,” he said. “I’ll get going on it first thing.” He opened the door, but he didn’t get out. “Doctor B?”

“Yeah?”

“How could somebody do that to a woman? Butcher her like an animal and dump her like garbage?”

I shook my head. “I can tell you her race, her stature, her handedness, and her age,” I said. “I might be able to tell you how she died. But why? I can’t answer that one.” I took a deep breath and exhaled slowly. “What was it the old maps used to say at the edges, out beyond the known territory? ‘Here be monsters’? I don’t understand it—I’ve got no scientific explanation for it—but there's evil in the world. Hiding around corners, lurking in doorways, coiling underneath rotting logs. Irrational, inexplicable, powerful evil."

A LIGHT WAS on in the living room when I pulled into my driveway at eleven fifteen, but the rest of the house was dark. Unclipping the garage-door remote from the visor, I clicked the button, eased beneath the rising door, and switched off the ignition. I sat for a moment, the truck's engine ticking with heat, my heart ticking with disappointment.

After seventeen years of marriage—and a decade of late-night returns from crime scenes—I no longer expected Kathleen to wait up for me; I'd even taken time to call her, when Tyler and I had stopped for gas, to tell her not to. But I'd been harboring hope that she would ignore the suggestion. Bodies and bones didn't usually bother me; I regarded them as puzzles to be solved—mental challenges, not human tragedies—but tonight I felt skittish and shaken. The brutality of the woman's slaying had gotten to me; so had the near miss with the rattlesnake. Had the ticking engine somehow reminded me of the snake's warning buzz? The deputy's rhetorical question as we'd loaded up—"Did you know that a rattlesnake's head moves at a hunnerd and seventy-five miles an hour when it's striking?"—popped into my mind, unbidden and unwelcome, for the dozenth time since dinner.

I stripped off my clothes in the garage—I'd shed the jumpsuit earlier, back at the stadium—and tossed them in the washing machine I'd installed in the back corner, at the end of my workbench. It was the old washer, the one Kathleen had exiled from the laundry room after finding decomp-soaked dungarees in it. Now, banished to the garage, it lived a contaminated and constrained life: no more satin pillowcases, silk blouses, sheer nightgowns, lacy undergarments; nothing but stinking shirts, muddy jeans, ruined towels, mildewed socks. My career had been good for America's appliance manufacturers, I reflected, dumping in extra detergent and twisting the Maytag's knobs to the longest, hottest cycle. Besides replacing the washing machine ten years ahead of schedule, I had also replaced a practically new stove several years earlier, after carelessly allowing a simmering skull to boil over: a mistake I'd made early in my career, before I learned not to bring my work home. I'd tried drenching the contaminated stove with Pine-Sol, Lysol, and Clorox, but to no avail; switching on any of the burners or the oven would fill the kitchen—swiftly and powerfully—with the pungent odor of human decomposition.

The garage was already chilly with the night air, and I was shivering by the time I got into the shower in the basement bathroom—my son, Jeff's, bathroom. I cranked the hot-water valve wide open, adding just enough cold to keep from getting scalded, letting the water pour over me, pummel me, and I hoped purify me. I stood beneath the steaming stream until I'd used every drop of hot water in the fifty-gallon tank. I could have used another fifty gallons and still wished for more.

Wrapped in a towel, I made my way quietly up the stairs, pausing in the living room only to switch off the lamp beside the sofa. At the far end of the darkened hall, the bedroom door was a rectangle of deeper darkness. Even before I reached the room, I heard the deep, sighing breaths of Kathleen's earnest, steady sleep. I stood in the doorway and listened. Behind me, in the living room, I heard the hollow, metronomic heartbeat of the regulator clock on the fireplace mantel. The clock had once kept time in my father's law office, and it skipped not so much as a single beat when Daddy opened his desk drawer, took out a pistol, raised it to his temple, and squeezed the trigger. The clock required winding every seven days, and I welcomed the ritual. I remembered watching my father wind it, gripping the key between his broad thumb and the knuckle of his forefinger; I remembered the time, not long before his death, when he let me wind it, my three-year-old fingers engulfed by his big, helping hand. The clock was my most tangible link to my dead father, and the weekly ritual of winding it allowed me to touch him, to be touched by him, in a way that nothing else could. The clock began striking midnight. I lingered in the doorway until the last stroke died away, then tiptoed into the bedroom, draped my towel on the bathroom doorknob, and slipped into bed with Kathleen.

Without waking, she rolled toward me, her head instinctively seeking out its accustomed resting place on my chest, her breasts and belly pressed against my side and hip. Her skin felt cool against mine, and she burrowed into the warmth I'd brought with me from the shower. I synchronized my breathing to hers—a trick I'd learned years before, while doing battle with my dissertation—and as her breath and mine became one, I felt my whirling mind and skittish spirit begin to settle. I heard my father's clock strike twelve fifteen, and twelve thirty, and twelve forty-five, but I did not hear it strike one.

DEEP IN MY sleep, I heard a groan and a cry of distress, and although they seemed to come from somewhere far away, I knew they had come from me. I felt myself struggling, too, but my limbs were weak and ineffectual.

"Bill. *Bill.* Honey, wake up. It's okay." Kathleen's voice reached down and took hold of me in the depths, hauling me to the surface of consciousness. Her hands held my wrists; I didn't know if she was shaking me or restraining me. Both, perhaps.

I drew a deep, shuddering breath and expelled it, then another. She let go of me and switched on the bedside lamp, then slid herself to a sitting position, leaning against the headboard, laying one hand on my heaving chest, another on my head. "You okay?"

"Yes," I said automatically, and then, a second later, "no," and by the time the word was out, I found myself sobbing. "Oh, God," I gasped. "I had a dream. An awful, awful dream."

"Oh, sweetie," she said, pulling me to her bosom, stroking my hair. "I'm so sorry. Tell me."

But I couldn't tell her; I couldn't speak at all, not yet. My breath came in ragged, shuddering gasps—as if it were some separate creature, wild and savage and untamed.

"Shh," she soothed. "I've got you. I've got you." She rocked and swayed, her fingers cradling my head, her breath washing over me, until bit by bit, breath by breath, my chest rose and fell with hers once more and my fear subsided.

"We were in the backyard," I said finally. "You. Me. Jeff. Jeff wasn't a teenager—Jeff was a little kid—but the time was now, somehow."

"I like that about dreams," Kathleen murmured. "They make up their own rules as they go along. They don't always make logical sense, but they make emotional sense. Go on."

"I was mowing the grass while y'all were kind of milling around," I said, "and as I was mowing the steep part of the bank, where it angles down toward the ditch, I saw a hole in the ground I'd never seen before. It was big—a foot in diameter—and while I was staring at it, trying to figure out why it was there, I saw a pair of eyes, like glowing red coals, deep inside, and then this immense snake came slithering slowly toward me, slithering out of the hole. It was as big around as the hole, and long—fifteen, twenty feet long." She held me tighter, running her fingers through my hair and scratching my head to keep me connected to her, to keep me grounded. "It was like the snake knew me—knew all of us. Like he'd been lurking in our midst for a long time, I'd just never noticed him before. And I could tell he was about to do something terrible—to kill one of us, or kill all of us—and I had to stop him. He'd already killed my father—I knew this because the snake's face looked a little bit like my father's face—and I knew that he'd been following me ever since he killed my dad. Lurking just out of sight. Biding his time, waiting for the sinister signal or the evil impulse—whatever it was that guided him—to hiss *now* and cause him to strike. So I ran and got the hoe, and I started chopping him with it. He was coming at me and I was chopping, and chopping, and chopping. I finally managed to cut off his head, but while I was busy chopping off his head, his tail was coiling around me, and by the time the head was off, I was completely trapped in the coils, and the head was looking at me, still alive, the eyes still glowing red. And then I saw more glowing red eyes, deep in the hole in the ground. Another huge snake came slithering out, and then another, and another, and another."

In the dream's final scene, the snakes dispersed throughout the yard, scattering and yet somehow moving in concert—a choreography of venomous intent—converging on my loved ones, who remained innocent and unaware of the approaching menace. The father-snake's eyes watched, the vertical slits narrowing, as I fought to break free, as I struggled to shout a warning, as the tightening coils rendered me immobile and mute, impotent to stop the impending evil.

The horror of the scene gripped me once more as I described it. "God," I said. "*God.*"

With the tips of her fingers, Kathleen gently closed my eyelids. Then she covered my face with soft kisses, saying, "Mmm, salty." Next she kissed my neck and my chest. Then, as I lay on my back, my eyes still closed, she knelt astride me, touching me, taking me in: reminding me that there was goodness and sweetness in the world, too—irrational, inexplicable, and remarkably powerful goodness, too.

CHAPTER 10

Satterfield

SATTERFIELD DAWDLED, TAKING HIS sweet time filling out the deposit slip, allowing two customers to get into the teller queue ahead of him.

"Next, please?"

His timing was perfect; Satterfield's favorite teller, Sheila, smiled in his direction as she said it. Sheila was a good-looking blonde, not young—hell, she might even be the other side of forty—but she was still hot, and she knew it; she worked it: lots of jewelry, tight skirts, silk blouses, the top two buttons always unbuttoned—enough to flash some cleavage and even some bra if she leaned forward just right.

"Must be my lucky day," Satterfield said, giving her his best smile as he strolled up to her window.

She smiled back, her eyes flicking downward long enough to check out the black T-shirt stretched tight across his chest and biceps. "What can we do for you today?"

“Well, for starters, you could deposit this. The eagle has landed.” He slid the Social Security check across the counter. She took it and turned it over, glancing at the spidery signature Satterfield had forged on the endorsement line.

“Did you want this in your mother’s account?”

“Sure. Her pension, her account.” In point of fact, it made no difference which account the money went to; Satterfield’s name was on her account, and he’d phone later—to a different branch—and have the money transferred into his. Meanwhile, it served his purposes to appear the doting, dutiful son to Sheila.

“How’s she doing? We haven’t seen her in a while.”

Satterfield shook his head sadly. “She’s really gone downhill since my stepdad died,” he said. “Just can’t get out and about anymore.” Both statements were true. After Satterfield had moved her to Knoxville, filed the change-of-address forms, and brought her into the bank to open the joint checking account, he’d strangled her in her bed, the very night they’d set up the account. “You let that sorry husband of yours treat me like shit,” he’d said, her eyes bugging and her mouth gaping, like those of a fish dying on a dock. “Your own kid. What’s that Bible verse you always loved to quote? ‘Train up a child in the way he should go, and when he is old, he will not depart from it’? Well, here I am, Mama, all trained up. I settled up with him, now I’m settling up with you.” There was now only one last account he needed to settle—one other person who’d done him grievous wrong—and Satterfield’s plan for vengeance, which had led him to Knoxville, was already showing much promise for creating intense and prolonged suffering.

Satterfield smiled again at the teller. "I'll tell Mama you asked about her," he said. "That'll cheer her up. She remembers you." He leaned forward and added in a low, confiding tone, "I always tell her I saw you, even when I don't. She likes the idea of a pretty woman being nice to her son, you know? Once a mother, always a mother." She raised an eyebrow, a half smile twitching at one corner of her mouth. *She is eating this up*, he thought. "You got kids?"

"Two."

"How old?"

"One in high school, one in college."

"Get outta here. You?" His eyes slid down her body, then back up. "You're messing with me. I see twenty-year-olds at the gym who'd kill to look like you."

She slid his deposit slip across the counter, leaning over farther than she needed to, giving him a peek down her blouse.

A stocky middle-aged woman—possibly no older than Sheila, but packing a lot more weight and a lot less heat—bustled up beside the teller, her face a mask of officiousness and disapproval. Her nametag read MELISSA PEYTON, HEAD TELLER. What she said was, "And how are you today, sir?" What she meant was, "Stop it, both of you."

"I'm just fine, Melissa," Satterfield crooned. "Your staff is always so nice. You've obviously done a good job training them. Leadership by example, we called that in the Navy." He flashed her the smile, then nodded and lifted a hand in farewell to both women as he turned to go. Once he was sure Sheila's boss couldn't see, he gave Sheila a private wink, which she returned.

HE'D PARKED THE Mustang on the far side of the parking lot, the side closest to Blockbuster Video, where the bank's employees were required to park so that customers could have the good spaces. He'd parked next to Sheila's car, a red Celica fastback—*hot woman, hot car*—and as he walked behind it, he stroked the rear spoiler with his fingertips, leaving tracks in the dust. Through the tinted windows he glimpsed the beads hanging from her rear-view mirror, five strands of cheap iridescent beads, shimmering pink and purple in the light. *Bet she goes wild at Mardi Gras, when she's someplace where nobody knows her.*

A couple of months before, after depositing his mother's check, Satterfield had hung out at Blockbuster until the bank closed, watching and waiting for Sheila to emerge. He'd trailed her, watching her drive, her right hand draped loosely on the wheel, her left arm—tanned and toned—resting on the windowsill, a cigarette slanting suggestively between the flashing rings and crimson nails of her long fingers. She lived in a condo complex, one populated mostly by single twenty-somethings looking for hookups around the pool. He'd gone back a few times on weekends; had seen her sunbathing, nursing a beer in a foam sleeve, lighting a series of cigarettes that she mostly just let dangle, sending up smoke signals of languor and availability. Usually she only hit the pool when her daughter was staying at the ex-husband's, though once he saw them both out there, both in bikinis. The daughter was hot, too. Satterfield had sensed friction between them. Not surprising, he guessed—the girl just starting to claim her sexual power, the mom clinging desperately to hers as it began to wane. Once Satterfield saw Sheila make a play for one of the young studs sunning his abs, asking him to rub suntan oil on her back, going *mmm* as he worked his way down to her hips, then up the backs of her legs. That night, after dark, the guy had shown up at her condo, a bottle of something in one hand, and she'd met him at the door wearing a short silk robe. The guy had stayed until midnight, and Satterfield had listened to their sounds through his parabolic microphone, which he aimed at the bedroom window like a weapon. A weapon of listening.

Satterfield had already checked the calendar, and he'd seen that October's Social Security check would likely arrive on Thursday or Friday. Maybe Sheila would get off work Friday afternoon and discover that she had a flat tire. Wouldn't she be grateful if Satterfield just happened to be coming out of Blockbuster with a few videos at that very moment; if he happened to see her distress and offer to help—change the tire and then follow her home, because those little donut spares are notoriously unreliable? Surely she'd invite him in for a drink.

If she invited him in, she was opening the door to what would come next. If she *didn't* invite him in, she was an ungrateful bitch, and she would deserve whatever she got.

SATTERFIELD'S LEFT ARM angled across the corner of the metal table, his open palm turned upward, fingers spread wide, as the man with the shaved head clasped Satterfield's hand in both of his and bent forward. The movement exposed the back of the man's head and neck, and Satterfield studied the tattooed tongues of red and yellow flame that licked the man's broad neck and the base of his skull.

The man straightened, eyeing Satterfield's face now. "You sure that's what you want?"

"Sure I'm sure," said Satterfield. "Why? Lots of people get stuff like this."

"I don't mean the design," the guy said. "I mean, you sure you want me to put the head in your palm? All those nerve endings, that's gonna hurt like hell."

Satterfield held the guy's gaze before answering. "Some guys get their *dicks* tattooed," he said. "Gotta be a lot more nerve endings down there. Besides, I'm pretty tough."

"Yeah," mused the guy, peering now at the constellation of small circles of pale scar tissue dotting Satterfield's forearm. "Yeah, I guess you are." His gaze shifted to the ink on Satterfield's right arm. "You a SEAL?"

"Was," Satterfield said tersely. "Not now. Not anymore."

The guy nodded; took the hint and didn't ask more questions. Then he looked again at the photograph Satterfield had laid on the table—the thick-bodied serpent, its tapered neck flaring to a broad, triangular head—and picked up the electric needle. As the hollow steel fang bit the flesh of his palm, striking again and again to inject the image, Satterfield's nostrils flared, and his eyes glittered with a cold, reptilian light.

CHAPTER 11

Brockton

I WAS FIVE MINUTES late getting to TBI headquarters in Nashville, but luckily I wasn't the only late arrival: I stepped into an elevator just as the door was closing, and found myself riding up with Special Agent Meffert. "Bubba," I said, shaking his hand, "how are you? Any leads yet?"

He gave a noncommittal shrug. "Some progress," he said. "We've ID'd her, but no real leads yet. I'll tell you more inside."

"Okay," I said. "Anything on the strip-mine girl, up in Morgan County?" He shook his head morosely.

The elevator stopped and we got out, heading down the hall to the TBI's main conference room.

A men's-room door in the hall opened and Carson Wallace, the TBI's deputy director, emerged. "Hey, Bubba. Dr. Brockton, thanks for coming." His handshake was wet, and it took some effort not to grimace in distaste. "I don't suppose y'all brought the feds with you?"

"Not unless they were hiding in the back of my truck," I joked.

"You never know, with them," Wallace said. "Those guys can be pretty stealthy." He opened the door of the conference room, then added, "See what I mean?" Already seated at one end of the table were two men wearing the dark suits and confident expressions of FBI agents. At the other end were two lesser lights—local police, I guessed, from the lack of razor-sharp creases in their sleeves and the fact that they each had a hair or two out of place.

I knew one of the FBI agents—Jim Brodsky, assigned to the Nashville field office—and greeted him with a handshake. My hand was still damp from Wallace's grip, and I saw Brodsky glance down in surprise, a look of faint distaste on his face. Then he and I both wiped our hands on our pants in unison. "Dr. Bill Brockton," he said, "meet Supervisory Special Agent Pete Brubaker." Brubaker held out a hand and gave mine a competitive squeeze. "Doc, Pete runs our Behavioral Sciences Unit up at Quantico. The profilers. You're familiar with them?"

"Sure," I said. "Who isn't, since *Silence of the Lambs*?" Brubaker gave me a tight, tolerant smile—a sign, I took it, that the Hollywood gloss on their work had worn a bit thin. "Actually, though," I added, "I worked with one of your colleagues back before Hollywood discovered y'all. Mitch Radnor and I both looked at those three dismemberments out in Kansas, back about five years ago."

A bigger, more genuine smile replaced the polite, cool one. "Oh, right," he said, "I remember that, now that you remind me. Great case. What was it the guy used to cut up the victims? Some kind of power saw. Not a chain saw, though. Not a circular saw, either."

"A Sawzall," I supplied. "A reciprocating saw with a demolition blade. Ten teeth per inch, if memory serves."

"That's *right*," he said, snapping his fingers. "Guy who did it was a contractor—a roofer, wasn't he?" I nodded. "I couldn't believe he was carrying that saw around in the back of his truck. Still had blood on the blade, didn't it?"

"From all three of his victims," I said. "Never trust a guy who doesn't clean his tools."

He shook his head. "Amazing, how you pegged that tool exactly."

"Not exactly," I corrected. "Just approximately. I couldn't tell what brand the saw was, just what type. And what kind of blade."

"How'd you do that?" asked Wallace, the TBI honcho. The two local cops listened, but made no attempt to elbow their way into the conversation.

"I just looked at the skeletal material," I said. "There were these perfect, uniform little zigzags carved in the bone. Lots of short, even strokes, so it was clearly a power saw. The zigzags meant the blade was going back and forth, not spinning. I illuminated the cut marks, at a really low angle, to highlight all the zigs and zags, and took a bunch of pictures. Then I went to Home Depot and compared the pictures with saw blades till I found one that matched."

"Radnor had a quote up on his wall for a while after that," said Brubaker. "Something you said about the difference between flesh and bone. What was it?"

"Was it 'You have to chew harder if it's bone'?" I said it deadpan, and he ruminated for a moment before getting the joke and smiling. "Or maybe 'Flesh forgets, bone remembers'?"

"*There* you go. That was it."

"Gentlemen," said Wallace, "I hate to interrupt the lovefest, but we've got some work to do here. We've got three unsolved murders in the past twelve months—three dead women, all of them dumped near rural interstate exits. The question is, are they unrelated? Or do we have a serial killer on the loose? Let's take the cases one by one."

The first case, from Memphis, was the murder of a forty-two-year-old Alabama woman, whose body was found in late spring in an industrial area along the banks of the Mississippi River. "She was half a mile from Interstate 55," said the Memphis detective, flashing through a series of visuals that began with a map of the city, then zoomed in to aerial views of the exit and the nearby industrial park. "She was stabbed in the neck. The knife cut the jugular vein and she bled out."

"Any defensive wounds?" asked Brubaker, the profiler.

"Both hands," the detective said, flashing through slides of the body at the scene and also during the autopsy.

"Back up," Brubaker said, then—at the photo showing the woman's bloody body sprawled on the ground—"Okay, stop. She's fully clothed?"

"Yes, sir."

"Any sign of sexual assault?"

"None."

"What about her personal effects?"

"Her money and jewelry were gone. Wedding ring, diamond engagement ring gone."

"Married? What about the husband?"

"He's clean. He was at home with the kids in Birmingham; she was in Memphis at a sales convention. Husband reported her missing the next day, when one of her coworkers called him to say she hadn't shown up for a presentation she was scheduled to give. Her driver's license and credit cards were gone, too, but so far nobody's used the cards. Last transaction was an ATM withdrawal of two hundred dollars on Beale Street the night she disappeared." He flipped forward through the slides again until he came to a grainy security-camera image of the dead woman.

"So she's alone," Brubaker said, receiving a nod in reply, "and she doesn't look scared. But what she *does* look is drunk."

"We do have witnesses who say she'd been drinking at one of the bars for a while."

"Anybody see her leave with someone?" The detective shook his head. "Any reason to think this was something other than a robbery that went bad when she resisted?" A shrug. "Any other armed robberies and stabbings in the past two years?"

"Sure," conceded the detective. "It's Memphis. We have a homicide every four days. A robbery every three hours. An aggravated assault every eighty minutes."

"Sounds like a swell place to live," said the profiler. "And an even sweller place to die. Okay, let's move on." He turned to the woman from the Chattanooga Police Department. "Tell us about your case."

"Twenty-nine-year-old white female," she began, "single, living alone. Reported missing by a coworker on June nineteenth when she didn't show up for work for a week, didn't return phone calls, didn't answer her door. She was found two days later, in the woods off I–24, about twelve miles southwest of Chattanooga."

Brubaker drummed his fingers on the table. "How was she killed?"

"Blunt-force trauma. Somebody beat her brains out." The Chattanooga detective slid packets of photos to all of us around the table. I heard a few grunts—including my own—as people reached the photos showing how thoroughly her cranium and face had been reduced to a bloody pulp. "Murder weapon was a cast-iron skillet."

"Excuse me?" interrupted the TBI's Carson. "Did you say a *skillet*?"

"Yes, sir," the detective replied. "If you'll flip a few more pages back in your packet, you'll see several photos of it." Like everyone else, I flipped, and I marveled at what I saw: a six-inch cast-iron skillet, the bottom and sides of it covered with a paste of blood, hair, and bits of bone and brain matter. The skillet was in two pieces. "As you see," the detective said, "at some point the handle snapped off at the rim from the force of the blows. The medical examiner was able to match the shape of the skillet with several of the fractures in the skull. There are pictures of that, too." Fascinated, I flipped forward until I came to a photo of a defleshed cranium, its shattered vault marked with distinctive curved lines. In one photo, someone with latex gloves held the skillet just above one of the curved indentations in the bone, and the arcs matched exactly.

"You said she was single," said Brubaker, and the detective nodded. "Ex-husband?"

"No, sir. Never married."

"Boyfriend?"

"Not at the time. And not for a while. Not in the prior two years."

He frowned. "Could there have been a new boyfriend, one she hadn't told anybody about?" The detective looked uncertain. "I think this is domestic," Brubaker explained. "Crime of passion. Look at the overkill—lots more violence than necessary, but it's not *sadistic* violence; it's just plain rage. Hell, she was probably dead after the first hit, but he just kept whaling away with that skillet till he *broke* the damned thing." He drummed his fingers again. "Was she killed at home?" The detective shook her head. "Where? Not in the woods, I'm thinking."

"Not in the woods, best we can tell," the detective said. "Somewhere else. We don't know where."

"She was killed in a kitchen, that's where," Brubaker said. "Where else can you lay your hands on a cast-iron skillet when you're mad as hell? Maybe the new boyfriend invited her over, then told her to cook dinner, and she refused—again—because she'd decided he was a loser and a jerk and a chauvinistic pig. I'm just making this up, obviously, but whatever it was, *something* set him off and he went ballistic."

The detective nodded, chewing her lip.

"You said she was reported missing by a co-worker?"

"Yes."

"Not her boss."

"No."

"The boss—a man, right?" She nodded. "Middle-aged? Married, I'm guessing?"

Her brow furrowed as she thought, and I could picture her trying to remember the boss's left hand. She looked up at Brubaker, surprised. "Yeah, now that you mention it, he *was* wearing a ring."

"Be interesting to know if the boss's wife was away when this happened," Brubaker said. "Also be interesting to check his kitchen for blood." Her eyes narrowed, and as they did, I could see wheels begin turning behind them.

We ended with the new case Meffert and I were working in Campbell County. Meffert started with an overview of the case, and with the update of the ID. "The victim was a twenty-six-year-old white female from Covington, Kentucky. Melissa Mahan; went by Crystal." He flashed a picture—a mug shot—showing a pretty but world-weary young woman. "She had a couple of arrests for soliciting. She worked part-time as an exotic dancer here"—he showed a slide of Adult World, the seedy establishment at the I–75 exit, a few miles from where we'd recovered her body. Next he showed the nearby truck stop. "She could have been picked up at either Adult World or the truck stop. Lotta truckers visit the porn palace; lotta hookers work the truck stop. She was a familiar face at the truck stop, I'm told."

"When was she reported missing?" asked Brubaker.

Meffert frowned. "She wasn't. Her last day of work at Adult World was September seventh. Over two weeks ago. But she wasn't scheduled to work again until September fourteenth, because her boss had suspended her for a week. So we don't actually know when she got picked up."

"You got anything that links her to a trucker?"

"Nothing definitive," said Meffert. "We found a fleck of red paint on the railing of the bridge she was dumped from. High on the rail—probably too high to have come from a car door. We've got the crime-lab guys analyzing it now, seeing if they can match it to a brand of paint or a brand of truck."

Brubaker turned to me. "Dr. Brockton, what can *you* tell us about how long she'd been dead?"

"Not enough," I said truthfully. "Obviously she was killed sometime after September seventh. And she was pretty badly decomposed by September twenty-third. I'm guessing she'd been there for a week, maybe close to two, before we found her. But whether she'd been dead for six days or sixteen days, I can't say for sure. There's just not much scientific basis for estimating time since death—not after the first few days, anyhow."

He drummed his fingers three times. Was he just thinking, or was he impatient; frustrated? Maybe all of those. "How many trucks a day pass by the strip joint or the truck stop?"

Meffert shrugged. "Lots. A hundred? Two hundred?"

"So if it *was* a trucker, and the time-since-death estimate has a ten-day range, your suspect pool could be as high as two thousand truckers." He shook his head. "That's a hell of a lot of truckers." He looked at me sharply. "*Ten days?* You really can't pin it down any tighter than that?"

I felt my face redden, and I wished I'd thought to begin studying maggot growth and development earlier than I had. I glanced at Meffert, remembering how he'd teased me about misjudging Colonel Shy's death by more than a century. Meffert was looking down at his notes—studying them with extreme attentiveness, it seemed to me.

Brubaker shifted gears. "What about the dismemberment? What was used to cut her up? Power saw? Hand saw? Hunting knife?"

"Don't know yet," I said, but I felt better about this line of questioning. "We put the bones in to simmer yesterday morning. I expect my assistant's cleaning them just about now. Ask me tomorrow, after I've had a chance to take a close look at the cut marks."

After another ten minutes of discussion—most of it focusing on the Stinking Creek woman, though with some follow-up Q&A about the Memphis and Chattanooga cases—Brubaker summarized his conclusions. The three murders were unrelated, he said. All three victims were women, true, and all three bodies had been found near interstate exits, but the similarities ended there.

"Well, thank God we're not looking for a serial

killer," said Wallace, the TBI honcho, putting words to the relief that I imagined all of us around the table were feeling.

That relief was short-lived. "Oh, but you are," said Brubaker. "I guarantee it." All heads turned in the direction of the FBI profiler.

"I don't understand," countered Wallace. "I thought you just agreed that these killings are unrelated."

"I did. They are." We stared at him. If he was hoping to get our attention, he'd succeeded. "These three *are* unrelated. But one of them's the work of a serial killer." I knew which one he meant even before he said it; in fact, at some level, I'd known since I'd first seen her bloody body. "The hooker who was cut up and dumped in the creek—she was almost certainly not that guy's first victim. You don't start with something like that. And she sure as hell won't be his last victim. Not unless he's caught very quickly."

Meffert raised his hand. "We've got another dead female in East Tennessee. Unidentified. Unknown cause of death."

Brubaker turned to him. "Killed when?"

"Don't know," said Meffert. "Doc, you want to jump in here?"

"An adolescent," I said. "Fourteen, fifteen. Dead at least two or three years, maybe lots more. Maybe as long as twenty years. Bare bones, bleached by the sun."

Brubaker's gaze swiveled between me and Meffert. "Was she dumped near an interstate?" Meffert shook his head. "Some other easily accessible spot?"

"No, sir," said the TBI agent. "Way the hell off the beaten track. At an abandoned strip mine up in the mountains. 'Bout as hard to access as it gets."

Brubaker shrugged. "Hard to say, if we don't know how or when she was killed. But unless something turns up that links the scenes, I'd guess it's unrelated."

Just then the door opened halfway. A woman caught Wallace's eye and beckoned to him; he pushed back from the table and stepped into the hallway. A moment later, he returned and tapped me on the shoulder. "Doc, you've got a phone call. Your assistant—Tyler somebody? He says he's found something you need to know ASAP."

Startled, I excused myself and followed the woman to a nearby office. On the desk was a phone with a blinking light indicating a call on hold. She pressed the button and handed me the receiver.

"Hello? Tyler?"

"Hey, Dr. B. Sorry to interrupt you. But you asked me to let you know if I found anything significant when I cleaned the bones."

I felt my senses go on high alert. "What is it?"

"I was just looking at the left humerus. It was cut about midway between the shoulder and the elbow?"

"I remember. Go on."

"Well, I looked at it in the dark, the way you showed us, with a flashlight beam skimming it at a really low angle."

The wait was killing me. "For Pete's sake, Tyler, just spit it *out*. What'd you see? Saw marks? Knife marks? An image of the Virgin Mary?"

"Well, cut marks, for sure," he went on, with

maddening indirection, "but not saw marks *or* knife marks, best I can tell. I compared 'em to all the examples we've got in the reference file. I finally found one photograph that matched the pattern."

"So what was the *tool*?" I looked down and found myself drumming my fingers on the desktop, unconsciously aping Brubaker's gesture of impatience.

"It was labeled 'Unknown.' From a case you worked in Alaska two years ago."

"SEXUAL SERIAL KILLERS don't do that," Brubaker said, with an assurance born of a quarter century of experience studying violent, twisted murderers.

"But why else would he cut her up that way," I persisted, "with a tool that I would recognize—that *only* I would recognize—if he's not trying to taunt me, or threaten me?"

"You said it yourself," he went on. "Even *you* don't know what the cutting tool was—not in this case; not in that Alaska case." He was pummeling not just my hypothesis but my confidence, too. "And you said the Alaska killer hung himself in prison, so we know *he* didn't kill this stripper. Not unless you missed the time-since-death estimate here by a lot more than ten days." That felt like a low blow, and it stung. When did the conference table turn into a boxing ring—and how had my forensic colleagues been transformed into spectators, watching me take a drubbing? "How the hell would some truck driver in Tennessee know about this cutting tool that's so mysterious even *you* can't figure out what it was?" I had no answer to that.

"Serial killers don't go after cops," he went on,

"and they *damned* sure don't go after anthropologists. They go after their dream victims. Bundy? He went after brown-haired women who looked like the girlfriend that dumped him. Gacy? Boys and young men. The Green River Killer, up near Seattle? Forty young women so far, nearly all in their teens and twenties." I nodded, grudgingly.

"Look," he added in a more conciliatory tone, "there are only so many ways to kill somebody. Put a hundred million killers at a hundred million crime scenes for a hundred million years, and sooner or later two of them will pick up the same cutting tool." I liked the reference—a riff on the old saying about monkeys and typewriters and the works of Shakespeare, which was really a saying about how random genetic variation eventually, inevitably, turned primordial slime into human beings—but I disliked the swiftness and certainty with which he'd rejected my idea: my suggestion that the Stinking Creek killer was somehow—some*why*—echoing one of my prior cases.

"You're the expert," I said, hoping my voice didn't convey the sullenness I was feeling.

"These guys go after victims that feed their sexual fantasies," he repeated. "Don't take this the wrong way; I mean, I *do* find you a *very* attractive man, Doctor"—he said it with a sly grin and a wink, to let everyone know it was a good-natured olive branch of a joke, as well as a signal that the discussion was over—"but I doubt that this guy's fantasies extend to you."

I prayed to God he was right. I hoped like hell he wasn't wrong.

CHAPTER 12

Desirée

SHE WAS LEANING AGAINST a streetlight—one foot propped on the post, the knee raised and her back arched, accentuating her curves—when the blue Mustang sidled to the curb and stopped. She waited until the passenger-side window came down, then pushed off from the post and sauntered to the curb. Music spilled from the car window—Elton John pleading "Don't let the sun go down on me"—then the volume ramped down, and she heard the guy inside call out, "Hey, good-lookin'. What's your name?"

"Desirée. What's yours?" He didn't answer.

Desirée was her street name, the name she donned along with the clothes; it made it easier to be who she had to be, to do what she had to do. She was wearing her Friday night outfit: a slinky gray top, worn off one shoulder; black spaghetti-strap bra peeking out from underneath; spiky red heels; fishnet thigh-highs; and a denim skirt so short it left an inch of toffee-colored skin exposed above the tops of the fishnets. Both stockings were torn—the front of the left thigh, the back of the right knee. She had two pairs of new ones in her dresser, but she'd noticed that she turned more heads—turned more tricks—looking like this. Men liked the ripped stockings; they seemed to get turned on by the idea that she'd been pawed or manhandled by other guys already. Made the sex seem dirtier; kinkier, she guessed.

Still standing on the curb, Desirée leaned down, forearms on the windowsill, giving the guy a good view of the lacy bra and the pale brown breasts. It was dark inside the car—a blue car with tinted windows—and the driver was wearing mirrored shades, so his eyes were hidden. But from the small reflections of herself dead center in the lenses, she could tell that he was eyeing her, or at least part of her. After she'd given him a long eyeful, she purred, "So, baby, you just lookin', or you want a date?"

"How much?" His voice all cool, like he didn't really care if he got any or not.

"Twenty if all you want's a quick hand job. Forty for oral. A hundred for a full-on, un-for-*get*-able ride."

He looked away briefly, then back at her, his fingers drumming the steering wheel in time to the music. "I'll give you fifty."

"Aww, don't lowball me, baby," she cooed. "Let me show you what I am *talkin'* about." She straightened, turned her back to the car, and planted the high heels wide, then slowly folded forward and put her hands on her knees, shimmying her legs and causing the skirt to creep up her thighs and buttocks. It was a trick she'd learned when she was dancing at the Mouse's Ear, the strip bar in West Knoxville where the suburban guys with money went when their wives were away or their big-spender customers were in town. Once the skirt was riding high and she knew he had a good view of her thong and her business, she began to undulate, rotating her head and her hips in opposite directions. Her hair radiated from her head in shimmering golden spokes—an ironic, hypnotic halo, one befitting a fallen saint seeking a paying partner in sin. Stopping mid-sway, she arched her back and blew a pouty kiss over her shoulder into the cavelike interior of the car. "Best hundred you will ever spend, lover boy."

"You remind me of somebody special," he said.

"I *am* somebody special."

"A girl in San Diego. My first time. A night I'll always remember." Desirée felt her hopes rising. "So I'll go sixty," he added.

She breathed a quiet sigh and clambered into the Mustang, the skirt still riding up as she settled into the low bucket seat. "Two blocks up, on the right, there's the Magnolia Inn. Go around back and pull in behind the Dumpster."

He turned toward her and shook his head. "No way, sister. I am not doing it behind a Dumpster in back of some hot-sheet motel."

"It's not about the Dumpster, baby," she cajoled. "It's nice and quiet back there. Dark. Private. Five minutes from now you will be in heaven."

"Forget it." The car wasn't moving. A bad sign.

She needed the sixty. Really, *really* needed the sixty, and if she didn't have it by midnight, she'd be headed down the rabbit hole of withdrawal. She tucked her hands under her thighs so he wouldn't see that she already had the shakes. "You wanna get a room, honey?" Trying to keep the desperation out of her voice. "That's cool. I've got a deal there. Twenty bucks for an hour. King-size bed. Clean sheets. I can do a lot more for you on a nice big bed."

He shook his head. "Naw. I got someplace better. Five minutes from here. No cops, no drunks, nobody. Just me and you. I got some pot, if you want to get high. Got some blow, too, if you're into that."

She felt a tingle of excitement mixed with relief. Sixty bucks plus a ride on the white horse? That was as good as a hundred in cash. Nearly, anyway. "Customer's always right," she said. "I need payment up front, though."

He laughed. "So you can snort the coke, snatch the dough, and run for it? Nice try, darlin'."

"Show me the money, honey. I need to know you've got it."

"Suspicious little thing, aren't you? You're hurting my feelings." He reached into a back pocket and fished out a wallet. Flipping it open, he riffled through the bills for her. She saw four or five twenties, maybe more; shit, she shouldn't have settled for sixty. But maybe she could squeeze another twenty out of him, once she had him revved up. All johns had a special itch, she'd found, and they'd usually pay extra to have it scratched. The trick was to find the itch without giving away the scratch. He plucked a twenty from the wallet, held it in front of her face. "Here. Earnest money. I'll give you the blow—the blow's what you want, right?—once we get there. You get the other forty bucks once you've made me happy."

He wasn't bad looking—not bad at all—and built, too. Strong looking, clean-cut. But that worried her: muscles and a short haircut. "You aren't a cop, are you? You look like a cop. How do I know you're not a cop?"

"Search me," he said, and laughed at his joke. "Too late, anyhow—you've already offered me sexual services for money. If I was a cop, you'd be busted already. But I'm not; I'm a soldier. Navy SEAL, just back from Iraq. Operation Desert Storm." He showed her his right forearm, which was tattooed with what looked like a bird of some sort—an eagle, she guessed—clutching a three-pronged spear. His other arm had a tat, too—what was that, a snake? God, she hoped not; Desirée hated snakes. "You oughta do me for free," the guy said. "One patriotic service person to another." He laughed again, and acted like he might take away the twenty.

"You serve your country for free, soldier boy?" She plucked the bill from his fingers and tucked it into her bra, then settled back in the seat and closed her eyes, anticipating the hum of the cocaine. She needed it—not just to quiet the jangle in her nerves, but to dull the ache in her tooth, too: a big abscess at the base of a molar, getting bigger and hurting like a sonofabitch. Jamming a bit of blow into the hole—*down the hatch*, that's what she thought now every time she tamped in the powder—would put out the fire in her jaw. Dull the jagged, broken-glass edge of the pain, at least for a while.

It was a long five minutes. She felt the car make

a couple of stops and a few turns, but mostly it was thrumming along a straightaway, the tires singing and the exhaust pipes purring like a big cat. When the car stopped, she opened her eyes. Straight ahead she saw tree trunks and leaves, the greens and browns washed-out looking in the glare of the headlights. Closer, between the car and the woods, rusting I beams reared from the ground; leaning forward, she saw a billboard looming over them. COMFORT INN, the fading letters read, but there was no hotel in sight. Off to the left, through the driver's window, she saw four lanes of cars and semis whizzing along a freeway, their headlights and taillights dimmed by the window's deep tint. *Through a glass darkly*, she thought. Bible verses still popped into her head sometimes, even after all these years. Always in her daddy's voice, big as God's, booming down from that pulpit. *For now we see through a glass, darkly; but then face to face.* She turned to see his face. "Where we at?"

"Cahaba Lane."

"Where the hell's Cahaba Lane?"

"Right here, darlin'. Right here. Come on, let's go." He opened his door, and the rushing sounds and harsh lights of the freeway traffic pressed in upon her—hundreds of people streaming by, close at hand yet worlds away, oblivious within the cocoons of their cars and trucks. He got out and came around to her side of the car and opened her door, almost like he was her real boyfriend. But she felt a chill—maybe the coolness of the night, or maybe something else—and she didn't move. "Come on," he said again, not so cheerful sounding this time.

"Let's go." He reached in and took hold of her elbow, pulling and lifting. He *was* strong. Her hand slid out from under her thigh, and her shirt rode up, exposing her lower ribs and the tuck of her waist and, below that, the jutting hipbone and shadowy hollow where her hip curved into her belly. "You want that other forty, don't you, darlin'? And that snowflake, too. I *know* you want that." He reached his left hand toward her, too—shit, the tattoo *was* a snake, and the head of the snake was in the hand that opened its jaws and then clamped down on her arm. He was pulling her with both hands now—dragging her—with a strength she was helpless to oppose. She came out of the car sideways, her knees and the fishnets raked by the pavement and a few shards of glass, before he raised her up, set her on her wobbly heels, and led her up a path that threaded between the I beams and up the slope.

Up into the woods.

Down into the darkness.

CHAPTER 13

Brockton

I WAS PROBING THE carpeting in the dean's outer office with the toe of a shoe—a clean, pig-shit-free shoe—and trying to estimate the thickness of the pile: an inch? inch and a half? I wasn't delighted to be cooling my heels here; he'd delayed and then canceled our meeting the prior week, so I was feeling low on the dean's priority list. Would he stand me up again today? Glancing up, I noticed Carissa, the dean's secretary, watching me, the phone in her hand, amusement on her face. "He's ready to see you now, Dr. Brockton."

I stood up and headed for the dean's doorway. My left toe snagged in the divot I'd pressed into the plush pile, and I stumbled briefly. Carissa worked to stifle a laugh, and I shrugged sheepishly. "Smooth," I said. "Do I know how to make an entrance, or what?" She smiled and to my surprise blushed. *Hmm*, I thought as I entered the dean's inner sanctum.

He stood behind his desk—a big walnut desk in

a big walnut-paneled office—and reached across to shake my hand. "Good to see you, Bill," he said. "I was just looking at the fall class enrollments. Looks like Anthropology's booming."

"We're holding our own," I said, trying to sound modest, but betrayed by a proud grin. Our numbers had doubled during each of my three years at UT; my 1991 session of Anthropology 101—the intro course—had moved from a classroom to a small lecture hall. This fall's section of Human Origins was meeting in a three-hundred-seat auditorium, and all three hundred seats were taken.

"What can I do for you? Wait, let me guess—you want to put a dome over the stadium and move your Intro class into the grandstands?"

"Hmm. Now that you mention it, that sounds like a great idea," I said. "Extend my office across the hall, punch a hole through the wall, and build me a little balcony over the south end zone. I could be like the pope, talking to his flock down in Saint Peter's Square."

"The Pope of Neyland Stadium. I like it. I'll need to run it by the Athletic Department—probably Religion, too—but I can't see why they'd object, can you?" His eyes flicked to a spot over my right shoulder—to the spot on the back wall where a clock ticked loudly—and I knew the banter was over. "So what brings you here today? Usually I only see you when I have to haul you in and slap your wrist for telling off-color jokes that make the freshman girls blush. I don't think I've had a complaint so far this fall. Of course, we're not far into the semester."

"I need some land," I said. "To put dead bodies on."

"I already *gave* you some land," he said. "Up at the Holston farm. Land, and a barn, too."

"You did, and I appreciate it. Really. We've got a good start on the skeletal collection—we're up to a dozen already—and the medical examiner in Johnson City just sent me another body the other day. Thing is, the location's a problem."

"How so?"

"Well, it'd be fine if all I wanted to do was store bodies while they skeletonized."

"But?"

"But I want us to start a research program." I pointed a finger at him, in what I hoped he would see as a good-natured manner. "*You* want us to start a research program, remember?" He nodded slightly; noncommittally. "And now I've got a plan."

"What kind of plan?"

"To study human decomposition in the extended postmortem interval. What happens to bodies after death? When does it happen? How do variables affect the process—variables like temperature, humidity, placement of the body, grave depth, insect activity, all sorts of things?"

"How is that anthropology?"

"It's *forensic* anthropology," I said. "Every time the police call me out to look at a decaying body, they want to know how long the person has been dead. It helps focus their search. Helps narrow the field of suspects. Helps confirm or refute alibis. Thing is, I usually can't tell them how long somebody's been dead. *Nobody* can tell them. Not with any scientific confidence."

His eyes narrowed a bit. "Is this about that Civil

War colonel? The one you thought had been dead only a year? Are you still smarting about that?"

"Yes and no," I said. "Do I hate having my nose rubbed in that when I'm on the witness stand in another case? Sure. But I'm a scientist. The takeaway message, besides the reminder that I'm not infallible, is that we need to do more research. A lot more research. And to do that, we need land close to campus."

"Why? What's wrong with the pig farm?"

"Besides the pig crap? It takes half an hour to get out there. If my graduate students have to drive all the way out there two or three times a day to get research data, it'll take 'em ten years to do their dissertations. We need someplace close." I pointed over his shoulder, out his window. "Look at all that empty space behind your office. We could put twenty, thirty bodies out there, easy." He looked alarmed. "*Or*," I quickly went on, "you could give me that patch of junk land near the hospital instead."

"*What* junk land near the hospital?"

"Right across the river—behind UT Medical Center—there's a place where the hospital used to burn their trash, back when medical waste could be dumped in an open pit and burned. There's two or three acres there. Plenty of room for what I've got in mind."

"Are you talking about the dairy farm? That's the Ag school's pride and joy."

"No, I'm not making a grab for the dairy farm. That's on the north side of the hospital. This is on the east side. At the far corner of the employees' parking lot. It's mostly woods, except for a little clearing where the burn pit used to be."

He tented his fingers, a gesture that I knew meant he was giving the matter serious thought. "Well," he mused, "that would certainly give the hospital a unique position in the world of medicine. There can't be another university medical center that's bordered by cows on one side and corpses on the other. A dairy farm and a body farm." He gave his head a slow shake and smiled wryly. "This is not exactly how I envisioned my contribution to higher learning, back when I was writing my dissertation on the decline and fall of the British Empire." He pressed his index fingers to his lips, and then flexed and straightened the tented fingers rhythmically, like a spider doing push-ups on a mirror. After half a dozen push-ups, he nodded and laid his hands on the desk. "Okay, I'll make some calls. On one condition."

"What's that?" Now it was my turn to feel nervous.

"No more tawdry jokes during class."

"Deal," I said, standing and making tracks for the door before he could change his mind. "I'll save them for afterward."

As I hurried through the outer office, I heard his voice behind me. "Hey, wait. . . ." Without turning, I waved good-bye to Carissa and kept moving.

THE BONE LAB was empty and locked. Peering through the small glass window in the steel door, I saw two trays of bones—pubic bones—sitting on a lab table, but no signs of life. *Crap,* I thought, *he's probably at the Annex.* I'd dialed the extension there and gotten no answer, but I knew that if Tyler wasn't in the bone lab, the odds were good that he was at the Annex. That meant another trek across the scorching parking lot, but my mood was too ebullient for me to care. Besides, I'd be totally drenched in sweat before long anyhow.

Tyler looked up from the sink, surprised, when I walked in. "Hey, Dr. B. Was that you that called a few minutes ago?"

"It was."

"Sorry I didn't pick up." By way of explanation, he held up a femur and a scrub brush. The femur—like the two hundred other bones still in the steam kettle—was from the guy we'd taken out to the pig barn two weeks before. In the space of just fourteen days, bacteria and bugs had consumed virtually all the soft tissue, leaving behind nothing but bare bones, a greasy stain in the dirt of the barn floor, and another body's worth of stench. Fortunately, my sense of smell was fairly poor—it was one of my best qualifications for my work—so the odors of death and decomposition didn't bother me as much as they bothered most people.

Tyler turned his attention back to the bone. "This guy must've had a hell of a limp," he said, giving the bone a final rinse. "This femur's two inches shorter than the other one. I *thought* he felt lopsided when we were carrying him. Here, take a look." He patted the bone dry with a surgical pad and handed it to me. It was warped and had a thick knot at mid-shaft, like a tree branch that's been cracked and has healed with a prominent and permanent deformity.

"Looks like he had a comminuted, displaced fracture," I said, "and never got it set. Must have been years ago, though. See how much the bone has remodeled to try to smooth out that discontinuity and those sharp edges?" He nodded. "Must've hurt for the rest of his life, though," I added. "Even with the remodeling, that had to interfere with the muscles and tendons." I handed the bone back to him, and he laid it on the counter, alongside the longer, straighter femur. I waited, expecting a question, but he seemed preoccupied with the bones. "Aren't you even going to ask?"

He glanced over his shoulder at me. "Ask what?"

"Why I'm here."

He shrugged. "So, Dr. B, why're you here?"

"Excellent question. Two reasons, actually. One, good news. I met with the dean earlier today, and he just now called me to let me know: We've got the land behind the hospital."

"Hey, that's great. When can we start setting things up?"

"Another excellent question. Today."

"Great. Wait. Today?" I nodded. "You mean *today* today?" I nodded again. "Today, when it feels like mid-August, not late September? With a heat index of 103?"

"We've got to get started before the bureaucrats come to their senses and change their minds," I said. "Strike while the iron's hot."

"Hot? The iron's gonna be *molten* out there today," he groaned.

"Quit whining. This is important. We're embarking on our research program. Here." Reaching a hand behind my back, I extricated the small paperback book I'd tucked into my belt. It was limper and damper than it had been before I'd made the sweltering walk from the stadium to the Annex.

Tyler took it and studied the cover, his face growing more puzzled by the moment. "Uh, thanks?" he said finally. "*The Washing Away of Wrongs.* Theology?" I shook my head. "And what's with the Sumo-wrestler cartoon on the cover? And all the Japanese symbols?"

"It's a forensic investigation manual," I said. "The world's first. Written in China, not Japan. In the thirteenth century." Tyler was starting to look interested. "And that's not a sumo wrestler, that's a dead guy. It's a coroner's diagram. From seven hundred and fifty years ago."

"Cool."

"Check out page sixty-eight—'The Case of the Bloody Sickle'—it's directly relevant to your thesis project. Your *new* thesis project. We can talk about it after you lay some yoga moves on the trees and underbrush out at our lavish new research complex."

THE STRENGTH IN my forearms was gone—I could scarcely hold up the chain saw—so I released the throttle trigger and the engine wound down to idle as the saw dropped. But the oiled chain continued to spin, the teeth still coasting, as the bar of the saw swung down toward my left leg. Almost as if I were outside my own body, I watched as the chain tore through the canvas of my coveralls and ripped into the flesh of my thigh. The teeth had nearly stopped by the time they reached the skin—the chain slid only a few more inches—but the chain was new and sharp, and my hide wasn't as tough as tree bark. For a few seconds I saw the clean edges of pink flesh—as if the tissue itself were as surprised as I was by the sudden turn of events—and then the blood welled up, filling the gash and oozing out, seeping into the fabric. "Well, *damn*," I muttered. I didn't feel any pain yet; for the moment, all I felt was stupid.

Setting down the saw, I shucked off my leather gloves and fished a sweaty bandanna from my back pocket to blot the cut so I could see how much damage I'd done. *Not too bad*, I thought with relief—scarcely more than a nick, in fact: an inch long and maybe an eighth-inch deep. I'd gotten off lucky. Very, very lucky. Rolling the bandanna diagonally into a long, flat band, I tied it snugly around my thigh to stanch the bleeding, then flexed and stretched my fingers prior to resuming my assault on the deadfall pines—a tangled half-dozen trees killed by pine beetles and then toppled by a storm. My thigh was now starting to ache, but we needed to finish what we'd started, and fast; I'd arranged for a concrete truck to arrive the next morning at nine, and unless we finished clearing the trees out of the way, the truck wouldn't be able to reach the site and pour the pad.

I reached down for the chain saw. As I tugged it off the ground, I noticed movement: blowflies—a dozen or more—taking flight from the blood-smeared chain. I smiled; it was a twentieth-century reminder of the thirteenth-century case I'd just told Tyler to read about.

ONE OF THE benefits of having offices in Stadium Hall, a former dormitory, was the abundance of showers. One of those showers was located in my own private bathroom in my own private hideaway: a second office, located a hundred yards—literally, the length of the football field—from the bustle and distractions of the main Anthropology Department offices. After Tyler and I had finished clearing and leveling the patch of ground that would become the new Anthropology Research Facility—a big, fancy name for a small, primitive place—I'd gone to my hideaway to shower and to glue my leg back together with Super Glue.

Just as I sat down on the toilet and picked up the tube of glue, my phone rang. "Oh, hell," I muttered, clutching a towel around me and scurrying to my desk. "Hello?"

"Howdy, Doc, is that you?"

"Sheriff Cotterell?"

"That's me. How are you, Doc?"

I caught my reflection in the mirror that hung on the bathroom door: practically naked, wrapped in an undersized and sodden towel, my face and neck crimson with sunburn, my thigh throbbing and bleeding again. I smiled, with a topspin of grimace. "I'm just fine, Sheriff. How about you? Any luck identifying that girl from the strip mine?"

"Not a goddamned bit, Doc, if you'll pardon my French. That's why I'm calling—see if maybe you could help us some more. Bubba and me was talking, and he asked me did you still have that girl's skull. I said, 'Well, I sure as hell *hope* so—he ain't never give it back to me.'" The sheriff paused.

I scanned my desktop for the skull, but it wasn't there. I felt a flash of panic—had someone made off with it?—but then I saw it sitting on my windowsill, and I vaguely recalled having moved it out of the way a few days before. Or was it a few weeks before? *Out of sight, out of mind,* I thought guiltily. "Of course I've still got it, Sheriff. Do you want it back?"

"Oh, hell no, Doc. I wouldn't know what to do with it. Thing is, Bubba was telling me about a TBI training he went to a while back. They had somebody from the FBI there talking about putting faces back on skulls—makin' 'em out of clay. Showing what the dead person looked like. Bubba 'n me was wondering if maybe you might know how to do that."

"I've tried it a time or two," I said, "but to be honest, I'm no good at it, Sheriff. My clay heads look like a fourth grader's art project. I'd only make it harder to ID the girl." I'd hoped that might draw a laugh from him, but instead, he sighed.

"Well. I figured it didn't hurt none to ask. We'll keep knocking on doors and asking questions. Thing is, Doc, we're running out of doors to knock on."

"That's the way sometimes with forensic cases," I commiserated. "Especially old ones. People forget. Out of sight, out of mind," I added, feeling another pang of guilt for having nothing helpful to offer him. I wished him luck and hung up, but I felt the dead girl's eyes—her vacant eyes—staring at me in reproach, her silent voice clear and accusatory in my head: *What about me?* she seemed to say. *Have you forgotten me, too? So soon?*

Wiping the blood from my thigh with the damp

towel, I blotted the wound with tissue, then applied a thin line of super glue to the edges of the skin and pressed them together. The glue—cyanoacrylate, said the label, which also warned that the chemical was a carcinogen—burned my nostrils and stung like a sonofabitch. *Serves you right*, I heard a voice in my head sniping. But whether it was the dead girl's voice or my own this time, I didn't know.

CHAPTER 14

Satterfield

"YOUR FIRST TIME IS special." People said it about all kinds of shit, Satterfield reflected, and maybe it was true—maybe every first *was* special. First kiss. First love. First killing.

Its specialness to Satterfield wasn't the *way* he'd done it; in truth, he'd done it clumsily, and far too swiftly. Its specialness lay in the fact that he *had* done it. The killing had been spontaneous—as surprising to him as it was to her—but it had been an epiphany, a life-changing revelation.

Three years had passed, but the images of it remained vivid. Indeed, the more times he replayed them, the more vivid they grew.

She was small and pretty—half Jap, half round eye, with a slender, finely chiseled face and thick, red-black hair. Satterfield saw her dancing in one of the skin bars near the base, and he liked what he saw. Before he knew it, he'd dropped fifty bucks on overpriced, watered-down drinks, and then another fifty on a lap dance that left him wild with want.

"Can we go somewhere?" he begged when she sat down beside him, her thigh pressing against his. "Can you take the rest of the night off? Or even just take a break and come outside with me?"

She laughed. "You want some private time with me? VIP room." She pointed a glossy red nail—her pinky finger—toward an unmarked black door set into a black wall. "Hundred dollars. Ten minutes."

He stared at her. "A hundred bucks? For ten *minutes*? That's robbery!"

She smiled coyly. "That not what other men say." She stood up and began undulating in time to the music, backing slowly away from his table, her face mirroring the lust that was coursing through him. A Marine at a neighboring table turned his chair toward her and slid another chair, an empty, in her direction. She glanced at the chair and then looked at Satterfield, smiling and cocking her head inquiringly.

He could stand it no more. Scrambling to his feet, he seized her by the wrist and pulled her close. "Three hundred," he said, "if you meet me in the parking lot in ten minutes."

THE GIRL HOOKED her thumbs through the elastic of her G-string and shimmied out of it, then lay back on the rear seat of his car, raised her arms over her head, and opened her knees.

Satterfield stared. Her body was the most beautiful thing he'd ever seen—far more beautiful than anything in the skin magazines his stepfather kept in the sleeper cab of the semi. Beneath the red-orange glow of the streetlight filtering through the car's tinted glass, her skin shone like molten copper. Her muscled legs testified to the strength and grace that hours of dancing each night had created. Her belly—flat when she was standing—was concave now that she lay on her back, and the strands of the golden tassel that hung from the piercing in her navel fanned out in the same way her hair fanned on the leather upholstery behind her head. "Okay, sailor boy," she said, fingering one of her nipple rings, "show me."

Satterfield was unmanned. Inside, when she'd been seductive but unavailable, he'd been about to explode. Now, though—the teasing done, replaced by a command to perform—he felt himself beginning to panic, to sweat, and to shrink. Mortified, he began rubbing his crotch, slowly at first, then with increasing desperation and fury.

She raised herself onto her elbows. "What? You not want me? Why you act like you want me, if you not want me?" Her eyes flitted from his face to his crotch and back up again. "You never been with woman, sailor boy?" Her lips curled into a smile—a smirking, scornful smile. "You scared, sailor boy? You a sissy, sailor boy? You wet bed at night, sailor boy?"

He was on her in an instant, delivering a backhanded slap, then a forehand slap. She opened her mouth to scream, but he clamped one hand over her mouth, and clamped the other around her throat. Her eyes bugging wide, she thrashed and bucked beneath him, but she was no match for him, and gradually her struggles lessened. He removed the hand from her mouth and loosened his grip on her throat. She gasped like a drowning victim surfacing from underwater; he allowed her a few sips of air, then bore down on her neck again. Her eyes were desperate and pleading now, and he felt himself growing aroused.

His orgasm came when her eyes rolled back in her head.

HE WAS INTERROGATED by the local cops but he was never charged. Nobody'd seen her leave with him, and she'd been seen doing lap dances for a lot of men around the time she went missing.

The military police had their suspicions, too—just routine lead checking at first, but then, once the bone detective got involved, they'd zeroed in on Satterfield. In the end, the Navy chose not to court-martial him, but it also chose not to keep him in its ranks. There's the right kind of killing and the wrong kind of killing; the kind that solves problems, and the kind that creates them.

Two years after enlisting—two years after he walked away from his mother and his stepfather and finally embarked on what felt like a life of power and prestige—Satterfield found himself unmoored. Two years of basic training and special-forces training were shot. His two-week career as a SEAL—two weeks of training, before he'd been washed out—was memorialized in a tattoo on his right forearm. He'd gotten the tat the day he'd heard he'd been accepted for SEAL training—a moment of overconfidence or of hope or even of gratitude. He'd gotten the celebratory tattoo that afternoon, then gone to the strip club that night.

Administrative discharge, "under circumstances other than honorable," with nothing to show but the tat. It made him a decorated veteran in his own ironic way. By the end of his military service, he'd acquired skills in stealth, survival, and attack—with bare hands, knife, pistol, rifle, even explosives.

He'd also acquired even more valuable things: insight and self-knowledge, which he'd gained in those moments when he first tasted the fruit of the tree of power—the power unleashed by the convergence of pain, sex, and fear. Especially fear.

Last but not least, he'd acquired a new nemesis: the man who'd focused the Navy investigator's suspicions on Satterfield. The man who'd ruined the life Satterfield had finally, against all odds, begun to create for himself.

The man whose reciprocal, retaliatory ruination Satterfield had come to Tennessee to set in motion.

CHAPTER 15

Brockton

"ART DEPARTMENT." THE FEMALE voice in my ear sounded young, alert, and amused, as if she'd heard the punch line of a joke just before she picked up the phone.

"Good morning," I said. "This is Dr. Brockton, in Anthropology. Is Dr. Hollingsworth in?"

"Dr. Hollingsworth?" There was a puzzled pause, followed by a suppressed snort of laughter. "Oh, you mean *Joe*?"

Flustered, I glanced at the campus directory again. Art Department: Chair, Joseph Hollingsworth. I'd probably met him at some faculty function or other, but if I had, I didn't remember. "He—Joe—he's the department chairman, right?"

"*Right*," she said, her amusement tinged with sarcasm now. Joe's department, I gathered, marched—or boogied?—to a different, hipper drummer from mine.

I backed up to take another run at it. "So. Joe—my main man, Joe—is he around?"

She wasn't buying. "One moment, *Dr. Brockton*. I'll see if Dr. Hollingsworth is available." *Ouch, man*, I thought as the receiver clicked me onto hold.

A moment later, it clicked again and the call was transferred. "Hel-*lo*, this is *Joe*," a cheery voice sing-songed.

"Good morning," I said. "This is Dr.—" I halted, my formality sounding stuffy now even to me. "Sorry. Joe, this is Bill Brockton, over in Anthropology?"

"Yessir, Mr. Bill. What can I do you for?"

"I'm looking for somebody who's good at portraits. Nothing fancy; just a sketch, really. Pencil or pen is okay; color or black and white. What matters is that the artist has a good feel for anatomy, musculature, facial features. I need something realistic, not . . . ," I hesitated, "not like Picasso, you know?"

"I think I get your drift," he said. "Thing is, 'bout everybody over here thinks even Picasso is old school, you know what I mean?" I suspected I did; I'd walked through the cavernous atrium of the Art and Architecture building a time or two, and I could make neither heads nor tails of most of the abstract paintings and sculpture on display. "Sounds like what you need," he went on, "is one of those guys that draws tourists at the beach, you know? Pay him five bucks, and five minutes later, he hands you a pretty decent caricature of yourself."

"Hmm," I mused. The nearest beach was eight hours away. "Well, but I don't want something cartoonish. Like I said, I need something realistic. Serious, too."

"Let's back up a little," he said. "A portrait, you said. Who's the subject?"

"I don't know."

"Come again?"

"I don't know who it is," I repeated. "That's the problem. Here's the thing, Joe. I've got a dead girl's skull in my lab. Thirteen, fourteen years old. Her bones were found at an old strip mine up near the Kentucky border. She's been dead a while; we're talking years, not months. I'd like to find somebody who could look at that girl's skull—see it through the eyes of an artist—and then sketch what that girl may have looked like when she was alive."

He was silent for a moment. "Wow," he said. "Y'all don't mess around over there in Anthropology, do you?" Another pause. "You know, it's not exactly Life Drawing—matter of fact, I guess it's the *opposite* of Life Drawing—but I had a girl in my class last spring who was damned good at the human figure. Faces, too; *especially* faces. Most folks just draw what they see on the surface, but her drawings? You could tell what was *under* the skin, too, you know? I don't know if she can do it the other way around—start with the inside and add what's on the outside—but I wouldn't be surprised."

"She sounds worth a try. What's the best way to get in touch with her?"

"Hmm. She wasn't an art major; come to think of it, I wanna say she was a high-school student. Her name . . . her name . . . oh, hell, I'm blanking on her name. Hang on." I heard a rustle as he covered the mouthpiece of the phone. "Hey, Rachel," I heard his muffled voice calling. "What the hell's the name of that high-school girl that took Life Drawing last spring? Tall. Lanky. Blond. Went barefoot all the time, even in February. Amelia something?" I heard the young woman's voice in the background, muffled and indistinct. "Ha! *That's* why I wanted to call her Amelia." Another rustle as he unmuffled the mouthpiece. "Her name's Jenny Earhart. She goes to Laurel High School—you know it?"

"That hippie private school? In the run-down house up on Laurel Avenue? Long-haired stoner kids hanging out on the front porch all the time?"

"Sounds like you know it. If you talk to her, tell her Joe-Joe said hey." He laughed. "Don't tell her the old coot forgot her name."

"LAUREL HIGH. PEACE." The young man who answered the phone sounded thoroughly sincere. And more than a little stoned.

"Uh . . . peace," I replied. "I'm trying to get in touch with a student there."

"Heyyyy, man, *I'm* a student. Troy."

"Uh, hi, Troy. Actually, I'm trying to get in touch with another student. A student named Jenny. Jenny Earhart. Is Jenny there?"

"Nah, you're out of luck, dude. Jenny's not here. Jenny's gone."

Luckily, Jenny hadn't gone far, according to the sheepish school administrator who took the phone from Troy. "Jenny's doing an art internship this semester," the woman told me. "She's working afternoons at a graphic-design agency in the Old City." She gave me the agency's name, and when I phoned,

Jenny herself answered the call, sounding perfectly poised and not at all stoned.

THE AROMA OF roasting coffee hung heavy and pleasant in the air, like wood smoke on a winter's day, as I parked my truck and stepped out onto the treacherous footing of Jackson Avenue. The street was brick, and the bricks were chipped, cracked, and in places altogether missing, thanks to a century of heavy traffic and chronic neglect. That was finally changing—the gritty warehouse district known as the Old City was finally, in the last decade of the twentieth century, being gentrified with bars and boutiques and loft apartments—but the change was slow and uneven. Especially underfoot.

The coffee aroma permeating the Old City came from the JFG Coffee Company, whose headquarters and roasting plant occupied most of a five-story building on Jackson Avenue. The building's ground floor had been rented out to newer, hipper tenants. One of these was the design agency where Jenny was interning; the other was the JFG Coffeehouse, where she'd suggested we meet.

Joe Hollingsworth had described her as tall, blond, and rangy; he'd also described her as perpetually shoeless. I didn't spot any bare feet in the café, but I did spot a young woman who was tall and blond, leaning over a sketch pad, finishing a pastel sketch of the JFG Coffee Building. The sketch portrayed the old building honestly: A couple of windows in the façade had been boarded up, and vestiges of an adjoining building remained, in the form of bricked-up openings and cut-off staircase supports that no longer supported anything. But the building's age and imperfections were offset by the youth and vitality of the people she'd shown enjoying themselves at café tables out front. I leaned in for a closer look at the faces, and even though the figures were small, their features were detailed and lifelike.

"Professor Hollingsworth—Joe—said you were good with faces," I told her. "I agree. And like I said on the phone, I need a good face." I'd set a hatbox on our table. Now I removed the lid, then reached in and lifted out the skull, which was resting upside down on a doughnut-shaped cushion, surrounded by Bubble Wrap. I righted the skull, rotating it toward her.

"Oh, my," she whispered. She inclined her head this way and that, studying the skull from multiple angles. "She looks so young. And so . . . *vulnerable*. What else can you tell me about her?"

"Not much, unfortunately. All we have is the bone, and there's a limit to what it tells us. She's been dead for at least two years, maybe more."

"How do you know?"

"Because when we found her, she had a two-year-old black locust growing in her left eye orbit."

"What?"

"Eye orbit. Eye socket, most people call it."

"No, I mean, what did you say was growing there? A *locust*?"

"A black locust. A tree, not a bug." I turned the skull toward the ceiling of the coffeehouse. "See what a nice little planter that makes? Just add a seed, a little dust, a little rain, and *voilà*." I shifted the skull so she had a better view into the eye orbit. "See that slot, way in the back?" She nodded. "That's where the optic nerve runs from the eyeball to the brain. The roots grew through that opening into the cranial vault."

"Wow."

"But wait, there's more. We also found a wasp nest in there, inside the cranium. Her skull was becoming its own little ecosystem."

"Amazing. That's beautiful. But heartbreaking, too. You said she was, what, fourteen?"

"Fourteen, thirteen, fifteen—one of those, almost certainly. White. Right-handed. No dental work, so the family was probably poor. Her bones are slight and the muscle markings aren't prominent, so I expect she was thin. Maybe even malnourished. She . . ." I hesitated.

She turned and looked at me. "She what?"

"I suspect she'd been abused."

Her eyes narrowed, and she searched my face. "Sexually abused? How can you tell?"

"I meant physically. Wouldn't surprise me if she was sexually abused, too, though. Her left arm was broken at some point, and it wasn't set properly, so it healed with a little kink in it. Maybe they just didn't have money for a doctor, but maybe they didn't want anybody to know about the injury. Lots of boys break their arms, but not many girls. She had a couple broken ribs, too. More recently than the arm, but still a good while before she died."

"How can you tell?"

"Because all the fractures had healed, and the bone had remodeled."

"Remodeled?"

"It means the repair job has blended in, recontoured over time. Like the rough edges have been filled in with putty and sanded smooth. Lots of recontouring in the girl's arm, not as much in the ribs. Just guessing, I'd say she was six or eight when her arm was broken, nine or ten when her ribs were busted."

"Jesus." She turned back to the skull, shaking her head. "Sounds like she had a really awful life."

"I'd say she had a bad death, too, however she died." I glanced at the pastel drawing beside the skull. In the foreground, healthy, happy people smiled at one another. "Truth is, Jenny, I don't think anybody ever gave a damn about this girl."

She looked up from the skull, looked me in the eye with a directness and frankness I found startling in a teenager. "You do," she said. "And now I do. It's not much, but maybe it's a start."

CHAPTER 16

Tyler

TYLER SLID THE BODY bag halfway out of the truck, then paused. "Ready, Dr. B?"

Dr. B leaned over the tailgate and grasped the corners at the bag's other end. "Ready."

"Okay, on three. One, two, *three*." As Tyler walked backward, the bag slid; just before it dropped off the edge of the tailgate, Dr. B hoisted the end, and together they trudged to the chain-link cube in the woods.

The cube—a sixteen-by-sixteen-foot cage, with a concrete floor and a chain-link roof—wouldn't win any architectural prizes, that was for sure. But they'd designed and built it themselves, for a few hundred bucks, and it would do the job it was designed to do: keep out raccoons and coyotes and buzzards, but let in blowflies and other bugs . . . and let in Tyler, to observe and document the insects' arrival, activity, and departure in the days and weeks to come.

The corpse—the unclaimed body of a seventy-year-old white male who'd committed suicide—had come from the medical examiner in Nashville. Most male suicides used firearms—"Men love guns, even when they hate themselves," Dr. B had said to Tyler once. Men preferred guns and nooses to kill themselves; women went for poison. This man, though, had cut his own throat, an act that spoke to Tyler of fierce determination and deep despair. Slashed wrists were often survivable, especially if the cuts were shallow and crosswise, rather than lengthwise and deep enough to shred arteries. But taking a straight razor to the neck, like this guy had done? No turning back, long as you nicked the jugular vein or the carotid artery.

They squeezed through the narrow gate, Tyler first, moving backward. "Walk softly," Dr. B reminded him. "The concrete's only been curing for forty-eight hours." Dr. B had wanted to wait a week before putting any load on the concrete, but as Tyler had pointed out—repeatedly—fall was coming, and if he didn't start the project before the weather turned cold, the only insect activity he'd be able to record for quite a while could be summed up in one word: *hibernation*.

By the time they laid the body bag on the wire-mesh rack Tyler had built—a cot, basically, made of two-by-fours and quarter-inch wire mesh—the bag was swarming with flies, and as he tugged the long, C-shaped zipper open, the eager insects began squirming through the gap to get at the body.

The blowflies' eagerness was no surprise to Tyler, nor were their numbers; he'd seen them plenty of times before, at death scenes and at the pig barn. What was new to him was that this time—with this *corpse*—the flies were not simply a nuisance to be endured, a buggy cross to be borne. This time, the flies were the stars of the show, the subjects of scientific scrutiny, their comings and goings and ages and stages to be attentively observed and meticulously chronicled.

Dr. B watched, and then posed, as Tyler took photos: the first photos of the first research study at the world's first laboratory focused on human decomposition. Then, satisfied or bored, he departed, leaving Tyler alone in the cage with the corpse. "I'll give you two some time to get acquainted," he'd joked as he headed toward the parking lot. "Keep in touch. And take plenty of pictures."

By the time the sound of Dr. B's truck had faded away, dabs of white, grainy paste were already appearing on the corpse. The dabs, whose appearance and timing Tyler duly recorded on film and in his field notes, were deposits of blowfly eggs, and by mid-afternoon the eggs had already begun to hatch, releasing thousands of tiny, wiggling, ravenous little maggots, whose miniature feeding frenzies Tyler watched through a magnifying glass and photographed with a close-up lens. The hatching eggs were clustered at the edges of the eyes, the nostrils, the mouth, the ears, and also—especially—along the bloody slash across the neck.

After shooting an entire roll to document the corpse's initial state, Tyler dug a collapsible tripod out of his backpack and positioned it beside the corpse, screwing a second camera on top—a camera with a built-in timer, set to take one photo every hour, day and night. Then, and only then, did he take time to unfold the metal chair he'd brought over from the stadium. Reaching into his backpack once more, he took out the Chinese forensic handbook Dr. B had given him, *The Washing Away of Wrongs*, and settled into the chair. He opened the book to a dog-eared page and read—aloud, as if the corpse could hear the story, and would appreciate its relevance—about a crime that a clever investigator had solved some seven and a half centuries before:

> *There was an inquest on the body of a man killed by the roadside. It was first suspected that he had been killed by robbers. At the time when the body was checked, all clothing and personal effects were there. On the whole body there were ten old wounds inflicted by a sickle. The inquest official said, "Robbers merely want men to die so that they can take their valuables. Now, the personal effects are there, while the body bears many wounds. If this is not a case of being killed by a hateful enemy, then what is it?" He then ordered those around him to withdraw, summoned the man's wife and said, "In the past what man was your husband's worst enemy?" She replied, "Hitherto my husband had no enemies. But only recently there was a certain X who came to borrow money. He did not get it. They had already fixed on a definite date and they discussed that. But there were no bitter enemies." The inquest official secretly familiarized himself with the victim's neighborhood. He thereupon sent a number of men separately to go and make proclamations. The nearest*

neighbors were to bring all their sickles, handing them in for examination. If anyone concealed a sickle, they would be considered the murderer and would be thoroughly investigated. In a short time, seventy or eighty sickles were brought in. The inquest official had them laid on the ground. At the time the weather was hot. The flies flew about and gathered on one sickle. The inquest official pointed to this sickle and said, "Whose is this?" One man abruptly acknowledged it. He was the same man who had set the debt time limit. Then he was interrogated, but still would not confess. The inquest official indicated the sickle and had the man look at it himself. "The sickles of the others in the crowd had no flies. Now, you have killed a man. There are traces of blood on the sickle, so the flies gather. How can this be concealed?" The bystanders were speechless, sighing with admiration. The murderer knocked his head on the ground and confessed.

BY SUNDOWN THE flies had dissipated: gone to ground, or to the trees, or to wherever they took their night's rest. But within the cage, upon the corpse on the wire-mesh cot, the maggots remained, restless and ravenous, their labors unceasing; their appetites insatiable.

THE DRONE OF the flies—so constant over the past two days that it had become white noise, soporific in its regularity and monotony—suddenly grew louder and more singular, as an intense tickle in his left nostril caused Tyler to leap from the folding chair and paw at his nose. "You little bastard," he said to the retreating blowfly, which narrowly avoided being crushed by the pinch Tyler gave his itching nose. He pointed down at the corpse, which rested on the cot of wire mesh, already beginning to drip with greasy effluvia. "*Him*, dumbass, not me."

Tyler had been observing blowflies for two days now—observing, photographing, and occasionally swatting, despite Dr. B's admonition to the contrary. Penned in the new research enclosure with the first corpse in his entomology study, he was beginning to feel like a prisoner, though his sentence was a self-imposed one: bug bites and a chain-link cage, for the sake of science.

He stepped outside the cage and locked the door behind him, then stripped off his fly-spotted clothes there in the woods, a stone's throw from the hospital employees' parking lot, too weary to care if any orderlies or nurses or janitors caught a glimpse of his pale ass shining through the trees. Funny thing, how tiring it was to sit in a chair for twelve hours, rising only to take photos, or take a piss in the woods, or scarf down a sandwich.

He bundled the clothes—stinking of sweat and decomp—into a plastic trash bag, hoping he wouldn't forget to put them in the washer when he got home. Then he hosed off, using the spigot that Dr. B had somehow cajoled a maintenance guy into installing beside the enclosure. He filled his palm with shampoo and worked it into his hair, over his face, under his arms, across his chest and belly, and into his crotch, scrubbing with fingertips and fingernails, scrubbing away fly tracks and fly eggs, real and imagined. The water was warm at first, the afternoon's heat still stored in the serpentine coils of the hose. Coil by coil it cooled, and by the time he was finished, he was shivering. Opening a second trash bag, he took out a threadbare beach towel and dried himself briskly, rubbing warmth back into his skin before slipping into ripped, velvety Levi's, a faded sweatshirt, and floppy leather moccasins.

As he wadded the towel and added it to the laundry bag, he found himself blindsided by a wave of loneliness and longing and tenderness. The towel was one of two that he and Roxanne had found at a beach—at what he thought of as *their* beach.

PLUM ISLAND, MASSACHUSETTS, August of '91—their first trip together, to visit Roxie's sister in Newburyport. They'd borrowed bikes and started pedaling, no plan or destination in mind, and after a while they found themselves on Plum Island, following their noses and the signs to the wildlife refuge that occupied most of the island. Refuge Road: surprisingly hot and buggy, walled off from the Atlantic's breezes by a ridge of dunes and scrub. Six sweaty miles down Refuge Road, they finally reached the southern tip of the island, Sandy Point, astonished to find that the small parking lot was empty. "I wish we'd thought to bring stuff to swim," Roxanne had said, but Tyler had smiled and pointed to the towels: two of them, neatly folded at the edge of the asphalt—obviously forgotten by other beachgoers, but seemingly placed there just for them.

"Come on," he'd said, grabbing the towels and running toward the water, shucking clothes as he ran.

"Tyler!" she'd shrieked. "We can't—what if we get arrested?" He'd simply turned, arms spread wide, a goofy grin on his face, unabashedly delighted to be free of his clothes and headed for the water. Dropping the towels at the high-tide line, he'd bounded into the water until it was up to his thighs, then plunged headlong into a breaker. By the time he'd surfaced and stood, his back to the surf, she was naked and prancing into the water, high-stepping like a Tennessee walking horse, her breasts and belly and the dark thatch of her pubic hair catching the golden afternoon light in a way that took his breath away. She'd shrieked a second time as a wave reared up and broke against her, toppling her backward. When she stood up, laughing, she flung her head back, whipping her hair over her shoulders and sending a shower of droplets skyward. For a fraction of a second, the droplets created a rainbow around her, and Tyler knew that he'd remember that fraction of a second for the rest of his life.

A few minutes later they were lying on the warm sand and the found towels. "Tyler, we can't," she'd said again, this time in a husky whisper. "We could get arrested."

"It's a wildlife refuge," he'd murmured, nibbling her neck. "We're just part of the wildlife. And you are my sweet refuge."

"Oh, my," she'd breathed. Then, as his hand slid slowly down her body, simply, "Oh. Oh. *Oh.*"

HE RETURNED TO the cage and the corpse at daybreak, arriving—as best he could tell in the pale light—before the first of the flies. During the night, as Tyler had drifted in and out of dreams of Roxanne, the temperature had dropped to 57 degrees, according to the bare-bones weather station he'd installed at one corner of the enclosure: a warm night for late September, but not warm enough, apparently, to hatch more of the fly eggs. Meanwhile, the prior day's maggots—mere specks, as of sundown—had grown visibly, thanks to their unceasing efforts during the night. *The graveyard shift*, he thought. The head start meant that they and their progeny—the generations they would swiftly beget—already had a leg up in the Darwinian race to survive and thrive, to be fruitful and multiply, to fill the earth and consume it.

As the first rays of sunlight slanted through the trees and slipped through the woven wire, Tyler caught a flash of iridescent green in the air, followed swiftly by another, another, and a hundred more.

And the evening and the morning were the third day, he thought, wondering what it was that he and Dr. B were creating here. *Not exactly the Garden of Eden. More like* Lord of the Flies.

THE GARDEN OF Eden: The words rattled around in his mind, knocking loose another memory of Roxanne, and of the Edenic week they'd spent house-sitting for the Brocktons, shortly after the Plum Island trip. They'd spent most of their time in bed, crawling out only for brief forays into the bathroom and the kitchen. Tenderness, awe, lust, hunger, thirst, elimination: the sublimest of emotions and the rawest of physical needs, coexisting not just peacefully but joyously and powerfully, during the heady days and nights of new love. Tyler and Rox had broken one of the bed slats during a final, frenzied coupling on their last afternoon there. The board had snapped with a crack like a rifle shot, and as the mattress gave way beneath them, their cries of passion gave way to gales of laughter. Rox had washed the sheets and towels while Tyler had dashed to Home Depot for a new slat, skidding into the store's parking lot just minutes before closing time. On a whim, as he was leaving—exiting through the store's lawn and garden section—he'd bought a small concrete statue for the Brocktons' back patio: a waist-high angel, its wings spread high and wide, a sword pointing heavenward. "To guard the gates of Paradise," he'd explained to Rox as he tucked it beside an azalea bush by the sliding-glass door.

They were wedging the new slat beneath the bedsprings when the whir of the garage-door opener signaled the Brocktons' return. "I think our guardian angel's already sleeping on the job," Roxanne had teased, leading him out of the bedroom—but not before giving his bruised lips a final kiss.

HE'D LEARNED HIS lunchtime lesson the day before, when he'd found himself sharing his sandwich with a bevy of blowflies in the cage. Some of them—hell, probably *all* of them—had doubtless checked out the corpse before coming to sample his salami-and-cheese sub. Did it count as micro-cannibalism, he wondered, if dead-guy molecules on a fly's feet rubbed off onto his sandwich? Better—less repulsive—to play it safe; today he'd dash back to the bone lab for lunch.

Before leaving, he took another round of photos—a few wide shots of the entire body, followed by medium shots of the face, neck, torso, and limbs, and then close-ups and macro shots of the various maggot colonies. Virtually all the prior day's eggs had hatched by noon—all except for one dab of grainy white, which a less-than-brilliant fly had laid in the desert, cadaverously speaking: She'd deposited them on the parchment-dry skin of the left shin, where the eggs—lacking moisture—had shriveled instead of hatching. *Location, location, location,* thought Tyler, snapping close-ups of the eggs that would never hatch. Meanwhile, in the more desirable real estate—the moist and bloody parcels of flesh—fresh dabs of eggs were appearing, shoehorned in amid the teeming larvae. Did maggots feed on smaller maggots, he wondered—was it a bug-eat-bug world? Or did harmony and understanding prevail in the midst of such abundance, such manna from heaven? It was the age-old story of research: You set out to answer one or two questions—what bugs show up to feed on corpses, and when?—and pretty soon, a thousand more questions rear their wriggling heads.

He finished a 36-exposure roll of slide film and stashed the camera in his backpack. Then, just before leaving the cage, he removed a one-pint glass jar from his pack and unscrewed the lid, then swept the open jar back and forth in a series of rapid figure eights above the body. Clapping the lid back on, he inspected his catch: a dozen or so puzzled and frustrated flies. He wedged the jar into the pack, where it nestled against today's sandwich, which he would not be unwrapping until he was safely indoors. "Eat your hearts out—your hollow, tubular little insect hearts," he goaded the flies. "Because the sweet, succulent sandwich? Today she is mine! *All mine!* Ha-*ha*!"

Jiminy Cricket, he thought, *I'm talking to* flies *now? I am* totally *cracking up*.

Leaving the enclosure, he latched and padlocked the chain-link door. "Yeah, right," he muttered, snapping the lock shut. "As if someone might want to steal a stinking corpse swarming with maggots." He'd parked a ways from the trees—hotter than the shade, but a lot less likely to get bombed by the birds.

The truck was on a slight incline, facing downhill, so instead of cranking it, he floored the clutch, put the transmission in second gear, and coasted down the slope. Just before he reached the bottom, he switched on the key and popped the clutch to roll-start the engine. The truck lurched as the clutch caught, and then the cylinders fired up. He used to tell himself he did this to lessen the wear and tear on the starter, but the truth—the real reason he did it—was that he got a kick out of it. Every single time. He hummed, then began to sing: "Back in nineteen fifty-eight . . . We drove an old V–8 . . . And when it'd gone a hundred thou we got out and pushed it a mile. . . ."

HE WAS LICKING the last of the mayonnaise and mustard off his fingers when Dr. B walked into the bone lab, looking surprised. "Tyler—I thought you were in lockdown across the river."

"I tunneled out," Tyler said. "Actually, I'm about to do an experiment." He reached into his backpack and fished out the jar. "These are my guinea pigs. I mean, my rigorously screened research subjects."

"What's the research question? What's your hypothesis?"

"The question is, how far away can blowflies smell a corpse? My hypothesis is, if I release these little guys over here, they'll follow their noses and show up over there again. Maybe even before I do."

"Hmm. Interesting." Brockton took the jar from him and peered through the glass, scrutinizing the bugs. "How will you know? I'm sure their mommas can recognize 'em, but to me, they look just like every other blowfly I've ever seen."

"Maybe now, but in five minutes, I bet that anybody—even you—can pick these flies out of a lineup."

"You're on," said Brockton. "I need to run upstairs and check the mail. When I come back, we'll put your recognition hypothesis to the test." He ducked out the steel door of the basement lab, and Tyler heard his footsteps jogging up the two flights of stairs to the Anthropology Department's main office.

Ten minutes later he heard footsteps jogging back down, and the steel door banged open. "Time's up. You ready?"

"One. More. *Second*. Okay, ready." Tyler straightened and rolled his chair sideways, so Dr. B could get at the jar. "There's been a slight revision to the research protocol," he added with exaggerated academic pomposity, "due to attrition in the study sample size. The original cohort was eleven. Now the *n* is five."

"Five?" said Brockton. "Out of eleven? Good God, your research subjects are dropping like flies." Tyler groaned, as Brockton had surely hoped he would. "Remind me never to be one of your guinea pigs." Dr. B picked up the jar and carried it to the large bank of windows lining the lab's south wall. Holding it up to the light, he tilted it, turned it, and then grinned at it. Six flies lay dead or dying in the bottom of the jar, but the other five were buzzing or crawling, vigorously and vividly. Each of them sported a small but prominent dot on its thorax: a distinctive dab of UT orange.

"GOD *DAMN* IT," Tyler muttered, pinching the sides of his nose fiercely. He had scarcely settled back into his folding chair after his lunch break, and already his nostrils were being invaded again. The first fifty times it had happened, he'd puffed air out his nose to blast the intruder loose without inflicting damage. By now, though, he was in a murderous mood, and was more than happy to turn his nasal passages into death chambers. Releasing the nostril that had been violated, he blew, and the crushed fly shot out and landed on the concrete. Tyler leaned down, the nail of his middle finger circling to the tip of his thumb, coiled to flick the fly through the fence and into the woods. Then he froze, staring, and burst into a laugh. "I'll be damned," he said.

The dead fly was wearing UT orange.

CHAPTER 17

Brockton

"EXCUSE ME?" I SAID into the telephone handset.

"I said, 'Good fences make good neighbors,'" the dean repeated, the edge in his voice growing even sharper.

"I heard what you said," I told him, "and I even know it comes from a poem, but I don't quite get what you mean by it."

"I mean what the *hell* were you thinking?"

"I'm sorry," I floundered, "but I *still* don't know what you mean."

"I mean I just spent half an hour on the phone with one of the groundskeepers from the Medical Center," he snapped. "He's trimming weeds at the edge of a parking lot, and he steps into the woods to take a leak. Guess what he sees?"

I had an uneasy feeling that I knew, but I decided to play innocent, in hopes that I was wrong. "Uh . . . a marijuana patch?"

"No. Wait—*what?* Are you growing pot in the woods now, too?"

"No!" Perhaps I should've chosen my alternative scenario more carefully. "No, of course we're not growing pot in the woods."

"Well, thank God for small favors," he said. "So this poor, unsuspecting bastard goes behind a tree to pee and nearly craps his pants instead, because he suddenly finds himself face-to-face with a human corpse. A very nasty-looking, nasty-smelling human corpse."

"Ooh," I managed. "I'm sorry to hear that."

"You'll be even sorrier if he files a lawsuit. Which he's threatening to do."

"Ouch," I said. "I'm *really* sorry to hear that." That was no exaggeration, though I said it not so much from contrition as from a sense of foreboding. "Reckon it'd help if I go see him? Grovel awhile—apologize a lot—and explain how important the research project is?"

"Try the groveling on me, first," he grumbled. "And while you're explaining, don't forget to explain the fence project."

"What fence project?"

"The new fence you're going to build around that whole patch of ground. Eight feet high. Wood, and solid—so nobody else gets traumatized."

Christ, I thought, *where do we get the money for that?* Fencing in the wooded area would cost far more than building the chain-link cube had cost. I was about to make that point to the dean—before embarking on the groveling and apologizing he'd demanded—when I heard a bloodcurdling shriek just outside my office door. This did not bode well as a first-day experience.

Ten feet away, my new secretary, Peggy something-or-other—Williams? no: Wilhoit—had settled into her chair and begun scaling the months-high mountains of mail, memos, and other departmental detritus that had accumulated over the past several months. For the past hour I'd heard her clucking and sighing her way through the task, lobbing an occasional question across the divide and through my open door. "Do you want to order personalized pocket protectors for all the faculty?" she lobbed. I didn't. "Do you want this catalog from the Edmund Scientific Company?" I did. "Do you already know about the faculty meeting next Tuesday?"

"What faculty meeting?"

That was when she shrieked: a full-throated, long-lasting scream. Hastily hanging up on the dean, I leaped up and rushed through the door to the outer office. My new secretary had pushed as far away from her desk as she could get, the back of her chair pressed against the windowsill. Her arms were extended in front of her, her fingers spread, her hands shaking. In front of her, in the small, semicircular clearing of desktop she'd managed to create, I saw an oversized manila envelope, an eight-by-ten photograph pulled halfway out of the opening. I didn't need to see the rest of the photo to recognize it—or to know why it had prompted such distress.

The photo showed a nude woman—a nude *dead* woman—lying on a hillside in the woods. Her legs, which had no feet, were opened wide, splayed on either side of a small tree; her crotch was jammed tightly against the sapling's trunk, in what appeared to be a shocking pose of sexual violation.

I snatched the envelope from the desk and quickly slid the picture back inside.

"*Why?*" whispered Peggy hoarsely.

"I'm so sorry," I said. Reaching behind me, through the doorway, I tucked the envelope into the bookshelf just inside my office.

"Why?" she repeated. "Why would someone send you that? And what kind of sick person would *take* such a picture?"

I winced. "Actually, I took it," I told her. "It's an old crime-scene photo, from a murder I worked up in Morgan County a couple years ago. December twenty-fourth, 1990. Christmas Eve." I sighed. "I don't know why this copy just came in the mail. I guess the sheriff's office or the TBI is cleaning out old case files. That, or they misread a request I sent out a few months ago, for copies of my forensic reports. A bunch of my files got thrown out last spring by mistake—by a temporary secretary, matter of fact." I frowned at her reflexively, as if the missing files were somehow *her* fault, then inwardly scolded myself. "I'm sorry you ran across that with no warning," I said. Pulling the envelope from the bookshelf, I looked to see whether it had been Sheriff Cotterell or Bubba Hardknot who'd scared the bejesus out of my new secretary, but there was no return address, and I tucked the envelope away again. She drew several deep breaths, each one sounding steadier than the one before. "Most of what we do here's pretty boring," I said, "but some of it's strong stuff—not for the faint of heart or weak of stomach."

She exhaled slowly through pursed lips, her cheeks puffing out as she did. "Well, you did warn me—sort of—when you interviewed me. I just hadn't expected something like . . . *this* . . . my first day on the job. 'A mean surprise'—that's what my mama would call it."

I smiled at the phrase. "Well, I'm sorry for the mean surprise, Betty."

"Peggy," she corrected.

"I'm sorry for the mean surprise, Peggy." I smiled in a way I hoped was reassuring. "Around here, you'll get used to things like that."

She didn't return the smile. "No offense, Dr. Brockton," she said, "but if I ever get used to things like that, it's time for me to look for a different job."

Suddenly I realized that I'd hung up on the dean in mid-scolding. "It might be time for *me* to look for a different job," I said ruefully, reaching for the phone and preparing to grovel.

"HELLO," I BARKED, snatching the handset from the cradle with a dripping, slippery hand.

"Uh . . . hello? Is this Dr. Brockton?" The caller sounded tentative and timid, as if she hoped I were someone else.

"*Yes*, this is Dr. Brockton," I snapped. I'd just returned from helping Tyler haul a fresh body from the morgue to the research facility. He now had two research subjects in the cage—"Double your data, double your smell," I'd joked—and I'd brought some of the aroma back with me. I'd ducked into the shower to wash it off, and the phone had begun to ring just as I'd lathered up. I'd ignored the first dozen rings, but finally the insistent jangling had gotten to me. For the second time in as many weeks, water pooled beneath my bare feet on the grimy concrete floor, the grime turning to slime.

There was silence on the other end of the line, and my annoyance ramped another notch higher. "I *said*, this is Dr. *Brockton*. How can I *help* you?"

"It's . . . it's Peggy."

"Peggy? Peggy *who*?"

"Peggy *Wilhoit*." The hesitancy and fear in her voice faded, displaced by what sounded like indignation. "Your new *secretary* Peggy." *Oops*, I thought. "Peggy, who opens your gruesome, disgusting mail."

"Oh, *Peggy*," I gushed. "Sorry, I couldn't quite hear you," I fibbed. "There's a leaf blower right outside my hideout." I waited for a response—a *No problem* or *That's okay* or other phrase of forgiveness—but instead, I heard only silence. Deafening, damning silence, on her end of the call and also on mine: no droning leaf blower backing up my story. I cleared my throat. "How are you settling in by now, Peggy?"

"Well, the backlog's a bit overwhelming, but I can see most of the desktop now. And I haven't come across anything else that's made me scream. Yet." She paused. "*Where* did you say you are?"

"In my hideout. My sanctuary. My secret office, up at the north end of the stadium. I only use the one next to yours when I'm being a bureaucrat," I explained. "Pushing papers, counseling students, chewing out junior faculty. I use this one when I need to get real work done."

"Ah. Well, perhaps you'll be so good as to show me where it is sometime. Meanwhile, you have a visitor here at Bureaucracy Central."

Oh, hell—not a visitor, I thought, but then I checked my watch: eleven thirty. "Ah," I said. "Tell him to meet me here."

"Him who?"

"Him *Jeff,*" I said, sighing at the woman's denseness. "My son. My visitor."

"Could this be a different visitor? A young woman?"

"You're asking *me* if it's a woman? Can't you tell the difference?"

"Yes, of course I can . . ." She paused, and when she resumed speaking, I felt frostbite nibbling my ear. "Let me start over. You have a visitor, Dr. Brockton. She is a young woman. Her name is Jenny Earhart."

"Oh—the artist?"

"I don't know, Dr. Brockton; I didn't ask her about her talents. But I'll do so now." I heard a murmured exchange, then, "Yes, Jenny Earhart, the artist."

"Does she have a sketch for me?"

Another murmured exchange. "Yes, she says she has a sketch for you."

"Excellent! Send her my way."

"Which way would that *be,* Dr. Brockton?" Clearly I had gotten off on the wrong foot with my new secretary.

"Oh. Right. Tell her I'll be right there. Thank you, *Peggy.*" Without waiting for a reply, I hung up the phone, toweled off, and yanked on clean clothes, which snagged and dragged on my damp skin. Then I jogged through the curving concrete corridor beneath the stadium, skidding to a stop outside Peggy's door just in time to avoid colliding with my son.

"*Jeff.* What are *you* doing here?"

"Gee, try to contain your excitement, Dad. It's a teacher-training day at school. You invited me to lunch, remember? Ribs at Calhoun's?"

"Sure. I knew that. I meant, what are you doing here *now*? Is it lunchtime already?" I brushed past him, squeezing through the doorway into the outer office. Behind the desk sat the new secretary, Peggy the Frosty, eyeing me coolly. In front of her, sitting sideways, wedged into the narrow gap between the desk and the doorway to my inner office, was Jenny, a leather portfolio and a skull-sized hatbox on her lap.

"Good morning," I said, taking the box off her lap and setting it on the corner of Peggy's desk. "Don't open that," I warned Peggy. "You won't like what's inside." I gave Jenny a conspiratorial smile. "That was quick," I said to her. "I figured it'd take you at least a week."

She shrugged. "I got really caught up in it—stayed up all night working on it. It was like she was . . . I don't know, trying to reach out to me." She blushed. "Sounds silly, I know."

"Actually, not at all," I assured her. "I sometimes imagine I hear the dead when I'm looking at their bones. Hear them whispering—telling me what happened."

"Yes, *yes*. Like that. Like . . . communing with the dead, almost. Amazing."

"*Sounds* amazing." Jeff's voice came from just behind me. He'd followed me into Peggy's office, and he leaned around me now, into Jenny's field of view, waving. "Hi. I'm Jeff. His son."

"Jeff, this is Jenny Earhart," I said. "An artist.

She's doing a facial sketch for me—that girl whose bones we found on Labor Day up at the strip mine." I turned back to her. "Why don't you come into my office, where there's a little more room, and show me what you've got?" I nodded toward the doorway, and she stood. "Give us a few minutes, son."

"Why don't we take her to lunch instead?" Jenny stopped in the doorway and turned to look at him. "You're an artist," he said. "That means you're starving, right? Metaphorically speaking," he added, flashing her a smile. I stared at him; was my son flirting with my forensic artist? And since when did he say things like *metaphorically speaking*? It must have worked, because she smiled back at him. "We're walking over to Calhoun's on the River," he hurried on. "You got time to go with us?" She looked at me; all I could do was shrug, leaving it up to her. "I'm *super*-interested in art," Jeff added. He caught my dubious glance. "Forensics, too, of course."

"That's good to know, son," I said. "We're putting a big wooden fence around the Body Farm. You can come help me paint it."

CALHOUN'S ON THE River was a five-minute walk from the Anthropology Department. Jeff, Jenny, and I took the stairwell down to the bone lab, exited at the base of the stadium—down at field level, near the south goal line—and angled across parking lots and four lanes of Neyland Drive to the big, barnlike restaurant perched on the north bank of the Tennessee River.

Calhoun's was a Knoxville landmark, noted for its barbecued ribs, its unsurpassed view of the river, and its proximity to Neyland Stadium; the place was nearly always hopping, but on days when the Vols—the Tennessee Volunteers—were playing at home, it was mobbed. People arrived by car, on foot, even by boat. A small wharf adjoined the restaurant, and on home-game weekends, boats would begin arriving days ahead of time, some chugging upriver all the way from Chattanooga or even Alabama. The tradition had begun with a single small boat back in 1962, but in the thirty years since, it had taken off, turning into an immense, floating block party: tailgating, Knoxville style. The first few boats would tie up to the wharf; subsequent arrivals would tie to them, and so on. By kickoff time, a vast flotilla—yachts, houseboats, pontoon boats, even runabouts—extended halfway across the river. To get to and from the shore, people clambered from vessel to vessel, bobbing and weaving from the combined effects of the river and the revelry. "The Vol Navy," this ad-hoc armada had been christened, and as an anthropologist, I found it a fascinating case study in social structure and cooperation.

On this day—three days before a much-anticipated match against the Florida Gators—a half-dozen early arrivals rocked gently in the water. Dangling high off the stern of one of the vessels, the reptilian eyes *X*ed out with black electrical tape, a ten-foot-long inflatable alligator swayed from an oversized hangman's noose. *Here's hoping*, I thought. The Vols looked promising this year.

The hostess seated us at a corner table overlooking the river—overhanging the river, in fact, as part of the restaurant extended above the water, supported by pilings. The windows on the river side extended from the floor to the ceiling; we sat down just in time to see a towboat and a load of empty barges, riding high in the water, making their way upriver. The headwaters of the Tennessee were only a few miles beyond, at the confluence of the Holston and French Broad Rivers. Both tributaries were navigable beyond Knoxville, but not for long, at least not for heavy traffic. A limestone quarry lay just above the confluence, on the French Broad—half a mile upstream from the UT pig farm—and my guess was, the barges were headed up there to take on a load of gravel. As the wake from the churning towboat reached the advance squadron of the Vol Navy, the boats rocked and heaved in the water.

"*So*," Jeff intoned dramatically, "you two are probably wondering why I called you here today."

"What?" I said, turning from the window. Jenny laughed.

SHE OPENED THE portfolio slowly, dropping her gaze and fumbling with the latch on the leather case as if it were a complicated mechanism. It might have been my imagination, but her fingers appeared to be trembling a bit. Reaching inside, she took out a sheaf of papers and slid them onto the table. On top was a photograph—actually, a photocopy of a photograph—showing a frontal view of the dead girl's skull, printed in high contrast to bring out the contours of the bone. "I wasn't sure how to do this, so I started by taking pictures," she said. She slid the frontal view aside; beneath it was another photocopied picture, this one showing the skull in three-quarter profile. "I used these as templates, underneath the paper I was drawing on, to make sure I didn't change the shape or proportions."

"Smart idea," I said. "So then you put tracing paper on top of these and drew on that?"

She shook her head. "I tried that, but I could see the skull *too* well through the tracing paper. It was overwhelming, and I couldn't visualize the face. Then I tried drawing on regular printer paper, but the skull was too faint through that—all I could see were the edges and the eyes. So finally I decided to try working on a light box, illuminating the skull and my drawing paper from underneath."

"Third time's the charm," said Jeff, who was leaning in—more closely than necessary, it seemed to me—from her other side. "Just like with Goldilocks and the three bears. It was *just right*." It was the cheesiest flirting I'd ever seen. I looked at Jenny, expecting to see her rolling her eyes in scorn.

Instead, she was beaming.

"Something like that."

She slid the second skull image aside, and I felt a jolt almost like electricity. Staring up at me from the table was a teenage girl—a skinny, ashen-faced girl who looked as if she hadn't had a good meal or a glimpse of the sun in months. Her hair hung straight, limp, and greasy looking. Her lips were thin and pursed. But it was the girl's eyes that gripped me; they locked onto mine, or so it seemed, and wouldn't let go.

"Wow," I said. "You've put a lot of despair in those eyes." Jenny looked at me for the first time since she'd slid the papers onto the table, and I saw concern in her eyes. "Don't worry," I hurried to assure her. "It's fine. It's better than fine; it's really good. From what I see in the bones—from what I imagine they're whispering—I'd say she had cause to despair, every day of her life. I'm just surprised you were able to convey that with a pencil and a piece of paper."

"I can't really take credit for that," she said. "I borrowed that." Seeing my puzzled look, she went on, "I've got a big book of photographs by Dorothea Lange. Do you know her work?"

"I do. She took a lot of portraits of hardscrabble folks during the Great Depression, didn't she?"

She nodded. "Tenant farmers. Migrant workers. Appalachian families. I was looking through that book, and I saw a picture of a farmer's wife holding their baby. The woman couldn't have been more than twenty, but she was totally beaten down by life already. You could see it in her eyes." She paused to clear her throat. "If this girl had made it to twenty and had a baby, I bet she'd have looked like the farmer's wife in that photo. So I borrowed that woman's despair. She had plenty to go around."

She set the frontal sketch aside to show me the next one, a three-quarter profile. It, too, was excellent—the girl's gauntness was emphasized by the deep hollows in her cheeks, which showed up more prominently in this one. "I really like it," I said slowly, "but the first one grabs me more. I'm not sure why."

"It's the eyes," Jeff chimed in, surprising me. "In this one, she's not looking at us."

"You're right," I agreed, impressed that he'd nailed it so fast. I picked up the frontal view for another look. "The way those eyes stare at you? It's like she's challenging you, saying, 'Hey, *look* at me. Do you know me?' You can't ignore that look."

"That's what I thought, too," Jenny said. "So next I did this one." She unveiled another drawing—another three-quarter profile—but in this one, the girl's gaze was locked on mine once more.

"Wonderful," I said. "That's the one to use."

"If you think so. But there's one more. I took a little artistic license with it, though. Maybe too much." She uncovered the final drawing. She'd gone back to the frontal view for this one. The eyes, as I'd come to expect, were arresting and haunting. But underneath one, she'd added a detail—an unexpected bit of shading that hit me like a punch in the gut: She had given the girl a black eye, and in the process, she'd somehow given the girl a story, given her a *life*. I remembered Jenny's assessment of the girl's life, as we'd sat at the table in the coffee shop—"Sounds like a pretty awful life," she'd said—and somehow she'd captured that in her sketch. As I held the soft nap of the drawing paper in my hand, I found myself staring into that life—even as I felt myself being stared into by the haunted, haunting eyes of the dead girl.

I COULD SMELL onions and potatoes frying even before I got to the top of the basement stairs and opened the kitchen door. "Yum," I said. "Smells great."

Kathleen looked over her shoulder, her spatula still stirring the sizzling contents of the cast-iron skillet. "How was your day?"

"Good. Interesting. I'll tell you about it, but not right now." I switched on the portable television that we kept on the kitchen counter and switched it to WBIR, the NBC affiliate, which dominated the local news. "I think they're doing a story about that Morgan County case I'm working. The strip-mine girl."

The newscast led off with a story about Saturday's football game between the Vols and the Gators. Even though the Vols' head coach, Johnny Majors, was still recuperating from a quintuple bypass, the Vols had won their first two games, including an upset win over fourteenth-ranked Georgia. This week, though, the Vols were taking on an even tougher opponent. The Gators were ranked number four in the nation, and they'd beaten UT the year before. Even though UT was a 10-point underdog, the story ended with a string of Vol fans professing their confidence. "Gator season is *open*!" yelled the final fan, an orange-clad man swaying on the rear deck of a houseboat. Behind him, I saw the familiar shape of Calhoun's in the distance, and—directly over the man's shoulder—the inflatable alligator hanging from its noose.

"Authorities in Campbell County are investigating the mysterious death of a teenage girl," said Bill Williams, WBIR's longtime news anchor. "The bones of the girl, whose age is estimated at twelve to fifteen years, were found on Labor Day beside an abandoned strip mine. Dr. Bill Brockton, a forensic anthropologist at the University of Tennessee, says the girl's body was dumped at the mine at least two years ago, possibly longer."

The camera shifted to Williams's coanchor, a woman named Edye Ellis. "Investigators today released an artist's conception of what the girl may have looked like." The screen filled with two of Jenny's sketches—the three-quarter profile and the frontal view that included the black eye—while Ellis continued, "Authorities have not been able to determine the cause of death." Now the image switched to a two-shot, with Ellis turning solemnly to Williams. "And Bill, investigators are treating this case as a homicide."

Williams nodded gravely. "Anyone with information about the girl's death or her identity is urged to call the Campbell County Sheriff's Office or the Tennessee Bureau of Investigation." The sketches flashed on the screen again, this time with phone numbers for the sheriff's office and the TBI.

The next story was a heartwarming piece about a fuzzy, adoptable puppy at the Humane Society shelter. "Cute dog," I said.

"Adorable," Kathleen agreed. "Sad thing is, there'll be more calls about the puppy than about the girl."

"Lots more calls," I agreed, switching off the set. "What'd you think of the sketches?"

"Good," she said. "Really good. Much better than usual. Those drawings of suspects they put out? Terrible."

"That's my doing," I preened. "The good ones, not the bad ones."

"Get out of here," she said. "You couldn't draw your way out of a paper bag."

"No, but I found an artist—a good artist—and I

loaned her the skull to work from. The chairman of the Art Department recommended her. Cute girl. Amelia somebody; no, wait—Jenny, not Amelia. Earhart. Jenny Earhart. I think maybe Jeff's gonna ask her out."

"Jeff? *Our* Jeff? Ask out a college girl?"

"No, she's still in high school. She goes to Laurel—you know, that hippie school? She took a drawing class at UT last spring, knocked the socks off the professor."

"What makes you think Jeff might ask her out?"

"He came by to have lunch with me today, right about the time she showed up with the sketches. So he invited her to Calhoun's with us. Flirted with her the whole time. I kept expecting to look under the table and see his hand on her thigh."

"Bill!" She turned and waved the spatula at me reprovingly. "You're incorrigible."

"What? I seem to remember putting my hand on *your* thigh under the table a time or two, back in the day."

"Back in the day? More like last week, at the provost's dinner."

I took a step toward her, pressing against her from behind, and slid my hands down to her thighs, giving them a fond squeeze. She swatted my hands away, but not immediately.

"You don't want me to burn the potatoes," she said. "Besides, Jeff will be upstairs any second now." She leaned back and rubbed her hair against my cheek. "But hold that thought." So I did.

I HEARD THE clock striking eleven as Kathleen lay curled against me, her head on my chest. "Bill?" Her voice was low and drowsy.

"Hmm?"

"Wouldn't it be great if Jeff found some nice girl?"

"He's *got* a girl," I pointed out. "Good old what's-her-name. Tiffany? Brittany?"

"Madison. Oh, please. That girl has the brains of a Dalmatian."

"True. But I've seen her in a bikini, and that girl has the body of a centerfold."

"That's the reason he's going out with her. The *only* reason he's going out with her."

"Seems like a damn good reason to me," I chuckled. I felt a sudden pain, as the point of an elbow gouged my ribs. "*Ow.*"

"Beauty's only skin deep," she murmured. "Stupidity goes all the way to the bone."

"You talking about the Dalmatian, or about me?"

Her only answer was a soft, sighing breath, which ruffled the hair on my chest, like breeze ruffling a Kansas wheat field.

THE PHONE RANG the next morning at seven thirty, just as I got back from my weekly trim at the barbershop. I snatched up the receiver, hoping to hear Sheriff Cotterell or Bubba Hardknot on the line; hoping that someone had ID'd the girl after seeing the sketches on WBIR or in this morning's *News Sentinel*.

My hopes were quickly dashed. "Hi, Dad."

"Jeff? Why aren't you in school?"

"I *am* in school. I'm calling from the pay phone in the hall." In the background, I heard the clamor of boisterous young voices.

"What's wrong? Are you sick? Are you in trouble?"

"No, no, I'm fine. I just didn't see you this morning. You'd gone to get a haircut when I came up for breakfast."

"Did you *need* to see me this morning?"

"Mom said you told her about Jenny last night."

"About Jenny? Yesssss," I said slowly, turning to look at Kathleen. She was stirring her coffee with unusual attentiveness. "We did talk about Jenny. Why?" Stretching the phone cord to its limit, I leaned in Kathleen's direction, into her field of view, and raised my eyebrows at her. She shrugged, as if she had no clue why Jeff was calling me. I took the gesture as proof positive that she'd put him up to it. To something.

"Quit beating around the bush, son. What's on your mind?"

"I want to ask her out."

"Go for it," I said. "You don't need my permission to ask a girl out."

"I want to ask her out for this Saturday."

"Fine by me. I wasn't expecting to see much of you Saturday anyhow. Your mom and I'll be at the UT-Florida game."

"Thing is, I was hoping to take Jenny to the UT-Florida game."

"Ha," I said. "Good luck with *that*. That game's been sold out for months. You couldn't find a ticket . . ." A thought struck me—a thought so awful, I knew instantly that it was the truth. "You can't be serious. Tell me you're not calling to ask me what I think you're calling to ask me."

"*Please*, Dad."

"You want my tickets to the UT-*Florida* game? You gotta be kidding. Wild alligators couldn't keep me away from that game. You can have my tickets to the Arkansas game," I said. "Or even the Alabama game. But Florida? You gotta be kidding." Now Kathleen was desperately trying to catch *my* attention. Frowning, I mimicked her earlier shrug. "I love you a lot, son, but not *that* much."

Kathleen sighed, shaking her head. Then she reached into the pocket of her bathrobe and fished out a cordless phone. "Jeff?"

"Hey, Mom."

"Pay no attention to your father. Of course you can have our tickets to the game."

"*What?* What the hell?" I squawked.

"Thanks, Mom. Thanks, Dad. Late for class—gotta go," he said, and the line went dead.

"What the hell?" I repeated. "I've been looking forward to that game for a year."

"Oh, come on," she said. "Don't be stingy. Look at it as an investment in Jeff's happiness."

"What about *my* happiness?"

"Doesn't it make you happy to see him asking out that nice girl?"

"You don't even *know* her," I blustered. "Now that I think about it, she's not so nice after all. In fact, I think she's a very bad girl. A terrible girl. Dumb, too—she makes Dalmatian-brain look like a genius."

"Oh, nonsense. Besides, maybe you can find happiness some other way on Saturday," she said. She opened the front of her bathrobe and gave me a slow, suggestive smile, swaying her hips as she did.

"But sweetie," I said. "*Darling.*" I felt a powerful surge of conflicting desires. "This is my only chance all year to see UT play Florida. You and I will have *lots* of chances to . . . you know . . . find happiness."

Still smiling, she wrapped the bathrobe across herself, two layers deep. "If Jeff doesn't get to take Jenny to that game Saturday," she said sweetly, "football might be the only happiness you find for the rest of the season." She puckered her lips, mimed a kiss in my direction, and then tied the bathrobe belt. In a knot.

CHAPTER 18

Satterfield

HE BACKED THE MUSTANG out of his garage and tucked it around back, behind the house and out of sight. Not that there was anything to see, and not that there was ever any traffic on his street anyhow. Still, the fewer tracks you left, the fewer tracks you had to cover. That was one of the survival-training lessons he'd learned during his brief stint in SEAL training. He'd forgotten that lesson once, with that first girl, and he'd paid a steep price. The disgrace of getting discharged—"under less than honorable conditions"—had cut deeply; it had cut to the bone, and it had left him scarred, as surely as his stepfather's cigarettes had scarred him. But scars were like combat medals, etched in the skin and the soul: badges of honor, or at least of survival. Satterfield had survived, and he'd begun settling accounts.

He backed the van out, then eased it back in, centering it on the concrete slab. He'd start with a base coat of olive drab, then finish the camouflage by adding splotches of pale green and muddy brown.

He found himself humming as he laid out the drop cloths and taped the glass and poured the viscous paint carefully into the sprayer. He hummed in part because he liked the preparations; liked transforming his meticulous plans into reality. Also, though, he hummed because he enjoyed the joke—found amusement in the ironic absurdity of dressing out a dweeby white work van in hunter's camouflage.

The real joke was that it wasn't really the van that he was camouflaging, though, it was himself: By disguising himself as the sort of dumb shit who believed that a bad camo paint job was cool—*Don't forget to do a shitty job,* he reminded himself—he enabled himself to creep closer to his quarry, to coil around her before she realized that she was the prey.

CHAPTER 19

Tina

TINA AWOKE IN SEMIDARKNESS, groaning and groggy and disoriented. Naked and cold, too. Her shoulders and hips and knees ached, but when she tried to stretch, she found that she could not move. Her wrists were bound behind her, her ankles tied to her wrists; Tina was hog-tied, she realized, and the realization caused a flood of memory and terror to surge in her. She'd climbed into the van on Magnolia sometime around midnight. It looked like a work van, with metal racks on the roof for ladders or pipes or lumber but with a bad paint job, a stupid paint job—camo paint on a work truck. It didn't make her feel all that impressed with the john—what kind of idiot would try to camouflage a work van?—but business was slow and her hot pants were anything but warm in the chill of the late-September night. Just as the van had pulled away from the curb, she'd glanced down and seen a coil of rope on the floorboards. The guy had caught her looking at the rope, and then at him, and the glint in his eyes—the cold and predatory glint they took on in response to the fear in her own—had set off every alarm in her head. She'd tried to get out of the van then, even though it was moving, but the door was locked, and the lock knob had come off—had been *taken* off, she'd realized with a sudden sick feeling. She'd begun beating helplessly on the glass of the window, like a luna moth battering itself against a windowpane or a streetlight. He'd pulled over fast, and the last thing she remembered was a strong hand seizing the back of her neck, another strong hand clamping a cloth over her nose and mouth, and pungent, sickly-sweet vapors coursing through her nostrils and mouth, down into her lungs, deep into her darkening brain.

"Rise and shine, Tina," said a voice nearby. *His* voice. The voice of the guy who'd picked her up in the stupid van. "Tina? Right? I hope you got a good rest, Tina. You need to be fresh." He paused. "You ever go hunting, Tina?"

She shook her head. "No," she whispered hoarsely.

"Not a lot of women do. It's more of a man thing. But we're fixin' to go hunting, you and me." He sighted along a long, slender shaft, pointing its triangular tip at her, and at the far end, she saw three slender vanes. Feathers. "Actually," he said, smiling, reaching down with one hand, "*I'm* fixin' to go hunting." He lifted something from the floor of the van, a shape that reminded her of a half moon: curved on one edge, straight on the other, but empty in between. She began to whimper and shudder, her trembling as rapid and desperate as the luna moth's, its powdery wings flailing and beginning to smoke as they beat against the pitiless glass of a searing searchlight.

The man with the moon was the devil himself, and the moon in his hands was a hunting bow.

CHAPTER 20

Roy Lee

"WHAT THE *FUCK*?!" PERCHED fifteen feet up the trunk of a pine tree, on the narrow platform of a tree stand, Roy Lee Cheatham blinked and peered again through the scope of his deer rifle, then released his trigger finger, flipped on the safety, and laid the .30–06 across his knees so he could look through his binoculars instead. The binoculars were more powerful than the rifle scope, and they had a wider field of view, too, which made it easier to keep them trained on moving animals.

"Come on, come on, where you at?" he whispered, then, "God a-*mighty*." Two hundred yards away, moving from tree to tree, was a woman. A buck-naked woman. He stared through the glasses, his vision—frequently blocked by tree trunks—shifting from her face to her bare breasts and flanks and back up to her face. Again and again she looked over her shoulder, as if she were being pursued, and her face looked wild and desperate. She was limping—staggering, almost—and Roy Lee understood suddenly that she was hurt. He got another brief glimpse, and this time he thought he saw blood streaming down her leg. "Holy *shit*." Laying the rifle flat on the platform of the tree stand, he scrambled down the ladder and ran toward her, calling, "Hey, lady! *Lady!* Hang on—I'm coming to help you." He ran on a diagonal track that he thought would intercept hers, but it was hard to be sure, as his line of sight was often obscured and his crashing run drowned out whatever sounds she was making. After he'd sprinted a hundred yards, he stopped to look and listen.

The woods were silent. She had stopped, too, he realized. He scanned slowly, his eyes and ears on full alert. Slightly to his left, perhaps thirty yards away, he heard a faint, ragged wheeze, and then he caught a flash of pale skin. "Hey," he called again, and started in that direction. She burst into view, like a quail flushed from dry grass, and began to run—away from him, not toward. "Wait," he called. "You look hurt. I'm trying to help."

She continued to flee, but she was moving far slower than Roy Lee was, so he gained ground on her swiftly. Blood was streaming down her leg, and as he got closer, he was stunned to see the shaft of an arrow protruding from the back of her thigh. He drew even with her within a minute. "Hey," he panted. "*Hey*. What happened?" She stared at him, wild-eyed, and continued to stumble forward. He took hold of her wrist. "I'm trying to help, can you understand that? We need to get you to a doctor. I'm not gonna hurt you." She stopped, her chest heaving, her breathing somewhere between gasping and sobbing. "Easy, now. *Easy*, now." He spoke as if he were soothing a spooked horse. "That's a girl. That's a girl. Don't be afraid. You're okay. Everything is gonna be okay."

"Is it?" Roy Lee's head snapped up at the words, spoken in a male voice somewhere ahead and off to his right. He scanned the trees but saw nothing. "Never make promises you can't keep, Goober," the unseen speaker continued. "Didn't your mama teach you that?"

"Git your ass outta your damn hidey-hole and we'll have us a little talk about what my mama did or didn't teach me," said Roy Lee. He caught a slight movement in his peripheral vision, and he turned just in time to see a camouflaged figure rise from a crouch and pull a compound bow to a full draw.

"I've got no interest in talking to you about your hillbilly mama," said the man with the bow. As he said the word *mama*, he relaxed the first two fingers of his right hand. Roy Lee heard a dull twang and a brief seething sound—the snap of a bowstring, followed by the whisper of feathers as the arrow flew toward him at 300 feet per second. Then he felt himself shoved against the naked woman as the razor-tipped arrow penetrated his chest, and his heart opened in a bloom of crimson to receive its thrust.

CHAPTER 21

Brockton

"*DIS*-PATCH. CAN I HEP you?" From the woman's voice—flat but twangy, like an out-of-tune banjo—I guessed that she'd lived in Wartburg, or at least somewhere in the hills of East Tennessee, all her life.

"Sheriff Cotterell, please."

"I'm sorry, sir, Sheriff Cotterell is away right now. I can probably track him down on the radio, if it's urgent."

I felt a twinge of disappointment. "No, it's not urgent. Could you give him a message, please?"

"I don't care to," she said, and even though I'd lived in Tennessee for three years now, it still took me a moment to translate her spoken words—which sounded like a refusal—into her actual meaning: *I don't mind.*

"I'd appreciate that. This is Dr. Bill Brockton, at the University of Tennessee."

"Yes, sir, Dr. Brockton, how are you? This is Mae. We met when you was up here awhile back, working that Donnelly woman's murder. I hear you're back with us on another'n now. That girl's bones, found up on Frozen Head. I seen her pitcher on the TV news th'other night."

"I hope a lot of other people up that way saw it, too," I said. "That's one of the reasons I was calling Sheriff Cotterell—to see if he's gotten any leads since"—I caught myself just before parroting the words "her pitcher"—"since the sketch came out."

"No, sir, I'm sorry to say we haven't. Not a peep. But us'n the TBI's takin' copies all over ever'where—churches, grocery stores, gas stations, Health Department, you name it. I made a prayer request at church last Sunday, too, that the Lord'll lay it on somebody's heart to come forward and tell us who she is and what happened to her."

"Well," I said, "between the sheriff's office, the TBI, and the Lord, sounds like y'all have all the jurisdictions covered." I waited for a laugh, but I didn't get one. "Other reason I was calling was to see if Sheriff Cotterell needed something from me on the Donnelly woman's murder."

"Denise Donnelly? What kind of follow-up? Sonofagun husband that killed her don't come up for parole for another eight years. He ain't filed any kind of appeal, far as I know, and I'd prob'ly know, since he's my cousin." A pause, then: "How come you to ask?"

"Oh, it's nothing, really," I said. "I got one of the Donnelly crime-scene photos in the mail the other day. No letter or anything with it—just the picture." As I spoke, I walked to the bookcase where I'd tucked the envelope a few days before, after snatching it from Peggy's trembling hands.

"You say the *sheriff* sent it to you?"

"Well, I *think* so," I said. "First I thought Bubba Hardknot sent it—Agent Meffert?—but Bubba says he didn't. So then I figured it had to've come from the sheriff. Figured maybe y'all were cleaning out your files."

"I'll ask him about it when he gets in," she said. "But I'd be real surprised if he sent you that pitcher. He ain't mentioned that case to me in a year or more. And he *sure* ain't give me nothing like that to mail."

"You reckon he might've mailed it himself?"

"Who? The *sheriff*? Well, they do say there's a first time for ever'thing." Now she laughed. It was a hearty, good-natured laugh, but as I slid the crime-scene photo from its envelope, the laugh seemed to turn mocking and sinister, and then it seemed to turn to shrieks: first, the echoes of my secretary's frightened scream; then the warning sirens in my own head; finally, the cries of the dead woman whose image I held in my hands.

A dead woman who was not Denise Donnelly. A dead woman whose crime scene had not yet been worked, because her body had not yet been found.

As I stared at the photo, I finally noticed things I'd overlooked the day I'd snatched it from Peggy and shoved it back in the envelope. I noticed that the trees were tinged with gold and orange and red—September trees, not December trees. *Right now* trees, I thought. I noticed that although the woman's feet were missing, her body showed no signs of decomposition, and her blood was fresh and bright.

Last but not least—far, far from least—I noticed that the photo had a small time stamp in the lower right corner. Unless the camera's internal clock was wrong, the photo had been taken—and the woman's life had been taken—just three days before my new secretary reported for work and opened the envelope.

"Hello? Hello? Are you still there?" The voice of the dispatcher seemed to come from far away, and I stared at the telephone receiver dumbly, seemingly baffled to find it in my hand.

"Please ask the sheriff to call me when he gets in," I said, then hung up and called the TBI, leaving a similar message for Meffert. All I'd be able to tell them was that somewhere out there—somewhere in the millions of acres of Tennessee woods—another woman lay dead and decomposing. And that somewhere out there, a killer might already be stalking his next victim—a victim whose body would end up bearing an uncanny and inexplicable resemblance to one of my prior cases.

CHAPTER 22

Janelle

GODDAMNED WASTE OF TIME, Janelle thought, glancing over her shoulder at the empty mile of Magnolia Avenue stretching between her and downtown. All four lanes were empty, except for scattered trash: wadded-up burger wrappers, smashed French fries, crushed paper cups and aluminum cans and plastic hubcaps.

Sometimes Janelle did good business at lunchtime on Fridays—white-collar guys cruising for a nooner; construction workers clocking out early, cashing their paychecks before the ink was all the way dry; family men looking to unwind before heading west to the burbs for a weekend of soccer coaching and honey-do chores. Today, though, Magnolia Avenue was looking like the main drag of Ghost Town, USA. Was there a wreck somewhere blocking traffic? Road work somewhere between here and downtown? Didn't appear to be. She kept walking east, her back to downtown—her swaying ass to downtown, more to the point—but the six-inch heels on her boots were better for posing than for walking, especially on the broken, glass-littered sidewalks of East Knoxville.

She was on the verge of giving up, heading back to her room for a nap—might as well rest up for the night ahead, when surely business would be better, *please God*—when she heard a rumbling engine and the quick toot of a horn. The car passed her slowly, then cut into the parking lot of the Dollar store, pulling up right alongside her. A nice ride: an early Mustang—*whoa, a '67*, she realized—with no dents or rust. Recent paint job, too, by the look of it, though Janelle didn't like the garish shade of orange; for her money, black or red would've been lots classier. Lots sexier.

The driver looked well kept, too, and maybe about the same age as the car: twenty-five, plus or minus. Close-cropped hair, form-fitting black T-shirt, good biceps and pecs: gym muscles, not ditch-digging muscles. He should be good for at least fifty. Maybe more, if she played him right. "I like the car," she cooed. "Whatcha got under the hood?"

"A big-bore slant six," he said, winking to make sure she caught the double meaning.

She raised her eyebrows and smiled, to signal that she did. "And is that an auto-matic, or do you prefer . . . *manual*?" She flashed him a naughty smile and cocked one leg out to the side. *Play it cool*, she told herself.

"You *know* it's a straight stick," he grinned. "You good with a clutch?"

Janelle knew cars, and she could play this game with the best of them. "Baby," she said, "when my master cylinder starts to working, your hydraulic pressure is gonna go sky-high, and your slave cylinder will *explode*."

He laughed. "You win. Hop in, I'll give you a test ride."

"Where we goin'?"

"Far as you want," he said. "How 'bout we go all the way?" The passenger door opened. "Come on."

She sashayed toward the car, feeling the seam in the jeans cleaving her in a way that he couldn't help but notice; feeling her breasts swaying in the filmy top; feeling his eyes roaming all over her. She was looking good today, long as he didn't look at her face too close—the lines and the dark circles were getting harder to hide in the daylight. It had been her experience, though, that most johns weren't all that interested in her face.

Stopping at the open door, she put one boot up on the sill. The boot came to the top of her calf, and the jeans—tight as second skin—were tucked in, giving her a leggy look that generally made men's heads turn when she walked down a sidewalk. She didn't lean down to talk to him; she kept her head above the roofline, so he'd focus on her body. "It takes some cash to fill up my tank. I got to keep the chassis nice and lubricated."

"How much cash?"

"You want the turbo package, baby?"

"Come on. I'll give you a hundred—fifty for you, fifty for the car lingo."

She slithered down into the bucket seat, the jeans forming taut, fan-shaped creases at the crotch as she did. "That might be the tightest pair of jeans I ever saw," he said. "Have much trouble gettin' out of those?"

"I don't *have* trouble gettin' out of these," she said, "I *cause* trouble."

"You just don't quit, do you, sister?"

"Brother, I am only just getting started."

HE PARKED THE car under the billboard and shut off the engine. She stared out the windshield at the traffic whizzing past on the interstate, then she swiveled in the seat to face him. "You're kidding me, right?"

"Nope. I'm dead serious."

"This is where you want to do it? A hundred feet off I–40, in broad daylight? No offense, but what the hell, man?"

"I got a nice little love nest right up that path there," he said. "You're gonna love it."

"No, I am *not* gonna love it. You want me to do it in the *woods*, laying on sticks and leaves? Take me back. This is some kind of fucked up."

He opened his door and came around to her side of the car. She reached for the lock, but there *was* no lock, and she thought, *Shit shit* shit, as the door opened wide. "Let's go, darlin'," he said, reaching for her hand. "Time for you to show me that turbo package you were braggin' about. You are gonna love my hot rod."

She slapped at his hand, but he reached in with the other one and grabbed her by the wrist. "Play nice, now." He folded her thumb forward, down toward the inside of her forearm, torquing her wrist to a right angle, twisting her arm out to the side. The pain made her cry out, and she leaned forward in the seat, then leaned out of the car to ease the pressure. "That's right, come on out. Unless you want me to break it." He increased the pressure, and she gasped, expecting a bone to snap. "We're gonna walk up into those woods together, and you're gonna act real nice, to make up for being rude to me just now. Remember, darlin', I am the customer. And the customer's always right. Am I right?" He gave another quick squeeze, and she whimpered, clenching her teeth to keep from screaming. "Tell me: Am I right?" He bore down slowly this time, increasing the torque with excruciating precision.

"Yes. *Yes*," she whispered.

"Yes what?"

"Yes, you're right."

He was squatting down now so his face was level with hers, watching her closely as he twisted again. Smiling as he saw the agony in her eyes. "Say 'Yes, *sir*, you're right.' "

"Yes, *sir*, you're right." She was starting to cry now, involuntary tears of pain and fury rolling down her cheeks. *God*, she hated being so helpless to resist, but more than that, even, she hated to cry—hated it for the weakness it showed; hated it, too, because she knew this asshole was getting off on it.

"Get out of the car, nice and easy. Here, I'll help you." He added some upward force, and she staggered out, almost vomiting from the pain in her thumb and her wrist. "That's it. Now up that little path there." He walked behind her, using the shrieking thumb and torqued arm to steer her, as if her arm were the tiller of a small boat.

Fifty yards up the trail he stopped and turned her

to face him. "All right now, show me how you wiggle out of those jeans." She glared at him, arms at her sides, not moving. He unbuckled his belt—a wide leather strap with a heavy brass buckle—and yanked the buckle. The strap seethed and snapped through the belt loops like an angry snake, then popped free of the final loop and writhed in the air between them, nearly hitting her in the face. "Don't make me tell you again," he said. Doubling the strap, he slapped it lightly against his thigh. Hands shaking, she fumbled with the button in her waistband, finally got it, and then unzipped the jeans and began pushing them down over her hips. "Not like that," he said. "Work it. Make it good. Put on a show for me."

"Fuck you, asshole," she hissed.

The backhanded swing of the doubled belt caught her on the right ear and cheek; the force of the blow knocked her to the ground, laying her cheek open and causing her to black out briefly. When she came to, he was dragging her to her feet. "Let's try this again," he said. "Show me how you wiggle out of those. Slow and sexy. Put some shimmy in it. You need to put the 'service' in 'customer service,' sweetheart."

Her breath coming in jerky gasps, she began to twitch her hips and sway. He kept time with both hands: his left hand flipping the belt against his leg, his right hand rubbing himself to an erection. His eyes feasted on the fear she knew was showing in hers.

NAKED NOW, SHE squatted in front of him, twigs and rocks jabbing the soles of her feet. His left hand encircled her throat; his right gripped the back of her head, his fingers entwined in her hair, so he could push or pull with equal ease. "Open up and say 'ah,'" he ordered. "And show me how much you want it. Suck it like your life depends on it."

His final words were accompanied by a steady tightening of the pressure on her windpipe. The pressure eased, but only slightly, when she gasped, "I want it. So much. Give it to me, baby. Please."

Wrapping her right hand around him, she opened her mouth, sizing him up, wondering, *Could I bite it off?* As she guided him in, between her lips, past her incisors, across her tongue, she imagined it all—the swift, savage clamp of her strong jaws, the gasp and then the howl of pain, the gratifying geyser of blood pulsing from his severed stump, the spurts diminishing until there was no more blood to be shed. *He'd still kill me,* she realized—a quick clench of the hand around her throat, first as a reflexive response to the pain, followed by the full force of his vengeful fury. *But he'll kill me no matter what. Unless I get away. But how?*

Fighting for breath, fighting back the need to gag, Janelle began cooing and moaning—softly at first, then steadily louder—feigning the desire he demanded. With her left hand, she caressed the front of his thigh, her nails lightly raking the skin. He seemed to like that—his thrusts grew more insistent, and his right hand kept time, slamming her face against his crotch harder and harder.

Releasing the shaft of his penis, Janelle now reached both hands behind him and squeezed his clenching buttocks, drawing a low groan from him. *That's right, asshole*, she thought, *you just think about gettin' off.* Slowly she ran her fingernails down the backs of his thighs, his knees, his calves, until her hands reached his ankles, where his pants were bunched. Taking the crotch of his bunched-up pants in both hands, she gripped it tight, then—drawing momentum from the next forward yank of the hand entwined in her hair—she drove her head into his belly. At the same instant she straightened her legs and yanked the pants toward her, turning all her terror into strength. The man grunted and toppled backward, arms flailing, whacking his head on the trunk of a fallen tree.

Janelle didn't wait to see if he was hurt. Oblivious to the damage being done to her bare feet, she ran down the trail, out of the woods, and then—stark naked—darted across the dead-end lane, up the grassy embankment, and onto the shoulder of Interstate 40, frantically waving her arms for help.

Two cars whizzed by, horns blaring, but then a tractor-trailer rig smoked to a stop just beyond her, and another tucked in behind the first. The astonished truckers clambered down from their cabs and converged on her just in time to see a neon-orange Mustang fishtail up the dead-end lane, skid around a corner, and vanish up a serpentine road into the backwoods of east Knox County.

PART 2

The Fall

> . . . your eyes shall be opened, and ye shall be as gods, knowing good and evil.
>
> —Genesis 3:5

OCTOBER 1992

CHAPTER 23

Satterfield

THE LIGHT AT MAGNOLIA Avenue and Cherry Street flipped to yellow, and Satterfield braked for once instead of punching the gas. For one thing, he was moving at a crawl anyhow, trolling for the woman who'd slipped from his grasp a few hours before; for another, he wasn't in the Mustang, but in the van, with its anemic engine and sissy automatic transmission. The camo paint was gone, scrubbed off; anybody who bothered to glance his way would see an ordinary work van—a painter's van—with a pair of battered, spattered aluminum ladders clattering on the roof racks.

At the far right corner of the intersection was a Family Dollar store, and Satterfield eyed it through the windshield. The Magnolia Avenue hookers tended to congregate there, or at least cross paths there. Maybe it was because Magnolia and Cherry was a high-traffic intersection, or maybe simply because Family Dollar was a cheap place to get snacks or nail polish or stockings or other tools of the trade. *Does Family Dollar sell rubbers?* he wondered idly. *Lube?* Ironic, that hookers were regulars in Family Dollar. He noticed a bail-bonding company conveniently located in the next block, and, across Magnolia, a run-down motel, probably a hot-sheet motel. *Hell, if there was a Waffle House and a beer joint and a VD clinic, you could just live right here,* he thought sardonically. He snapped to attention when a leggy woman in a short skirt strutted out of Family Dollar, a blond wig swaying as she walked. The strut was right and the skirt was tight, but the skin was wrong—it was black skin. As he scanned the fringes of the store's parking lot, Satterfield's jaw muscles throbbed, pulsing like venom glands. He'd spotted two or three other hookers along Magnolia in his first pass out and back, but not the one he wanted to find. The one he really, really needed to find.

He'd made a mistake. It was the only one he'd made—the only one, at least, since that beginner's mistake, with that first woman. That one had cost him dearly; had cost him a career and a future. This one might be as bad. Would she go to the cops? *Probably not,* he told himself, for the hundredth time. *Hookers hate cops.* He drummed his fingers on the wheel. *Then again,* he fretted, *hookers don't fight back. And they damned sure don't win. Don't get away. Not from me, they don't.* But she did; she had. So clearly she wasn't like most hookers. And even if she didn't go to the cops, she could put the word out on the street about him, warn the others against him, and sooner or later that could circle back to bite him in the ass. If he didn't spot her by midnight, he'd have to start asking around, loosening some lips with some cash or some crack. The girl—shit, he hadn't even bothered to ask her street name—was a serious loose end, one that had to be tied up, fast and tight. *This is not good,* the voice in his head shouted again. *Not good.*

Behind him, a horn honked—he hadn't noticed the light turn green—and Satterfield thrust his arm out the window and gave the guy the finger. The gesture was answered by the squawk of a police siren and the strobing of blue lights. "Shit," he hissed. Distracted and distraught, he hadn't even noticed the KPD cruiser come up behind him at the red light. "Shit, shit, *shit.*" He eased the van forward and turned into the Family Dollar lot so he wouldn't block traffic. "Stupid, stupid, stupid." He slapped the right side of his face so hard he saw stars. "*Stupid.*" The stinging pain helped focus his mind.

Keeping his eyes locked now on the outside mirror, he watched the cruiser pull into the lot behind him. Satterfield tugged his wallet from his back pocket and flipped it open, removing the driver's license from the clear sleeve and laying both items on the dash, the license on top of the wallet. Then he reached behind him and tucked his hand into the deep pocket on the back of the seat. There, his searching fingers closed around the serrated slide of the Glock, and he slid out the pistol, which felt heavy and reassuring in his hand. He racked the slide to chamber a round and laid the gun across his lap, the muzzle pointing at the center of the driver's door. Then he covered it with the wrapper from the Hardee's burger he'd just eaten. The shreds of lettuce littering the wrapper were still crisp, the smears of ketchup still bright as blood.

In the mirror, he watched as the door of the cruiser opened and the cop got out—a red-faced kid, probably no more than a year out of the academy, Satterfield guessed. He was already porking up, his blue shirt straining and bulging over his belt from a surfeit of sausage biscuits or Krispy Kremes or Coors; a few years from now, by the time he was Satterfield's age, the porky kid would probably be on blood-pressure and cholesterol meds. Was his face flushed because he had a drinking problem, too, on top of the eating problem? Or was that just sunburn, or maybe a rookie's anger at being flipped off?

Satterfield was on high alert—coiled—debating between playing it cool and striking preemptively. Maybe all he'd need to do was grovel. *Gosh, officer, I am* so *sorry*, he rehearsed. *Some punk was tailgating me a couple blocks back, and I thought . . .* But what if the girl had already gone to the police? What if all the patrol units already had his description? And what if this guy, eager to prove himself, had memorized the description—had seen Satterfield trolling for her and had recognized him?

Satterfield's finger tightened as the blue uniform loomed closer and larger, now filling the mirror. If he fired through the door, Porky would never even see it coming. His piglike eyes and jowls would open wide in surprise, and then—just as the sound of the shot registered in his brain—he'd crumple to the asphalt. Shooting him through the door might require a second shot to finish him, though—time-consuming and riskier, potentially exposing Satterfield to more witnesses. What if he held on to his license when the cop tried to take it? Would that distract the guy long enough for Satterfield to raise the gun and take a clean headshot?

"Sir, I need to see your license and registration," Porky said, peering through the window at Satterfield's face.

"Officer, I am *so* sorry," Satterfield began, reaching for the license with his left hand, shaking his head in a show of embarrassment and contrition. "I had no idea that was you behind me." He picked up the license by one corner, gripping it tightly as he extended it toward the window. "My father was a police officer," he added, laying it on thick as syrup. "I respect the hell out of you guys."

Instead of taking the bait—and instead of taking the license—the cop said, "Sir, would you remove your sunglasses, please?"

Satterfield hadn't expected that. *Shit, now what?* he thought. *Do I put down the license, or let go of the gun? Or do I shoot now?* He stalled for time. "Excuse me?"

"I said take off your sunglasses, please."

Fuck. Is he just seeing if I'm stoned, or does he have a description? The day was cool, but Satterfield felt a crown of sweat beading his scalp, felt moisture gather under his arms and trickle down his sides. The Glock had a six-pound trigger pull, and Satterfield's finger pressure was already pushing three pounds, easy—maybe four—and climbing.

Suddenly the cop's face swiveled toward the cruiser, and Satterfield heard a radio call blaring through the loudspeaker. "All units, all units. Armed robbery in progress, Home Federal Bank, 3001 East Magnolia."

Without a word, the cop spun and lumbered away. Slamming the cruiser into gear, he whipped it around, almost clipping the van's bumper, and fishtailed out of the Family Dollar lot, tires smoking and siren shrieking.

Satterfield took a deep breath and exhaled slowly, then bent forward and rested his head on the steering wheel. After three more such breaths, he straightened up. Lifting the hinged lid of the console, he took out a pack of unfiltered Camels and a lighter. With shaking hands he tapped out a cigarette and lit it, taking a deep drag and holding it, forcing the nicotine into his bloodstream as he replaced the pack and the lighter and closed the lid. Then, expelling a tight plume of smoke, he turned his right palm upward on the console. "You stupid piece of shit," he whispered, in a voice that he hadn't heard in years.

The flesh hissed and smoked as he pressed the burning cigarette to his palm. Satterfield flinched, but he did not whimper or cry out. He hadn't whimpered since he was twelve, and he'd be damned to hell if he'd ever whimper again.

CHAPTER 24

Kittredge

KITTREDGE FROWNED, RUBBING HIS left hand across his mouth, the stubble on his upper lip and chin rasping like sandpaper across his fingers and palm. The stubble rubbing was the detective's version of a worry stone; the sound and sensation distracted his mind, turned down the distracting, unhelpful inner chatter. Kittredge rubbed his chin religiously, ritualistically, the way a baseball player might tap dirt from his spikes with the bat before stepping into the batter's box, focusing on his shoes instead of the cowhide-covered cannonball about to come screaming in at ninety-five miles an hour—and by distracting himself from it, giving himself a better shot at *hitting* the damned thing.

"I'm having a little trouble here, Ms. . . ." Kittredge stole a glance at the complaint form on his desk. "Ms. Mayfield. You're saying this man raped you. But you also say you got into his car with him. Agreed to have sex with him. For money. You see my problem here? How am I supposed to arrest a man for raping a woman who agreed to have sex with him?"

The woman looked away, appeared to be wavering. Probably deciding to cut her losses, Kittredge figured—just get up and walk out, knowing she was lucky to be alive. Instead, she turned and looked him in the eye. "But I *un*agreed," she said. "I canceled the deal. I said no." Now her gaze did not waver. "Look, Detective, I know I'm just a whore," she said bluntly. "I sell my body on the street. I let strangers screw me for fifty bucks—twenty if I'm desperate." She pressed on. "It's not much of a life, and you probably think I'm scum. *I* sure as hell do, lots of the time. But there's one tiny little scrap of dignity I still cling to, and you know what that is, Detective?" He could tell she didn't expect him to answer—didn't even *want* him to answer—so he waited. "It's that I get to decide. I get to say yes—and God knows, I say yes just about every chance I get. But every once in a great while, I say no. Out there today, I said no, and you know what happened when I said no? That sick sonofabitch damn near broke my arm, and then he busted my face open with a belt. And then he forced me to strip naked and kneel down at his feet and take his dick in my mouth. After I said no. *After*."

She stared at her hands, which had started to tremble on the table, as silent tears rolled down her cheeks and plopped onto the metal surface. Kittredge expected to see sadness in her face, but what he saw instead was fury. Fury at what had happened to her out in the woods? Fury at how her life had gone off the rails so badly? Fury at her own complicity in annihilating goodness and grace from her life? "I said no," she repeated through clenched teeth, still looking down, as if speaking to her quaking fingers. Then she looked up at Kittredge again and resumed speaking, her voice clear and strong now: "Tell me, Detective. If some strange man did that to you—knocked the shit out of you, and made you strip and kneel down and suck his dick, and tell him you *loved* it—how would you like it?"

Kittredge had never thought about it, and didn't want to think about it now, but there it was, the unwelcome and disgusting image in his mind, like some sort of brain STD he'd just caught from her. "I wouldn't like it," he finally said. It was a vast, absurd understatement. Kittredge felt something shifting inside him—something besides the contagion of the image. Kittredge felt something opening up, making room to accommodate this woman's sense of injustice, enough to admire her for not giving up and just taking what the guy had done. "Honest truth, Janelle? I'd hate it like hell."

"SO," KITTREDGE SAID as they took the Asheville Highway exit off I–40, "left here?"

"Yeah," she said. "Cross the river, then take the first right."

Kittredge slowed to thirty crossing the Holston. The river was spanned here by a steel truss bridge, fifty years old if it was a day. The bridge was narrow and rickety, but Kittredge liked the angles and rivets, liked the way the emerald-green paint matched the color of the river below. He also liked being able to see through the railings and down to the water. Modern bridges, like the I–40 bridge that spanned the river a half mile downstream from here, blocked your view of the water; all you could see was the concrete sides. When Kittredge crossed a river, he wanted to *see* the river.

"They're tearing this bridge down next year," he said to her, partly just to break the silence, but partly to make up for the way he'd treated her earlier. He'd been stingy with his humanity at first. He'd been unintentionally cruel, forcing her to expose herself to *him*, too—expose her pain and her shame—before he started treating her like a crime victim, like someone deserving of respect and compassion and at least some attempt at justice.

She glanced out at the antiquated girders strobing past. "If they want to tear this thing down, they better hurry. Looks like it might collapse before they get to it."

"Naw," he scoffed. "Keep this thing painted, it'll last another hundred years. The new one'll be wider and stronger. Safer, sure. But nowhere near as interesting." He surprised himself then, stopping the car midway across. She seemed surprised, too—her head snapped around in his direction, her expression a mixture of puzzlement and alarm, her right hand edging toward the door latch. He pointed out her window. "See that little dip in the railing right there?"

She studied his face for a moment before turning to look. "Yeah?"

"I jumped off of there once. A long damn time ago. Night I graduated from high school."

"You jumped from there? That's a long ways down. You drunk?"

He chuckled. "Shit-faced. Wouldn't've done it sober. Never did, anyhow—not before, not since. Glad I did it the once, though." He let out a low *hnh*, a monosyllabic grunt. "If the Lord looks out for fools and drunkards, I had double coverage that night." He glanced in the mirror and saw a truck coming up behind them, so he nudged the Crown Vic on across the bridge. He signaled and took the right onto John Sevier for a half mile, following the river downstream a ways before turning off the highway; before turning on to the back road that the map showed leading to Cahaba Lane, where she said he'd taken her. "This guy took you off the beaten track, that's for sure," he said. "Was he just wandering around, looking for someplace private to park?"

"No. He knew right where he was going."

"What makes you so sure?"

"He knew the roads. I could tell by the way he was driving. He knows his way around out here. Maybe he lives out here somewhere."

"Could be," Kittredge said. "I'll check with the gas stations and quick-stops around here, see if anybody knows the car. You said it's a Mustang, kinda old?"

"A '67," she said. "Third year of production."

"He told you that?"

"Didn't have to. I knew it." He glanced a question at her. "I had one, once upon a time," she said. "A long damn time ago." Her words—"a long damn time ago"—were an echo of his. *Is she making fun of me?* he wondered. *Couldn't blame her. But maybe she's deciding to trust me.* "They widened the radiator grille on the '67," she went on. "That's how you can tell it from the '65 and the '66. Made those fake air scoops on the sides bigger, too." She took a long breath; blew it out. "It wasn't really mine. It was my stepfather's. I stole it when I ran away from home."

"How old were you?"

"Fourteen."

"*Fourteen?* Jesus. You must've wanted to get away from home mighty bad. How come?"

"Take a wild guess, Detective." He winced, cursing himself for his stupidity, but didn't say anything; didn't want to risk interrupting her story again. "My mama worked nights," she said. "He started in on my sister first. She was two years older than me, and she protected me. Took the bullet, so to speak. At the time, I didn't realize what a sacrifice that was. 'Greater love,' and all that. But after a while she couldn't take it anymore. She ran away at fifteen; tried to talk me into going with her. I should've. Would've, if I'd known what it would be like once she was gone. Once I was home alone with him."

"I'm sorry," he said. "Took some guts to steal his car. How far'd you get?"

"Not far." She laughed, surprising Kittredge. "I wrapped that car around a telephone pole about five miles down the road. Wasn't far, but it was far enough—I knew I couldn't go back. Not after what I did to his precious Mustang. That damn car was the only thing he loved in this world, far as I could see." Kittredge nodded. "I crawled out through the busted windshield—neither door would open—and looked at what I'd done. The radiator was spewing steam; the gas tank was dripping gas. I had a pack of matches in my pocket, and I struck a match and threw it under the car—*whoomph*—and walked away. Just kept going. I burnt my bridges but *good* that day."

"I guess you showed him," Kittredge said, and she laughed again.

"I guess so; don't know, though. I hitchhiked to Miami, and never saw the bastard again."

"Why Miami?"

"Why not? Warm all year. Pretty beaches. Men with money."

"Why'd you come back, then?"

"My mom." She looked out the window before turning back to him. "She got sick while I was in Miami. Ovarian cancer, fast and mean. By the time they tracked me down, she was just about dead. My asshole stepfather was long gone, of course—he split soon as she got sick."

They passed beneath I–40, where a pair of long concrete bridges spanned the Holston River and the road they were on. Just after they emerged from the underpass, they turned left. The small green street sign—Cahaba Lane—was dwarfed by a big white sign that announced Sunnyview Baptist Church and pointed down the road. "This look right?" She nodded grimly. "And you think you can find the spot in the woods where he took you?"

"Be hard to miss, won't it? The spot with a pile of my clothes laying there. Can y'all get fingerprints off of fabric?"

"We'll ask the crime-lab guys. If your stuff's still there. Don't you think he might've taken it, though?"

"What, a souvenir? To remind him of our special first date?"

"Some guys do. The really creepy ones. But I was just thinking he might've taken it to cover his tracks."

She shook her head. "Not unless he came back for it later. That dude was haulin' ass out of the woods, same as me. Chasin' me, at first. Gaining fast. But then those truckers stopped to help, and he jumped in his car and got the hell out of Dodge."

He eased the car to a stop at the end of the lane, the tires crunching shards of broken bottles. Overhead loomed a faded Comfort Inn billboard, supported by rusting I beams, their bases like trash magnets, fringed with coffee cups, beer cans, and other debris. Kittredge narrowly missed stepping on a used condom that lay crumpled on the ground. *Nice*, he thought. Her door swung open before he got there to open it for her. She stepped out, glancing down at the condom, an expression of weary disgust on her face.

As they started up the narrow path that led through the posts and up the wooded slope, Kittredge felt a chill. He touched the holster on his belt, making sure his weapon was still there.

CHAPTER 25

Janelle

WALKING UP THE WOODED slope, Janelle felt almost like two people; two Janelles. A TV ad from her childhood started playing in her mind—*"It's two, two, two mints in one!"*—and it wouldn't stop. *Two Janelles in one!*

Janelle Number One was scared shitless, remembering the feel of the path under her feet, remembering the pain of the bent wrist and the twisted arm; remembering the humiliation of what he'd made her do after that.

Janelle Number Two, though, was mad as hell. Was something else, too. Brave? Strong? Those weren't words she felt entitled to use—not about herself, anyhow. But whatever the feeling was, she recognized and welcomed it; it was the same feeling she'd had the afternoon she'd run off in her stepfather's Mustang, the same feeling she'd had when she'd tossed the match beneath the car, when she'd decided to keep going instead of slinking back home, tail between her legs, to shut up and lie down and just *take* it, the way her life and her sack-of-shit stepdaddy had tried to teach her to do.

It helped that the cop, Kittredge, was treating her like an actual human being, not like some piece of shit that deserved whatever was done to her. Helped, too, that he was nervous out here, same as her—not that he said anything, but she saw him reach back and touch his gun when he thought she wasn't looking. *See,* she told herself, *you're not so pathetic. Big badass cop with a gun, and he's scared, too.*

She was walking in front, the way she had a few hours before. She found the view disorienting, so she bent down, looked down, the way she had earlier in the day, when her arm had been twisted behind her. Looking down helped her remember. She felt the trail level off briefly—that felt right—then turn upward again. A memory floated slowly up toward the surface of her consciousness, like a bubble in hot pancake batter on a griddle; just as the memory bubble popped and her eyes and her mouth were opening, she stumbled—again—on a fat root that snaked across the trail.

"Careful," said Kittredge from behind her.

"There," she said, pointing down. "I tripped on that same root before. Right after that, we went thataway." She turned to her left and struck out sideways, across the slope, her head up now, her gaze ranging far and wide.

"You sure?"

Instead of answering, she stopped and gasped, raising both hands in front of her, as if to ward off something; as if to ward off the ghost of Janelle

Number Three. A hundred yards ahead of them—fifty yards beyond the clothing Janelle had scattered on the ground a few hours before—lay a dead woman. She was sprawled faceup, but much of her face was gone, and her legs—splayed on either side of a tree—had no feet.

CHAPTER 26

Brockton

***DET. KITTREDGE,* I SCRAWLED** on the notepad beside the telephone, and I felt the hairs on the back of my neck rising as Detective Kittredge described the death scene where he was standing.

"Excuse me," I said, interrupting him. "The tree—it's a sapling, isn't it." I was telling him, not asking him. "Three, four inches thick. Her crotch is pressed right up against the trunk."

A silence, then: "What makes you think that?"

"What makes me think that is the fact that I'm looking at a photograph of it right now, Detective." As I said it, I slid the picture the rest of the way out of the envelope. It was the manila envelope that had arrived in the mail a week or so before, traumatizing Peggy her first day on the job.

"Could you please say that again, sir?"

"I said I'm looking at a photograph of the death scene right now. The dead woman in the woods. The tree she's pressed up against."

"I'm not sure I'm following you here, Dr. Brockton. How could you possibly be looking at a crime-scene photo? The photographer isn't even here yet."

"Somebody mailed it to me a week or so ago," I said. "Probably right after he killed her." A thought struck me, and I added, "Killed her and cut off her feet." I was still embarrassed that I'd failed to recognize that the photo hadn't come from the case files of Sheriff Cotterell or Bubba Hardknot; that the image was fresh, taken no more than a few days before it had arrived in my office.

"This picture you say somebody mailed you." The detective's wording was careful and conditional—almost accusatory—as if he were cross-examining me in court. "Did you contact the police when you received this, sir?"

"No. Well, sort of." I felt flustered suddenly. Stupid suddenly. "But I mentioned it to a TBI agent a day or two later."

"*Mentioned* it? You see that a woman has been murdered and dismembered, and all you do is *mention* it?"

"I thought he'd sent me an old crime-scene photo," I tried explaining. "From a case he and I worked a couple years ago, up in Morgan County. It looks exactly like it. Well, *almost* exactly like it. As close as a killer could get, I guess, without waiting a month or two."

The detective was silent for several long seconds. "Doctor, I don't mean to sound dense," he said, "and I don't mean to sound disrespectful—my colleagues at KPD speak very highly of you—but what you're saying isn't making much sense to me."

"It's not making a lot of sense to me, either, Detective, but bear with me for half a minute, and I'll try to help us both make better sense of it." Stretching the phone cord as far as it would go, I rolled my chair across the office to a battered filing cabinet and opened the drawer that held my slides. Thumbing back through the tabs of the file folders, I stopped at 90–11—my eleventh forensic case of 1990—and tugged the fat folder free. I opened the file, which contained clear plastic sleeves of 35-millimeter slides, along with a few eight-by-ten enlargements. "Back in December of 1990," I said, pulling out one of the enlargements, "Sheriff Jim Cotterell, up in Morgan County, called me out to a death scene. A TBI agent, Wellington Meffert, was there, too. You know either of those guys?"

"No, sir, I don't. I'm still not quite—"

"Hang on," I said. "I'm getting there. A woman's body was found there in the woods. She was naked, and her feet had been chewed off by dogs or coyotes, and her crotch was jammed up against a tree. I'm looking now at one of the photos from *that* case—the December 1990 case—and the trees are all bare. In the picture somebody sent me last week—the picture of the woman I think you've just found—all the trees still have leaves, and they're just starting to turn. I didn't look closely at this picture last week—I thought it was just an extra print from that 1990 case—but I'm sure looking now." I took a magnifying glass from the center drawer of my desk and inspected the woman in the photo. "Hard to say for sure, but it doesn't look like this woman's feet were chewed off. Looks more like they've been severed." He didn't respond, so I went on, talking about what

I saw, now that I was finally looking. "The tree she's up against—looks like a maple." I moved the lens to focus on the nearest cluster of leaves; they were shaped like five-pointed stars, but with no other serrations. "No, not a maple," I amended. "A sweet gum, I think, now that I look closer." Detective Kittredge still wasn't saying anything, and I wondered if I should just shut up. Instead, I plowed ahead. "Looks like the bottom branch is snapped, but in this picture, the leaves aren't dead yet. So I'm guessing it got broken just before the picture was taken."

A pause. Finally, as if he'd made up his mind about something—as if he'd made up his mind that I wasn't crazy, or a killer—he said, "Yes, sir, she's up against a sweet gum. And the leaves on the bottom branch are withered now. All the other leaves are turning, and some have already fallen, but these withered on the branch." Another pause. "Could you tell me a little more about that other case? Morgan County, you said?"

"Sure," I said, glad that he seemed to be coming around. "This was about two years ago—twenty-two months, actually—outside Petros, the little town where Brushy Mountain State Prison is. A man kills his unfaithful wife and dumps her body in the woods. A couple weeks later, a hunter finds it and calls the sheriff, and the sheriff calls me. The body's lying against a tree, one leg on each side, with the woman's crotch pressed against the trunk. At first we think the killer has posed her that way—some kind of sexual display—but then I notice a dark, greasy spot about ten feet up the hill, and I realize that *that's* where he dumped her; that's where her body started to decompose. Then I saw the tooth marks on her feet—what little was left of her feet—and I realized what had happened. After she got nice and ripe up there on higher ground, she was found by wild dogs, or coyotes, and dragged downhill a ways, until she snagged on the tree and the coyotes couldn't drag her any farther."

"Hmm." Another pause. "I'm still playing catch-up with you here, Dr. Brockton. Are you suggesting that this woman I'm looking at right now was killed by the same guy as the woman in Morgan County two years ago?"

"No, that's not what I'm saying at all. That's not possible—at least, I don't *think* it's possible. That guy confessed. He's two years into a ten-year sentence."

"So . . . let me try this again," the detective said. "You're saying I'm looking at some kind of copycat killing here?"

"Copycat killing?" As I repeated his words, something about them sounded slightly wrong. I laid one of my Morgan County crime-scene enlargements alongside the photo I'd received in the mail. They were strikingly similar; chillingly similar. "I don't know if it's a copycat *killing*," I said slowly, "but it's for damn sure a copycat death scene." My eyes locked on to the broken branch, and I noticed that it had been pulled toward the far side of the sapling. "Jesus," I said. "That branch was blocking the shot. Whoever took this picture broke the branch to get it out of the way. So *his* picture would look just like *my* picture."

"Come again?"

"Detective, whoever killed this woman staged her body to look just like the crime scene I worked two years ago. And he photographed her from the same angle. It's almost like he had a copy of my picture with him, out there in the woods." A realization struck me, swift and forceful as a fist. "Dear God. This is the same guy."

"But . . . you just said the guy's in *prison*."

"No," I said, my heart a cold stone in my chest. "Not that guy. Not the guy in prison. The other guy. It's the same guy."

"*What* same guy?"

"The same guy who killed and dismembered a woman up in Campbell County about a month ago. With a tool that left cut marks he knew I'd recognize."

I PAGED TYLER, adding the prefix 999 to my phone number—code for "We've got a case; get your butt over here ASAP!" I figured it would take him at least ten minutes to lock the research cage and get back across the river to the stadium. Plenty of time for me to make a phone call. As I dialed the number, I prayed I wouldn't be routed to a voice-mail box or a secretary. What was the chance that a senior-level FBI profiler was still at his desk at four on a Friday afternoon?

"Behavioral Sciences, Brubaker." Even over the phone, the FBI agent's confidence and air of authority were unmistakable.

"Thank God you're there," I said. "This is Bill Brockton, at UT—the University of Tennessee."

"Hello, Doc. What's up? You sound stressed."

Apparently his psychological insight wasn't limited to psychotic killers.

"Things have just gotten really strange here," I said. "Remember the meeting in Nashville, when I said that dismemberment case up near Kentucky looked like one of my Kansas cases?"

"I remember. The cut marks. Curved cut marks. What about it?"

"There's just been another killing here. Another woman. And it mirrors another one of my cases."

There was a brief silence before he spoke. "With all due respect, Doc, there are only so many ways to kill a person. Law of averages—sometimes killings resemble other killings. Coincidence is not the same as causality."

"Damn it," I snapped, "this is not resemblance, and it's not coincidence. This death scene is an exact replica. I got a photo of this latest victim in the mail a week ago—a week before her body was found. I thought it was one of my photos, from two years ago. Even the damn camera angle was the same." The line went silent. *Did he just hang up on me?* "Are you still there?" I was reaching for the switchhook and the redial button when he spoke.

"Yeah, I'm here. I'm thinking." More silence. "So let's say you're right. Who would do this, and why?" Now I was the one struck silent. "Doc? Are *you* still there?"

"Yeah," I said. "I'm just confused. Aren't you the one who figures out the who and the why?"

"I try. But if you're right—if these killings have some connection to you—then you're the key. What's the message he's sending you?"

The call wasn't going the way I'd hoped it would. "Well," I floundered. "Could he be trying to impress me?"

Even from five hundred miles away, the derision in his voice was clear. "Impress you? You've been watching too many Hollywood movies, Doc. He's messing with you, more like. Or threatening you."

"Threatening me? Why would he be threatening me?" Up to now, I'd felt puzzled and disturbed. Suddenly I felt something much worse.

"I don't blame you for sounding nervous," he said. "If any of the creeps I've profiled ever hatched a vendetta against me, and were out in the world instead of locked up? Trust me, I'd be nervous as hell. Luckily, I've got no prior relationship to any of 'em. No reason for them to come after me."

Somewhere in a far, dark corner of my mind, I began to hear a low humming sound. "Wait. *Wait.* Are you saying that this could be someone I *know*?"

"Possibly. I'm just thinking out loud here, Doc. Maybe somebody you had a connection with; somebody who felt like you betrayed him somehow, did him a grievous wrong."

"But if that's the case, why's he killing these women? If he's got a grudge, why doesn't he just come shoot me? Why these murders that echo cases of mine?"

"Dunno. He might be trying to make some sort of grand philosophical statement. Something about the hydra-headed nature of evil."

"The which-headed?"

"Hydra-headed. Hydra, the mythological monster with all the heads—nine? twelve? A bunch.

Hercules was sent to kill the Hydra. Which was supposedly impossible, because any time one of the heads got cut off, a new one grew back."

"Got it," I said. "I do remember that myth, now that you mention it. So you're saying this guy might be trying to make the point that it doesn't matter if I solve one murder? That another one, just like it, will take its place? But what does that have to do with me?"

"It's more complicated than that," he said. "More personal. He's not broadcasting the message. He's narrowcasting it."

"Narrowcasting?"

"Whatever he's saying, he's saying it to you, about you. It's between him and you. We don't know why." He paused. "Not yet. But I'm afraid we will."

His words chilled me. "So I need to conjure up the name of everybody I ever cut off in traffic? Every student I ever flunked?"

"No, it would go deeper than that. Somebody you had some sort of strong connection with. Somebody who feels like you betrayed him somehow. Ruined his life."

I felt baffled. Angry, too. So this unfolding nightmare—this set of gruesome murders—was somehow *my* fault? I felt myself flush. "I'm not exactly a treacherous kind of guy," I said testily. "I've never cheated on my wife. I've never lied on a job application. I've never stabbed anyone in the back, literally or figuratively. Hell, I've never even gotten a speeding ticket."

"Easy, Doc. Easy. Let me be clearer. I'm not saying you *did* betray this guy—this hypothetical guy. I'm just playing *What if:* What if you had some connection to somebody who ended up coming unhinged? What if he decided, rightly or wrongly—completely, one-hundred-percent wrongly—that you'd let him down, betrayed him, wrecked his life? That sort of scenario, that kind of guy, might fit the facts. Anybody like that come to mind?"

"No."

"Well, sleep on it."

"How am I supposed to sleep, with this hanging over my head?"

"You might want to try to engage him," he mused. "Draw him out. Engage him. *Goad* him."

"How would I do that? Put up a billboard by I–40? 'Hey, serial-killer guy, you stink'?"

"Something like that. Guys like this tend to be very narcissistic. He's almost certainly reading the newspaper and watching TV, looking for coverage of the killings. He gets off on it—it gives him a sense of power. If the police, or especially you, disparage him to the media—talk about his carelessness, his stupidity—he'll probably be very agitated. He might respond, maybe get in touch with the paper or a TV station. If he does, that gives us another thread to follow."

I heard a rap on the doorframe. Tyler stuck his head in, gave me a *Let's roll* look. "I gotta go pick up a dead woman," I told Brubaker. "Another thread to follow. I'm hoping the thread doesn't end up leading to my door."

LATE THAT NIGHT—after Tyler and I had gathered up the woman's body from the base of the sweet gum sapling at Cahaba Lane; after I'd talked to a newspaper reporter and a WBIR reporter; after we'd taken the corpse to the Annex; after we'd plucked and pickled the five biggest maggots; after we'd put the remains in to simmer, so we could render them to bare bone; after I'd showered at the stadium and dragged my weary self home and wolfed down a leftover turkey sandwich and crawled into bed beside Kathleen, who'd given up on me for the evening—I finally fell into a fitful sleep.

In my dream, I found myself once more in my backyard, approaching the opening where the gigantic snake lurked. In one hand I held a half-sized garden hoe, a pitifully undersized weapon with which to do battle. Leaning down, I peered into the hole, switching on the flashlight I held in my other hand. The beam of light disappeared into unfathomable darkness.

Straightening, I turned to go, but a movement at the edge of the yard caught my eye. A track of flattened grass led from where I stood to the edge of the woods—the sort of track an immense serpent would create as it slithered across the lawn. Just inside the tree line, where the grass ended and the track disappeared, I saw the body of a woman—a headless and footless woman—her legs twitching and bucking on either side of a tree trunk. In the shadows beyond, I saw more women lying in the woods. All of them splayed against tree trunks; all of them dead; none of them lying peacefully.

I bolted awake, drenched in sweat, my heart racing. The digital clock on the nightstand read 3:47. Slipping out from beneath the covers, I tiptoed from the bedroom and through the living room, my footsteps keeping time with the hollow ticking of the regulator clock on the mantel. The kitchen was lit by the blue-green numerals of the microwave and—once I lifted the telephone from its cradle on the wall—by the faint glow of the keypad. "Nine-one-one," the dispatcher answered. "What's your emergency?"

"It's not an emergency," I said. "But it's important. This is Dr. Bill Brockton, at UT. I need to leave a message for a KPD homicide detective. Detective Kittredge."

"Sir, this is 911 emergency dispatch. We don't take messages."

"It's about the Cahaba Lane murder," I went on. "Tell Detective Kittredge he needs to search that whole hillside."

"Sir—"

"Tell Detective Kittredge there are more bodies—more dead women—out there in the woods."

CHAPTER 27

Satterfield

SATTERFIELD SMOOTHED THE NEWSPAPER on the kitchen table, taking care not to smudge the ink. The story was briefer than he'd have liked, but it was prominently displayed—at the top of the front page—and it was accompanied by a large photo. He reread the text:

KPD, TBI Seek Serial Killer

The body of a Knoxville prostitute was discovered in a wooded area in eastern Knox County near Interstate 40 yesterday, and the murder is the work of a serial killer, say two law-enforcement sources. The Knoxville Police Department, Knox County Sheriff's Office, Campbell County Sheriff's Office, and Tennessee Bureau of Investigation are seeking the killer, who is considered responsible for the deaths of at least two women, both believed to be prostitutes—one from Knoxville and one from Campbell County. The murders are "definitely the work of the same killer," according to one investigator, speaking off the record. Neither victim's name has been released, pending notification of family members.

Officially, both the KPD and the TBI remain tight-lipped, refusing to confirm or deny that the murders are the work of a serial killer. "We investigate every possible lead in every murder," said KPD spokesman Warren Fountain. "Any time we have multiple unsolved homicides, we consider the possibility that they might be linked. That's standard procedure for every law-enforcement agency." But a second source told the *News Sentinel* that an FBI "profiler"—an agent specializing in serial killers—is consulting with Tennessee authorities to help catch the murderer. The FBI would not comment on its role in the investigations.

My, my, Satterfield thought. *Calling in the cavalry.* He took it as a compliment. He stopped reading long enough to look at the photo. It showed four uniformed policemen carrying a stretcher out of the Cahaba Lane woods, threading between the I beams that supported the COMFORT INN billboard. On the stretcher was a misshapen lump, which the photo caption identified as "a body bag containing the mutilated corpse of a murdered Knoxville prostitute." He was disappointed that the body was covered, though of course he'd seen the woman—he'd had sex with the woman—before she died. Afterward, too.

Satterfield resumed reading the story.

Also consulting with KPD and TBI investigators is Dr. Bill Brockton, a forensic anthropologist at the University of Tennessee. "My role is to try to figure out how and when she was killed," said Brockton. Brockton voiced confidence that the killer would be caught soon. "Luckily, most criminals aren't very smart. In fact, most of them are just plain dumb. This guy has already made some careless, foolish mistakes. I feel sure he'll be caught soon."

Satterfield stared at the page, wishing the heat of his focused fury could cause the paper to burst into flames. He stared again at the photo. In the background, trailing the policemen with the stretcher, was a now-familiar, very loathsome face: Brockton's.

An X-Acto knife rested on the kitchen table, to one side of the newspaper, and Satterfield reached for it. Gripping its precisely knurled aluminum handle with the tips of his left thumb and first two fingers, he jabbed the needle-sharp tip of the blade into the newspaper photograph twice—first into Brockton's left eye, then into the right eye. Then, and only then, did he slit the article from the page and slide it into a clear plastic sleeve, the kind with the reinforced strip along one edge and three holes punched in it, so it could be clipped into a three-ring binder. Clipped into Satterfield's binder.

He walked into the den, to the big shelving unit that held the television, VCR, and stereo. Just above the wire-mesh terrarium where the snake lay—the thick body draped heavily over a piece of driftwood and a couple of the sandstone slabs—was a bookshelf. As Satterfield reached across the top of the enclosure, the ribbon of tongue slid from the snake's mouth and flicked, licking molecules of Satterfield from the air—exhalations from his lungs; skin cells sloughing from his scalp and his arms, perhaps even from the scab in his palm; perhaps the snake was tasting the tattoo of its own head and tongue. Satterfield rubbed his palms together, to send a shower of cells wafting down upon the snake, then reached for two volumes from the bookshelf.

Back at the table, he opened the first volume—*The University of Tennessee Faculty and Staff Directory*—and turned to the dog-eared page where Brockton's name was highlighted in yellow. Uncapping a pink marker, Satterfield now highlighted another name, the name directly above Brockton's: *Brockton, Kathleen; Nutrition Science.* Next, he opened the second volume—the Knoxville telephone directory—and located the family's phone number and address.

From his scrapbook, Satterfield removed a Knoxville street map, which was tucked into a pocket at the back, and unfolded and smoothed it on the tabletop. Then, scrolling down the street index, he located the Brocktons' street coordinates and marked their address with a pair of small, neat *X*s in red ink. Finally, he sliced the pink and yellow names from the faculty directory and taped them to the map beside the *X*s.

Before folding the map and putting it back in its pocket, Satterfield looked at a spot ten miles northeast of the Brocktons' street: a small, roadless parcel at the end of Cahaba Lane. The parcel was bounded on the north by Interstate 40 and on the south by John Sevier Highway. Within the blank parcel, three small red *X*s had been added in Satterfield's precise calligraphy.

CHAPTER 28

Kittredge

KITTREDGE WATCHED IN SILENCE. Skeptical, discouraged silence. He and Janelle—the prostitute lucky enough to be alive—were huddled in an interview room with a crime-lab tech, who was using an Identi-Kit to piece together a face from Janelle's description of her attacker.

Janelle peered at the latest assemblage of features, the tech's third try, and shook her head. "Nothing personal," she said. "I know you're trying to help, and I appreciate it. But none of these looks like a real person." The tech frowned. "They all look like cartoons," she added. "Of retards."

Kittredge coughed to cover a laugh, and Janelle and the tech looked up. Kittredge feigned another cough while slipping Janelle a conspiratorial wink, then he shrugged at the tech. It wasn't the tech Kittredge blamed; it was the Identi-Kit. In theory, it seemed like a good idea: Offer a smorgasbord of predrawn facial features to choose from, so a victim's verbal description of a suspect—wide eyes or squinty eyes? blue eyes or brown? broad nose or thin, a beak or a ski jump? thin lips or full?—could be translated into an actual face assembled out of transparent overlays, each overlay printed with one specific feature.

That was the persuasive theory behind the Identi-Kit. In flawed practice, though, Janelle's dubious dismissal was dead-on. Few police departments had the money to hire professional artists—KPD certainly didn't—and the Identi-Kit didn't require much in the way of training or artistic talent. Unfortunately, it didn't deliver much, either, in Kittredge's experience. The Identi-Kit was made by Smith & Wesson, he'd been surprised to learn a while back. *Should've stuck to handguns*, he'd thought. Still, even though it was a long shot, the Identi-Kit seemed a shot worth taking, given that the stakes had just gone sky-high. Janelle had seen the face of a sick, sadistic killer and had lived to tell about it; that made her description their best hope of finding him before he killed again. *But maybe he already has.* And what if the anthropologist, Dr. Brockton, was right—what if there were already more bodies out there in the woods around Cahaba Lane? *We'll know soon enough*, he thought grimly, checking his watch. He'd be rendezvousing at Cahaba Lane in an hour with a team of cadets from the Police Academy, leading them in a line search. Meanwhile, he desperately needed a suspect sketch.

"Hang in there—don't give up on it yet," Kittredge said. He wasn't sure who needed the encouragement more, Janelle, the tech, or himself.

"Who did that other one?" Janelle asked him.

"That other *what*?"

"That other drawing. That good one." Kittredge and the tech looked at each other, puzzled. "A week or two ago," she said. "Or maybe a month. I saw it on TV. It was a girl, a drawing of a dead girl. They found her in the woods, too—just bones—and one of y'all's artists drew what she looked like. It was good. It looked like a real person."

"Oh, gotcha," Kittredge said to Janelle, then—to the tech—"A cold case up in Morgan County. Skeletal remains from an old strip mine outside Wartburg. The UT bone expert, Dr. Brockton—he's working on that one, too." To Janelle: "I think that girl's sketch came from the bone expert."

"Well, he's an art expert, too, then," she said. "Could we get him in here to work with me?"

"He didn't actually draw it himself," the detective clarified. "I think he found an artist to do it. Based on what the skull looked like."

"Well," she persisted, "who was that artist he got? Can we get him for me, too?"

Kittredge felt exasperation at her pain-in-the-assedness, admiration for her doggedness.

Kittredge excused himself for a moment, to go call Brockton: to ask for the name of an artist who could do a good drawing. One that didn't look like a cartoon of a retard.

CHAPTER 29

Janelle

JANELLE FELT THE AIR whoosh out of her hopes when the girl walked into the room. She was just a kid, sixteen or seventeen. "*You're* the one? You did the picture of that dead girl?"

"Yes, ma'am," said the girl.

Janelle snorted. "Nobody's ever called me 'ma'am' before," she said, then added, "not unless they were mocking me." She eyed the girl warily. "Are you mocking me?"

"No, ma'am," said the girl. "No. *No.* Why would I mock you?"

"Why wouldn't you, darlin'," she said, her voice soft and sad. "Why the hell wouldn't you."

The girl laid a hand on Janelle's arm. "I'm sorry about what happened to you," she said. "Really, really sorry."

Janelle moved her arm, reached for a tissue. "Story of my life," she said. "This damned thing's just one more chapter." She blew her nose, then turned away and folded into herself, collecting herself. When she turned back, she saw that the girl had picked up her pencil and pad and started drawing. Janelle frowned. "I haven't told you what he looks like yet."

The girl turned the pad to show her the drawing. It was a sketch of Janelle herself, nothing but a few quick lines, but somehow it captured everything that mattered; somehow it revealed Janelle to herself: a worn and wary beauty, her cheek stitched together, her soul pulling apart. "Damn," Janelle breathed. "You *are* an artist, girl. What'd they say your name was, hon? Jenny?"

"Yes, ma'am."

"I'm Janelle, and I'm not quite as old and broken-down as I look. So stop calling me 'ma'am', or I might have to turn you across my knee. Got it?"

Jenny grinned. "Yes'm," she said slyly, the *m* audible enough to be heard but faint enough to deny. Janelle felt the skin of her face moving, tugging at the stitches in her cheek. After a moment, she recognized the movement as a smile.

"OKAY, TAKE A look, see if this is anywhere close." Jenny laid the tablet on the table and slid it across to Janelle.

Janelle hesitated, looking in the girl's eyes. The girl smiled shyly, shrugged slightly, in a no-promises sort of way. For some reason, Janelle found the gesture reassuring—its combination of helpfulness and humility. She picked up the sketch and looked down, then drew a quick gasp as a wave of panic swept over her, tumbling her in its grip. "Son of a *bitch*," she breathed.

CHAPTER 30

Brockton

I'D BARELY BEGUN RAKING—my lawn's first dusting of red-orange maple leaves—when Kathleen opened the front door and called to me. "Bill, there's a Detective Kittredge on the phone for you. He says it's important." I laid down the rake and hurried inside.

"You were right, Doc," he said without any preamble. "We just found two more bodies in the woods behind Cahaba Lane. Deeper in. Several hundred yards away from the woman with no feet." I wasn't surprised to hear there were more victims, but I was surprised to hear that one of them was a man.

I took no satisfaction in being right; in fact, I hated it. I would much rather have heard that the search was a wild-goose chase, my nightmare not a premonition but simply the product of an overheated imagination. *Two more dead,* I thought. *Please, God, let these be the last.* I prayed it, but I didn't expect it.

Kittredge gave me directions to the scene; this time, we'd go in from the back side, by means of a different road. "Brace yourself, Doc," the detective added. "It's bad. The worst I've seen. The woman—"

"Don't tell me," I interrupted. "I want to see it with fresh eyes. No preconceptions."

"You got it. See you soon."

Tyler met me at the stadium; we tucked an extra body bag in the back of the truck and headed east along the river, along Neyland Drive and Riverside Drive. I could have done that stretch of road in my sleep; Riverside dead-ended at the pig farm where I'd warehoused bodies until recently. A mile before the farm, we turned left onto Holston Hills Road, which paralleled the Holston River. We passed a mile of woods and farm fields, then crossed the river at Boyd's Bridge, zigzagging eastward on a series of progressively smaller roads. Normally I liked back roads; this time, though, the roads seemed to be leading us somewhere sinister. Leading us into the heart of darkness.

Neither of us had spoken since leaving the stadium. "You're quiet," I said finally. "You pissed off because we're working on Saturday?"

There was a pause before he answered. "I'm tired," he said. "I was up late. Writing up my research notes."

"Uh-*huh*. Did your research notes give you that hickey?" Tyler had mentioned that Roxanne was in town for the weekend, and I suspected they'd made the most of their night.

"No comment." He *was* pissed off. *Not surprising,* I thought. *He hasn't seen her in weeks, and I'm dragging him off to a death scene.*

We lapsed back into silence, and in the silence, I heard Kittredge's words echoing: "The worst

I've seen." Would it turn out to be worse than the things *I'd* seen? If so, what adjective could describe it? When the normal progression—bad, worse, worst—couldn't do justice to the horror, what could? Worst, more worst, most worst?

Even with Kittredge's directions, I found the route mazy. This time, because of the location of the bodies, we'd be approaching the woods from the east. I'd highlighted the route in my *Tennessee Atlas & Gazetteer.* Given the propensity for bodies in East Tennessee to wind up off the beaten track, I'd found the *Gazetteer* indispensable, since it showed not just paved roads and dirt roads, but even major trails and topographic contour lines. During the three years since my arrival at UT, I had put two dozen red *X*s in my *Gazetteer*, each *X* neatly marking a death scene I'd worked.

I followed the route Kittredge had dictated—Moshina Road, Pine Grove Road, and finally Ratliff Lane. By the time we turned on to Ratliff, Tyler was slumped against his door, his head askew, his mouth open, a string of drool swaying from his chin. I smiled, thinking, *Roxanne drove all the way from Memphis for this?*

Ratliff Lane started out as asphalt, soon turned to gravel, and finally became a pair of red-clay ruts. It dead-ended at a clearing that was occupied by a rusting mobile home and a rusty Ford pickup, plus two Knox County sheriff's cruisers, a KPD mobile crime lab, an unmarked Crown Victoria, and a black Chevy Suburban. The Crown Vic, I guessed, was issued to Detective Kittredge. The crime-lab van, I hoped, was brought by Art Bohanan. Art was a senior KPD forensic tech; he was also one of the nation's leading experts on fingerprints, I'd learned in the course of several prior cases with him. The Suburban, I knew for sure, belonged to Knox County's medical examiner, Dr. Garland Hamilton. Hamilton's vehicle was unmistakable, at least from the rear: Prominently positioned alongside the government-issue tag was an ironically apt bumper sticker—a skull wearing a crown of thorns, captioned GRATEFUL DEAD.

A sheriff's deputy directed me past the other vehicles to the lower side of the clearing, where I shoehorned the truck into a space that would have been better suited to a Honda Civic. Branches snapped and screeched along the passenger side as I bulled my way into the underbrush, waking Tyler with a start. He stared at the fractured twigs clawing across his window, then rubbed his eyes and shook his head, causing the string of drool to twitch and sway beneath his chin. "Wow," he said. "I guess I nodded off for a minute there."

"I guess so," I replied. "Unless you've started drooling when you're awake."

He rubbed his mouth and chin, grimacing when he got to the drool. "What the hell?" he squawked. "This isn't supposed to start happening till I'm, like, *your* age."

"I guess you're precocious," I said. "You know what they say about drooling, right?"

"Can't say as I do."

"Once the drooling starts, impotence and incontinence aren't far behind."

"*Hey.* Don't even joke about that stuff," he muttered, making the sign of the cross.

"Joking? Who said I was joking?" I slid from the truck and closed the door before he had a chance to retort.

I opened the back of the truck and tucked the two body bags into the plastic bin that contained our field kit—camera, gloves, trowels, tweezers, paint-brushes, evidence bags, clipboard. Tyler emerged from the underbrush, bits of twigs and leaves in his hair, and I slid the bin across the tailgate to him. Leaning back in, I retrieved a rake and a shovel, which I angled over my shoulder like some outsized, double-barreled farming implement. *Swords to plow-shares*, I thought, *shotguns to shovels.*

The deputy met us midway across the clearing. "They're up yonder," he said, nodding in the general direction of the unmarked Crown Vic that was last in the line of vehicles. "Couple hunnerd yards in. Just follow the blazes of tape." A pine tree at the clearing's edge had a strip of crime-scene tape tied around its trunk at shoulder height. Peering farther into the woods, I could see another bright band twenty yards beyond, and a third farther still.

I headed up the gentle incline, my usual surge of adrenaline accompanied by an unexpected topspin of something else—apprehension? dread? Some-times, walking into a crime scene with a shovel over my shoulder, I would hear myself singing softly: "Heigh-ho, heigh-ho, it's off to work we go."

This time, as I followed the blazes deeper into the woods, I did not hear singing. This time, I heard crackling under my feet, thudding in my chest, and alarm bells in my head.

CHAPTER 31

Satterfield

THE POLICE SCANNER WAS still going crazy as Satterfield turned off Kingston Pike and on to Cherokee Boulevard, looping and swooping along the serpentine road toward the river. Toward the Brockton house.

From the flurry of transmissions on the police scanner, he knew they'd found the two other bodies in the woods. He would love to have seen the face of whoever had found the corpses, especially the woman's; for that matter, he'd love to see the faces of everyone working the scene. *Fools and weaklings*, he thought. Most of all, he'd love to see Brockton's face, now and also later, when the surprise Satterfield had left for him was discovered.

He slowed as he neared the house. The garage door was up, and through the opening, he saw that the Camry—the woman's car—was still inside. Satterfield eased to the curb and parked in front of the house. He sat for a moment, looking for signs of movement at the windows, then got out, went to the rear of the van, and took two orange highway cones from the back. He placed one ten feet behind the van, the other ten feet in front, the way he'd seen the telephone linemen do. *Stupid*, he thought. *If you can't see the damn truck without the cones, you're not gonna see the damn truck* with *the cones.*

Satterfield was counting on the truck being seen—specifically, being seen by the lady of the house. He'd spent hours preparing it to be seen: spraying the horizontal stripes of blue and gold along both sides and across the back—the stripes were the easy part—then, using the stencils he'd cut, adding the BellSouth name and logo. As always, he'd worked meticulously, and although the signage wasn't perfect, he believed it would fool anyone but an actual BellSouth worker . . . and he *knew* it would fool a woman looking out the window of a Sequoyah Hills home: a privileged woman; a woman accustomed to having men in work vans show up to attend to her lawn and her TV cable and her telephone lines.

Angling across the lawn, he headed for the end of the house farthest from the driveway—the end where the phone line ran from the street to the service box on the outside of the house. As he walked, Satterfield glanced occasionally at a clipboard he carried in one hand. In his other hand he carried a telephone—one of the handsets from his cordless home phone—and he pretended to be carrying on a conversation. Every few steps, he nodded his head, as if listening intently, then uttered a terse, technical-sounding phrase, in case the woman in the house was watching and listening. "It could be the capacitor in the sub-relay," he said into the phone.

"It's not quite up to specs. Voltmeter's showing only 17 ohms." He nodded again, striding purposefully, almost to the corner now. "Naw, the junction-box circuits all check out fine. Could be a bad ground, though." There: He'd rounded the corner of the house, apparently unnoticed. A few feet along the wall, just beyond the electricity meter, was a gray plastic box, not much bigger than a book, its front embossed with the BellSouth logo. Satterfield took a screwdriver from the tool belt he was wearing and unscrewed a single screw, then unsnapped the latch and swung the cover open. Inside was a tangle of thin, brightly colored wires—blue, white, red, yellow, green—just like the ones he'd seen when he'd studied the box on his own house. He left those alone, and reached instead for the wide, flat cable, which he unclipped, disconnecting the house from the outside world—from help—as simply as disconnecting a phone from a wall. *So easy*, he marveled.

He crossed the grassy front yard to the center of the house and trotted up the brick steps, then rang the doorbell and listened. When he heard footsteps inside, he made a show of flipping through the forms on the clipboard. Out of the corner of his eye, he saw the curtain beside the door move slightly, then felt eyes on his face and his clipboard, his counterfeit BellSouth badge, and his counterfeit BellSouth shirt. He assumed the eyes were noticing the counterfeit BellSouth van at the curb, too. They must have, for he heard the snick of a dead bolt, followed by the squeak of rubber weather stripping as the door swung off the sill and opened a foot. "Yes?" Her voice was tight; was she scared, or was she just annoyed at being called to the door on a Saturday morning?

"Good morning . . ." He glanced down at the clipboard, then back up at her face. No bombshell, but not bad looking at all. " . . . Ms. Brockton."

"Yes?"

"Wayne Taylor, BellSouth. Sorry to bother you, ma'am, but we've had some reports of rolling service outages along your street. You noticed any trouble on your line today?"

"Today? No. I used the phone an hour ago. It was fine."

"*Hmm*," he said, sounding puzzled. "I just touched base with the central office, and *they* say the *computer* says your line's cutting in and out. Intermittently. Would you do me a favor and just check for a dial tone real quick? I'd hate to have you find out your line's dead after I'm already gone. Might be Monday or Tuesday before we could come back." He gave her a friendly, apologetic smile.

"I didn't even know you guys worked on weekends." She sounded less guarded now.

"We don't, in most neighborhoods, you know? Problem like this in East Knoxville? We'd get to it in a month or two." He chuckled knowingly; conspiratorially; as if to say, *Nice to be rich white folks, huh?* "I'll just wait out here while you check it."

She shrugged, then nodded. "Okay, I'll be right back." She closed the door; after a beat, he heard the dead bolt slide into place—slowly, almost sneakily, as if she didn't want him to know she was locking the door. He smiled at that. Thirty seconds later, her footfalls returned and the door opened again, a little quicker and a little wider this time. "Well, you're right," she said. "The computer's right. There's no dial tone. Did you say everybody on the street is having problems? Wouldn't that mean it's somewhere farther up the line? A substation or transformer or whatever you call it?"

"You'd think so, but it's not that simple. You get trouble in one house—a short, some kind of interference—and it can run right up the line, cause a ripple effect, knock out a whole block." He shook his head in an expression of good-natured exasperation. "You mind if I run a quick check on your wiring?"

She frowned. "How long will it take? I need to leave in half an hour."

"Oh, I should be long gone by then," he said. "I don't need much time. Five minutes, maybe ten."

"Okay, come on in." She stepped back and swung the door wide.

That's right, Satterfield thought, stepping across the threshold and into the living room. *You have to invite me in the first time.* "Do you know where all your jacks are, ma'am?"

"There's probably one in every room, isn't there?"

"Not necessarily, a house this old. How long have y'all been here?"

"Not long. Not quite three years."

"Added any more lines or jacks since then?"

"No."

"Well, show me the jacks you know about, and I'll see what I find."

She nodded, then pointed to a cordless-phone base station on an end table beside a sofa. "The jack for that's behind the sofa." She turned and went into the dining room, scanning the baseboards. Satterfield watched her walk. She was wearing sweatpants—baggy in the legs, but snug across her ass. *Nice ass, for a woman pushing forty*, he thought. *Running? StairMaster?* She disappeared around a corner. He followed, and found himself in a large kitchen, with a wooden table and four chairs. On the table was a dirty plate—crusts of toasted bread, smears of jam, a few bits of egg, a greasy knife and fork. "There's one," she said, pointing to a wall phone with an extra-long cord, its coils kinked and twisted together.

Next, she led him down a hallway to a pair of bedrooms—a sparsely furnished guest room first, then what was clearly the master bedroom, big and lived-in and rumpled. The doorway faced the bed, which was loosely made; a quilt was pulled up crookedly, and four pillows were piled against the headboard. A pair of nightstands flanked the bed. One, obviously hers, was crammed: a stack of books, another of magazines; bottles and tubes of lotion; a fragile-looking antique lamp, trimmed with teardrops of crystal, its frilly shade made of something that looked like silk. The other nightstand held a digital alarm clock, a pair of toenail clippers, a simple wooden lamp with a paper shade, and a phone in a charging cradle. "That's another cordless," she said, "but there's a jack down in that corner."

He nodded, then glanced around the room, taking in the details: a tall chest of drawers and a low, wide dresser, its marble top strewn with bracelets and necklaces. In the far corner stood a tall wooden coat tree, a half-dozen hooks hung with jackets and bathrobes—a big robe of navy-blue terrycloth, a smaller one of powder-blue satin, with a matching satin belt hanging from one loop of the robe, stretching almost to the floor. "Any other jacks in this room?" Satterfield strolled toward the coat tree as he said it, pretending to check the baseboards. "Sometimes a big room like this'll have a couple jacks in it." His eyes were locked on the belt. *So easy,* he thought again.

"I don't think so," she said. "But there are a couple in the basement. I'll show you those, then I'll get out of your way and let you work."

"Yes, ma'am," he said. "I'll check the basement first, work my way back up. Basements cause a lot of the problems I see. Basements and squirrels." He turned away from the shimmering robe. It would still be there when he returned. Meanwhile, he could imagine ways to put the satin belt to good use.

As he followed her to the bedroom door, he reached out and snagged an object off the tall chest of drawers—a pocketknife. He could put that to good use, too.

SATTERFIELD WAS DIRECTLY beneath the master bedroom, in what appeared to be a teenage boy's room—piles of jeans and socks and T-shirts strewn everywhere; the bed unmade; posters of swimsuit models on the walls. He could hear the woman overhead, opening drawers and walking around her bedroom, as he poked idly through the boy's belongings. He imagined her changing clothes: tugging off the sweatpants and the shirt, naked underneath;

slipping on panties, cupping her breasts into a bra. *Victoria's Secret, or granny panties and a boob-sling?* Probably somewhere in between, he guessed, based on her body—tight, but not flashy.

When he heard the sound of her footsteps leaving the bedroom, he headed upstairs, taking time for a quick look at the basement rec room and garage, so he'd have the entire layout in his head. Jogging up the stairs toward the kitchen, he called out, "Ma'am? Hello?"

"Yes?" She was at the sink, rinsing the bits of egg and toast into the garbage disposal. A tennis racket lay on the wooden table, and she was wearing a sweater and a short skirt and tennis shoes. Her legs looked freshly shaved, and the muscles in her calves and thighs looked chiseled—*cut*, he thought, pleased by the double entendre.

"I got lucky downstairs," he said. "Loose connection in that bedroom jack. Shortin' out somethin' awful."

She wiped her hands on a dish towel. "That's it? We're all set?" She lifted the receiver from the wall phone and held it to her ear, then frowned. "It's still dead."

"I just need to run out to your service box and reset the line. Wait sixty seconds and try it again. If it's not working, holler at me. If it's working—and it will be—I'm outta here." He winked. "For now."

CHAPTER 32

Brockton

THE DEEPER INTO THE woods we went, the more crime-scene tape I saw. The outer perimeter of the scene took the form of an irregular polygon, its perimeter composed of dozens of straight segments of crime-scene tape, stretched from tree to tree to tree, enclosing an area some fifty feet across by a hundred feet long.

Just inside the nearest segments stood a ladderlike structure—a hunter's tree stand, I realized—its legs wrapped in spirals of tape, like yellow and black candy canes of crime. Leaning against the lower rungs of the stand was a hunting rifle with a powerful scope. A handful of evidence flags and evidence bags clustered around the base of the tree, but the real action—if the thicket of people was any indication—was at the far end of the scene.

Tyler and I skirted the perimeter, so we'd walk through as little of the enclosed area as possible. As we neared the far end, I saw two smaller ovals taped off within the overall scene—inner perimeters, which I guessed corresponded to the positions of the two victims.

A uniformed deputy whom I vaguely recalled from a prior case stood sentry at the outer edge of the scene. *Jenkins*, I nearly called him, but I had a flash of doubt, so I snuck a glance at his brass name bar. "Officer . . . Dinkins. Good to see you again. This is my graduate assistant, Tyler Wainwright."

"Howdy, Doc. Good to see *you*. Nice to meet you, Tyler." Dinkins recorded our names and arrival time on a log of people at the scene, then lifted the tape so we could enter without having to stoop much.

By the time I'd straightened, Kittredge was heading our way to lead us in.

The closer of the two inner scenes was twenty feet away, but even a distant glimpse of the body—a tall, barrel-chested corpse clad from head to foot in camouflage—convinced me that this was the male victim. As we got closer, I saw that he lay faceup on the ground, arms and legs sprawled outward, his body and even his face lightly dusted with red, gold, and brown leaves. His face was largely gone, and his abdomen had collapsed—a sure sign that he'd already passed through the "bloat" phase of decay, when bacteria and enzymes in the gut release gases that inflate the abdomen almost like a balloon, or like the belly of a woman who's eight months pregnant. Once the bloating is over—once the digestive system has digested itself, after a fashion—the belly deflates and shrivels, as this man's had. I couldn't be sure, but my top-of-the-head guess, from the shrunken look of the abdomen, the bony fingers, and the extensive decay of the face, was that the man had been dead for at least a few days, maybe a week or more.

It didn't take a forensic genius to make an educated guess about the manner of death. Protruding from the man's chest, slightly left of center, was a foot-long shaft of camouflaged aluminum, topped by three feathered vanes—"fletchings," if I remembered the archery term correctly from my Cub Scout days—and a notched plastic tip where the arrow gripped the string of a hunting bow.

"Come on over here, Doc," called a voice that I recognized as the medical examiner's. Dr. Hamilton and half a dozen other people were clustered around the second of the inner perimeters. As Tyler and I approached, their forms blocked our view of what lay inside the tape. Then, just as we reached the group, they parted—a human curtain—and I heard myself gasp.

"Jesus God Al-*mighty*," I heard Tyler say, and then I heard him vomit.

THE WOMAN'S BODY was nude, her arms raised above her head, crossed at the wrists and pinned in place by three arrows: one through each palm and another piercing both the wrists, plus more in her legs. The position of the body and the arrows made me think of Christ on the cross, as well as one of the Catholic martyrs—Saint Sebastian? Was he the one who'd been killed by arrows? Unlike the man lying nearby on the forest floor, the woman's body showed little decay, most of it confined to her feet, which had been reduced largely to bone by the teeming mass of maggots clustered there. I made a mental note to remind Tyler to collect the largest of the maggots from each body.

The blood from the woman's wounds—her stigmata, I couldn't help thinking—was still plainly visible: black streaks coursing down her wrists and forearms, her upper and lower legs, her sides. But why were there no arrows in her chest or belly? Was the killer that bad a shot? Then it hit me like a fist: He was that *good* a shot. He'd wanted her to die slowly, so he'd aimed for the outer edges of his human target, not the center. There was one horrifying exception: a single arrow protruding from between her thighs. Judging by the angle, I felt sure that arrow had not been fired from the bow, but placed—pushed—by hand, in an ultimate act of sadism and misogyny. The combination of nakedness, helplessness, and savage injury combined to make the woman seem more thoroughly violated and debased than any murder victim I'd ever seen.

No one had spoken as I'd studied the scene from ten feet away, at the edge of the tape. I drew a deep breath and blew it out slowly, then turned from the grisly scene and scanned the faces around me. "What else do y'all need to do before Tyler and I go in?"

"I've pronounced her, so I'm done for now," said the M.E., Dr. Hamilton. "I'll do an autopsy, although she's a little far gone for me. Maybe I can pin down the sequence of wounds, not that it matters a lot. She was probably already dead by the time he pushed that last arrow into her."

"I hope so, Garland," I replied. "God, I hope so."

I forced myself to look more closely. The insides of her thighs were smeared with blood, but not a copious amount. I checked the arrow and the ground beneath, just to be sure. Blood had trickled down the shaft and dripped to the ground, but it was far from the hemorrhage that would have occurred if her heart had still been pumping during that final assault. I breathed a sigh of relief and a silent prayer of thanks.

I looked away, caught the eye of Art Bohanan, the ranking crime-scene tech. "Art, how about you? You still working it?"

"I've taken pictures and gone over it once," he said. "I'll take another look once the body's out. Y'all go ahead." I noticed several evidence flags and bags on the ground at the base of the tree, as well as a few numbered index cards tacked high on the trunk, behind the woman's hands. Peering closer, I saw strands of rope or twine snagged in the bark, and I realized the killer must have tied her hands in place before firing the arrows, then removed the ties once she was pinned to the tree.

I looked at Tyler, who was standing beside me again now, ashen but upright. "You okay?" He managed a weak nod. "Okay, let's go. Start with pictures."

Art had already taken KPD's crime-scene photos, but his focus—photographically as well as forensically—always differed slightly from mine, so I wanted my own.

Leaning close to the face, I noticed several contusions, which I assumed indicated that she'd been struck, possibly while fighting back. Her head slumped forward, pressing her chin against the medial ends of the clavicles, but something about the angle of the jaw and shape of the mouth struck me as odd. I'd donned a pair of gloves before stepping inside the tape; now, cradling her face in both hands, I tilted her head upright, allowing her slackened jaw to open. Stuffed inside her mouth was a wadded white rag. *Poor thing*, I thought, *couldn't even scream*. Without turning my head, I said, "Art, looks like she's got a rag in her mouth. You want it now, or later?"

"Sure, I'll take it now."

With my left hand, I pulled the mandible gently to open the mouth wider; with my right, I reached deep inside. Clamping my fingers together to compress the material, I wiggled and tugged gently to remove the improvised gag. "Hmm," I grunted, surprised at what I'd fished out. "It's not a rag after all. It's a big wad of paper."

"Well, maybe we'll get lucky," said Art. "Maybe it's a signed confession, with the perp's name and address on it."

"You want me to unwad it?"

"Better if I do it back at the lab. Probably help if I moisten it a little more."

Nodding, I turned and held it toward him, then dropped it into the paper evidence bag he opened beneath my hand.

I turned my attention back to the corpse. Up close, focused now on the details, I was able to stop thinking of her as a tortured and violated woman and to begin scrutinizing her as a corpse, a case, and a challenge. Moving downward from the face, I was struck by a number of small, circular marks on her breasts. "Garland, are these what I think they are?"

"They are if you think they're cigarette burns," he said.

"I hate it when I'm right that way," I said. "I'm guessing they're antemortem, not postmortem?"

"Probably," he said. "Point of burning somebody with a cigarette is to hurt and humiliate 'em. Doesn't work as well if they're dead."

I nodded, already moving on, focusing on the legs and feet. I'd leave the examination of the mutilated genitals to Garland and his autopsy. I noticed that each thigh was pierced completely and pegged to the tree by a single arrow. An additional arrow jutted from the back of the right thigh, the base of the arrowhead barely visible through the entry wound. That meant, I assumed, that the point was lodged deep in the bone. It reminded me of an Arikara Indian skeleton I'd excavated years before: a robust male who had lived—and limped—for years with a Sioux arrowhead embedded in his femur, the bone healing and remodeling, doggedly but imperfectly, around the flint point. The position of the arrowheads could not have been more similar; the circumstances of the wounds could not have been more different: one received during a battle between warriors, the other as a defenseless woman fled from a sadistic psychopath.

The woman's feet intrigued me. Actually, what intrigued me was the contrast between her feet and the rest of her body. The decomposition in the feet was consistent with what I'd seen in the face and hands of the dead hunter; consistent with what I'd observed in numerous corpses a week after death. The decay in the rest of her body, on the other hand, was more consistent with what I'd seen in corpses that had been dead only two or three days. It was as if one corpse's feet had been grafted onto a fresher corpse's legs. "Tyler, did you notice the differential decay?"

"Sure did," he said. "Interesting."

"Be sure you get plenty of pictures."

"I'm on it," he said. The click of the shutter, nearly as regular and frequent as the ticking of my mantelpiece clock, confirmed that he was.

"Got a theory?" As I posed the question, I was wondering if *I* had a theory.

"Gimme a minute to think on it," he said.

In my mind's eye, I scanned back through various cases—various corpses—characterized by differential decay, or a dramatic difference in the degree of decomposition exhibited by certain regions of the body. In every case I could think of, the differential decay could be explained by trauma. In one case—a Cocke County man who'd been stabbed to death a week before we found him—the soft tissues of the left hand remained largely intact; the right hand, by contrast, was down to bare bone. When I cleaned and examined the bones of the right hand, I found cut marks in the metacarpal bones and phalanges. In attempting to ward off the attack, the victim had sustained defense wounds in the right hand. Those bloody wounds had drawn droves of blowflies, which had laid countless eggs in the wounds, and the larvae—maggots—that hatched from those eggs had swiftly consumed the soft tissue of the right hand. A similar explanation, I expected, would account for the differential decay I'd seen the day before, in the first of the Cahaba Lane bodies, the one with no feet: Virtually all the soft tissue was gone from the woman's neck—probably because she'd been strangled, causing bruises and bloody scrapes that attracted blowflies, the way Sung T'zu's thirteenth-century sickle had; the way my bloody chain saw had.

But the pattern here was different. The feet—which *weren't* pierced by arrows, and presumably weren't bleeding profusely—were far more decayed than regions that *had* been pierced, that *had* bled: regions that should, therefore, have been swarming with hungry maggots.

"By the way, Tyler, you did take samples of the maggots from the woman yesterday, didn't you?"

"Sure," he said. "The ten biggest ones, just like you said."

"Good. Be sure you do the same today—from both bodies. If we compare the sizes, we should be able to tell which murder happened first. Let's compare 'em to the ones out at the research cage, too—might help us pin down the time since death a little closer."

Kittredge interrupted. "So you use the bugs to tell time? Like a stopwatch?"

"Exactly," I said.

"Cool."

Tyler resumed our conversation. "Okay, I have a theory on the differential decay."

"Let's hear it."

"Is it possible," he said, "that she's in a cooler microclimate over here than the dude over there? Cool breezes eddying up this little draw?"

I turned and stared at him. "A *micro*climate?" He shrugged sheepishly. "Tyler, that might be the dumbest thing I've ever heard you say."

He flushed; at least the color was returning to his cheeks. "It was a reach, I grant you. You got a better theory, Herr Professor?"

"Well . . . ," I said slowly, stalling for time, searching my memory banks. I recalled the case of a man who'd hanged himself in the woods, and whose body was in remarkably good condition a month after death. Just then my peripheral vision flickered. Something very small and very close had fallen downward through my field of vision from somewhere above. I checked the area around my feet without spotting anything unusual, then I heard myself say, "Hmm. *Hmm.*" Centered on the glossy black toe of my left boot I saw a single grain of rice. Only it wasn't a grain of rice; it was a baby maggot—the small, freshly hatched stage called the "first instar." As I looked at it, pondering its unexpected appearance on the toe of my boot, my eye caught another downward flicker of motion—rather like a shooting star plunging to earth. But it wasn't a star; it was another first-instar maggot, whose trajectory brought it squarely onto my boot, cheek by jowl with the first one. My eyes instinctively swept upward. If it was raining maggots, there must be a cloud up there somewhere.

It didn't take long to locate it. My left toe was positioned directly beneath the arrow wound in the right thigh. Peering closely at the wound, I saw a handful of maggots clinging to the bloody tissue there. Even as I watched, another of the maggots lost its grip—its toehold or mouthhold or whatever hold it had—and fell. This one landed slightly to one side, squarely on the exposed bones of the victim's right foot. "Yes, as a matter of fact," I said to Tyler, as insight dawned, accompanied by a slow smile spreading across my face. "I do indeed have a better theory. And once you've finished your master's thesis, you can start your dissertation project and prove I'm right. Maggots—like Isaac Newton's apple—must obey the law of gravity."

OUR JOB AT the scene was complicated by the need to free the woman's corpse, which was pinned to the tree by deeply embedded arrows. I tried wiggling the arrows while tugging, but to no avail. "Art," I called, "are you hoping to get prints off these? What I mean is, do we need to handle them gently?"

"I'm always hoping to get prints," he said. "Expecting, no; hoping, sure."

"In that case," I suggested, "we might want to think about cutting the arrows right behind the head. Then the shafts would slide right out of her." I saw heads nodding in agreement. "One of y'all got bolt cutters in your cruiser?"

The youngest and slimmest of the deputies turned and began jogging down through the woods toward the vehicles. While we waited for him to return, we bagged the man's body.

Unlike the woman, the man had bled out from a single wound. His camo shirt was soaked, and blood had poured off his chest and pooled on the ground beneath him. "Those arrows mean business," I remarked.

"I'd rather get gun shot than arrow shot," said Dr. Hamilton. "You ever taken a close look at a hunting arrow?"

"Depends," I said. "Do eighteenth-century Arikara Indian arrows count?"

"No comparison," he said. "We're not talking a chip of flint tied to a stick. These things are killing machines—engineered to inflict massive, lethal damage on big, big animals. They can shatter bone, rip muscle, shred arteries. Most of 'em have four blades angling back from the point—razor-sharp blades, flaring to an inch or more wide." He looked around at his audience, seemed satisfied with our attentiveness. "The entry wound from one of these arrows is twice the size of a .45-caliber bullet. Granted, a .45 slug traveling eight hundred feet a second packs more wallop than an arrow at three hundred feet a second. Still, think about the damage done by something that can bore a one-inch hole through a caribou." He nodded at the corpse. "This guy's heart virtually exploded. His brain might've had time to realize how thoroughly he was screwed. But the screwing itself?" He snapped his fingers. "A nanosecond."

"So quick bright things come to confusion," said Kittredge.

"Huh?" I said.

"A line from Shakespeare," he explained. "It's just a fancy way of saying you can be screwed in a heartbeat."

IT WAS ONLY after we cut her down—only as I was zipping the body bag; only as I was moving her left hand out of the path of the zipper—that I noticed: The dead woman's little finger was missing, amputated at the base so neatly that it left no stump; only a circle of crusty black blood and—within the outer black ring—a small circle of sheared-off bone, like a bull's-eye in a target. It was a startling contrast with the remaining fingers. The nine nails looked freshly coated with scarlet polish, as if the woman had just come from a nail salon—a manicure to primp for her date with death.

We carried them out together, these two people whom I suspected never actually met in life, only in death. Tyler and I, along with Art Bohanan and Garland Hamilton, carried the woman's body; Detective Kittredge and three uniformed deputies carried the man's.

When we reached the clearing where the vehicles were parked, I saw movement at a window beside the trailer's front door. Fingers curled around a curtain and pulled it aside, and a woman's face stared out at me. It was the dead man's widow—Kittredge had told me she was inside. Even through the grimy glass, the bleakness in her expression was unmistakable, and I found myself averting my gaze—out of respect, I told myself, but also, truth be told, out of discomfort. I had nothing to offer her: no comfort, no explanation, no way of setting the world right by her. Judging by the shabby trailer, the shabby truck, and the shabby patch of ground, life had been dealing low cards to her for years now; this one was simply the latest. I didn't know why the deck seemed to be so thoroughly stacked against some people—and so completely in favor of others—but I'd seen lots of lousy hands dealt to good-hearted people by now. Seen plenty of gold-plated hands go to liars and jerks, too. What was the Bible verse my minister, Reverend Michaelson, had chosen as his text last Sunday? "God sends his rain on the just and on the unjust?" Reverend Mike's gloss on the text was an uplifting one, a glass-half-full gloss: God's blessings and grace don't have to be earned; they're *there*, just like the beauty of fall foliage and summer sunsets, freely available to even the most undeserving.

But what about the converse, I couldn't help wondering: What about the misfortune and suffering—sometimes even black-hearted evil—that seemed to rain down relentlessly on people who were long overdue for some sunshine?

CHAPTER 33

Tyler

SQUINTING AGAINST THE GLARE from the porch light, Tyler batted a moth from his face and unlocked his front door. "Hey, babe, I'm back," he called. "Finally. Sorry it took so long." He switched on the living room light and closed the front door, but not before the moth darted into the apartment with him. "Roxanne? Rox? Are you here?" His voice echoed in the living room, and he felt a flash of fear—that Roxanne was gone, that she'd bolted back to Memphis to study with her classmates. *Hell, maybe she was never even here*, he thought. *Maybe I just dreamed her.* A fever dream, born of the loneliness and longing and lust that had been his trio of constant companions ever since she'd moved to Memphis for med school back in August, two months before. Two months going on forever.

"Hey," a distracted voice answered him. "Here. In the bedroom."

She was sprawled diagonally across the bed, lying on her stomach, propped on her elbows, her nose buried in one of the half-dozen doorstop textbooks she'd schlepped with her. She was naked. Her slender, graceful back was arched, and the pillow beneath her pelvis had slightly lifted her butt, which was round and firm from years of ballet and jazz classes, displaying it to best advantage, which was considerable. The dimples at the top of her hips—"dimples of Venus"; Tyler *loved* that name—seemed to be smiling just for him.

She turned her head toward the doorway, where he'd stopped to admire the view, and gave him a smoldering look over her shoulder. "I'm studying anatomy," she said, arching one eyebrow at him. "The human reproductive system. Come and be my lab partner." She parted her lips and ran her tongue across the upper lip. "Better yet," she murmured, "be my lab partner and come."

She closed the book and shoved it off the mattress. It landed with a *thunk* that made the nightstand lamp quiver. Tyler stepped toward her, already feeling his breath quicken and his desire stir.

And then it happened. She rolled over onto her back, and raised her arms above her head, displaying herself—offering herself—in all her nakedness and vulnerability and sweetness, and it was his utter undoing. In his mind's eye, she became the woman in the woods, and for a horrifying moment he envisioned Roxanne's lovely body bloodied and bristling with arrows. His heart pounded, his head swam, and his legs began to give way beneath him. Stumbling forward and clutching the footboard of the bed, he dropped to his knees and tucked his head, his breath coming in quick, spasmodic gulps.

She scrambled down the mattress and leaned over to stare down at him. "*Tyler?* Sweetie, baby, what's wrong?"

He could not answer. Folded in on himself, he shivered and hyperventilated. She scrambled down to his side, wrapped him in her arms, and stroked his head. "*Sshh,*" she whispered. "*Shhh.*" She pressed the back of a hand to his cheek. "Are you sick?" Wordlessly he shook his head. "Have you . . . *done* something? Something awful? Slept with somebody else? Run over a child?" Another shake of his head. "Then come get in bed, and let me hold you."

She helped him up, led him to the side of the bed, and eased him onto the mattress, then curled around him from behind. They lay like that for a long time. Muscle by muscle, nerve by nerve, breath by breath, he calmed, and the reality of the room—the warm pool of light from the lamp, the warm skin and soft breath of the woman pressed against him—reasserted itself.

Finally she spoke. "What's got you so upset? Tell me."

And so he did. He told it almost as if in a trance; almost as if he were reliving it, or showing her the slides he'd shot at the scene, all 108 of them—three full rolls of gruesome film. He told his way in, and he told his way out. But by the time he was telling his way out, he'd gotten separated from her. Somewhere during the telling in, she'd stiffened, so slightly that he'd failed to notice it at first. Heedless, he'd kept on, describing the woman pinned to the tree, naked and martyred. Meanwhile, the other naked woman—the naked woman in his bed, who had offered herself to him at her most unguarded—had gradually edged away, easing the sheet up her leg and hip and torso. And when at last he revealed the obscenity of the final arrow, Roxanne rolled away and sat on the edge of the bed, no longer touching him, and wound the sheet around herself like a shroud, tucking it tightly beneath both arms.

She drew a long, slow breath through her nostrils. She held it for several seconds before exhaling, with equal control, again through her nostrils. In the stillness of the room, the breath seemed deafening. "God *damn* it, Tyler. Why did you tell me that?"

He rolled to face her. "What do you mean, why did I tell you? Because you *asked* me to, Rox."

"I wish I hadn't. I take it back. Un-tell it, Tyler—I don't want to know. I don't want it in our bed. I don't want it in my head."

"I know," he said. "I don't, either." He held out a hand, hoping that she'd take it; hoping that from their shared distress, they could build a bridge across the chasm that had opened between them. His hand lay open, untaken; Roxanne remained rigid on the edge of the bed, as still as a stone. "Come on, Rox, don't do this. Give me a break here."

Without looking, she swung her left arm behind her, striking him in the chest so hard he grunted. "*Damn* it," she repeated. "Why are men such *shits*? Especially to *women*? I swear to God, Tyler, it makes me sick."

"I don't know why," he said. "You're right—men do awful, awful things to women. I hate it, too. It makes me sick, too. I puked in the woods out there today. I did. Ask Brockton; he'll tell you." She sat, unmoving. Unmoved. He waited, and it became clear that the wait could last forever. "You know what, though, Rox?" His voice took on an edge. "I am not the bad guy. I am nothing *like* the bad guy. As a matter of fact, I'm the *good* guy—one of them, anyhow—and I'm doing my damnedest to help *catch* the bad guy. So cut me some slack here, could you please? Because in case you hadn't noticed, I had a shitty day. A really, really, *really* shitty day."

She softened—some—and came back to him, turning onto her side and laying her head and one hand on his chest. But she did not unshroud herself. The fruit of the knowledge of evil had left bitterness in her mouth and coldness in her body. Hours later, when Tyler twitched and began to snore, she slipped from the bed. By the watery, soundless light of dawn, she dressed and packed and let herself out.

By the time she turned onto I–40 for the four-hundred-mile drive west, the rising sun was blazing red-orange in the rearview mirror, like the flaming sword at the gates of Eden, after Adam and Eve had been cast out for knowing too much.

CHAPTER 34

Brockton

LEAVING THE STADIUM, I turned right on to Neyland Drive, driving slowly beside the emerald waters of the Tennessee, my thoughts spinning like the eddies and whorls spooling downriver as the silent current poured over ledges and pits lurking deep and invisible beneath the surface.

At Kingston Pike I made the left toward Sequoyah Hills and home, but then, to my surprise, I found myself turning in to the parking lot of Second Presbyterian. Two cars were parked in front of the office: an aging Ford Escort, which I seemed to recall belonged to Mary Cowan, the church secretary; and a new Toyota Camry, recently bought by the senior minister, Rev. Mike Michaelson.

Mary—on her way out just as I was headed in—stumbled and nearly fell as I tugged the office door from her grasp. "Oh, sorry," I said, catching her elbow to steady her. "Didn't mean to pull you off balance."

She laughed. "I've been klutzy all day today. I

would've tripped no matter what. I'm just praying I make it home in one piece." She started down the sidewalk, raising a hand and waving as she walked away.

I paused in the doorway and called after her, "Looks like he's in?"

"He's got a finance committee meeting in an hour," she said over her shoulder. "Go on in—he'd be *thrilled* to talk about something besides balance sheets and revenue projections."

Passing through the outer office, I noticed that his door was ajar. Rapping gently with one knuckle on the oak, I said, "Mike?"

"Hello? Come in." I stepped into a pool of golden light, created by two floor lamps, a mica-shaded desk lamp, and walls of honey-colored sandstone. I couldn't help smiling at the contrast between the pastor's warm, elegant study and my own shabby, grimy corner of the Ivory Tower. If I felt a brief twinge of envy, it was good-natured and short-lived envy. Reverend Michaelson looked up from a daunting spreadsheet. "Bill, what a nice surprise. Have a seat. How are you?"

"I'm fine," I said, sinking into a large leather armchair. "Busy. A lot going on."

He nodded, looking thoughtful. Was that an instinctive response, I wondered, or was it part of his training—Empathy 101? Pastoral Counseling 202? I'd always been impressed by how well he kept current on the activities of his parishioners, so I wasn't surprised when he said, "Seems like you've been in the news a lot lately. I can't pick up the *Sentinel* or turn on Channel 10 without coming across you."

"Yeah. Unfortunately."

He leaned his head slightly to one side. "Tell me, is it difficult, doing what you do?"

I shrugged. "I had good teachers. And great opportunities to learn—two summers at the Smithsonian, a bunch of summers digging up Indian bones in South Dakota. Sometimes I get stumped, but often I stumble onto the right answer."

He smiled. "Clearly. But I didn't mean intellectually difficult. I meant emotionally difficult; spiritually difficult. What kind of toll does it take, doing what you do? Seeing what you see?"

"Huh." I half laughed, half grunted. "They teach you guys mind reading in seminary?"

"No, it's probably better they don't. I'd be afraid of what I'd find out." He leaned back in his chair, a high-backed swivel rocker, and tented his fingers, the same way my boss, the dean, tended to. "It takes courage to confront the dark side of life on a daily basis. Not many people are up to it. I'm not sure *I* would be."

"Thing is," I said, "some days it's more daily than others. Lately . . . " My words trailed off, and I waited for him to jump in with a question or some shepherdly counsel or comfort. Instead, he just sat there, his eyes attentive above the finger tent. I backed up and took another run at it. "Lately, though, it feels extra daily. And darker. Much darker." He nodded, still waiting. "I worked a double homicide yesterday in East Knox County. Two bodies in the woods. The man, he died almost instantly; no suffering to speak of, except on the part of the wife he left behind. But the woman? She died slowly. In agony. The guy who killed her did unspeakable things to her." I paused, unsure where to go next. Surprisingly, I went to Tyler. "My graduate assistant worked the scene with me. Smart, good-hearted kid. Name's Tyler. Tyler threw up when he saw what had been done to the woman. I'm not sure Tyler's 'up to it,' as you put it."

"Nothing to be ashamed of, if he's not."

"I know he doesn't owe it to me to follow in my footsteps, though I'll be disappointed if he doesn't. But that's not what's eating at me."

"What *is* eating at you?"

"Tyler said something today that I can't get out of my head."

"What'd he say?"

"Actually, it was his girlfriend who said it. Or maybe his ex-girlfriend. Roxanne. After he told her about the woman in the woods, Roxanne left in the middle of the night, while he was sleeping. No note; no phone call. The last thing she said—pardon my French—was 'Why are men such shits to women?' Tyler didn't have an answer. *I* don't have an answer." I leaned forward, my elbows on my knees. "Do *you* have an answer?"

KATHLEEN WAS LOADING the dishwasher when I got in. "We waited for a while, then finally gave up," she said, not looking up from the dishes. "Where've you been? Why didn't you call?"

"I'm sorry," I said. "I got sidetracked on the way home. I thought it would only take a few minutes. Ended up taking an hour."

"Would've been nice if you'd found a way to call. Jeff brought Jenny for dinner."

"Jenny?"

"Jenny. The artist. His new girlfriend." Her tone was sharp.

"I know who she is. I just didn't know she was coming to dinner. I didn't see them down in the rec room. They're not making out in his room, I hope."

"They're gone," she said peevishly. "They left ten minutes ago. If you'd called to say you were on your way, I expect they'd have waited."

"I'm sorry, Kathleen. Really sorry. I didn't mean to be late."

"Where were you?" she repeated. "What were you doing?" She turned to face me for the first time, her eyes narrowing. "Are you having an affair?"

I burst into laughter—a mistake, apparently, because she threw the wet dish towel at me. I kept laughing. "I'm sorry, hon," I said. "I'm not laughing at you. It's just . . . I was talking to a minister. I stopped by church on the way home."

"What church? *Our* church?" I nodded. "Whatever for?"

"Long story," I said.

"Obviously." She hipped the dishwasher door closed—with more energy than the job required—and turned to face me, motioning to a pair of chairs at the kitchen table. "Spill it. I'm all ears." She was still peeved, but she was intrigued now, and that seemed like progress.

The night before, I'd spared her the grisly details of the death scene in the woods. Now I told her a bit more, and then told her about Roxanne's sudden departure, and the bitter question she'd posed to

Tyler. "It's been bugging me all day. So I stopped to see if Mike might have some insight."

She stared at me from across the table. "Let me see if I've got this straight. You were hoping a theologian could solve the conjoined-twin problems of evil and misogyny in a five-minute, oh-by-the-way mini-lecture?" I shrugged sheepishly; I hadn't gone into his study with such a clearly articulated and clearly ludicrous agenda, but she'd summed it up pretty well. "Honestly, Bill, you do put the *idiot* in *idiot savant* sometimes."

"You know," I began, in feeble protest. But I didn't have a leg to stand on, and we both knew it. "It's true," I conceded, shaking my head. "You're right. Absolutely, utterly right." She smiled then, reaching across the table to give my hand a squeeze. One of the things I appreciated most about Kathleen was her readiness to forgive, to let go of a grievance at the first sign of contrition.

"And what words of wisdom and divine insight did the Right Reverend Michaelson impart while your steak was turning to shoe leather?"

"Steak? I missed steak?"

"On the grill. Grilled potatoes, too."

"Ah, *man*," I moaned. "My favorite dinner? I can't believe I missed it. Proof positive that the devil is alive and well. Messing with the world in general and me in particular."

"Maybe it's not beyond redemption."

"The world?"

"The steak. I pulled it off while it was still medium rare. Believe it or not, it no longer surprises me when you're late for dinner."

"You're an angel," I said. "And the age of miracles is not yet over."

"I'll fix you a plate if you'll tell me what Mike had to say." She scooted back from the table, went to the fridge, and began pulling out Tupperware containers.

"I'm not sure I can remember all the details."

"Then give me the Cliffs Notes version."

"Here's the Cliffs Notes version: 'It's complicated.'"

She frowned across the plate of steak and potatoes. "I think I'll give this to the dog next door. Because that's *not* complicated; it's simple, and the dog will adore me."

"Hang on, I'll try to give you the gist," I squawked. "But it *is* complicated. I asked Mike, 'Why are men such shits to women?' and—"

"I hope you rephrased the question."

"No," I admitted, "I gave him the unvarnished version." She shook her head despairingly. "Anyhow, his answer started with the Judeo-Christian concept of the Fall of Man—"

"The Fall of Man? Did he blame it on Eve?" she asked sharply.

"No, actually. Matter of fact, he took a few shots at the early church fathers for painting it as the woman's fault."

"Well, praise the Lord," she said sarcastically. "It's about time Eve's criminal record got expunged."

"Anyhow, after the Fall, he—Mike, not the Lord—veered off into evolutionary biology and primate behavior. Male aggression, territorialism, competition for mates, mate guarding. He knows more zoology than I do. Then we got into psychology and cultural anthropology and sociology and politics: patriarchies, matriarchies, oligarchies, preserving the power structure . . ."

"All right, you win," she sighed, popping the plate in the microwave and tapping the one-minute button. "I should've let you stop with 'It's complicated.' But did it make you feel better, wandering down those trails with him?"

"Kinda," I hedged. "But he didn't really answer the question. Like I said—and like *he* said—it's complicated."

"No it's not," she said.

"Wait—you just *agreed* that it was complicated."

"I agreed that his *answer* was complicated," she said. "But *my* answer's simple." I stared at her. "Men treat women like shit for the same reason they treat children or animals like shit: Because they *can*. It's a power trip. 'I'll feel stronger and better if I prove that you're weaker,' right?"

"Well . . ."

"Every guy wants to be the big man on campus," she went on. "Bed the prettiest women; *breed* with the prettiest woman. It's like a pride of lions. If you're not the big lion—if you're only a medium-sized lion—you take it out on the little lions. Men like that would probably rather be shits to other men, but they can't be, so they're shits to women and children and animals."

Kathleen's blunt gloss on the issue lacked the intellectual nuance of Reverend Mike's—no detours down scenic side trails of theology and sociology and anthropology—but what it lacked in sophistication, it made up for in ringing clarity. "So you're saying it all comes down to pecking order?"

"No. I'm saying it all comes down to *pecker* order; pecker size. Men who treat women badly are men with small peckers—metaphorically, at least. Probably literally, too."

I laughed, mildly shocked but mightily impressed. "Next time Mike needs a guest preacher, you should fill the pulpit. The congregation would get some straight talk. And they'd get to Calhoun's half an hour before the Baptists." She smiled. "But now I'm puzzled about something else. If Mike didn't answer the question, how come I came out of there feeling so much better?"

"That's easy, too," she said. "It's in the Gospel According to James."

"James? There *isn't* a Gospel According to James." I ticked off the four gospel writers: "Matthew, Mark, Luke, John."

"I'm talking about the Gospel According to James Taylor."

"James Taylor? The folksinger?"

"Folksinger and prophet of the human heart. 'Shower the People'?" She wagged a finger at me and began to sing. "Once you tell somebody the way that you feel, you can feel it beginning to ease." She cocked her head. "Right? Isn't that why you feel better?"

"Crap, Kathleen. How'd you get to be so much smarter than I am?"

"Not just smarter," she said. "*Wiser*. It's a woman thing." She tapped her belly with an index finger. "It's the uterus. It gives us superpowers of wisdom and insight." Without looking, she reached behind her back and popped the door of the microwave, cutting off the timer a nanosecond before it began its annoying beeps. "Want salad?" I shook my head. She set the plate down in front of me, singing, "Better to shower the people you love with love, show them the way you feel . . ."

The steak smelled gloriously of mesquite smoke and marinade, as if it had only that moment been lifted off the grill. Rich, reddish-brown juice seeped from the seared meat, pooling beneath the crisp potatoes. "Perfect," I said. "Thank you."

"You're welcome. And Bill?" I glanced up, my fork and knife already poised above the plate. "Thanks for not being a shit to women. Or kids. Or animals." I smiled at her. "You've got a big heart." She smiled back. "And you *know* what they say about the size of a man's heart."

"Oh *my*," I said, as I caught the drift of her innuendo. "Is it true, what they say?"

"Better than true. It's an understatement."

Beaming, I bowed my head and tucked into the feast.

CHAPTER 35

Satterfield

SATTERFIELD WAS A SHADOW among shadows, flowing through the night like some coalescence of darkness—like darkness made flesh—along the perimeter of the quarry yard. The night watchman had just made his 1:00 A.M. circuit, and he wouldn't make another for an hour—maybe longer, if he fell asleep in the guard shack, as he sometimes did.

Satterfield didn't need an hour; didn't need even half an hour. The blasting caps were locked in a windowless steel building—it was called a "magazine," but essentially it was a vault—tucked into a recess in one of the quarry's limestone walls. The dynamite was locked in an identical magazine in a second recess, fifty yards from the first one. Satterfield had not actually been inside either magazine, but earlier in the day, he'd watched through his spotting scope as a wiry guy had gone into the first structure and emerged a few minutes later with a handful of caps, dangling from their electrical wires like silver firecrackers swinging from long, slender fuses of red and blue. After driving a brief distance along the rim of the gaping pit, he'd gone into the second magazine and then emerged carrying a box covered with warning labels—labels Satterfield had seen many times during his demolition training in the Navy.

Satterfield had been researching lock picking, so he could come and go without leaving a visible trace. He'd seen locks picked in plenty of movies—the long, slender picks, worked into the keyhole, wiggled and twisted in some artful, arcane manner—but as it turned out, it looked like it was going to be easier than that. The prior night, when the watchman had gone to make his rounds, Satterfield had slipped into the guard shack and rummaged around. Sure enough, in the gritty center drawer of a gritty metal desk, he'd found an assortment of gritty spare keys. One of them bore the promising label "demo." For a moment he'd doubted his luck—had they really been stupid enough to use identical locks on both bunker doors?—but then he realized that yes, of course they had. If they were dumb enough to leave the keys to the whole operation in an unlocked desk—an unlocked desk in an unlocked *guard* shack, for crissakes—they were plenty dumb enough to use identical locks for the blasting caps and the explosives.

The guard's 2:00 A.M. rounds would take him first to the blasting-cap magazine, so Satterfield started there, to make sure he'd be finished well ahead of time. The building was low and squat, maybe ten feet square by seven feet high, the steel outer walls lined with several inches of hardwood, if the quarry's magazines were built like the Navy's. The door looked like something from a warship: Also made of heavy steel plate, it was low and narrow, mounted on massive hinges.

Satterfield slid the key into the padlock's keyway, feeling the pins bump across the teeth, one by one. When the key bottomed out, he twisted gently. The lock opened grudgingly, grittily, the coating of limestone dust resisting as the shackle slid out of the brass body. It took most of his strength to wrest the door open, and he felt a flash of admiration for the wiry blaster he'd watched through his scope; the guy was several inches shorter than Satterfield, and probably weighed twenty or thirty pounds less. *Not an ounce of fat on that guy*, he thought. The door rasped on the hinges, but the sound was slight—almost as though it were absorbed by the velvet blackness of the magazine's interior.

Once inside, he tugged the door shut behind him, then clicked on the small Mag-Lite. As he scanned the room, he smiled. Three walls were lined with wooden shelves, and the shelves were like a high-explosives candy store. The blasting caps—hundreds of them; hell, *thousands* of them—were stored in wooden bins. Some sported pigtails of bright orange det cord; others—the ones he wanted—trailed electrical leads, the pairs of wires looped and fastened into tight coils.

He slipped three caps into one of the thigh pockets of the black BDUs—no point getting greedy, since he had the key to the store, and he didn't want to risk creating a noticeable shortage in the inventory—then turned to go.

He pushed his way out the heavy door, then closed it behind him, snapping the balky lock shut. Five minutes later he was inside the second cavelike magazine, this one containing cases of dynamite and wooden spools of detonating cord. From an open case of dynamite, he took two sticks—more than he needed—and tucked them into a deep pocket, then turned to go. At the door, though, he hesitated, then turned back, irresistibly drawn to the spools of det cord: Primacord—500- and 1,000- and 2,000-foot spools of linear explosive, in a rainbow of colors: orange, yellow, red, green, purple, in solids and stripes, each color and pattern denoting a different load of explosive inside the bright plastic sleeve. Some of the cord was no thicker than clothesline; on one spool, though, the cord was nearly as fat as his pinky. PRIMALINE 85, read the label on that one, which meant that every meter of cord contained 85 grams of high-explosive PETN.

God, I love this shit, Satterfield thought. He loved Primacord for what it could do; hell, with that one spool of Primaline 85, he could probably take down every major bridge in Knoxville. He also loved Primacord for its neatness and precision. Dynamite was dirty and messy, though undeniably macho; Primacord was clean and neat. Consistent, too: No matter which spool you unwound, no matter which loading you used, you could be sure that the explosion would rip through the cord at 23,000 feet a second, 16,000 miles an hour: New York to L.A. in *ten minutes*. He'd done the math during his demo training at Coronado, working the problem three times to make sure he hadn't misplaced the decimal. How the hell did they do that, extrude high-proof explosives with such perfection that the blast traveled through the cord ten times faster than a bullet, but precisely, reliably fast? You could set your watch—hell, you could set a damn atomic clock—by precision like that.

He wasn't here for the Primacord, but the temptation was too strong to resist. Slipping the KA-BAR knife from its sheath, he unspooled ten feet of the Primaline 85, sliced it off, and then wound it around his waist, cinching it into three tight coils. He took a moment to imagine what would happen if something set it off while he was wearing it. *Shit*, he thought, shaking his head and grinning, *your head would come down in Kentucky and your feet in Alabama; one hand in Maryland, the other in Oklahoma. Don't get hit by lightning on the way home.*

This bunker's door was even harder to close than the other. Satterfield made a mental note to bring some WD–40 next time he came, to lube the hinges. Be a damned shame to throw out his back.

CHAPTER 36

Brockton

HOLDING MY BREATH TO protect my lungs, I jogged into the cloud of smoke that shrouded the entry to the Knoxville Police Department. The air was thick with carcinogens—at least a pack's worth of second-hand smoke, judging by the throng of smokers loitering outside the grimy glass doors. The KPD was a squat, brooding fortress of putty-colored brick set atop Summit Hill Drive. The police shared the building with traffic court, and I suspected that most of the smokers were speeders and DUI defendants, taking advantage of the noon recess to calm their jitters with a jolt of nicotine.

"Excuse me, sir?" I was accosted by a disheveled young man whose stringy, greasy brown hair had been cut, at some point in the distant past, in a style that was named after a saltwater fish whose name I struggled to recall. I held up my hand to deflect his sob story and request for spare change. Instead of panhandling, though, he simply asked, "Could you tell me the time, please?" Ashamed of my brusque response, I stopped, one hand on the door handle, and checked my watch.

"Ten of one," I croaked, expending as little of my lungful of air as possible.

"Dude," he said as I tugged open the door. "What happened to your voice?"

"Throat cancer." I clutched my larynx as I rasped out the brazen lie. "Smoking." Before he had a chance to engage me further, I ducked through the door, hurrying toward the smoke-free air inside. Glancing over my shoulder, I saw the mullet-head scrutinizing the ashy end of his cigarette, his eyes narrowed with suspicion. Then he dropped it to the concrete and ground it out. Before he did, though, he took one long last drag.

Traffic court occupied a single floor on the left-hand side of the complex; the police department commanded a four-story wing to the right. I signed in with the receptionist, who made a quick phone call and then buzzed me in. "Crime lab. Take the elevator to the second floor."

In the lab, Art Bohanan sat at a long metal lab table, peering through a magnifying lens at the blood-smeared shaft of a hunting arrow. On a metal tray to one side were the other headless shafts, decapitated with bolt cutters to allow the dead woman's body to be taken down from the tree. A second tray held the sharp-tipped, razor-edged arrowheads—all except for the one that had lodged deep in the femur. "Hey, Art," I said. "Any prints?" Without looking up, he shook his head. "In that case, you probably won't find any on this one, either." Reaching into the pocket of my windbreaker, I pulled out a clear plastic jar, two inches wide and three inches tall, containing the arrowhead I'd extracted from the femur. "Dr. Hamilton did as much autopsy as he could this morning," I said, "and he pulled this out. But she was too far gone for him to tell much, so he's turned her and the man over to me. We'll start cleaning her bones tomorrow; right now we're still processing the woman that was splayed against the tree."

"You think she'll be done today?" asked Art. I'd worked with him on enough cases to feel sure that his use of the word "done" was a deliberate double entendre. Art had commented, on more than one visit to the Anthropology Annex, that we processed bones exactly the way his wife made beef stock: cut off most of the meat, then put the bones into a big pot to simmer. After my costly lesson about the penchant of unwatched pots to boil, I'd taken steps to ensure that I wouldn't ruin any more of Kathleen's stoves: I'd sworn never again to process skeletal material at home, and I'd dipped deeply into the department's budget to buy the Annex a 20-gallon steam-jacketed kettle—the kind commercial kitchens used to cook meals for the masses. With the thermostat set at 150 degrees and a bit of meat tenderizer, Biz, and Downy added to the water, the soft tissue—even the brain—softened and dissolved, leaving the bone clean, undamaged, and smelling more like laundry than roadkill.

"Might be done today; more likely tomorrow. She had a fair amount of tissue left."

He nodded at me, then shook his head glumly at the arrow shaft he'd been examining, laying it on the tray alongside the others. "This guy was careful," he said. "Either he wore gloves, or he wiped everything down pretty well."

"You said you had something to show me?"

"Couple things, actually. Hang on a sec." He switched off the lamp and rolled to the other end of the table, where he picked up a phone and punched in an extension number. "Hey, it's Art," he said. "I just finished going over the arrows. . . . Nah, nothing. Nada. Zero. Zip." He glanced at me. "Dr. Brockton just walked in. I'm gonna show him the stuff I showed you this morning. . . . Okay. Bye." He replaced the handset. "That was Kittredge. He's on his way down."

Art rolled his chair back toward the center of the table and picked up a square white card, slightly smaller than the width of a sheet of printer paper. The card was covered with oblong smudges, as if it had been pawed by a jam-fingered child. Even from a distance, I recognized the whorls and loops of fingerprints. There were two horizontal rows of small square boxes—ten boxes in all. Nine of the boxes contained prints; the tenth box was as empty as the space that had once been occupied by the woman's amputated finger. "I printed her at the scene," he said, "before you got there." I nodded; I'd already figured that. "Pretty good, if I do say so myself."

"Her hands were in great shape, compared to the guy's," I said. "His were almost down to the bone."

Art handed me another card, this one with a complete set of prints from both hands. Holding them side by side, I compared the two cards. The prints on the second card, the complete card, were sharper and crisper than those taken from the woman's corpse; no surprise there. But even I could tell that both sets of prints—the crisp antemortem prints and the blurred postmortem prints—had been made by the same hand. "You got a match already?" He nodded. "That's great." I read the name at the top of the complete card. "Pamela Stone. Who is she? *Was* she?"

"Thirty-two-year-old hooker. Street name was Desirée. Kittredge is checking with vice and patrol to see what else they know, and when she was last seen."

As if summoned by the mention of his name, Kittredge entered the crime lab. He nodded to Art and reached out to shake my hand. "Doc. How's it going?"

"Okay. I brought y'all the arrowhead from the thigh. Dr. Hamilton examined her first thing this morning. I was just telling Art, we'll start cleaning off the bones tomorrow, soon as the prior victim's done."

"Forgive my ignorance," he said, "but do you have to get the family's permission for that?"

I shook my head. "As a forensic case, it—she—is now in the medical examiner's system. Processing the remains, getting them down to bone, is standard investigative protocol."

He nodded. "What'd the M.E. find? Anything helpful?"

"I'm not sure how helpful this is," I said, "but it's interesting. She lost a lot of blood, but not enough to kill her. He thinks she died of a coronary."

"A heart attack?" Kittredge looked puzzled.

"Yeah. The M.E. thinks she died of fright."

He whistled softly. "That's a first, for me. But I can believe it, considering what the guy was doing to her. Anything else?"

"Not yet," I said. "I want to take a closer look at the right hand once it's cleaned up. Something about that missing digit bugs me, but I can't quite put my finger on it. No pun intended."

Kittredge nodded slowly. "I'd like you to take a look at what was in her mouth," he said. "I don't know what to make of it. Maybe you'll have an idea."

"I'll try. Always happy to help, if I can."

Kittredge leaned across the table and picked up a flat plastic sleeve, holding it up to display one side. Inside the sleeve was a sheet of what had been crisp white paper in a past life, but was now stained and smeared and wrinkled. In addition to what appeared to be random blotches, the sheet bore numerous fingerprints, these etched in bright purple, a hue somewhere between raspberry and grape jelly. I turned to Art. "You got prints off that wad of paper? Damn, you're good."

Art shrugged modestly. "Ninhydrin. Binds to the amino acids in proteins. Any time you handle something, you leave behind a few skin cells, and there's protein in those cells. A quick spritz"—he nodded toward a spray bottle on the table—"and presto."

"Presto indeed," I said. "That's a lot of prints."

"At least three different sets," he said. "Two men and one woman, looks like."

"And good enough to run through AFIS?" I was

proud that I knew the acronym for the Automated Fingerprint Identification System.

"Good enough to give us a match already," Kittredge interjected. "One of the men."

"You're kidding."

The detective shook his head. "Nope. Dead serious."

"Amazing."

"What's even more amazing," said Kittredge, "is that the guy's name is right here on the page."

"His *name*?"

"Yep. Full name. Signature, too."

"He wrote a note and actually *signed* it?"

"Not a note, exactly. Take a look, tell me what you think." The detective handed me the plastic sleeve.

I flipped it over, and my heart nearly stopped.

Neatly typed on a sheet of UT letterhead, the name—and the scrawled but familiar signature beside it—read "William M. Brockton."

I stared at the stained and rumpled piece of paper—the first page of a forensic report I'd written and submitted—its edges thick with purple fingerprints. *My* fingerprints. I looked from Kittredge's face to Art Bohanan's and back again. "How the *hell*," I finally said, "did that end up in the mouth of a dead woman?"

Art said nothing; Kittredge said, "My question exactly, Doc. I was hoping you might be able to answer it for me." Still reeling from shock, I nodded numbly, then drew a deep breath and took another, longer look.

I had recognized the format the moment I'd

glimpsed the page. It was a forensic report, the kind I'd written and signed dozens of times, in dozens of cases. This particular report, I saw upon closer inspection, was addressed to a state trooper in Alaska—Corp. Byron Keller—and the subject line read "Re: Forensic case 90–02."

I remembered the case well; in fact, I'd mentioned it to Tyler, though not by number, less than twenty-four hours before, as we'd driven back to the morgue with the two bodies from the woods. Keller's case had begun when a pair of Alaska hunters had found a skeleton, half buried in a gravel bar at the shore of a river. Keller had initially thought the skeleton might be that of a hiker who'd gotten lost and starved to death, or perhaps been killed by a bear. But there'd been no reports of missing hikers in the area; in addition, there were no traces of backpacking equipment or apparel: no boots, and in fact, no clothing of any kind.

Corporal Keller had contacted me after reading a newspaper story about one of my early Kansas cases—the Sawzall dismemberment case, the one where I'd teamed up with an FBI profiler—and called to ask if I'd take a look at the bones from the gravel bar. Intrigued by the lack of clothing or other contextual clues—*taphonomy*, in technical terms—I'd agreed, and two days later, a FedEx courier had delivered the bones to Neyland Stadium. The bones, as my report to Keller had detailed, were those of a twenty-five- to thirty-five-year-old white female, approximately five feet five inches tall. Three amalgam fillings in her teeth indicated that she'd been born sometime after 1950, and that she'd received good dental care during her youth; two unfilled cavities in her third molars suggested that she'd stopped going to the dentist as an adult, probably because she lacked the money. "Based on prior, similar cases," I'd written, "it is possible that the victim was a prostitute, one whose disappearance might never have been reported."

The memorable feature of the case, and the reason I'd mentioned it to Tyler, was that the victim—eventually identified as a missing Anchorage prostitute—had been abducted and flown to the wilderness by a local man who was both a hunter and a bush pilot. "An X-ray of the remains reveals a smear of lead on vertebra T-7," I wrote, "indicating that she had been shot." After receiving the report, Corporal Keller had returned to the riverbank with a metal detector, and found a gray bullet nestled in the gray gravel. Had she been transported to the wilderness and released as prey? The suspect denied it, but on the basis of the remains I'd examined—plus three more shallow graves that had been marked by *X*s on an aviation chart in the man's airplane—he'd been convicted and sentenced to life in prison.

The details of the Alaska case had come back to me in a flash, the moment I'd seen Corporal Keller's name on the report; indeed, it was almost as if the sun-bleached, river-rinsed bones of 90–02 were hovering in the air before me like a hologram. Then the hologram shimmered and shifted, the skull becoming a face, the empty eye orbits morphing into the piercing gaze of KPD Detective Kittredge. "So, Doc," he prompted, "what can you tell me?"

"I can tell you I'm stunned," I said. "As baffled as

you. Maybe more." He waited, his eyebrows raised to make sure I knew that he expected more. I racked my brain.

"The first time we talked," Kittredge said slowly, "you described the crime scene at Cahaba Lane perfectly, before you'd ever been there. You had a picture of it in your hand before our photographer was even at the scene."

"I got that photo in the mail," I reminded him. "The killer sent it to me."

"So you said. That night, you called 911 to say there were more bodies in the woods there."

"It was a hunch," I said, "not a confession."

"Now, one of your reports—signed by you, handled by you—turns up in the mouth of one of the other bodies you said we'd find in the woods."

"And I'm the one that found it in her mouth," I pointed out. "Fished it out and handed it to Art. Remember? Why the hell would I hand over something that incriminating, if I were the one who'd put it there?"

He shrugged. "You own a hunting bow, Doc?"

"God no," I said, relieved to be able to answer with a simple, unequivocal negative.

"So if we searched your house right now, we wouldn't find one?"

"Are you kidding? I haven't shot a bow and arrow since Cub Scouts. You're welcome to come search the house. Let's go, right now. Talk to my wife and son. They'd laugh if you asked them if I was a crack shot with a bow and arrow." I held out my hands, palms up. "Do these look like fingertips that spend a lot of time on a bowstring? Feel them." I stretched my hands toward Kittredge, and he probed my white-collar, desk-job fingers. "Hell, my wife has more calluses than I do," I said.

Kittredge drummed his fingers on the edge of the table. "So who would have had access to that report? That's not a copy, that's the original. You signed it, and you handled it. Who could've gotten hold of that? And why would he wad it up and stuff it in a woman's mouth before using her for target practice?"

Glancing again at the report I held in my left hand, I shrugged, turning my right palm upward, empty-handed. "I sent the original to Keller at the Alaska State Police. I would've handled that one, because I signed it." I glanced at the one in my hand. "But this isn't the original," I added. "It's a copy."

"How do you know it's a copy?"

"Because my signature here is black. I sign the originals in blue." I looked again at the smudges. "Art, you say there are three sets of prints on here—mine and two others?"

"At least three. Possibly more, but if I were a betting man, I'd say three."

"And you're sure one set is mine?"

"I'm sure one set matches what we've got on file as yours."

"Then they're my prints. If you say they're mine, they're mine. So this has to be a copy I handled." I looked at the distribution list on the report. Often I sent copies of reports to several recipients—multiple investigators, the coroner or medical examiner, one or more prosecutors. This one had gone only to the state trooper. I felt another wave of surprise and confusion, bordering on panic. "This is *my* copy. Has to be. This came out of my own filing cabinet." I stared at the page, as if the answers to my swirling questions might somehow materialize in the margins, superimposing themselves on the purple fingerprints—mine and the two mystery sets. Suddenly, it was almost as if an answer *did* materialize. "My God," I breathed. "She was telling the truth."

Kittredge and Art looked at me as if I'd gone over the edge, off the cliff of madness.

"She?" said Kittredge.

"The temp." The detective still looked puzzled and dubious. "I had a temporary secretary for a month last spring," I explained. "Trish, my regular secretary, was on medical leave. Ended up taking early retirement. But I had a temp for a few weeks, and while she was there, we did some office shuffling. The day the files got moved I was gone all day, giving a talk over at the TBI lab, near Nashville. The temp—Darla? Darlene? Charlene?—she boxed up all my case files and stacked them in the hall. I would never have let her put them there. Anyhow, the next day, she came to see me, all upset; said one of the boxes had gone missing, gotten lost somehow. I reamed her out, accused her of throwing 'em out by mistake, but she cried and cried, swore she'd packed and stacked everything really carefully. I didn't believe her. Sent her back to Human Resources with a bad reference."

"How many files did you lose?"

"Dozens," I said. "All the forensic cases I'd worked since I came to UT. Not the photos, luckily—I keep those in a separate filing cabinet, in a different office—but all the written reports. Took all semester to rebuild those files—I had to call and get copies of those reports from everybody I'd done cases for." I shook my head, remembering the tedious effort. "Oh, including Keller, the Alaska state trooper. I called to ask him for a copy. He'll probably remember that, much as I bitched and moaned over the phone."

Kittredge nodded. "Any guess who might've taken the files? And why?"

I remembered what Brubaker, the FBI profiler, had said two days before: "Somebody who thinks I ruined his life."

CHAPTER 37

Tyler

TYLER LEANED BACK IN the rusting metal chair, his head pressing the chain-link fence, the mesh grating slightly as it bowed outward from the pressure. Overhead, low clouds scudded across a gray sky, and Tyler felt coldness seeping into his core—coldness that included, but was not limited to, the chill in the air.

There was a strange stillness and quietude in the cage; an absence so intense, it was almost a *presence*. Looking down at the increasingly skeletal corpse on the wire cot, he realized what it was: The maggots—most of them—were gone. A wide trail, brown and greasy, led from the concrete pad into the woods and across the ground before disappearing amid and beneath the fallen leaves. *The Exodus,* he thought in a flight of bizarre, blasphemous fancy. *Some Moses maggot has led them to the Promised Land to pupate. "Follow me, and you shall be transformed. You shall be winged, like the angels, and take to the heavens . . ."* Even more bizarre than his blasphemous fantasy was the bleak realization that he would miss the maggots.

Tyler turned to the back of his lab notebook—most of its pages now crammed with figures documenting time, temperature, humidity, barometric pressure, maggot length, and the myriad of other minutiae he'd immersed himself in for weeks now—and began to write. He filled this page not with data, but with desolation.

October 27, 1992

Dear Roxanne,

A helicopter thuds overhead—LifeStar is airlifting someone to the emergency room at UT hospital—and the downdraft sends the tarp flapping off the roof of the enclosure, raining a shower of leaves down onto me and my constant, closest companion: not you, but Corpse 06–92.

I spend my days in a cage in the woods, watching the inexorable decay of a man who once lived and breathed and likely dreamed and loved. As I chart his decline, as I chart the rise of the insect multitudes into which he's being transubstantiated, I wonder if I'm becoming that man—if I'm being transformed into something other than what I once was; something less than what I want to be; something corrupt and malodorous. "You; him," the flies that swarm my face seem to say, "in the end, you both belong to us, and already there's very little difference."

Forgive me for dragging you into the sickening scene I witnessed. It haunted me—haunts me still—but I should have been more considerate; should not have spread that contagion to you. I've reimagined that scene every day since I saw it; it grieves me to think that perhaps you have, too. Was I naïve to hope that I could walk through the valleys and alleys of the shadow of death—even wrapped in the armor of truth and justice—and then simply walk blithely out again, scot-free, without something nasty sticking to the sole of my shoe; sticking to the shoe of my soul?

Now that the tarp is off the top of the cube, I can look up, through the chain-link, and see the sky for the first time in days. The airspace above the cage is crisscrossed with birds, stirred up by the passing helicopter, I suppose, and something about their flight strikes me for the first time. Birds on the wing rise and fall, rise and fall, a hundred times or more a minute. Not the loafing coasters, of course—not the lazy buzzards gliding overhead, sizing me up with appraising eyes—but the ordinary, diligent little fliers. In our mind's eye, smoothing algorithms are overlaid, flattening the birds' trajectories, minimizing their myriad midair miracles. We see their flights as perfect forward motion, but nothing could be further from the truth. In truth, every flap is followed by a tuck and a sweep, hasty and high stakes; hot on the heels of every flickering gain in altitude comes a small, heart-thudding drop.

So go their brave and lovely lives aloft:
They—like us—rise and fall and rise again.
Continually risking. Continually failing.
Continually triumphing.

Or so I still hope, here within my cage.

I miss you, sweet Roxie, and I miss the man—I miss the "me"—I get to be when I'm with you.

Please let me see you at Thanksgiving. Please give me a reason to give thanks.

Please.

Please.

Please.

Tyler

THAT EVENING, AFTER scrubbing bones from the steam kettle, then scrubbing his skin until it was raw, Tyler put on exercise clothes and slipped into the back row of a yoga class—a room filled with bodies more limber than his, minds less troubled than his. During Tree Pose, he looked at the woman directly ahead of him and shuddered: For a moment, as she clasped one foot and folded her leg, Tyler thought her leg had been severed at the knee; thought the droplets falling from the knee were blood, not sweat.

At the end of the class, he lay on his back—Corpse Pose—and felt droplets falling from his face: not sweat, but tears. Then pressure on his fingers—the woman beside him had reached out, taken his hand, offered a comforting squeeze.

He could not return the squeeze. Corpses cannot return kindness.

At the end of class, he rolled onto his side: Rebirth Pose. By the time he opened his eyes, the room was empty and he was alone.

CHAPTER 38

Kathleen

SHE GAVE THE OFFICE door an exploratory nudge, then—when it moved—she hipped it open with a practiced bump. She was mildly annoyed that the latch still hadn't been fixed, but at the same time, she was grateful that she didn't need to set down her briefcase or coffee to open it.

Kathleen wanted to believe that Bill was being coy at breakfast: that he hadn't mentioned their anniversary because he was planning to surprise her with a romantic dinner at Regas or, better yet, the Orangery—closer to home and much more elegant, though twice as expensive. Despite her hopes, though, she suspected that he'd simply forgotten the date. It wasn't that Bill was a thoughtless husband—not compared with most of her colleagues' husbands, at any rate, not if their reports were accurate. But lately he'd been busy, preoccupied, and tense.

She felt a commingled rush of surprise, delight, and guilt, therefore, when she saw the vase of roses and the gift-wrapped box on her desk. Sweet man—

he *hadn't* forgotten. She plunked down her briefcase and picked up the phone to call him. While she waited for Bill's secretary to transfer the call—the girl was new, and not terribly efficient yet—Kathleen shouldered the phone to her ear and plucked the box from the desktop. It was small—the size of a pack of cigarettes—and she gave it a shake, listening for the telltale rattle of earrings or a necklace. She untied the gold foil ribbon, then used a fingernail to slit the tape on one of the end-flaps of blue wrapping paper.

"Hello there," Bill said breezily when he came on the line. "To what do I owe the pleasure? Did you just hear from the tenure committee, or did Jeff just get expelled?"

"You *sneak*," she said. She tilted the package, and the box slid slowly from its tight paper cocoon. "You fooled me completely. I was sure you'd forgotten." Still clutching the paper, she lifted the box by its lid, allowing the lower half to drop into the upturned palm of her left hand. The box's contents were cushioned and concealed by a puffy rectangle of cotton batting.

"Forgotten what?" he asked as she laid down the lid and paper and plucked out the batting to unveil the gift.

Kathleen's scream rose, the handset falling from her shoulder and clattering to the floor.

Inside the jewelry box, resting on another bed of white batting, were two objects. One was an antique pocketknife—Bill's pocketknife, the one he'd inherited from his father. The other object was a slender human finger, its severed base black with crusted blood, its nail bright with scarlet polish.

CHAPTER 39

Brockton

KATHLEEN'S SHAKING HAD FINALLY stopped, but mine was just starting. The difference was, my wife had been shaking with fear; I was shaking with fury. I stared at Kittredge. "What do you mean," I snapped, "you'll 'put in the request'? That's not nearly good enough, Detective." Kittredge opened his mouth to speak, but I cut him off angrily. "A killer—a sadistic serial killer—has just delivered a human finger to *my wife*, and the best you've got to offer is 'I'll put in the *request*'?" Kittredge and I were huddled in the hallway outside Kathleen's office, and we weren't alone; uniformed officers guarded each end of the hallway, and they could probably hear every angry word I spoke, but I was too distraught for diplomacy. "You should be saying to me, 'We will guard her night and day until we catch this guy.' What the hell would he have to do to get that kind of response, instead of 'I'll put in the *request*'?"

"I know you're upset, Dr. Brockton," Kittredge began.

"You better *believe* I'm upset," I interrupted. "This is my wife he's threatening now. You've seen what this guy can do. You've seen what he's already done."

He nodded. "I know. I *know.* Look, if I were in charge of patrol, I'd give the order in a heartbeat. But I'm *not* in charge of patrol, so I have to run the request up the chain of command. Please understand that. I feel sure everybody up the line will agree it's important. But that's the protocol I've got to follow." I wanted to break something, possibly Detective Kittredge's neck. "Look, let me call it in right now. You and your wife can stay here while we wait to hear back. There's a dozen KPD and UT cops here now. Hell, that's as much protection as the president gets."

WHILE WE WAITED, Kittredge interviewed Kathleen in a vacant Nutrition Science classroom. I paced the hall outside, but not for long. After two laps of the hall, I knocked on the door, then entered the room. "Sorry to interrupt," I said to Kittredge. "Any idea how long this'll take?" I saw surprise and annoyance in the detective's eyes.

"Probably not more than half an hour," he said in a level voice, "but I want to make sure we don't miss anything—some little something that might give us a lead. I'm sure you can appreciate the need to be thorough."

"I'm not rushing you," I said. "Just checking. I need to dash back to Anthropology for a few minutes. I just wanted to make sure I'd have time." He nodded. "I'd like to see you again before you leave,"

I added. "I'd like an update on what the plan is." He nodded again—curtly this time—as I turned to go.

I jogged back to the stadium and scurried down the outside stairs, between the crisscrossed steel girders, then entered the basement and unlocked the door of the bone lab. The lab was empty—empty of the quick, that is, though full of the dead. The newest arrival was the freshly scrubbed skeleton of the woman whose photograph—arriving in the mail shortly after her death—had been a message that I had failed to grasp. A message from a killer who seemed to be lurking just around the corner of my subconsciousness, and drawing closer all the time.

There was something else significant about this woman, something lurking around another corner of my mind, just out of conscious reach—some other sign or message. I knew it was there, but I couldn't quite put my finger on it. I'd realized this while pacing the hall as Kathleen and Kittredge had talked. Whatever the message was, it was not printed on photographic paper; this one was written on the woman's bones. It had to be.

The bones were laid out in anatomical order on the long table beneath the windows—Tyler had brought them up from the Annex early in the morning, before heading across the river for another day of bug watching—and as I crossed the lab, I noticed that the angled slats of the Venetian blinds cast lengthwise shadows on the bones, creating the illusion that the dead woman was behind bars. *Sentenced to death without parole*, I thought grimly.

The emptiness at the distal ends of the lower

legs was striking—even more striking now than when I'd seen her lying on the ground, legs splayed around the sapling. The absence there was almost palpable, in the same way that a sudden, unexpected silence seems loud. But it wasn't the missing feet, or even the cut marks at the ends of the legs, that had brought me hurrying back. What had brought me hurrying back was the neck; specifically, the hyoid, the thin, U-shaped bone from the throat.

By the time we'd found the body in the woods, the soft tissues of the neck had already decomposed extensively—far more than other regions, except for the ankles, where the feet had been severed. The differential decomposition told me that there'd been trauma to her neck. Unlike the thirteenth-century Chinese villager killed by a sickle, this woman had not had her throat cut; I knew that from the photograph I'd gotten in the mail, which showed no sharp trauma to the neck. That meant her neck had sustained a more subtle injury, yet one serious enough to scrape or bruise the skin there—and therefore to make it especially attractive to blowflies. The day we'd recovered the remains from Cahaba Lane, I'd told Tyler to look closely at the hyoid when he cleaned the material. "I bet you anything that bone is fractured," I'd said. "I bet she was strangled."

I'd been right about the fracture; I'd confirmed it a few hours before, when I'd taken my first look at the processed skeleton. But I'd barely begun my examination—in fact, I had just picked up the hyoid and taken a cursory glance at it—when Peggy had transferred Kathleen's call to me. Seconds later, I'd dashed out of the lab, the dead woman forgotten in my urgency. But as I'd paced the hall outside the conference room where Kittredge was interviewing Kathleen, my mind had strayed back to the bone lab. Back to the dead woman. Back to the fragile, broken bone from her throat.

In life, the hyoid—a support for the muscles and ligaments of the tongue and larynx—had helped give this woman a voice, had helped her speak. Now, in death, I prayed that the hyoid could tell me not only how she'd died, but also who had killed her.

THE HYOID WAS gone.

I stared at the skeleton—at the cervical spine, where the bone should have been; where the bone *had* been, only a few hours before. It was gone.

I felt myself break into a sweat. Had he been here—the killer? Had he forced the bone lab's lock, recognized the mutilated skeleton somehow, and made off with the hyoid—the evidence that he'd strangled her? The scenario seemed far-fetched, but what other explanation could there be? I picked up the phone from the desk and dialed the departmental office two flights above me. "Peggy," I said without preamble, "do you know if Tyler's been back to the bone lab since this morning?"

"Tyler? Not that I've seen. Why? Do you need me to track him down?"

"I do," I said. "I need to know if he came back and took the hyoid from this skeleton."

"What's the hyoid?"

"A bone from the neck. Thin. Arched. Shaped like a short, wide version of the letter U."

"You mean that little bone you had in your hand when your wife called?"

"Exactly," I said. "That bone's gone missing, and I've got to find it. It's . . ." I paused, suddenly confused and spooked. "How did you know I had it in my hand when she called?"

"Right after I transferred the call, I saw you go tearing up the steps. You had something in your hand. Check your pockets."

"What?"

"Check your pockets," she repeated. "I bet you put it in one of them."

"That's absurd," I said, reaching my right hand to my shirt pocket, then—more to myself than to Peggy—"I'll be damned." I'd had it with me all along.

"You're welcome," I heard her saying as I hung up the phone.

Plucking the bone gingerly from my pocket, I took it to one of the magnifying lamps and switched on the light. The fluorescent ring flickered on, and I held the bone beneath the lens, my hand looming, large and momentous, through the glass.

The thicker, central body of the bone—its ends defined by a pair of toothlike processes, the "lesser horns"—was intact. The damage was confined to the junction where the body met the thinner, more fragile ends of the arch—the "greater horns," the ends were called. But only one of them was damaged: the left one, folded inward, almost at a 90-degree angle to its normal position, the ligamentous joint splintered. My right hand trembling slightly, I walked back to the skeleton and held the bone in position above the neck. Then, with my left hand, I reached down and closed my fingers partway, encircling the neck without quite touching it. If I had tightened my grip, my left thumb would have pressed on the greater horn, folding it inward, creating exactly this fracture.

A wave of dread and panic crashed over me. I'd seen a woman's hyoid broken exactly this way once before: three years earlier, in 1989. That woman had died in California, and this one had died in Knoxville. But though two thousand miles separated them, I felt sure the two women had died by the same hand.

The words of Brubaker, the FBI profiler, came shrieking into my mind. At the time he'd spoken them, I'd shrugged them off; now, they cut me to the bone. "You're the key," Brubaker had said. "It's personal between you and him."

THIS TIME, I didn't even pause to knock when I burst into the classroom where Kittredge and Kathleen were talking. They looked startled by my entrance; they looked stunned by my announcement: "I know who," I said. "And I know why."

KITTREDGE WAS RUBBING his chin. He'd been rubbing it for the past five minutes—ever since I'd burst into the room—and the skin was starting to look red and raw. "And you're saying you know this guy—Satterfield, you say?" I nodded. "Knew him before these bodies started turning up."

"Didn't actually know him," I clarified. "Knew *of* him. He was a suspect in a woman's murder out near San Diego three years ago—a woman who was a stripper and a prostitute. He was in the Navy, and a naval investigator asked me to consult on the case."

"Why was that?"

"The investigator—with the NIS, the Naval Intelligence Service—had been a student of mine in Kansas in the mid-eighties. He worked a couple summers with me, digging up Indian bones. He knew I'd seen a lot of skeletal trauma there, and knew I'd starting working forensic cases, so he arranged to have the woman's bones sent to me."

"And what did you find?"

"I found that she'd been strangled," I told him. "With just one hand."

He looked puzzled. "How could you tell that?"

"The medical examiner hadn't been able to determine the cause of death," I said. "No obvious trauma, to the soft tissue or the bones. But male killers often strangle women, so I took a closer look at the hyoid—put it under a scanning electron microscope—and I found microfractures in the left side of the arch." He still looked puzzled. "May I demonstrate? Do you mind if I put my hand on your throat?" I'd considered asking Kathleen, but she was already spooked, and the last thing I wanted to do was add to her fear.

He shrugged. "Sure, go ahead. If I start turning blue, do let go."

"Deal." I reached out and gripped his neck with my left hand. "See how my fingers reach around behind your neck, but my thumb's closer to the front, on the left side?"

"Uh-huh." His response sounded slightly strained.

"So now, if I squeeze"—I tightened my grip—"it puts more pressure on the left side of the windpipe, and on the left side of the hyoid bone." I moved my thumb up and down slightly, sliding it repeatedly across the thin arch of bone. "The California woman was young—early twenties—so the hyoid hadn't fully ossified. It wasn't brittle enough to snap, which is why the medical examiner didn't notice the damage. But the killer squeezed hard enough to suffocate her; hard enough to bend the bone and tear the ligament." I gave my thumb a final twitch, then let go. "The investigator had a list of seven sailors who'd been with the woman around the time she went missing," I went on. "I told him to rule out right-handed suspects. 'The killer's left-handed,' I said. That left only one suspect. This guy Satterfield."

Kittredge cleared his throat several times before speaking. "Okay," he rasped, then cleared his throat again. "Got it."

Kathleen spoke up. "Detective, are you all right? You look a little flushed."

"Yes ma'am, I'm fine," he croaked. "But just for the record? I'm glad your husband wasn't teaching me about stab wounds." He looked back to me. "So this guy Satterfield—he was court-martialed? But not convicted?"

"Wasn't even court-martialed," I said. "The investigator was sure he'd done it. He was left-handed; he'd been seen with the stripper, about a week before her body was found. And Satterfield was kind of a head case. A couple of the guys in SEAL training with him said he was really edgy—'a ticking time bomb,' one of 'em said."

"Wait, wait," Kittredge said. "This guy's a Navy *SEAL*?"

"Not quite, but almost," I said. "He'd gotten into the training program, but when the NIS flagged him as a murder suspect—a week or two in—the SEALs dropped him like a hot potato. He went back to his regular unit—the Special Boat Unit, it's called. Those guys get a lot of the same training the SEALs get. Explosives, martial arts, survival, all that macho stuff."

"*Shit*," said Kittredge. "Sorry, Mrs. Brockton. But why the hell wasn't he charged?"

"Not enough evidence," I said. "He'd been seen with the woman the night after he got tapped for SEAL training—celebrating, I guess. But like I said, her body wasn't found until a week or so after that. I . . . " My voice trailed off.

"You what?"

"The prosecutor asked me if I could prove that she died the night Satterfield was seen with her. I told him I couldn't. All I could say was that I believed she'd been dead for three days or more. 'I can't get a conviction based on that,' he said." I shook my head. "I've felt bad about that case for three years now."

"And so Satterfield just walked?"

"Not entirely. I was told the Navy discharged him."

"Honorably?"

"No. I forget the term. Administratively? With some note about 'less than honorably,' I think. Apparently you lose your benefits, and there's a big black mark on your record forever."

Kittredge had resumed rubbing his chin. "And he knew you were involved in the case?"

"I don't know," I said, but as I said it, I knew it was wrong. "He must have. He had a lawyer, and I guess he was entitled to know the evidence against him."

"So he could have found out that you focused the investigation on him. That you made him the prime suspect. That you played a big part in getting him booted out of SEAL training, and then booted out of the Navy. With an indelible stain on his record."

I nodded, feeling sick. The detective added a grimace to the chin rubbing. "Shit," he repeated, this time with no apology for the language. He shook his head. "Okay, I promise you, we'll get more protection for you and your family. You got a gun?"

I shook my head. "Never needed one. Any time I'm working a death scene, I'm surrounded by cops. Besides, I'm usually on my hands and knees with my butt in the air. Makes it kinda tough to get the drop on an assassin."

He looked from me to Kathleen and back again. "Might be a good time to get a gun," he said. Then, as if the thought had just struck him. "And you say the bone—the hyloid—"

"Hyoid," I corrected.

"You're saying the hyoid from that Cahaba Lane body is what made you think of this guy?" I nodded. He looked puzzled. "I don't get it," he said. "Why didn't the sketch make you think of him? Don't you know what this Satterfield guy looks like?"

"What sketch?" Now I was the puzzled one.

"The sketch the Earhart girl did for us."

I felt a rush of . . . what? Confusion? Embarrassment? Anger at being left out of the loop? "Why didn't you tell me you had a sketch?"

"Jesus, Doc, I've been a little busy, you know? Trying to find witnesses. And I didn't figure you were likely to *be* one, since he seemed to spend his time with the hookers on Magnolia Avenue." He narrowed his eyebrows at me. "Didn't you see the sketch in the paper?"

I stared at him, dumbfounded. "When?"

"This morning. Page one."

"We didn't get a paper this morning," I said, glancing at Kathleen. She shook her head—she hadn't seen it either.

Kittredge reached beneath the pages of the yellow pad on which he'd been taking notes and pulled out a folded piece of newsprint—the front page of the *News Sentinel*.

I felt the ground open beneath my feet when I saw the face in the sketch. I felt the darkness engulf me totally when I heard Kathleen gasp, saw the horror of recognition on her face, and felt her body begin to quake once more.

CHAPTER 40

Satterfield

***SOON,* THOUGHT SATTERFIELD, GRIPPING** the tan, waxy cylinder of dynamite with his right hand as he bore down with his left, sliding the serrated blade back and forth with neat, measured strokes across the middle of the eight-inch stick. *They'll be coming soon. Maybe not today, maybe not even tomorrow. But soon.*

The *News Sentinel* lay faceup on the kitchen table beside the cutting board, and Satterfield's face—only a sketch, but a good likeness, no question about it—stared up at him from the front page. Above it, a headline in inch-high type shrieked, "KPD SEEKS SERIAL-KILLER SUSPECT."

The one that got away: She'd gone to the cops, all right, and now the net was closing. He'd cursed himself a hundred times for the carelessness and stupidity that had allowed the girl to get away. In addition to the cigarette burn in his palm, he now had a dozen more, on various parts of his body. But when he'd unrolled the newspaper and seen himself—seen that the final clockwork had been set in motion—he'd felt something shift inside himself, and he'd thrown away the cigarettes. Burning himself was a trivial and self-indulgent gesture; it was a waste of time, and he had no time to waste.

He eased up on the blade as the sharp tips of the serrations began grazing the cutting board, etching a razor-thin line across the grain of the maple. A few more feather-light strokes—one, two, three—and the dynamite parted. A few shreds of the waxy wrapping clung to the blade, and Satterfield wiped the knife on his leg to brush them off, careful not to snag the denim.

He laid the knife aside and picked up one of the pieces of dynamite, holding it up to the light to inspect the cross-section. The cut was clean, the small zigzags from the blade's serrations etched neatly in the soft, glistening explosive, which had the consistency and the sheen of sausage. Holding the half stick to his eye, he sighted along it, as if it were the barrel of a weapon; as if he were taking aim at someone or something—something very near in space or time. Then, reaching across the table with his left, he picked up a slender silver cylinder—an electric blasting cap, the size and shape of a firecracker, with a pair of thin, insulated wires projecting from one end. Centering the blunt, wireless end of the cap on the freshly cut face of the dynamite, he pressed, twisting slightly. As the cap penetrated, Satterfield felt a thrill, as he always did when handling dynamite. The very name—coined by Alfred Nobel himself, from the Greek word "*dynamis*"—meant "power." Nobel was a man who understood power—

destructive power—and devoted decades to mastering it. Satterfield considered him a role model: a man who'd triumphed through intelligence, vision, and sheer will.

Satterfield pushed back from the kitchen table and stood, then walked into the den and settled into the leather recliner in the center of the room, facing the television. A slight movement caught his eye; in the wire-mesh terrarium, the broad, triangular head of the snake had swiveled in his direction, and the black ribbon of tongue was testing the air, tasting his presence in the room. As the snake's unblinking, ancient eyes watched, Satterfield lifted the half stick of dynamite and stared at it, then opened his jaws and took it in, wrapping his lips around it as it slid across his tongue and deep into his mouth. When he felt it against the back of his throat, he closed his eyes and lifted his other hand to his face. Clasped them both across his mouth, he imagined the force that would be unleashed when the current raced from the 9-volt battery into the blasting cap, the cap's small explosion setting off the dynamite's large one.

This wasn't how he'd planned or wanted it to end: forced into a corner, his back to the wall. Still, he had to admit, there was relief in knowing that it would be over soon. And there was power in ending things on his own terms; on terms that were—to borrow Nobel's word—dynamic.

CHAPTER 41

Decker

"LIEUTENANT! WE'VE GOT A vehicle passing our position, headed toward the house." The voice, from a spotter positioned at the mouth of the dead-end road, was an urgent whisper in his earpiece, and Lt. Brian Decker, commander of KPD's SWAT team, snapped to alertness.

"Vehicle's approaching the suspect's residence," added a second voice a half-minute later. Even through the tiny, tinny speaker, there was no mistaking the tension in the whisper from McElroy, the spotter watching the front of the Satterfield house. "Turning into the driveway."

Decker held up a hand, and the air around him grew electric, the slack boredom on the men's faces replaced by nervousness and excitement. Like all the men in the SWAT unit, Decker detested waiting—not just because he preferred action, but because waiting dulled a man's edge, and a dull edge was more dangerous than a sharp one. Decker's men—two teams, a primary and an emergency, plus a couple of snipers with scoped rifles—had slipped into their positions at 11:00 A.M., expecting to serve the high-risk warrant and take the suspect into custody by noon; one, at the latest. The five-man Primary Team, which would execute the takedown plan once the warrant was signed, lay concealed in the woods just across the road from the residence. Decker and the four others on the Emergency Reactionary Team had crept into closer positions, in the bushes at the east end of the house, so they could storm the front door if the situation suddenly went to shit for some reason.

But things wouldn't go to shit. Decker felt confident about the takedown plan. A quarter-mile up the road, a truck—a bucket truck labeled KNOXVILLE UTILITIES BOARD, with big KUB logos on the doors—was parked at the mouth of a dirt side road, beneath a power line and transformer, awaiting the green light from Decker. On his signal, the two men in the truck, wearing KUB coveralls, would pull up to the house in the bucket truck and fire up the chain saws, then start hacking branches off the best-looking tree near the power line. If Decker's own behavior as a property owner was typical—and he felt pretty sure it was—the suspect would come racing out the door, mad as a hornet, by the time the first limb hit the ground. The Primary Team would swarm out of the woods and take him down before he had any inkling what was happening.

The plan was rock solid; bureaucracy was the problem. Noon had come and gone without the warrant, and so had another two hours, as Decker's spotters had kept watch on a curtain-shrouded house on a dead-end street, where nothing moved except falling leaves, plunking acorns, and a few squirrels. The one consolation was that they had music to pass the time: 1970s rock-and-roll wafted faintly from inside the house—Pink Floyd's *Dark Side of the Moon* first, followed by Led Zeppelin. Even so, as the autumn leaves had corkscrewed down, Decker's boredom had spiraled upward. So had his stress, the two contradictory moods rising side by side, like a pair of vultures carried aloft on powerful, parallel updrafts.

The arrival of a vehicle, therefore, was welcome news. It meant that finally something was happening, even if it was just some lost driver turning around at the end of the cul-de-sac.

"Talk to me, Mac." Decker radioed the spotter, wishing his view wasn't blocked by the corner of the house. "What kind of vehicle?"

"A piece-of-shit Ford Escort," McElroy answered. "Held together by pink Bondo and gray primer and Domino's Pizza signs."

"He's ordered a *pizza*?" Decker rolled his eyes in disgust. He saw his afternoon and evening—his whole *life*—stretching before him, a vast, unbroken plain of boredom and inactivity. Then he had an inspiration, and switching frequencies, he radioed Captain Hackworth, the watch commander, with a question to which he already knew the answer. "Hey, Cap, has that warrant come through yet?"

"Not yet, Deck." Hackworth sounded as frustrated as Decker felt. "I told you, you'll hear the minute I hear."

"Question, Cap. We've got a pizza delivery

going down right now. Can we go in? Call it 'exigent circumstances'?" It was a legal loophole, an end run around the requirement for a warrant.

There was a pause before Hackworth answered. "Who's delivering it?"

Decker was puzzled by the question. "Uh, Domino's," he said. "What the hell's that got to do with it?"

"Not the *brand*, Deck; the *person*. Man or woman?"

"Oh, sorry. Dunno. Let me find out." Switching to the team's frequency, Decker called McElroy. "Hey, Mac. The pizza guy—male guy or female guy?"

"Can't tell yet," the spotter replied. "Still in the car. Bad glare and dirty windows."

Decker switched back to Hackworth. "Don't know yet, Cap."

"If it's a woman," said Hackworth, "and she goes inside, she *might* be in imminent danger. That would let you go without the warrant. Risky, though—might turn into a hostage situation. Or worse."

"Got it." He switched back to McElroy just as he heard the faint thud of a car door slamming.

"Lieutenant?"

"Go ahead, Mac."

"The pizza guy? Definitely a guy. Or a chick with one hell of a beard."

"Got it," said Decker, feeling both relieved and disappointed at the knowledge that they'd have to sit tight until the warrant came through.

"He's ringing the doorbell now," McElroy narrated. "Front door's opening." Led Zeppelin's volume ratcheted up a notch. "I see the suspect. Talking to pizza guy. Pizza guy's going inside. Door's closing." The music softened and blurred again.

"Can you hear anything?"

"Nah. The music's drowning 'em out."

Decker cursed their lack of gear. If they had parabolic microphones, McElroy would be able to pick up every word that was spoken, even from across the road. "Okay, keep watching, Mac. Tell me everything you see."

"Roger that."

Two faint songs later—"The Battle of Evermore" and "Stairway to Heaven"—Decker radioed Hackworth again. "Cap? Deck here."

"Go ahead, Deck. What's happening?"

"That's the thing, Cap—nothing's happening. Pizza guy's been in there a long damn time." Decker checked his watch. "Eight minutes. Shouldn't take but two, three minutes to pay for a pizza, right? Five, tops."

"Maybe. Maybe not," Hackworth said. "What if our guy couldn't find his wallet? What if he's writing a check, and the Domino's dude has to get a license number? What if they're just feeling chatty?"

"What if this creep swings both ways?" countered Decker. "What if he's killing the pizza guy right now?"

"I never heard of a sex killer who went after women *and* men," said Hackworth. "They like one or the other. Women, nine times out of ten. Anyhow, we got nothing on the suspect that suggests the pizza guy's at risk."

It wasn't what Decker had wanted to hear, but it was what he'd expected to hear. He was pretty sure, even before he radioed, what Hackworth would say. He was also pretty sure, despite his chafing impatience, that the watch commander was right. A moment later, McElroy's whisper proved it. "Lieutenant? Pizza guy's coming out." A minute later, the Bondo-patched, primer-splotched car was gone.

AT THREE, DECKER radioed Hackworth again. "Before you ask," the captain said, "the answer's *no*—we still don't have the warrant. How much longer is the chain saw plan workable?"

"Not much. Thirty minutes, tops. There's only an hour of daylight left. Besides, when's the last time you saw a tree-trimming crew start work at four? That's quittin' time, boss."

"Don't give up on it," said Hackworth. "We'll get that warrant yet. Maybe you can take him down first thing in the morning. Wake him up with a chain-saw serenade—that might knock him off balance even more."

"If we have to stay out here all night, Cap, tree branches might not be the only limbs we go after with the chain saw."

"Ha. Steady on, Deck. You'll know the second we've got the warrant. Stay sharp. And stay safe."

WHEN FOUR O'CLOCK came and went without the warrant, Decker sighed and shelved the tree-trimming plan, then gave the order to break out the night-vision gear—one rifle-mounted scope for each team leader and each sniper, plus one for McElroy.

The scopes were big and heavy—1960s technology, military surplus leftovers from Vietnam—and the image they gave was grainy as hell. Still, grainy night vision was better than no night vision, when lives were on the line. Decker was constantly lobbying for newer, better gear, and constantly being shot down, but he owed it to his guys to try.

Things had remained quiet at the house; the rock music had stopped once the Led Zeppelin album ended, and a light had come on in a room at the back of the house, according to the rear spotter, Cody. Judging by the light's random flickering—and the audio Cody could hear smatterings of—the suspect was watching the local news.

Decker's two best options, as he saw it, were to storm the house sometime after Satterfield went to bed, or to sit tight till morning and send in the tree trimmers then. He hated the thought of waiting another fourteen hours, but he also hated the thought of sending a team into a pitch-black house to capture an ex-soldier, even with night-vision gear. Better to wait it out, much as he despised waiting.

He was just about to radio this assessment to Hackworth when his earpiece erupted. "Lieutenant! It's Cody! I hear a woman in the back of the house—in the den or whatever that room with the big window is. She's screaming her head off!"

"I'm hearing it, too, Lieutenant," said McElroy. "She's screaming bloody murder." Even Decker could hear it: a series of shrieks that made his stomach lurch—shrieks that combined fear and pain like he'd never heard.

Decker snapped his fingers to get the attention of the emergency team. "Guys, let's *go*!" he said. "Front door. Go go *go*." He turned and pointed to one of the men. "E.J.," he said. "You haul ass around back. When you hear us hit the front door, you put a flashbang through that big rear window." He headed around the front corner of the house at a crouch, three of the men following close on his heels, as E.J. peeled off toward the back of the house.

Decker took the four front steps in two strides. "Fireplug, you ready?"

"Ready," came the answer from one step behind him. Fireplug was a squat, burly former Marine; he carried the team's forty-pound battering ram as easily as Decker could have carried a baseball bat.

"In five," Decker counted, "four, three, two, *one*!" Fireplug had begun his windup on "three," rotating his torso away from the door, swinging the battering ram like a pendulum. Then, as the arc reversed, he spun toward the door, his entire body—two hundred pounds of muscle and sinew—pivoting into the swing. The broad, flat head of the ram slammed into the knob, punching it through the wooden door and across the room to the opposite wall. The door crashed open and Decker scurried through, moving in a half crouch, the H&K submachine gun sweeping the room in tight arcs that tracked the direction of his gaze. He'd have felt safer with the short-barrel shotgun, but in a potential hostage situation, the shotgun's swath of devastation was too broad and indiscriminate.

When Decker was two steps in, the foyer lit up as

brightly as if a camera flash had just fired in the next room, and the house shuddered from the concussion of the flashbang—the stun grenade—that E.J. had thrown through the rear window, right on cue.

Without even having to think, Decker began mentally ticking off the seconds: *one Mississippi, two Mississippi . . .* If the suspect had been within ten feet of the stun grenade, the flash and the concussion would have blinded and stunned him, and Decker would have five seconds or so to find him and overpower him.

Three Mississippi. Decker risked a quick look through the doorway where the flashbang had gone off, then withdrew his head swiftly, so he wouldn't be exposed during the split second it took his brain to process the images his eyes had captured.

Four Mississippi. He'd glimpsed a wall-sized entertainment center filling one wall, the big TV shattered by the flashbang. Shredded curtains dangling beside the missing window. *Five Mississippi.* A human figure—a man!— sitting in a recliner in the center of the room. At *six Mississippi*, Decker made his move. "Police! Don't move!" he shouted, pivoting into the doorway, the H&K up and trained on the seated figure.

Seven Mississippi: The fist of God slammed into Decker, knocking him back, hurling him across the foyer, slamming him against the front wall. Stunned but still running on reflex, he reset his mental stopwatch: *One Mississippi, two Mississippi . . .* The cadence seemed slow and irregular, he noticed with an odd, detached objectivity, as if he were somehow outside himself as well as inside. Gradually he became aware of a second voice in his head—this one his as well—shrieking, *What the hell? Why did E.J. use two flashbangs instead of one?* Then: *Shit. That wasn't a flashbang. That wasn't us. That was him.* He shook his head to clear the cobwebs, struggling to piece the fragments into a picture that would explain why he was lying here in a heap against the wall. Either the flashbang hadn't fully incapacitated the guy—had it landed behind him? Did the recliner shield him? Or Decker had screwed it up—counting too slow, moving too slow, giving the guy time to recover? Time to recover and do *what*, though? Had he fired a weapon? Was Decker shot—thrown across the room by a bullet or a shotgun blast slamming into his vest? *No, not a shot*, he realized. *A blast. An explosion. But what—a grenade? Not the flashbang, but a real one, a frag?* "Fall back, fall back," Decker shouted. "Take cover."

He took inventory: *I'm alive. I can see.* He wiggled fingers. Toes. Everything seemed to be there, unless he was already feeling phantom pain in missing limbs. He glanced down, saw arms and legs where they belonged, still attached. A chunk of splintered wood, three inches long and a quarter-inch thick, jutted from his right deltoid. Decker reached across with his left arm—not easy to do, as bulky and confining as the flak jacket was—and gave an exploratory tug. A flash of pain seared his shoulder, but the wood slid out, wet and shiny with blood.

Decker heard more words, muffled and faint, and he realized these were coming from outside his own head, not inside. "Lieutenant! Lieutenant!" It was Fireplug, crouching against the foyer's inside wall.

"Hang on—I'm coming to get you." Decker held up a hand to stop him, but Fireplug was already scuttling across the room, and Decker felt strong hands gripping the shoulder straps of his vest, then felt himself being dragged backward, back toward the front door. "Holy *fuck*," Decker heard Fireplug say. Just before the wall blocked his view, Decker managed to turn his head and catch a quick glimpse through the doorway and into the room beyond.

"Holy *fuck*," Decker echoed.

The man was still seated in the recliner, arms dangling. The man no longer had hands. The man no longer had a head.

The woman was screaming—again, or still? Decker didn't know which. Her shrieks filled the air, piercing the smoke that clouded the rooms, piercing the haze that clouded Decker's brain.

DECKER WINCED AS he eased his butt onto the low wall at the end of the garage, leaning back gingerly against the suspect's house. Inside, the bloodcurdling shrieks continued—emanating, E.J. had reported, from a pair of stereo speakers. *A goddamn recording*, Decker had realized the moment E.J. had relayed this information. *A trick. A trap. A lure.* And Decker had gobbled down the bait, the hook, the line, and the sinker. In the distance, as if answering the screams, two sirens—no, three—wailed louder as they approached.

Decker took inventory of his aches. Ringing ears. A couple sore ribs, cracked or possibly broken; maybe a mild concussion, too. And an oozing puncture wound in his right deltoid, where the sliver of splintered wood had burrowed into him. One of the sirens was probably an ambulance, but Decker was damned if he'd leave the scene except under his own steam, with his own team. The bomb squad was on the way, too, or would be soon, but they moved slow; Kevin's team had even more crap to carry than the SWAT team did.

God, he thought suddenly, almost sick with fear. *Kev. Please not Kev. Please let Kev be off today.*

THE BOMB SQUAD'S truck lumbered into the driveway. Decker stood, and the instant he saw the driver's face—his brother Kev's face—he knew that his prayer had been ignored.

The truck lurched to a stop and Kevin Decker—"Boomer," to his bomb-squad colleagues, "Kev" to his big brother Brian—leaped out and ran to him. "Jesus, Bry, you okay?" Before Decker could answer, Boomer wrapped him in a hug. Decker grunted from the pain in his ribs, and Boomer released him. "Shit, you're hurt?"

"It's nothing. Bruised ribs. But my head hurts like a sonofabitch."

Kev sniffed Deck's face and hair. "Bang head, I bet," he said.

"I don't remember whacking it on anything."

"Not a banged head," said Kev. "*Bang head.* I get it all the time."

"What the hell's bang head?"

"A nitroglycerin headache," Boomer explained. "Means the device was dynamite. Nitroglycerin—the explosive in dynamite?—makes blood vessels dilate. You can get a headache just from handling the stuff, absorbing it through the skin. The fumes are the worst, though—they go up your nose, into the capillaries, and straight to your brain." He frowned at the house. "Guess that means I've got a vise-clamp headache with my name on it waiting for me in there, too, huh?" He looked back at Decker. "God, I'm glad you got out okay. Sounds like a close one."

"Closer than I liked."

From inside the bomb-squad truck came a series of short, sharp barks. Kevin's head snapped around. "Izzy. *Quiet*," he commanded. The barks were replaced by high-pitched whines. "*Izzy*." Izzy, named after a character on *Miami Vice*, was Boomer's dog, a big German shepherd whose job—whose passion, whose very reason for living—was sniffing out explosives. Until recently, the bomb squad had relied mainly on a robot, which sounded great but worked like crap, always getting stuck or running out of battery power, requiring somebody to go in and retrieve it. The robot was so unreliable, in fact, that Decker's SWAT team—the ones generally tapped to go fetch the malfunctioning machine—had acquired a nickname that was all too accurate: the "Robot Rescue Team." Decker generally hated seeing the robot get hauled out and sent in; today, though, he would welcome it.

"You starting with R2D2?" he said hopefully.

"Nah. If there's already debris, the robot would get snagged for sure. Faster and better to go right in with Izzy."

"How's his nose today?"

"Awesome. As always."

Decker gave Kev's shoulder a squeeze. "Y'all be careful in there."

Kev nodded reflexively, but he didn't answer, and Decker noticed that his brother looked distracted, as if he were listening to something other than the words of brotherly love and caution. "Is it true? The guy's still sitting in there?" Decker nodded. "Head blown off? No shit?"

"No shit."

"*Good*," snapped Boomer, with a vehemence that surprised Decker. "I just wish he'd died slower. Sick son of a bitch."

"Hey, now," Decker said. "Don't make it personal. Forget about me; forget about him. Just do your job. What's that thing you're always saying, about how the dog knows when you're off kilter?"

"What, 'The dog is only as good as the handler'?"

"No, the other thing you're always saying."

"Oh, you mean 'Shit flows down the leash'?"

Deck nodded. "Yeah. That. You stay focused in there, so Izzy can, too."

SHIT FLOWS DOWN *the leash.* The words were stuck in Decker's mind now, replaying like a broken record. Like a premonition. Or maybe, he preferred to think, like a mantra, a message he was sending to Kev via brother-bond ESP.

He pictured the dog sniffing its way around the walls of the foyer and toward the blasted den; pictured Kev casting furtive glances over his shoulder at the headless, handless corpse slumped in the La-Z-Boy. *Shit flows down the leash, bro*, he messaged. *Keep your head in the game.*

Decker couldn't stand it. Ducking under the crime-scene tape Fireplug had stretched across the front sidewalk, he climbed the stairs and positioned himself in the open front door. The interior still reeked of explosives, though the smoke had dissipated. Boomer and Izzy had made it halfway across the foyer by now, working their way along the front wall of the house, when suddenly the dog's head snapped up and he stood on his hind legs, his front paws on the wall, his nose homing in on something. Decker leaned in and saw a dark smear on the wall. *Blood,* Decker thought, touching his shoulder. *My blood.* Did the dog know the blood was Decker's? Could he smell the kinship with Kevin? *Hell, yeah,* he thought. *Blood brothers. Brother's blood. Thicker than water. For sure he knows it's mine.* "Leave it," he heard Kev say, saw Kev give the leash a twitch. "Keep working." The dog resumed snuffling, following the baseboard around the room, to the doorway of the den. "Good boy," Kev praised. "Good work."

The dog disappeared through the doorway, into the den, and Kev followed, a leash-length behind. The den would be a bigger challenge for them to check and clear, Decker knew. For one thing, it was a bigger, more complex room, with chairs and tables and lamps and other mangled furniture, plus the smells and soot from the SWAT team's flash grenade and the dead guy's dynamite. Then there was the stink of the dead guy himself—seared flesh and vaporized hair and leaked-out shit and piss—not to mention the creepy *presence* of the guy, too. Despite the lack of eyes, or even a head, for crissakes, Decker somehow imagined the dead guy watching, tracking Boomer and Izzy as they made their way along the wall. "Check," Decker heard his brother say in a low voice every few seconds, and even at a distance—even through the residual ringing in his ears—Decker could hear the strain in his brother's voice. *C'mon, Kev,* he messaged. *Focus.*

Suddenly he heard the dog yelp with pain and fear—fear, from a creature trained to hurl himself without hesitation at a 250-pound thug. A split-second later, he heard Boomer shout, "No!" Decker braced for a blast, but there was none; only shrieks from both the dog and the man.

Ignoring protocol, Decker raced into the house and across the foyer, skidding around the corner and into the den. There he saw a surreal nightmare unfolding. Kev and Izzy were on the far side of the room, near some kind of splintered cage of wood and wire. Rearing up on his hind legs like a horse, the dog was thrashing wildly, whipping his head back and forth, struggling to shake something off his snout. *A snake,* realized Decker. *A huge fucking snake!* The triangle of the reptile's head was like some awful reflection of the dog's own angular head; the long, thick body disappeared beneath the edge of the broken cage. "No!" Deck heard Kevin scream again over the dog's howls. "Izzy!" As Decker lunged across the room to help, he saw Boomer drop to his knees, hands scrabbling up the back of the snake, tugging at the neck, then—desperate to free the terrified dog—grabbing hold of the jaws themselves. He had just managed to pry the reptile loose when the dog—finally free to fight back—bit blindly, the powerful jaws closing on Boomer's right hand. Now it was Boomer howling, first as the bones of his right hand snapped, then as the fangs of the snake sought and found his left wrist, piercing the pale skin and then the ropy blue vein. The vein that carried blood up Kev's arm and into his lungs.

As Decker reached his brother's side, he saw the knotty glands at the base of the snake's head pulsing—once, twice, three times. "Kevin!" shouted Decker. "*No!*" Now it was Decker grabbing the snake's jaws, prying ferociously, ripping tendons and ligaments with the force of his fear and fury. Gripping the reptile's head with both hands, he smashed it to the floor, again and again and again, reducing it to a bloody, bony pulp.

On the floor beside him, the dog began to convulse, blood foaming from his mouth and nose, and Decker saw his brother lift the dog and clasp it to his chest, sobbing. "Izzy," Kev gasped. "I'm sorry. Oh, God, Izzy, I'm so, so sorry."

Then—as if stricken with guilt at his failure to repay the dog's devotion with diligence and vigilance and safekeeping; as if the two were joined by bonds even stronger than family—Decker's brother began to froth blood as well. Decker watched, paralyzed and helpless, as his younger brother toppled forward onto the twitching body of the dog.

Death crawls up the leash.

CHAPTER 42

Brockton

I WAS RUNNING OVERTIME in my four o'clock Human Origins class, delivering a lecture on evolutionary changes in the human skull. "How many of you have seen the Coneheads, on *Saturday Night Live*?" I asked. Half the three hundred students raised their hands. "In another twenty thousand years," I said, "if the cranium keeps getting taller and narrower, you and I will look just like the Coneheads." The students were still laughing when a uniformed KPD officer came through the double doors at the back of the auditorium. Most anthropology courses were taught in the small, shabby classrooms in Stadium Hall, but the three big intro classes—Human Origins, Archaeology, and Cultural Anthropology—required a bigger venue, which I'd found in McClung Museum, a pleasant quarter-mile walk from the stadium.

The officer, a patrolman named Maddox, had been assigned to watch my back until Satterfield was safely in custody. Another officer was watching Kathleen, and a third was keeping tabs on Jeff. "So our brains have gotten bigger," I continued, "as our jaws have gotten smaller—*because* our jaws have gotten smaller, in fact. Thirty-two used to be the normal number of teeth for adults, but as a species, we're gradually losing our third molars, our wisdom teeth. So if you don't have wisdom teeth, it doesn't mean you're dumb; it actually means just the opposite—it means you're more highly evolved than some moron with a mouthful of teeth." From the back of the auditorium, Maddox beckoned to me.

"Excuse me, class," I said, trying to sound lighthearted. "It appears that the long arm of the law has finally caught up with me." Heads swiveled, faces curious. "Y'all start counting your teeth. If you've had any pulled, or lost any, count those, too." I beckoned to a girl seated in the front row. "Rebecca? Would you come up to the board and take a tally for us? In this sample of three hundred humans, how many have thirty-two teeth, and how many have only twenty-eight? What's the breakdown, by number and by percentage?" As I started up the aisle, I saw students tooth counting—some using the tongue-probe method, others running a fingertip inside their mouths.

Maddox led me out of the auditorium and into the hallway. I searched his expression for some hint of what he had to say. "What's up, Officer?"

"Got some news," he said in a low voice. He glanced around the wide hallway, which was empty but exposed. "But let's go someplace a little less public." I took him down a narrow side hallway that led to the museum's offices, stopping in a corner that offered privacy, as well as a good view of anyone approaching from either direction.

"From the look on your face," I said, "whatever the news is, it isn't good."

"Some of it's good, some bad. The good news is, the SWAT team went in, and the suspect's dead." The words sent a flood of feelings coursing through me: blessed relief, grim satisfaction, and guilt.

Suddenly my heart clenched as I realized just how bad the bad news might be. "Dear God," I said, clutching his arm. "Has something happened to Kathleen? Or Jeff?"

He shook his head. "No, no, nothing like that," he assured me. "But the scene turned into a total cluster-fuck, if you'll pardon my language. Sumbitch had the place booby-trapped—that, or he ate a stick of dynamite. Blew his own damn head off. Nearly took the SWAT team out with him."

"That's awful."

He made a face. "That ain't the bad part. The SWAT guys are okay. But there was some kind of damn snake loose in the house, too—rattlesnake or cobra or who the hell knows what. Bomb-squad guy was in there with his dog, sniffing for more explosives. Damn snake bit the dog. Handler, too. Dead, both of 'em. Died quicker'n you can say Jack Robinson."

"God in heaven. What kind of monster keeps killing even after he's dead?" Maddox shook his head in sorrow and bafflement. "Do you know if my family knows about what's happened at the scene? My wife and my son? If they don't, I'd rather be the one to tell them. In person."

Maddox radioed the officers who were keeping watch over Kathleen and Jeff. "No sir, they don't know it yet. Your wife's in a meeting, and your boy's at cross-country practice."

I nodded gratefully. "Could you relay a message to them? Ask them to be home by six?" He nodded. "And Officer? Please make sure they know I'm fine."

I didn't *feel* fine; I felt like I might be sick. But it seemed important to say it—to my family, and to myself. *I'm fine. I'm fine. I'm fine.*

CHAPTER 43

Kittredge

KITTREDGE FROWNED AT THE driver's license the forensic tech, Bohanan, was holding between a gloved thumb and forefinger. *Nicholas Eugene Satterfield*, said the license, which had come from the dead man's wallet. The face in the photo bore a strong resemblance to the artist's sketch of the Cahaba Lane rapist—the Cahaba Lane killer. The frown-inducing problem was that Kittredge couldn't match the face on the license or the face in the sketch to the face of the dead guy slumped in the La-Z-Boy, because the dead guy slumped in the La-Z-Boy *had* no face.

Bohanan tucked the license into an evidence bag. "We got dental records on Mr. Satterfield?"

"Not yet," said the detective. "Military does, but we don't. I'm still trying to find out who's got 'em—the Navy, or the Military Personnel Records Center, in St. Louis." The detective leaned in and peered at the bloody stump of spine. "Ick. What good will dental records do us, anyhow? We got no teeth."

"O ye of little faith," said Bohanan. "Just because his teeth aren't in his head anymore—"

"His *head's* not in his head anymore," Kittredge pointed out.

"Teeth are tough," Bohanan persisted. "They might be somewhere in this mess. Some of 'em, anyhow. *Parts* of some of 'em. A bit of bridgework, maybe, or a weird-shaped filling."

"What about DNA?" said the detective. "Everything I read these days goes on and on about how great DNA is. Genetic fingerprints, no two alike. The future of forensics, supposedly."

"Exactly," said Bohanan. "The *future*. Sure, it's possible, in some fancy-schmancy genetics lab. But routine forensic casework, in Knoxville, Tennessee? That's five years down the road. Maybe ten." Bohanan rocked back on his heels, studying the corpse. "We got anything else to base an ID on? Anything that doesn't require, you know, a head or hands? Surgical scars, tattoos, six toes, anything?"

Kittredge snapped his fingers. "*Damn.* Yeah—he's got tats. Both forearms. A snake on one. A devil's pitchfork on the other."

Bohanan lifted the handless right arm and slid the shredded sleeve up to the elbow. On the inside of the forearm was a crudely inked image of an eagle, its wings spread, its talons clutching a ship's anchor and a three-pronged spear. "Not a pitchfork," Bohanan said. "A trident. Symbol of Neptune—god of the sea. I've got an uncle with one kinda like this. He was a SEAL during the Vietnam War."

"That fits," said Kittredge. "Let's see the other arm."

Bohanan reached across the recliner and raised the left arm. Stretching upward above the shredded remnants of the wrist was a snake. Like the man, the reptile had been decapitated by the blast.

"Bingo," said Kittredge, reaching for his radio. "Cap? It's him. . . . ID in his wallet, tats on his arms. . . . Yeah, both tats, exactly like she described." He glanced again at the snake. *Burn in hell, asshole*, he thought.

CHAPTER 44

Brockton

TWO POLICE CARS WERE idling outside my house when I arrived—the officers who'd kept watch over Jeff and Kathleen—and I stopped in the street and got out to thank them. Behind me, my watchdog, Maddox, eased his cruiser to the curb and parked. As I eyed the three police cars, I wondered what the neighbors must be thinking. *Quite a fight*, I pictured the crone across the street murmuring as she peered out her window. *Mind your business, woman*, I imagined her withered husband admonishing from the couch, then adding, *I told you that Brockton fella had a mean streak in him, didn't I?*

My family's guards, whom I hadn't met, got out and walked toward me in the twilight, greeting me by name and extending their hands to shake mine. "I sure do appreciate y'all keeping an eye on my wife and my son," I said. "I can't tell you how much that helped my peace of mind." Behind me, I heard Maddox's door open and close, then heard his footsteps on the darkened asphalt.

"Glad to do it," said the one who'd been assigned to Kathleen. "That dude was some bad business." The other two nodded.

"I just got an update," Maddox said. "They've got a positive ID on him now. It's over."

I didn't know whether to cheer or weep. Instead, I asked, "How?"

"Driver's license," he said. "And tattoos."

"And burns? Seems like I remember hearing that he had scars on his arms from cigarette burns as a kid."

He shrugged. "I guess, but I'll ask, if you want. They said it was positive, so if he had 'em, they must've seen 'em."

"I trust y'all," I said. "So I reckon we've seen the last of y'all for awhile?" He nodded. "Y'all can call your wives, tell 'em you'll be home for supper after all."

Maddox glanced at the other two, then back at me. "Actually, some of us are getting together at Patrick Sullivan's Saloon," he said. "That was Boomer's favorite hangout. Come join us, if you want to."

"I appreciate the invitation," I said, lifting my hand in farewell and turning to go. "But I ought to stay here, be with my family. They need me right now."

Was that true? I didn't actually know, I realized as I clambered back into my truck and turned into the driveway. What I *did* know was that I needed them.

"Dammit, Jeff," I muttered, threading between the Toyota and the shrubbery. "Don't take your half in the *middle*." The driveway was sixteen feet wide—more than enough for two vehicles to pass, with room to spare—but Jeff had parked the old Corolla we'd bought him smack in the center. If I detoured around him on the right, I'd make ruts in the lawn; hugging the left side of the driveway, as I was doing, meant raking the fingernails of the boxwoods down the side of the truck. The screeching set my teeth on edge and sent involuntary shivers up my spine.

My irritation gave way to relief, though, as the garage door ratcheted upward to reveal Kathleen's Camry tucked in the near bay of the garage. I eased in alongside and hopped out, feeling gladder to be home than I could remember feeling in . . . when? Forever? As I trudged up the basement stairs and into the kitchen, I said a prayer of thanks.

Kathleen was at the sink, pouring pasta from a steaming pot into a colander. Jeff was at the stove, stirring sauce; to my surprise, Jenny Earhart was at the table, setting places for four. "Hello, hello," I said, "Jenny, how nice to see you."

The pot clattered into the sink as Kathleen whirled toward me. "*Bill.* Oh, thank God. Are you all right?" She wiped her hands on her apron, then wiped her eyes with the backs of her hands as she hurried to me and folded against my chest.

"Oh, honey, I'm *fine,*" I said, taking her in my arms. "Didn't your watchdog tell you I was okay? He was supposed to."

"He did," she said, "but I didn't believe him. The way he said it—'Don't you worry, ma'am, your husband is fine, *just fine*'—it sounded like the *opposite* of fine. Like you were alive, but paralyzed or something. He wouldn't tell me anything else. I thought about turning on the news, but I was afraid to."

"Oh, sweetheart." Still holding her in my arms, I stroked her head to soothe her. "I'm so sorry you worried. Things got bad—not for me, but for the police, at his house. Satterfield's house." I squeezed her tightly. "The good news is, he's dead."

She leaned back to look at me, her eyes wide. "The police shot him?"

I shook my head. "He killed himself."

"*Good.*" Her quick vehemence surprised me.

"But he did some damage on his way out. He was holding a bomb or a hand grenade or something. He set it off when the SWAT team went in. Blew himself up."

Her hands flew to her mouth. "Oh, my God! He killed the SWAT team?"

"No. No, not them. It was stranger than that. Bizarre. Like a nightmare." I led her to the table and motioned for all of them to sit, partly so I could see them all while I told the story, but also so that I could sit down, too. I drew a breath and began to tell what I knew, or at any rate what I'd heard—possibly at third hand, possibly at thirteenth hand—about the blast, and the bomb squad, and the snake and the dog and the dog's dead handler. About how Satterfield had reached up from the grave, or from hell itself, to take more innocent people down with him.

CHAPTER 45

Satterfield

SATTERFIELD REACHED UP TO scratch an itch on his head, and the dial of his watch swam past his face in a smear of luminescence. Beneath the cargo hatch, the space was low and pitch black, and it smelled faintly of death. *Like a coffin,* he thought. *A family-sized coffin. On wheels.* Should he put them in here, once he was finished with them? *No. Leave them out—on display—for all the world to see.* He raised his left hand, the luminous dial floating upward a few more inches in the blackness, until his fingers brushed the lid, eighteen inches above his face.

It had been easy—*so easy,* he thought—but then, he'd had a big advantage: He had known they'd be coming, but they hadn't known he knew. *Fools. They should have known better. They should have done better.*

The pizza guy, on the other hand—no way *that* poor bastard could have known better. A quick, lethal snap of the neck, administered by someone who ordered pizza once or twice a week, and always tipped five bucks? No way to see that coming. Swapping clothes, slapping on the fake beard, stenciling the tats on the arms, tightening the trip wire on his way out the front door, tripping the timers on the lights and TV and the recording of the woman's screams—all that had taken less than ten minutes. *Practice makes perfect*, he praised himself.

Driving away from the house in the kid's piece-of-shit Escort, he'd checked the rearview mirror repeatedly, smiling every time he looked and found it empty. Half an hour after answering his front door and beckoning the unsuspecting pizza guy inside, Satterfield had parked the Escort near the stadium, jimmied the latch on Brockton's cargo hatch, and clambered in, pulling the hatch closed above him.

Now—after three hours of patiently lying in wait in the pitch-black bed of Brockton's truck—Satterfield was ready to emerge from the coffinlike blackness; ready to rise from the dead and rejoin the land of the living. Ready to take Brockton and his family out of it.

How long should he wait? Part of him wanted to draw it out. The longer he waited, the more times and more ways he could envision it, savor it, play out in his mind the infinite permutations that were still possible for now, before the fact. Once it was done, only one version would remain in his head: the real version—one finite actuality, which would sweep away all the manifold and intricate and pleasant hypotheticals.

But waiting increased the chances that something might miscarry. Satterfield had bought time—hours, at least; possibly even days—with the explosion and the decoy corpse, but the longer he waited, the greater the risk that the police would unravel his ruse.

He ran a thumbnail beneath the hinge of his jaw and scraped at the edge of the rubber cement. Once he'd pried away a bit of the glue-matted hair, he tugged off the beard and flicked it into the corner of the pickup's bed. The insulated pizza bag lay beside him, and Satterfield slowly opened the Velcro straps, the ripping-apart almost deafening in the close darkness, and then opened the flap. With his fingertips, he took inventory of the contents once more, though he already knew the items by heart and by touch: the four-cell Mag-Lite, blindingly bright and heavy as a club; the straight razor; a small, orange ball of baling twine; the twelve-inch zip ties; the flattened roll of duct tape; and a small pair of pruning shears. The 9-mm Glock was already out of the bag, tucked into his waistband.

SATTERFIELD'S EYELIDS BLOOMED red-orange, crisscrossed by a spiderweb of dark veins, when he clicked the switch and the Mag-Lite blazed to life. Squinting against the glare, he propped the flashlight against the truck's wheel well and reached overhead for the long, thin rods that held the cargo hatch closed. Gripping each rod at its midpoint, he pulled downward, bending them both enough to free their ends and unlock the cargo hatch. He pushed gently, and the hatch pivoted upward, opening like a vast maw to disgorge Satterfield. To unleash him upon them.

He lay still and listened before moving. A few faint tickings from the engine of the truck and from the Camry parked beside it. The dull whir of the furnace blower. The gurgle of water draining from a sink. The murmur of a voice—indistinct words, but distinctly Brockton's voice—filtering down through the joists and the flooring above the garage.

Moving fluidly and noiselessly, he rolled onto his side and curled his legs to his chest—coiling—then pivoted into a crouch and eased over the tailgate. By the light of the flashlight, still propped against the wheel well, he sorted his gear, tucking the razor and the pruning shears into his right hip pocket, the coil of baling twine into his right front pocket, the zip ties into his left front pocket, and the fat, flattened roll of duct tape into his left hip pocket.

Once the items were stowed within easy reach, he picked up the flashlight and started around the end of the truck, heading for the front of the garage. Then, on an impulse, he leaned into the bed of the truck once more to retrieve the Domino's cap and the empty insulated bag. Tucking the bag under his left arm, he donned the cap, twisting and tilting it slightly—*a jaunty angle,* he thought.

Metal edges and handles glinted as he played the flashlight across the garage's back wall, where tools were neatly arrayed on pegboards, one on either side of the door that led into the basement. Household tools occupied the pegboard to the left of the door: a Dustbuster, three sizes of pipe wrenches, an assortment of pliers, a set of screwdrivers, rolls of electrical tape, coils of insulated wire. Woodworking tools and lawn-care implements filled the other side: saws, hammers, clamps, planes, chisels, pruning shears, a hatchet, an ax, a sledgehammer, splitting wedges. *Christ*, Satterfield thought, *the fucker's a one-man Home Depot.* He played the flashlight along the knee-high shelf beneath the workbench lining the wall, the beam lingering on a belt sander, a circular saw, and a chain saw. Hell, if he'd known there'd be such a wealth of implements to choose from, he'd have brought fewer things with him. His hands were already full, and he didn't want to deviate from his initial plan, but he made a mental note to return to the garage in a few hours and pick a few choice items to liven things up, to stave off boredom.

He checked the wall beside the door that led into the house. There was a switch plate with three light switches, plus a doorbell-style button beneath it—the garage-door opener, probably. No keypad, so no security alarm, which he already knew from his scouting trip a few days before, when he'd "fixed" the telephone line.

The basement door was metal, with a dead bolt as well as a lock in the knob. Switching off the flashlight, Satterfield tried the knob. It turned, and when he pushed lightly, the door opened a crack. *Idiots.*

The large room inside the door—a basement den—was faintly lit by the blue clock of a VCR. Beyond, a hallway bisected the far half of the basement, leading, he recalled, to a bathroom, the kid's bedroom, and a spare bedroom jammed with junk. Easing down the dark hall, he found all three doors ajar, all three rooms empty. Retracing his steps, he returned to the stairwell and started up, testing each step for any hint of a squeak before committing his full weight to it.

A line of golden light showed beneath the door at the top of the stairs, the sound of voices mingling with the clink of cutlery on ceramic. "Jeff, mind your manners," he heard the woman say. "Leave a little for the rest of us."

"Sorry, Mom."

He conjured up his mental picture of the layout. The door from the basement opened directly across from an exterior door—a sliding-glass door—that led to a patio and a garden in back of the house. To the right of the stairwell was the dining room; to his left, the kitchen. Judging by the direction of the sounds, they were eating in the kitchen.

Satterfield slipped the Mag-Lite into the pizza bag and pulled the pistol from his waistband. Hanging the pizza bag from his left wrist by the nylon strap, he took tender hold of the doorknob and twisted, his thumb moving as slowly as the second hand on a clock. The door opened inward, into the stairwell—much better for him than if it swung outward, into view. He eased it open an inch, then waited and listened. "Bill, have some more salad," the woman said.

Another careful inch.

"Thanks, hon, but I'm not really hungry."

A foot this time.

"I'll take some more," the boy said.

Satterfield swung the door fully open.

"Please?" prompted Brockton.

"It's okay, Dad—you don't have to beg me." A half second later: "Hey, come on. That was funny."

"No, not really," Satterfield said, taking two quick steps—through the doorway and then around the corner, into the kitchen. "Who wants pizza?" Their faces, startled and stupid with surprise, swiveled toward him. Four startled faces, not three. *A girl. Who the hell's the girl?* Brockton, seated at the near end of the table, started to his feet, the look of surprise on his face giving way to anger and fear as his gaze shifted from the Domino's shirt and pizza bag to the face of the man. The face of Satterfield.

Satterfield swung the pizza bag sideways by its strap, the heavy rectangle slicing through the air and smashing into Brockton's face, the weight of the heavy flashlight inside adding to the force. Brockton toppled backward, knocking over his chair as he fell, and then struggled to rise from the floor. Satterfield kicked him to put him back down, then took a step back and waved the pistol. "I'm sorry to have to break it to you," he said, "but I lied—I don't really have pizza for you."

CHAPTER 46

Decker

DECKER KNEW THAT THE detective and the forensic techs didn't want him there—he was lurking and watching, radiating anguish and rage—but nobody wanted to get in his face about it; nobody wanted to be the jerk that told a guy whose brother had just died to get the hell out of the way. The detective, Kittredge, was squatting beside Bohanan, the senior forensic tech, who was kneeling near the feet of the headless corpse, using tweezers to pluck filaments of wire from the floor.

"Detective?" The voice came from behind Decker—from the direction of the kitchen, where one of the junior forensic techs was taking photos—and floated past him, into the living room, to Kittredge.

"Yeah?" Kittredge looked up, past Decker, toward the kitchen doorway.

"You just want pictures of the garbage? Or do you want me to bag it up and bring it back to the lab?"

"What's in it?"

"A bunch of pizza, mostly."

"How much pizza?"

"A lot. Looks like a whole pie."

"Uneaten?" Decker saw Kittredge frown, furrow his brow, reach up and rub the stubble on his chin. Bohanan glanced up, too, his tweezers poised in midair.

"If it were eaten, it wouldn't be here. You hungry, detective?"

"Hang on. I'm coming to take a look." Kittredge didn't head straight to the kitchen, though; Decker watched as the detective detoured to the near side of the den and squatted beside a battered Domino's box. Using the tip of a pen, Kittredge lifted the lid. Decker leaned in far enough to see what Kittredge saw: that the box contained three ragged pieces of pizza crust. Kittredge picked up one with a gloved hand. On his way into the kitchen, the detective edged passed Decker, avoiding eye contact.

The tech was right, Decker saw when he followed Kittredge into the kitchen—there *was* a lot of pizza in the trash. Enough to feed everybody working the scene, and then some. The detective plucked one of the slices from the can—a slice that had no crust—and held the fragment from the box alongside it. The edges fit together perfectly, like pieces of a puzzle. "What the hell?" he heard Kittredge mutter, and then: "Oh shit. No, no, no. *Please* no." Drawn by the stir of activity, Bohanan joined Decker in the doorway.

As Decker and the two techs watched, Kittredge reached into the trash can and fished out a navy-blue magic marker, along with a thin piece of cardboard stained with ink. The cardboard had been delicately and precisely incised with two stencil patterns. One was a bird—an eagle—its wings spread, its talons clutching an anchor and a three-pronged spear. The other stencil was a snake with a broad triangular head.

"We've got a problem here," said Kittredge.

"A big problem," said Bohanan.

Decker didn't say anything. He was already gone, sprinting for the front door.

"LIEUTENANT!" DECKER HEARD Cody's voice from the direction of the SWAT truck. "Hey, Lieutenant! Everything okay? What's going on in there?" Decker didn't stop to talk; he didn't even turn to look; he just lifted a hand and kept running.

As he'd hoped, the keys were still in the ignition of Kittredge's unmarked Crown Vic. You'd think a detective, a guy who'd probably spent years investigating robberies and auto thefts, would be careful with his keys. *Or maybe*, Decker thought as he slid across the ripped upholstery and cranked the balky engine, *he's hoping somebody will actually steal this piece of shit.* Jerking the gearshift into reverse, he smoked down the driveway, nearly backing over a startled uniformed officer, who was half sitting on the hood of the patrol unit parked in the street. Decker gave a brief wave of apology and roared away, his right hand reaching for the radio as soon as he was traveling straight. "Dispatch, this is Lieutenant Decker. Can you give me a physical address for Dr. Brockton? Bill Brockton—William, maybe? The UT bone doc?"

"Stand by, Lieutenant."

Decker was hurtling north, which was the only way it was possible to head from the dead end where Satterfield lived. In less than a mile, though—thirty seconds, at the rate he was going—he'd reach an intersection and have to choose: west, toward downtown and UT and most of the Knoxville suburbs, or east, toward Holston Hills and Seymour and Strawberry Plains. "Come on, come *on*," he muttered as the stop sign loomed a hundred yards ahead. He considered stopping at the intersection and waiting for the answer, but if he was right—if Satterfield was alive and gunning for Brockton—there wasn't time. Guessing, Decker took the left turn in a power slide, aiming the car west, envisioning its eight cylinders firing like the barrels of a Gatling gun.

"Dispatch to Decker." *Finally.*

"Decker. Go ahead."

"That address is 3791 Clifton Drive. That's in Sequoyah Hills."

"Can you give me directions from Kingston Pike and Neyland?"

"Stand by."

Decker was less impatient this time; it would take five minutes to reach downtown, and another five from there to Sequoyah. By the time the dispatcher radioed back with directions, the Crown Vic was wailing along the river on Neyland, past the stadium and the basketball arena and the sewage plant. He killed the siren and the blue lights when he turned off Kingston Pike on to Cherokee—not out of respect for the fancy neighborhood's peace and quiet, but to avoid announcing his arrival. He was swooping down the curving boulevard toward the riverfront when the dispatcher called him. "Lieutenant Decker, do you need backup? Is there a situation at Dr. Brockton's residence?"

"Negative," he replied at once. Backup and bureaucracy were the last things he needed. "I just need to drop something off. Hey, is there a patrol unit posted there?"

"Not anymore. Was, anyhow, till a few minutes ago. The watch commander pulled the plug once they got the ID on the suspect's body."

"Makes sense."

A moment later, the radio intruded on him. "Deck, this is Hackworth. Where the hell are you, and why? Am I to understand that you're no longer at the Satterfield house? That you're en route to the Brockton house?"

This was trickier. Being evasive with the dispatcher was one thing; lying to the captain was another, far bigger thing. "Yes sir, I am en route there."

"You? The whole team? What the hell are you doing, Deck? You're supposed to be guarding the perimeter of the Satterfield house."

"Yes, sir. My men are still on that. All over it." He kept talking, improvising, not wanting to give the captain an opening. "It's a personal errand, sir. Kevin took a class from Dr. Brockton a couple years ago." That much was true. "The Doc was one of Boomer's idols." Also true. "I'm taking something over there, to the Doc. A memento, sort of. Something I think Kevin would've wanted me to do." It was lame, but even that had some truth to it: safety; protection; justice—Kevin would certainly have wanted his big brother to deliver those things.

"Stand by, Deck."

Shit, thought Decker. *He's calling Kittredge. If Kittredge tells him the ID's no good, he'll figure it out. He'll know what I'm doing, and he'll tell me to stand down.* "Shit." He said it aloud this time. He didn't want to stand down; didn't want to wait for backup. *Wouldn't* stand down; *wouldn't* wait.

Careening down the final curve, he saw the river glittering through the trees on his left, separated from the road by a ribbon of shoreline park. He slung the car around the traffic circle; around the big, lighted fountain with its geyser of glowing water. Then he reached out and switched off the radio, so he would not hear the order that he was about to violate.

CHAPTER 47

Tyler

SLUMPING BACK AGAINST THE streetlight, Tyler pressed two fingertips to his neck and checked his watch: 30 heartbeats in 10 seconds; 180 beats per minute. Not his max, but damn good. So why didn't he feel better? Normally a run this hard—five fast miles, pounding up Cherokee Boulevard to Kingston Pike and then back along the riverfront—would clear his mind completely, put him into a zenlike state of blissful exhaustion. Tonight, though, all he had was the exhaustion, not the zenlike bliss. Zenlike bliss? What the hell was that? He couldn't even remember it, let alone feel it.

Shit, he thought, *I have to do it.* He'd been fighting it, resisting it for three days, even though he knew it was the right thing. He pushed off from the lamppost and found himself jogging—slogging, more like—up a side street, away from the gravel lot at the end of the boulevard where his truck was parked. Away from his truck; toward Dr. B's house. Sweaty and sticky though he was, he couldn't put it off any longer; he had to tell Brockton he was quitting. There was no guarantee that quitting the program would make it possible to fix what had gone wrong between him and Roxanne; what was going wrong within himself. But staying in the program—walking through the valley of the shadow of death, again and again—would almost certainly wreck things forever. "You might think it's hypocritical of me," Rox had written to him in her last note. "After all, as a doctor, I'll spend decades keeping company with death. But I'll be pushing against it—opposing it, not embracing it."

Tyler had tried to figure out how Dr. B did it: The guy was up to his elbows in death and dismemberment, yet he had one of the sunniest dispositions Tyler had ever seen. How did he do it? How did he keep from being dragged down by the cases, by the oppressive weight of evil? *Damned if I know*, he thought.

The Brocktons' house was two blocks off the boulevard, in a pocket of houses that were much smaller and less showy than the mansions along Cherokee. The house was tucked deep in the lot, surrounded by maples and hemlocks. From the curb Tyler wasn't sure anyone was home—the front windows were dark—so he jogged down the driveway and toward the back, to check for lights in the kitchen, dining room, den, or master bedroom. Tyler had fond memories of the master bedroom—of the seven Edenic days and nights he and Roxanne had spent there, ostensibly keeping an eye on the place, but in reality having eyes only for one another. *Lotta water under the bridge since then*, he thought—most of it muddy and malevolent, or so it seemed at the moment.

Parked halfway down the darkened driveway was an old Corolla; was that what Dr. B had ended up buying for Jeff, after Tyler refused to sell the truck? Tyler stopped and peered through the driver's window. *A five-speed; good*, he thought.

Now that he'd stopped moving again, his legs turned leaden, and a sharp pain began gnawing at the meniscus cartilage on the inside of his left knee. He thought about turning tail, waiting until tomorrow, catching Dr. B in his office first thing. But the prospect of leaving things hanging for another night—another sleepless night—was unbearable, so he turned toward the house again, limping past the garage and up the stairs to the backyard and the patio off the kitchen. *Pitiful*, he thought. Not just the limp, but the whole sorry mess he'd made of things, first with Roxanne and now with Dr. B.

Golden light poured through the windows of the kitchen and back door, pooling on the flagstones of the patio, and Tyler suddenly felt himself drowning in that pool of light and warmth, drowning with longing and loneliness. A figure—Jeff?—emerged from the stairwell and turned toward the kitchen. He listened for voices, but the sounds inside the house were drowned by the noise of the heat pump, its compressor whooshing in the shrubbery beside him.

A picnic table flanked the near side of the patio, and Tyler sat on one of the benches to compose his thoughts, compose his verbal resignation. He considered and rejected half a dozen different opening lines.

Quit stalling, he berated himself. *Just knock, and get it over with.*

CHAPTER 48

Satterfield

SATTERFIELD GLANCED FROM FACE to face, reveling in how well things were going—better, even, than he'd imagined they would. The three Brocktons and the girl were seated around the kitchen table in a bizarre variation on family dinner: four half-finished plates of pasta and salad in front of them, duct tape over their mouths, zip ties cinching their ankles and wrists to the frames of the ladderback chairs.

The girl had been a surprise. "She has nothing to do with this," Brockton had tried arguing. "Neither does Kathleen or Jeff. This is just between you and me. Let them go." Satterfield had cocked his head, pretending to consider the stupid request; then he'd smiled, shaken his head, and yanked the tape tight across Brockton's mouth. The girl was a juicy little bonus; a windfall apple. *Manna from heaven*, he thought.

Brockton would be the last to die, of course. A big part of his suffering—though far, far from all of his suffering—would be to witness the agonies of the others, knowing that he himself was to blame. Utterly and solely to blame.

Laying the gun on the end of the table, Satterfield reached into his back pocket for the gardening shears. He held them toward the light, squeezing the spring-loaded handles, admiring the tight precision with which the blades closed and opened. Their curved edges—the upper blade convex, the lower one concave—reminded him of a cartoon fish, grinning with its oversized mouth. The coiled spring that pushed the handles apart made a soft, musical squeak each time the cartoon-fish mouth opened or closed. Pointing the tool toward each of them in turn, he recited, "Eeny meeny miny mo . . ." He paused and looked at Brockton again. "Or do *you* want to choose? Tell me—shall I start with the girl?" He smiled as Brockton grunted and shook his head frantically. "No? With your son, then?" He leaned across the table, the shears opening in his hand as he dropped the jaws below the table and toward the boy's crotch.

"*Nnnnhhh*," shrilled Brockton, struggling and thrashing so hard that his chair threatened to tip.

"No? Not him? Okay, whatever you say." Satterfield stepped to Kathleen's side and snipped the zip tie binding her right wrist to the chair. "I don't know who I'll send this one to," he said, taking hold of her hand, lifting it by the little finger. "But I'll think of someone." He squeezed, and the handles of the shears came together, and the grinning fish closed its jaws on her finger.

CHAPTER 49

Tyler

QUIT STALLING, **TYLER BERATED** himself again, and forced himself to stand and walk to the patio door. He was raising his hand to knock when he froze, his knuckle an inch from the door. On the other side of the glass, Jeff had reached out and taken hold of a small, slender hand—Kathleen's hand, Tyler assumed—and clasped the pinky finger between the thumb and forefinger of his left hand. Then he turned slightly—a few degrees, no more—but it was enough for Tyler to see that it was not Jeff at all. As his brain scrambled to interpret the data and identify the face, he felt a rush of panic. A moment later, his conscious mind caught up with the faster circuitry of his subconscious, and he recognized the face: the murder suspect, Satterfield! Just then he saw Satterfield reach toward Kathleen's finger with his right hand. Light glinted on steel, and then Kathleen's arm swung free, arced toward the floor, slinging blood as it dropped. Satterfield still clasped her little finger in his left hand, a pair of bloody gardening shears in the other. Her head jerked, and through her nostrils and the tape across her mouth came a muffled, whinnying scream.

Tyler gasped and staggered backward as if he'd been struck. He fought back the impulse to scream and the need to vomit, knowing that revealing his presence was almost certain to trigger a massacre inside. *Think,* he commanded himself. *Think!* God, why hadn't he gotten a cell phone when Roxanne had suggested it? He spun, scanning in vain for the glimmer of lights in neighboring houses. Should he run back to the street and start banging on doors? Was there even time for that? How long would it take for the police to get here in force—ten minutes? half an hour? The image of the arrow-pierced bodies flashed into his mind—two brutal deaths in quick succession—and he knew that the Brocktons might not have ten minutes. *It's up to me,* he thought. *I have to stop it. But how? Jesus God, how?* Satterfield surely had a gun—maybe more than one. Tyler had nothing, not even a set of keys. Sweaty running clothes and his bare hands, that was all he had. It wasn't enough. Not nearly enough.

CHAPTER 50

Brockton

I HEARD A CHORUS of muffled screams, including my own, when Satterfield cut off Kathleen's finger. My heart was racing and my chest was heaving; with the duct tape over my mouth, I couldn't get enough air, and felt close to blacking out. *Calm down*, I commanded myself. *Calm down. Breathe. Think. If you panic instead of thinking, everybody dies.* At death scenes—even gruesome ones, like the woman's body pinned to the tree by arrows—I was generally able to distance myself from the horror; to look at the scene as a puzzle. Could I do that now? I didn't know, but it seemed our only hope.

Satterfield laid Kathleen's finger on the table, along with the gardening shears, and picked up his gun again. I forced myself to observe his face, his movements, his surroundings, as if he were a research subject.

Over his shoulder, I suddenly glimpsed movement—a reflection in the sliding-glass door? *No*, I realized with a shock. *Something—someone—outside the door, out on the patio.* I waited and watched, tuning out the sights and sounds and horrors closer at hand. *There it was again—a face! My God—Tyler's face!* Perhaps there was a glimmer of hope.

But it was faint, and it was fleeting. We didn't have much time—maybe not even time for Tyler to go next door and call the police. If the police did come, and if Satterfield heard them, he'd kill us swiftly, before they could stop him.

It's up to Tyler, I thought desperately, and then thought despairingly, *How? It would take a miracle.* The word itself—*miracle*—gave me an idea. It was an absurd idea, but it was the only idea I had.

I shifted my focus back to Satterfield. I had to get his attention; I had to persuade him to take the tape off my mouth. I grunted his name, as best I could through the tape: *Nnn-nn-nnn. NNN-nn-nnn.* He looked at me quizzically. *NNN-nn-nnn!*

Now his expression changed to amusement. "Are you speaking to me?" I nodded, praying. "You have something important to say?" I nodded again. "What could you possibly say that would interest me now? 'I'm sorry?' Too late. 'Kill me first?' Not a chance." I shook my head firmly. "You really mean it, don't you? You actually think you have something to say." I nodded. *Don't look desperate,* I urged myself. *Look strong. Look smart. Look like you know something he needs to know.* "Tell you what," he said finally. "We'll play a game. I'll let you talk for ten seconds. If you scream, I shoot your wife. If you bore me, I shoot your son. Deal?"

I nodded again. It was an easy deal to make; we were all dead anyhow.

With his left hand, he pressed the muzzle of the gun to my temple. With his right, he picked up the gardening shears and brought the tips of the blades to my face. For a moment I expected him to cut off my nose, but he turned the tool sideways and slit the duct tape. I drew a deep breath—the air felt precious—and then I began to speak, softly at first, then gradually louder: "And the Lord God said, Behold, the man is become as one of us, with knowledge of good and evil. And the Lord looked at the garden, and he drove them from it." Satterfield stared at me as if I'd lost my mind, and perhaps I had. I wasn't counting the seconds, but he hadn't shot anyone—not yet, at least. The next part was the important part. *Please be out there, Tyler,* I prayed. *Please listen. Please understand.* "And in the garden he placed an angel," I went on, with rising fervor, like an old-time preacher. "An angel with spreading wings and a mighty sword. So that if any evildoer should come therein, the angel could fly at him with the sword, and smite the evil one, like the whirling hammer of the Lord God Almighty."

CHAPTER 51

Tyler

***JESUS GOD,* THOUGHT TYLER,** his mind racing and his heart pounding as Brockton's ravings—his coded message—sank in. How many years since Tyler's last track meet? Three? No, four: his sophomore year of undergrad. Could he even do it anymore? No point worrying about it; given the situation, it was do or die. *More like try and die*, he thought grimly.

Squatting beside the concrete angel in the garden—this had to be what Brockton meant—he curled his fingers beneath the wings and hoisted the statue a few inches off the ground, swinging it slowly back and forth like a pendulum, getting the feel of it. It didn't feel right: The wings were too wide; his hands were too far apart, and the angel's head was pressing into his belly. Worse, he could tell that if he released one wing before the other—even a microsecond before the other—the statue would tumble out of control and miss its mark. Frowning, he laid it down and studied it, circling it like a wary dog. Halfway around, he had an idea. Squatting again, he gripped the angel by the thin, circular base beneath the feet and straightened, then swayed to set it swinging, this time head down. *Better,* he thought. *Much better.* The mass and balance weren't exactly the same as the hammer's—the statue felt much heavier; maybe thirty pounds rather than sixteen—but he wouldn't be throwing for distance, only for accuracy. It would do. It had to do.

He shifted his grip slightly, propping the statue on the patio as he did, the tips of the wings and the sword forming a temporary tripod. *The fall of Lucifer,* he thought; then—straightening and lifting once more—*Angels and ministers of grace defend us!*

He did a test throw in slow motion, mentally coaching himself through the movements: the swaying windup, then the four-and-a-half spins—the accelerating dervish dance needed to power the flight of the angel, the hammer of God. Halfway through the practice spins, he stumbled and nearly fell, regaining his balance just in time to avoid a noisy crash. *Who are you kidding?* he asked himself scornfully, but then he heard another voice—a kinder voice: his high-school coach's voice wafting across a decade, cheerfully scolding him in exactly the same words he'd used a hundred times or more at practice: *Turn off your brain, Tyler. It's like making love, son—if you're thinking, you're not doing it right.*

The remembered admonition calmed Tyler; it even made him smile briefly. He drew a long, slow breath, feeling and hearing the air: rushing through his nostrils, flowing down the back of his throat, filling his lungs. He drew another, and a familiar, distinctive mixture of oxygen and adrenaline made its way into his muscles, awakening sensations and skills that lay deep and dormant within him. Turning his back on the window, he began to rock, swinging the statue to and fro, in pendulum arcs that gradually rose higher and higher: left, right, left, right, the wingtips and sword almost grazing the ground at the bottom of each arc. After half a dozen swings, the arc reached shoulder height on each side, and Tyler boosted the angel over the top: above his left shoulder, over his head, and then swooping down to the right. As it swooped he began to spin, shifting the plane of the statue's motion from vertical toward horizontal. It swung outward now, angling away from his body as he spun. Whirling faster and faster, he leaned back, leaned into the turns, he and the angel counterbalancing one another like skaters or dancers in a dizzying duet—two turns, three turns, four—the winged figure straining to take flight.

As Tyler completed his fourth turn, the back of his left shoe came down on a pea-sized pebble. Pinched between his heel and the patio, the pebble shot free, pinging against the glass of the sliding door. It hit just as Tyler came out of the turn, whirling toward the house, toward his release point—the point where he would relax his fingers and release the statue; where he would let the angel take flight.

At the edge of his whirling field of vision, Tyler suddenly saw Satterfield spinning, too: spinning toward Tyler, a nightmarish reflection of Tyler's own motion.

Time slowed; Tyler's vision narrowed, tunneled, excluding all but three things: the sheen of the glass door, the malice on Satterfield's face, and the pistol in the outstretched, tightening grip.

CHAPTER 52

Brockton

AS I WATCHED IN horror, Satterfield spun toward Tyler, raised the pistol, and fired.

The glass exploded—the room itself seemed to explode—and then Satterfield was lifted off his feet. He flew backward, slamming against the far wall of the dining room, hurled there—*pinned* there—by the angel from the garden. The wing tips pierced his wrists, pinning him to the wall like Christ on the cross, like the woman against the tree. The angel's head was pressed tightly against Satterfield's chest, the tip of the sword nestled in the hollow of his throat.

I glanced across the table at Kathleen, who was staring at the bizarre tableau, her shock at losing her finger momentarily forgotten, it seemed. Then, out of the corner of my eye, I glimpsed more movement outside. A man—his running shorts and T-shirt seeming surreally out of place here amid the carnage—stepped through the jagged, glass-fringed opening where the sliding door had just exploded. It was Tyler, looking as startled and stunned as I felt.

"It's okay, it's okay," he gasped. "You're gonna be okay."

"Tyler, thank God," I said. "Are you hit? Are you hurt?"

"I don't think so."

He knelt beside Kathleen and lifted her dangling, dripping hand. "Jesus. Jesus, Mrs. B, I can't believe he did that." He snatched a napkin from the floor and wrapped it around the stump of her finger, then raised the hand and angled it across her chest, resting it on her left shoulder. "Can you hold it here?" She stared, wild-eyed and confused. "Can you hold your hand up like that—just for a minute?—while I find something better to stop the bleeding?" Slowly her eyes focused on his face, and she nodded. "Good. That's really, really good, Mrs. B. Hang in there. You're gonna be just fine." Standing, he scanned the kitchen, then headed to the freezer. He opened the door, and I heard ice clattering as he rummaged in the bin.

Satterfield groaned and twitched. I was surprised that he was alive; I had thought—and hoped—that the statue had struck him with enough force to crush his chest and stop his heart. But no: Satterfield shook his head and opened his eyes, staring at the angel that pinned him to the wall. I saw him wince as he strained to free his arms, then—to my horror—I saw him lift his feet from the floor, flexing his legs to bring his feet up to the base of the statue, working them underneath it for leverage. "Tyler!" I yelled.

Tyler turned, the freezer door still open. "*Shit,*" he said, skidding back across the kitchen in a trail of ice cubes. He scooped up the gun that had flown from Satterfield's hand when the statue slammed into him. "*Stop,*" he ordered, raising the gun. Satterfield froze, but he didn't lower his legs. "I will *totally* shoot you, asshole," Tyler added. "Put your feet down—*now*—or I will gladly shoot your balls off."

Satterfield's feet slid from the statue and his legs eased down to the floor. Tyler kept the pistol trained on him, his hand shaking.

Suddenly I saw another flicker of movement in the back doorway—a face appearing and quickly withdrawing. Then a man in green military fatigues—a soldier? a cop?—stepped into the opening, dropped into a shooter's crouch, and aimed a pistol at Tyler's head. "*No!*" I screamed again. Tyler stared at me in confusion. I flung my head and shoulders backward, rocking the front legs of my chair off the floor, then jerked forward with all the strength I possessed. The chair bucked onto its front legs; I hung there, balanced at the tipping point, then—with agonizing slowness—toppled forward: toppled toward Tyler, falling against him, my head slamming into his belly just as I heard a gunshot from the doorway, and another, and three more in quick succession.

Tyler doubled over and collapsed onto me. Facedown on the floor, I could not see if he was alive or dead.

CHAPTER 53

Decker

DECKER STEPPED THROUGH THE doorway, the gun still raised, wondering what the hell had just happened; wondering what the hell was happening *still.* Brockton and Satterfield lay tangled together on the floor, thanks to Brockton spoiling his shot, knocking Satterfield down, the guy's head snapping downward just as Deck was squeezing off the shots. All five rounds had missed; all five had burrowed instead into—what the *fuck?*—an angel, a goddamned *angel*, which was holding someone, was *pinning* someone, against the back wall of the dining room. Someone who had tats on both of his raised forearms; someone who had the face of the suspect, Satterfield. *Christ*, Deck realized, nearly throwing up when it hit him, *I almost shot the wrong guy.*

He stepped to the far end of the table and pressed the muzzle of his weapon against Satterfield's forehead: the right guy's forehead this time, no doubt about it. As he did, he heard the keening of sirens, faint at first, their pitch and volume rising as they drew nearer. "This is for Kevin," Deck said softly, his finger pressing the trigger once more. "My dead brother."

"Wait," urged a voice. Brockton's voice, from the floor. "Don't shoot him. That's not the way."

"An eye for an eye," said Decker. "A life for a life. He owes lots of lives."

"It'll ruin you if you do it," said Brockton. "It would make you a murderer, too. Just like him."

"Not just like him," said Decker, the gun still on the guy's forehead.

"He'll go to prison for life," said Brockton. "Maybe get the death penalty. Let the court do that. It's too big a load for you to carry."

"I'm willing to take that chance," Decker answered, his finger tightening.

"Deck?" He heard another voice speaking now—the voice of the watch commander, Captain Hackworth, calling his name softly from the shattered glass door. "Hey, Deck, I'm coming in," Hackworth said evenly. "How about you let me take your sidearm now, okay?" Decker felt a hand on his shoulder, then saw another hand reaching in, fingers encircling the barrel of the gun. "You got him, Deck," the captain said as he gently raised the barrel and then freed the gun from Decker's grasp. "You got him. It's over."

"It's not over till I say it's over," Decker heard Satterfield hiss. "I'll be back to finish this."

Decker felt his fingers clench, and wished the gun were still in his hand; still pressed to Satterfield's forehead.

PART 3

After the Fall

And the Lord God said, Behold, the man is become as one of us, to know good and evil: and now, lest he put forth his hand, and take also of the tree of life, and eat, and live for ever:

Therefore the Lord God sent him forth from the garden of Eden, to till the ground from whence he was taken.

So he drove out the man; and he placed at the east of the garden of Eden Cherubims, and a flaming sword which turned every way, to keep the way of the tree of life.

—Genesis 3:22–24

JANUARY 1993

CHAPTER 54

Brockton

"I STILL CAN'T BELIEVE it," Jeff squawked, for the third time—or was it the fourth?—since we'd sat down in Calhoun's. "That guy really needs to fry." He punctuated his opinion by licking a blob of barbecue sauce from his thumb.

"Jeff." Kathleen's voice was soft, but it carried an unmistakable motherly reprimand—one she underscored by wagging a finger at him. It was her pinky finger—an eighth-inch shorter than before, its range of motion still limited, but on the mend, thank God. "We're here to celebrate," she added, "not second-guess the jury."

"I know. Sorry, Mom; sorry, Dad," he said. Through the plate-glass window behind him, I watched a towboat bulling a raft of barges upriver, the wake angling out from the stern and rushing toward the pilings on which the restaurant rested. Jeff plucked a French fry from his plate and raised it toward his mouth, then began gesturing with the potato, like a symphony conductor with a baton.

"But he killed six people—six people that we *know* of—including his own mother and stepfather. If a guy like that doesn't deserve to die, I don't know who does. *They* sure didn't deserve to die."

"They didn't," agreed Kittredge, "but it's not just about whether he deserved it." The KPD detective had joined us for the post-sentencing lunch; so had Janelle Mayfield, who'd fought Satterfield for her life and had won. With Kittredge's support, Janelle had been hired by KPD as an advocate for victims of sex crimes—a brave move on the part of both KPD and Janelle, I thought. "If he'd gotten a death sentence, he might never be executed anyhow," Kittredge went on. "There'd be appeals—years and years of appeals. Millions of dollars worth of appeals. Maybe it's just as good, and a lot cheaper, to lock him up and throw away the key."

I checked my watch; it was twelve forty-five. "Roxanne, what time's your flight?"

"Not till three thirty," she said. "If Tyler and I head for the airport by two thirty, we'll be fine."

"Are you kidding?" I teased. "The way he creeps along in that truck? You should've left forty-five minutes ago. Be quicker to walk."

"Ha ha," said Tyler. "You're just jealous because I won't sell it to you."

"What, that old thing?" I retorted. "No shoulder harnesses, no air bags—that thing's a death trap, man." I grinned, but then I felt a pang. I was going to miss Tyler—miss his work, and miss his company. "You sure you don't want to rethink, now that your thesis is done? Maybe take the spring and summer off, then decide?"

"Bill." Kathleen's voice was soft—even softer than it'd been with Jeff a moment before. I knew when to shut up, and the time was now.

"Another thing," said Jeff, taking advantage of the momentary lull. "How come Satterfield gets a free lawyer? A really *mean* free lawyer? That guy DeVriess—'Grease'—man, he was fierce. Made it sound like *Dad* was the scumbag on trial."

"*Jeff*." This time Kathleen's voice made no pretense at softness. This time even Jeff got the message. Across the table, Jenny's hand reached for Jeff's, her fingers giving his a squeeze. Chiding, or affectionate? Maybe both, I realized, when Jeff looked at her with a sheepish smile. Their communication—much of it conveyed by looks and touches—seemed surprisingly evolved for a pair of high-school kids. Was that because they'd had a brush with death? Or was it just because they were smart, good-hearted, and happy with one another? Whatever the reason, I was pleased for them.

"Show them," Jeff said to her.

"Now?" Jenny blushed, suddenly looking shy.

"Sure, why not? Show 'em."

"Show us what, sweetheart?" asked Kathleen.

"Oh, nothing, really," she said. "Just . . . a couple of sketches I did in the courtroom today." Jeff nudged her, and she reached down beside her chair and retrieved a small leather portfolio, setting it in her lap and opening the flap. She took out two pieces of drawing paper. "Janelle, one's for you."

"For me?" Janelle looked nervous. "Why?"

Jenny smiled. "You remember the drawing I did that day at the police department?"

"How could I forget?" said the woman. "Scared the crap out of me when I saw that awful face staring up from the page."

"Not the drawing of *him*," said Jenny. "The drawing of *you*."

"Honey, I am *talking* about the drawing of me," Janelle replied, drawing a good laugh from all of us. Then her face turned serious. "Sure, I remember the drawing you did of me. I looked pretty bad, too."

"Not bad," said Jenny. "Scared. Hurt. Sad. Mad."

Janelle nodded. "Sounds about right."

"Today I drew you again." Jenny handed her the top sketch. I couldn't have said which sprang to Janelle's face first, the smile or the tears. She tried to speak, but quickly gave up. Instead, she laid one hand on her heart; with the other, she held up the drawing so we could all see it. There were still traces of hurt—more lines around the mouth and eyes than a woman her age should have, and a zigzag scar across the cheekbone—but mostly, the face gazing out from the page radiated courage and confidence.

"That is *beautiful*," said Kathleen. "A perfect likeness."

Jenny beamed at Kathleen and Janelle, then looked at me. "Dr. B, the other one's for you."

"Me? Why'd you waste a perfectly good piece of paper drawing me?"

"It's not *of* you," she said. "It's *for* you." She handed me the drawing, facedown. I hesitated, then turned it up.

It was like nothing I'd ever seen: A girl's face—the unidentified strip-mine girl's face—turned upward, toward the sky. Her features were serene, almost beatific; underneath them, the skull shone through, faintly but distinctly, in a way that somehow did not diminish or detract from the beauty of the face. She was shown in profile, one eye open wide, the other hidden by the bridge of the nose. But from that other, unseen eye grew a tree: a miniature but fully formed tree, its crown luxuriant with leaves and blossoms and songbirds. In the background, and on all sides, other trees grew, from ground that had once been scarred and barren, but had long since softened and gone to green. Beneath the ground, the trees were linked by a web of roots—roots that entwined delicately, seamlessly, with the girl's golden hair; roots that somehow *were* the girl's golden hair. Amid death, the image seemed to suggest—in spite of death, or perhaps even *because* of death, in some mysterious way I did not yet understand—there was life.

Even life abundant.

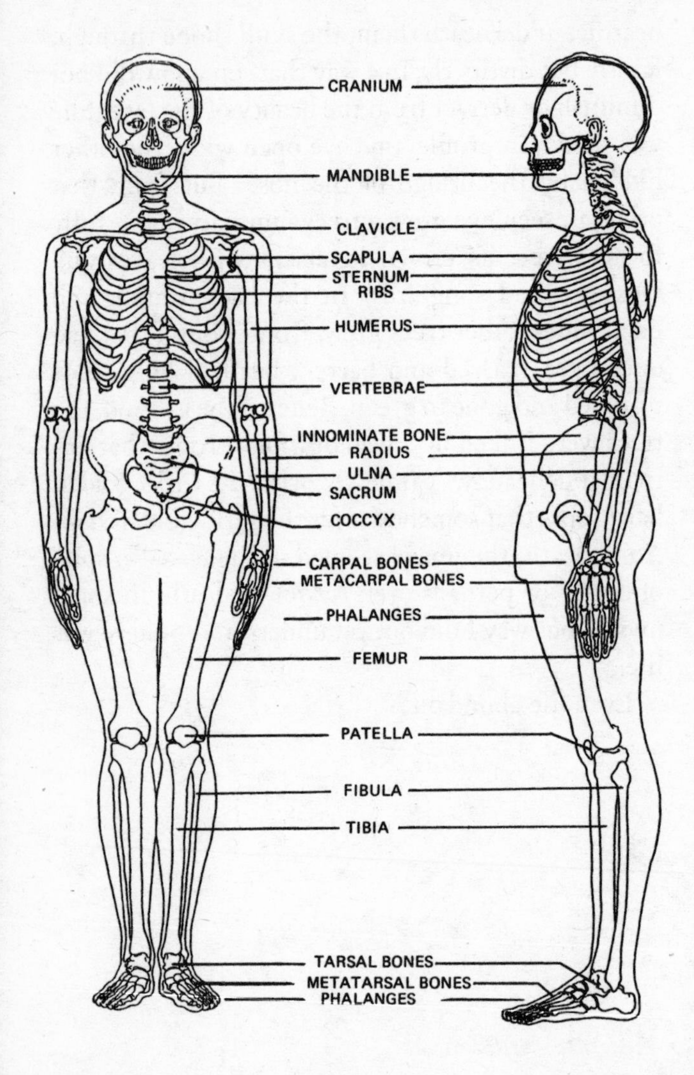
CRANIUM
MANDIBLE
CLAVICLE
SCAPULA
STERNUM
RIBS
HUMERUS
VERTEBRAE
INNOMINATE BONE
RADIUS
ULNA
SACRUM
COCCYX
CARPAL BONES
METACARPAL BONES
PHALANGES
FEMUR
PATELLA
FIBULA
TIBIA
TARSAL BONES
METATARSAL BONES
PHALANGES

THE SKULL

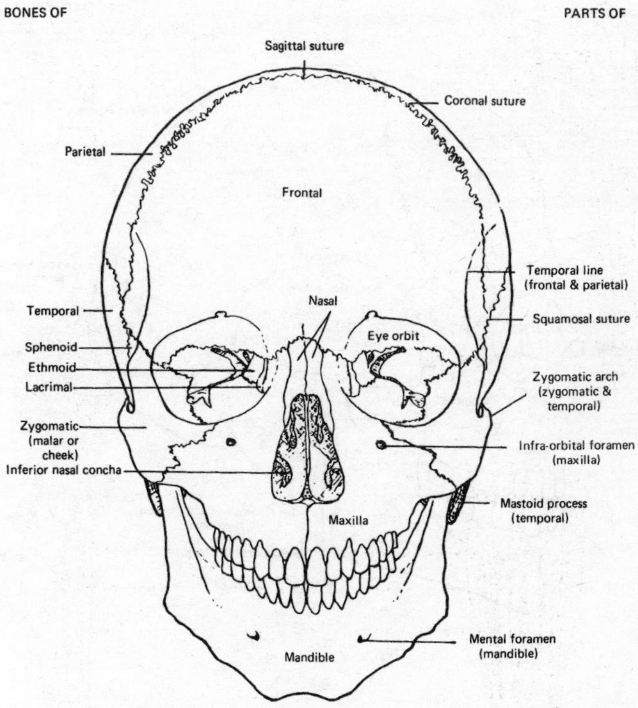

BONES OF
PARTS OF
Sagittal suture
Coronal suture
Parietal
Frontal
Temporal line
(frontal & parietal)
Temporal
Nasal
Squamosal suture
Sphenoid
Eye orbit
Ethmoid
Lacrimal
Zygomatic arch
(zygomatic &
temporal)
Zygomatic
(malar or
cheek)
Infra-orbital foramen
(maxilla)
Inferior nasal concha
Mastoid process
(temporal)
Maxilla
Mental foramen
(mandible)
Mandible

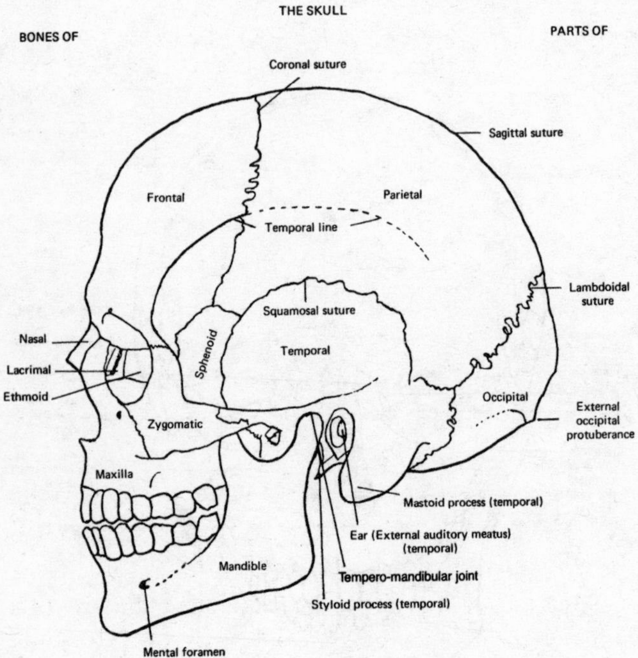
THE SKULL
BONES OF
PARTS OF
Coronal suture
Sagittal suture
Frontal
Parietal
Temporal line
Lambdoidal suture
Squamosal suture
Nasal
Sphenoid
Temporal
Lacrimal
Ethmoid
Occipital
External occipital protuberance
Zygomatic
Maxilla
Mastoid process (temporal)
Ear (External auditory meatus) (temporal)
Mandible
Tempero-mandibular joint
Styloid process (temporal)
Mental foramen

AUTHOR'S NOTE: ON FACT AND FICTION

Those of you who are astute at arithmetic may have noted that Dr. Bill Brockton, our fictional hero, is slightly younger—by some thirty years—than Dr. Bill Bass, who turned a remarkably youthful eighty-five in August 2013. Making Brockton so much younger has much to recommend it, fictionally speaking, as it allows Brockton (and us!) to be still employed, rather than retired.

But all choices have consequences, and in this book's case—specifically, the case of the Body Farm's genesis—Brockton's relative youth has required us to fudge the birth year of the real-life research facility. In *Cut to the Bone*, we give that year as 1992. In real life, it's considerably earlier, as well as more complex. The sow barn described in the book is quite real, but it was back in 1971 that it became the location for the Body Farm's first incarnation: a distant, smelly place where decomposing bodies could be stashed before they were processed into clean skeletal remains.

The Body Farm's second incarnation—its metamorphosis, to borrow an entomological term from the realm of blowflies and maggots—didn't occur until a decade later. In the spring of 1981, the first research project began in a new sixteen-by-sixteen-foot chain-link cube at the facility's current location, behind the University of Tennessee Medical Center, on the south shore of the Tennessee River. That project, which commenced with donated body 1-81, was a pioneering study of insect activity in human corpses. Corpse 1-81 and its successors (2-81, 3-81, and 4-81) served as the research subjects for a master's degree thesis by Dr. Bass's student William Rodriguez. Rodriguez's pioneering research, documenting the relationship between the insects' activity and the cadavers' decay rates, remains a classic—one of the most frequently cited studies in both forensic anthropology and forensic entomology.

There are, of course, more stories behind those stories. Readers who are interested in the factual history of the Body Farm might enjoy our first book, the nonfiction memoir *Death's Acre.* That book also contains a chapter on the "Zoo Man" case, a series of murders that electrified and terrified Knoxville in the early 1990s. Our fictional story here borrows freely from the factual case, in which Knoxville prostitutes were taken into the woods off Cahaba Lane and then murdered. We feel entitled to borrow, as both Dr. Bill Bass and KPD fingerprint expert Art Bohanan played key roles in the prosecution of Thomas "Zoo Man" Huskey for the Cahaba Lane murders.

We've endeavored to be accurate in our depiction

of KPD's SWAT team, which was relatively new at the time of our story. We have, however, taken one large liberty in our depiction of KPD's bomb squad, which did not yet have a bomb-sniffing dog in 1992.

The book's central premises were true then, and, sadly, remain true now: Women—especially young, poor women driven by desperation to prostitution—are among the most vulnerable members of our society; they're often preyed upon, largely scorned, and easily overlooked if they go missing. And sadistic sexual predators—embodiments of cunning and evil, created by a tangled, terrible confluence of nature and "nurture"—still coil unseen among and around us. As ever, there are serpents in the garden in which we dwell. Even so, it is a lush and lovely garden.

ACKNOWLEDGMENTS

Solving crimes requires the intelligence and cooperation of many people. So does creating crime novels. Luckily, many smart people have been kind enough to help us with that latter task.

Art Bohanan—the real one, not the fictional one—was, as always, a good sport and a great source of insight into crime-scene and crime-lab work. So was forensic ace Amy George. Dawn Coppock and James Rochelle—smart, good-hearted people who love the mountains of east Tennessee—offered helpful information on strip mining and its environmental effects, especially the severe and lasting effects of mountaintop removal. Precision blaster John Koehler—a man who can topple a smokestack like a tree, or collapse a building into its own basement—provided a fascinating glimpse into the world of explosives.

Lt. Keith Debow, commander of the Knoxville Police Department's SWAT team, was remarkably informative, patient, and good-humored in answering a fusillade of questions about the book's SWAT-team scenario; so was Lt. Doug Stiles, the team's previous commander. We appreciate their gracious help; we also appreciate their willingness to put themselves in harm's way—in *serious* harm's way—to protect the lives of others. Thanks also to Ed Buice and Special Agent Mike Keleher, at the Naval Criminal Investigative Service, who offered insights and suggestions about how a sailor who came unhinged might be investigated.

No book about a recent serial killer would be complete or credible without drawing on the work of the FBI's Behavioral Analysis Unit, whose "profilers" are justly renowned for their insights into the darkest of criminal minds. Supervisory Special Agent James J. McNamara (retired), who headed the BSU's serial-killer division for years, was generous with his time and helpful with his advice about what might motivate a sexual killer to add Dr. Bill Brockton to his list of potential victims. Sincere thanks to Jim McNamara, as well as to special agents Ann Todd and Angela Bell for making the connection with him possible. Tallahassee psychologist and researcher Thomas Joiner—author of *The Perversion of Virtue: Understanding Murder-Suicide*—also helped illuminate the dark corners and crevices of the soul.

To switch from serial murder to a *slightly* less frightening arena—the arena of publishing—we express our continuing gratitude to our agent, Giles Anderson, for keeping us gainfully and happily employed for the past decade (time *does* fly when you're having fun!). Editorial consultant Heather Whitaker read an early draft of this novel and offered suggestions that made the book far more coherent and far more suspenseful, and the eagle-eyed Casey Whitworth proofread the galley pages and made them far more corrct. Er, *correct.*

We're deeply grateful to a whole host of people at William Morrow and HarperCollins who make these books possible, especially our editor, Lyssa Keusch, and her associates, Amanda Bergeron and Rebecca Lucash; our publisher, Liate Stehlik, and deputy publisher, Lynn Grady; publicity wizard Danielle Bartlett; marketing director Kathy Gordon; online marketing guru Shawn Nicholls; the seldom-sung heroes in art and production, who turn computer files into actual books (and e-books)—production editor Julia Meltzer; designer Richard Aquan (*great* cover art for the dust jacket!); paperback art director Thomas Egner; and—of course—the sales staffers who actually persuade people to part with their hard-earned money to purchase our books, led by Doug Jones and Brian Grogan.

Last, to our wives, Carol Bass and Jane McPherson, for so many things that, if we listed them all, would make this book twice as long.

The ink on his contract with the University of Tennessee barely dry, Dr. Bill Brockton is called to a rural county to identify a dead woman and determine how she died. But the case—one of Brockton's first murders in Tennessee—could also prove to be his last as he runs afoul of both the county sheriff and an angry mob, intent on administering their own swift, rough brand of "justice." With his back to the wall, Brockton is forced to think fast, talk faster, and hope for a miracle.

Turn the page to read

JORDAN'S STORMY BANKS

an original novella by Jefferson Bass.

Perimortem, Part I

perimortem *(adjective): at or around the time of death*

December 24, 1990

THE FLAMES FLARED WITHIN the darkness, swirling red and orange and oily black, as the cross caught fire on the courthouse lawn. Lit and shadowed by the fiery undulations, as if in a nightmare, I saw angry faces, oiled guns, and the tight, heavy coils of a noose.

But it was no nightmare. I was wide-awake, it was Christmas Eve, and it was not entirely clear to me who would be found swaying from the noose by the light of Christmas morning: the black man huddled inside the Morgan County jail, or the meddlesome scientist standing on the building's steps, his back—*my* back—pressed tight against the wooden door.

How had it come to this? Was I wrong about the century I inhabited? Had I somehow been transported back in time a hundred years, from 1990 to 1890? How had matters come to this—for the man behind bars, and especially for me? Had I spoken out of turn, or rushed in where angels fear to tread? Maybe I should have stayed in Kansas instead of taking the job in Tennessee.

Or maybe it was all just because of the memo. That damned memo . . .

1

Antemortem

antemortem *(adjective): occurring before the time of death*

July 4, 1990

I STARED AT THE stinky, sodden mess on the stainless-steel gurney, my eyes watering and my brain reeling. "What am I supposed to do with this?" I asked the man who'd just delivered the mess, which was a corpse he'd pulled from the back of a hearse and wheeled into the basement of Neyland Stadium. Above our heads reared the stadium itself, the University of Tennessee's massive shrine to college football. Around us—in the dingy basement room I'd grandly named the Osteology Laboratory—clustered a few government-surplus lab tables and a few thousand boxes of Indian bones, so recently arrived and unloaded that they'd not even been shelved yet.

The hearse driver, who worked for a funeral home in Crossville, seventy miles west of Knoxville, shrugged. He pulled a piece of paper from his shirt pocket, unfolded it, and glanced at the wording. "I guess you're supposed to do whatever the Chief M.E. says you'll do," he said. He handed the page to me. "Welcome to Tennessee," he said, then spun on his heel and scuttled away in the hearse before I could stop him.

I read the memo with a mixture of puzzlement and rising alarm.

Date: July 1, 1990
To: Tennessee Medical Examiners
From: Dr. Gerald Francis, M.D.,
Chief Medical Examiner
Subject: Dr. Bill Brockton, State
Forensic Anthropologist

I am pleased to announce that I have appointed Dr. Bill Brockton to the newly created position of Tennessee State Forensic Anthropologist, effective immediately.

Dr. Brockton has just been hired as chairman of the Anthropology Department at the University of Tennessee in Knoxville. He comes to UT after ten years on the faculty at the University of Kansas in Lawrence, as well as ten summers of field work in South Dakota, where he and his students excavated thousands of eighteenth and nineteenth century Arikara Indian skeletons. Dr. Brockton received his Ph.D. at the University of Pennsylvania; his mentor, Dr. Wilton Krogman, was one of the nation's foremost physical anthropologists, sometimes called "the Sherlock Holmes of bones."

As State Forensic Anthropologist, Dr. Brockton is available to examine any unidentified remains found in your county, as well as identified corpses that have, or might have, skeletal trauma. I am confident that Dr. Brockton will be a strong and valuable addition to our staff, and I trust that you will all extend him a warm Tennessee welcome.

Cc: Tennessee District Attorneys General
Tennessee Sheriffs
Dr. Bill Brockton, Ph.D.

I reread the memo. Three times. "Crap, Gerry," I muttered, as if Gerry—Chief Medical Examiner Gerald Francis—could hear me, despite the fact that he was 180 miles away, in Nashville. "Why didn't you run that past me before you sent it out all over the damn state?" Thanks to the memo, every M.E. and D.A. and sheriff, in however-the-hell-many counties my new home state had, had gotten the wrong idea about me.

The appointment itself was no surprise—I'd agreed to take the post—and it wasn't the memo's description of my education and experience that had me fretting. When it came to analyzing skeletal remains and skeletal trauma, I felt competent and even confident; I had, after all, studied some ten thousand skeletons over the past dozen years, half of them in the dusty collections of the Smithsonian Institution, half of them in the fine-grained soil of the Great Plains, where I'd found and excavated them just ahead of rising waters, on rivers newly dammed by the U.S. Army Corps of Engineers. "The legions of the dammed," one of my waggish students had dubbed the five thousand or so Indian skeletons I'd saved from watery graves.

No, what troubled me about the memo was its promise of what I could do—what I *would* do—for the state's far-flung M.E.'s: "examine any unidentified remains," as well as "identified corpses that have, or might have, skeletal trauma."

I'd consulted with law enforcement investigators for years in Kansas, before moving to Tennessee; that consulting work, in fact, was how Gerry Francis knew me—from a case I'd described at a forensic conference a few years before. My collaborations with law enforcement had begun by accident, or, more accurately, by happenstance: One summer early in my teaching career at Kansas, as my students and I were pulling Indian bones from the shoreline, a South Dakota sheriff's deputy had jounced to a stop at the dig site and asked if I'd be willing to examine a skeleton a rancher had found in a dry wash on his property and tell him whatever I could about it. "A skeleton's a skeleton," I'd told the deputy. "Sure, let's go."

The skeleton—a robust white male—bore a striking resemblance to many of the male Indian skeletons I'd dug from their compact, circular graves: the skull struck by a heavy blunt object, which had left an oval depression—remarkably similar to that created by a Sioux war club. As it turned out, the dead white man actually *had* been struck by a Sioux war club. The man was a relic poacher, and—in a case of ironic just desserts—he'd been killed by a rival collector in a struggle over the club: a trophy that had emerged from a century of retirement to become once more a lethal weapon.

After I helped the sheriff's office with that case, one thing had led to another, as things have a way of doing, and by the time I'd left Kansas for Tennessee, I was averaging six or eight forensic cases a year for local police, county sheriffs, and the Kansas Bureau of Investigation.

But those six or eight cases invariably involved dry, weathered bones, not slimy, stinking corpses like the one that had just been delivered to me. *Dumped on me, more like it*, I thought. I could picture the relief—the utter delight—the Cumberland County medical examiner must have felt when he read his boss's memo and realized that he could wash his hands of this body, literally and figuratively, by sending it to Knoxville. To me.

As I unzipped the body bag and folded back the large, C-shaped flap that formed the bag's upper surface, I jumped back, startled and repulsed by the sudden sight and sound of thousands of maggots—blowfly larva—swarming and squirming and writhing to escape the light to which I'd suddenly exposed them. Diving for cover, they quickly slithered into the large openings they'd created in the face, neck, and lower abdomen of the body; as I watched their swift migration, my revulsion gave way to scientific fascination. Once they were out of sight, though, my gaze strayed back to the memo. *God, how many more bodies like this am I gonna get?* I wondered silently. Aloud, looking back at the body once more, I repeated, "What am I supposed to do with this?"

I was still without an answer an hour later when the phone rang. I started to ignore it—it was July Fourth, after all—but remembered that I'd given Kathleen, my wife, the bone lab's number. "I'll only be a minute," I'd told her. "Just long enough to sign for some skeletal remains. Call me if you need me to pick up anything on the way home."

"Hello?"

"Bill?" She sounded surprised to hear my voice, and that in turn surprised me, since I'd given her the number and told her that this was where I'd be.

"Hi, honey," I said. "What's up? Need something?"

"I need *you*. We have fifty people showing up for this cookout in twenty minutes. Your new colleagues and my new colleagues and our new neighbors. You said you'd be home half an hour ago to help."

I checked my watch and felt myself wince. "Oh, crap—I'm sorry. This turned out to be more complicated than I expected. I'm leaving right now."

As I hung up the phone, my earlier, unresolved question continued to hang in the air, nearly as tangible as the odor from the body on the gurney. Then inspiration came to me. "Ah," I said to the corpse. "*That's* what I'll do with you."

2

IT HAD SEEMED LIKE a good idea at the time, but in hindsight, perhaps what I'd done with the corpse hadn't been so inspired after all.

The building that was shoehorned beneath the grandstands of Neyland Stadium—a wedge-shaped warren of grimy rooms named Stadium Hall—had begun its life, decades before, as an athletic dormitory. Now, deemed too dilapidated to house athletes, it housed the Anthropology Department. Stadium Hall's chief virtues, as best I could tell during my first week on the job, were two: It contained plenty of rooms—hundreds of rooms—to accommodate what I hoped would be a fast-growing population of Anthropology faculty and graduate students. It also contained an abundance of bathrooms and showers, and it was in one of these showers—the one in the stairwell adjoining the basement bone lab—that I'd decided to stash the corpse over the July Fourth holiday, until I could figure out how best to clean and examine the bones of the dead man.

I returned to the stadium to reclaim the remains at 9:00 A.M. on July fifth. Unfortunately, the building's janitor had returned at *8:00* A.M., and by the time I showed up, he was mad as a hornet. The university police officers summoned by the janitor were none too happy, either.

I explained the situation to the police officers briefly, showing them the memo about my appointment as State Forensic Anthropologist, and then phoned the Cumberland County medical examiner, so he could corroborate my story—something he did with evident amusement. *Great*, I thought as the grinning police officers departed. *I'll never hear the end of this—not from the campus police, and not from the M.E.'s, either.*

It had taken only twenty minutes to resolve the police officers' concerns. Not so those of the janitor, who, rightly or wrongly, considered Stadium Hall his territory, not mine, and who threatened me with a smorgasbord of dire fates if he ever found another rotting corpse in his building. "I don't mind all them Indian bones you got in them boxes," he said. "But this-here nastiness ain't got no place in my building. I want it out of here, and I don't mean tomorrow."

"It'll be gone by the end of the day," I assured him, wondering how on earth I would manage to keep that promise.

"YOU'VE GOT A *what* in one of the showers in Stadium Hall?" The dean of the College of Arts and

Sciences—my new boss, as of four days before—sounded groggy when he answered the phone, and the thought that I'd awakened him during a five-day holiday weekend made me wince.

"A decomposing body," I repeated. I explained the situation to him. It was the third time in an hour I'd summarized the series of unexpected events, hasty decisions, and unhappy consequences.

"And what, exactly, do you want me to do about this?" He no longer sounded groggy; he sounded wide-awake and more than a little annoyed.

"Here's the thing," I said. "I think I need some land to put bodies on. The Cumberland County medical examiner isn't the only one likely to send me rotting John Does. The way this memo reads, bodies will be coming in from all over the state. It wasn't a problem out in Kansas—Kansas is twice the size of Tennessee, with only half as many people. So out there, it takes a while for folks to be found, and by that time they're generally down to nice, dry bone. Here, on the other hand . . ."

He sighed. "I'll make some calls." I felt my spirits lift, but they plummeted a moment later when he added, "First thing Monday."

"Monday? But that's four days from now," I squawked. "What am I supposed to do with this guy for the next four days?"

"You're a bright young man," he said. "You'll think of something."

"YOU'VE GOT A *what* in the back of your truck?" Kathleen stared at me as if I'd lost my mind.

"A decomposing body." I explained the situation

yet again; by now I could have told the story in my sleep.

"Where—*here*? In *our garage*?"

"No, no. Of course not. I'm not *that* dumb."

"How dumb are you? Did you leave it parked somewhere at UT?"

"Uh, not exactly," I hedged. She gave me a gimlet-eyed look, waiting me out. "It's in the driveway. Halfway between the house and the street."

"Bill *Brockton*," she groaned. "What am I supposed to do with you?"

"Hey, it could be worse," I pointed out.

"How, exactly?"

"I could've brought him home *before* the cookout."

She shook her head and heaved a sigh. "Thank heaven for small favors," she muttered.

THE DEAN SUMMONED me to his office at midmorning Monday. By that time the cab of my truck smelled to high heaven, even though the body bag was back in the cargo bed. I'd driven to campus with the windows down and my head in the wind, like a dog's.

As I left the stadium for the walk up the hill to the dean's office, I noticed a thick cloud of flies surrounding the truck; on the camper shell's window screens, they were packed wing-to-wing, as tightly as planes on an aircraft carrier's deck.

An hour later, trailing a plume of flies in my wake, I pulled away from the stadium and threaded my way up the Tennessee River, a map open on the seat beside me. Six miles to the east—where the

French Broad and the Holston rivers converged to form the Tennessee—the university owned a farm where, for half a century, the College of Agriculture had raised pigs. The pig-farming venture had ended a few years before, and the old sow barn, where countless piglets had been born and nursed, now sat empty and idle. That barn, the dean had informed me in our brief, curt meeting, was the place—the *only* place—where I was to warehouse any corpses I happened to receive from my colleagues in the medical examiner's system.

"Empty and idle" were accurate descriptors, as far as they went, but they were not comprehensive. A complete description of the sow barn—*my* sow barn—required "crumbling and stinking," too. *Fair enough*, I realized, considering that I'd be contributing more than a little decay and odor to the property myself.

I backed the truck up to the barn, opened the cargo shell and tailgate, then slid the body bag out. It dropped to the ground with a dull, squishy thud. By the time I dragged it across the wooden threshold and into the dim, foul-smelling interior of the barn, the bag and I were already being buzzed by a new squadron of flies.

"Welcome to Tennessee," I said to myself.

3

December 21, 1990

TURNING BACK FROM THE office doorway, I snatched up the ringing phone. "Hi, honey," I said. "I'll be right there. I'm leaving this instant." It was the Friday before Christmas, and all through the stadium I was the only creature stirring; everyone else was already home for the holidays, or at least en route.

I was answered by a gravelly, homespun voice, half an octave deeper than my own. "Well, darlin', I sure 'preciate that," the man chuckled. "But before you go, you reckon you could connect me with a Dr. Brockman? Dr. Bill Brockman?"

I felt my face redden. "Sorry," I said. "I thought you were my wife. This is Dr. Brockton. How can I help you?"

"This is Sheriff Dixon, Dr. Brockman. Up in Morgan County."

"Hello, Sheriff," I said. "It's Brock-*ton*, by the way, not Brockman. What can I do for you?" Turning to the framed Tennessee map mounted on the wall, I scanned for Morgan County. The state had ninety-five counties, and in the six months since my arrival in Knoxville, I'd worked ten forensic cases—five of them in Knox County; one each in Chattanooga, Nashville, and Memphis; the janitor-infuriating case from Cumberland County, fifty miles to the west; and one from a rural county southeast of Knoxville. I seemed to recall that Morgan County was nearby, but I was having trouble finding it.

"Looks like maybe we've got a homicide up here. A hiker found a body in the woods, up in Frozen Head State Park. Unidentified nigrah woman. In pretty rough shape. The medical examiner took one look and told me to call and have you come get her. Reckon you could come on up this way?"

I felt a tinge of annoyance—*that damned memo*, I thought again—followed by a wave of excitement and then a ripple of guilt. My addiction to forensic adrenaline was, I suspected, as strong as any alcoholic's thirst, and the truth was, I was happy to have a chance to slake it. But I'd promised Kathleen I'd be home by five o'clock, to help prepare for a Christmas party at six. "Where's the body now, Sheriff?"

"Still in the woods. Just up the slope from a creek. Jordan Branch. It's about five miles outside Wartburg. The M.E. said to leave it at the scene for you."

I spotted Wartburg on the map—a small dot about fifty miles northwest of Knoxville—and then found the irregular green rectangle that marked the state park. Glancing out the office windows, through the grime on the glass and the latticework of girders supporting the stadium's grandstands, I saw that the sky had already gone dark. "I don't mean to put you off, Sheriff," I said, "but I'd rather work the scene in the daylight. No matter how good your lights are, it's easy to miss things in the dark. Any chance you could post somebody out there tonight, to keep an eye on things? Let me meet you there first thing in the morning?"

He considered this for a moment. "I reckon I could put Cotterell out there. One of my deputies. He ain't got nothin' better to do."

I got directions and agreed to meet him at the Morgan County courthouse the next morning at nine. After hanging up, I called Kathleen. "Hi, honey," I said with a sense of déjà vu, sheepishness, and amusement. "I'll be right there. I'm leaving this instant."

4

"PRETTY ROUGH SHAPE" WAS putting it mildly. *Very* mildly. The truth was, in ten years of forensic casework, I'd never seen such a shocking death scene as the one Sheriff Dixon led me to.

We'd met at the Morgan County courthouse, a quaint brick building topped by an elegant, four-sided white cupola, each side dominated by a large clock face reading 9:05.

Ten minutes later, after backtracking several miles along the Knoxville highway, we'd turned onto a small side road that led to two destinations, according to a green sign at the turnoff: Frozen Head State Park, and Morgan County Correctional Center. The prison was first, a sprawling complex of dull brown brick and gleaming razor wire. A mile or so later, after a sharp turn and a narrow bridge over a tumbling creek—Jordan Branch, I guessed—we'd entered a narrow wooded valley. FROZEN HEAD

STATE PARK, read a sign, its white-painted letters etched into dark brown boards. Two miles beyond the sign—past a gate marked AUTHORIZED VEHICLES ONLY, where asphalt gave way to gravel—we'd stopped behind a Morgan County Sheriff's Office cruiser and a black Ford Crown Victoria sporting a state government tag, a trunk-mounted radio antenna, and a side spotlight near the left outside mirror.

The body lay barely thirty yards from the road, within a ragged rectangle of crime-scene tape strung from tree trunks. The ground sloped down toward the creek, and as we picked our way through the rocky terrain, I saw that the legs were angled downhill, toward the stream.

The corpse—a woman's corpse—was nude, and when we got close enough to make out details, I felt my stomach lurch. The body was bloated, the abdomen swollen with gases produced by bacteria and enzymes in the digestive tract. The skin of the torso, arms, and legs was largely intact, but virtually no soft tissue remained on the neck and face; the jaws and teeth were bared in a macabre grin, and the cheekbones and eye orbits—now vacant—were exposed as well, along with the vertebrae of the neck. So were the lower ends of the legs, the tibia and fibula of each leg jutting, footless, from the shredded flesh of the shins.

But gruesome as all those features were, they weren't what I found shocking about the scene. What I found shocking was the way the woman's body had been posed. Her legs were splayed on either side of a small tree, and her crotch—her decaying, decomposing crotch—was pressed tight against the trunk, as if, even long after death, she were still being sexually violated.

"Hey. *Doc.*" The sheriff's gravelly voice tugged at the sleeve of my consciousness, and the insistent tone made me suspect that he'd called my name more than once.

"Sorry, what?" I looked in the direction his voice had come from, and saw him standing by two other men—one in uniform, the other in civilian clothes.

"This here's my deputy, Jim Cotterell. And this troublemaker"—he said it in a tone that might have been joking, or might not—"is Bubba Hardknot, our friendly neighborhood agent from the Tennessee Bureau of Investigation."

"Deputy," I said, shaking the hand of the man in uniform. Then I extended my hand to the TBI agent. "Sorry, I didn't quite catch your name?"

"Special Agent Meffert," he said, smiling slantwise, in a way I couldn't quite interpret. "Wellington Meffert. It's a little fancy for everyday use in Morgan County. Most folks around here call me Bubba Hardknot. When they're being polite."

"I'm kindly surprised to see you way up here in the woods on a Saturday morning, Bubba," said the sheriff flatly. "I thought you TBI types kept banker's hours. Cotterell call you?" He glanced at his deputy; the look seemed accusatory or even hostile, and I gathered there was no love lost between the sheriff and the TBI agent—and possibly not between the sheriff and his own deputy.

"Naw, the park rangers called me," Meffert replied casually. "State property, state agency. Go figure."

"Hmm," grunted Dixon.

My camera was slung around my neck, and I removed the lens cap and began taking pictures—wide shots of the entire scene first, then increasingly tight ones, spiraling in so that I photographed the body from all angles. I finished the 36-exposure roll with close-ups of the footless legs, the fleshless neck and face, and the obscenely posed crotch. Satisfied that I'd captured the key images, I stood from my crouch and turned to the law enforcement officers. "Any idea who she is?"

The sheriff answered. "Not yet. Shouldn't take too long to find out, though. We don't get too many dead nigrahs around here." He chuckled, then added, "Not near enough, right fellas?" He gave me a sly grin and a wink. I blinked, puzzled—and disbelieving, once I replayed his words and decided that I'd understood the joke correctly. I glanced at the other men's faces. Deputy Cotterell was looking away, his cheeks flaming; Agent Meffert's face was a blank mask, as expressionless as stone.

I cleared my throat and turned back toward the body. "She might not actually be negroid," I said. "Once a person's been dead a few days, you can't always tell the race from the color of the skin. The skin of Caucasoids—whites—often darkens as they decay." The sheriff frowned, perhaps because he doubted what I'd said, perhaps because he didn't like the idea that the dead woman might be white. I couldn't tell which was the case, and I didn't want to know. "Any women been reported missing?"

The sheriff shook his head. "Naw. No nigrahs I've heard tell of. For sure no white women."

Reaching into my back pocket, I pulled out a pair of latex gloves and tugged them on, then knelt beside the head for a closer look at the exposed bones of the face. The woman's teeth had a strongly vertical orientation, and the nasal opening was narrow, with a thin sill of bone jutting slightly from the base of the opening. "Now that I look closer," I said, "I'm pretty sure she's white."

"The hell you say," muttered the sheriff.

"What makes you think that, Doc?" asked Meffert quickly.

I glanced over my shoulder. "You got a pen on you, Agent Meffert?" He nodded. I held a gloved index finger to my lips, as if I were a librarian, mid-shush. "Put one end of the pen at the base of your nose and lay it across your lips." Looking intrigued, he did as I'd directed. "It touches your chin, right?" He nodded again, the pen still in place. "If you were black, it wouldn't."

"Wouldn't what?" interrupted the sheriff.

"Wouldn't touch the chin. Black people's teeth and jaws slope forward—the fancy, five-dollar term for that is 'prognathic.' White people's teeth and jaws are more vertical—'orthognic.' This woman's got a narrow nasal opening, too; blacks have a wide one, with vertical grooves—gutters—so they can take in more air through their nose. That's evolution at work, adapting them to tropical climates."

Meffert nodded, looking thoughtful. The sheriff scowled, looking . . . *scowly.* He opened his mouth to speak, and I half expected to hear the term "jungle bunnies" in response to my evolutionary explanation. Instead, he asked, "You a bettin' man, Doc?"

"Excuse me?"

"You a bettin' man? A gambler?"

"Not really," I said.

"Well, if you was, what kind of odds would you lay on this being a white woman?"

"How certain I am that she's white, based on the teeth and jaws and nasal opening?"

"Right."

I shrugged. "I hate to say a hundred percent, because if I turn out to be wrong, I'll look like a hundred-percent idiot. I'll be able to look at a couple other things once I get her back to the lab and clean off the bones. But right here, right now? Ninety-five percent." I tugged downward on the mandible, opening the jaws so I could inspect the lower teeth, especially the molars. "Middle or upper income, too, probably. She's had good dental care."

The sheriff rubbed the corners of his mouth with one hand, his thumb and fingers widening and narrowing repeatedly, his lips alternately stretching and pursing in artificial simulacra of smiles and frowns. Then he turned slightly to one side and spat, a long stream of tobacco juice and saliva arcing onto the ground a foot from where I knelt. "Son of a bitch," he said. "He done this to a *white* woman? They's some serious shit about to hit the fan here. Ain't no doubt about it. We got to catch that boy, y'all hear me?"

"You think this murder was committed by a *juvenile*?" By the time I finished asking the question, I realized how foolish it was.

"A man—a black man—escaped from Brushy four days ago," said Meffert. "He's still on the loose."

"Brushy?"

"Brushy Mountain State Prison."

"The one we passed on the way in?"

"No. The old prison, in Petros." He pointed across the creek, as if I might be able to see it if I looked. "It's close—three, four, five miles, as the crow flies—but there's one hell of a mountain between here and there."

The prison's name rang a bell in the back of my mind. "Seems like I remember that somebody famous did time in Brushy Mountain."

Meffert nodded. "Still *doing* time. James Earl Ray. Guy that assassinated Martin Luther King. Sentenced to ninety-nine years."

"It's a hunnerd, now," interjected the deputy, Cotterell. "Remember? They tacked on one more year after he escaped."

"Oh yeah," I said. "What about that? I thought that prison was famous for being escape-proof."

"Ain't no prison escape-proof," scoffed the sheriff. "Not if it's built by human hands, guarded by human guards. Ray and six others scaled a fence in the back corner of the yard one day. Maybe the guards was sleepin' on the job. Maybe they was *paid* to be sleepin' on the job. Dumbasses went the wrong damn way after they got out, though."

"They headed north," Meffert explained. "This way. Into the mountains. They were caught two days later, in some of the toughest terrain in Tennessee. Story goes, by the time they found him, Ray was so exhausted and hungry and tore up, he was *begging* to go back to Brushy."

"And this guy who escaped four days ago," I said. "What's his story? Also a killer?"

"If he weren't before, he for damn sure is *now*," said the sheriff. "He is a sack of human excrement." The other two nodded.

"Serial sex offender," said the TBI agent.

"Bad luck for this poor gal, crossing paths with him," the sheriff resumed. "She didn't never have no chance."

As the lawmen continued chatting and head-shaking, I unfolded a body bag and laid it beside the woman's remains. The task of getting her into the bag was complicated by the presence of the sapling between her legs. I considered lifting one of her legs to vertical and then swinging it clear of the tree—the corpse had already passed through rigor mortis—but I feared that bending the leg so far might tear it from the hip. Instead, I squatted above the head and worked my hands under the shoulders, into the armpits, and slid the corpse several feet up the hill, so that both legs were clear of the tree. Then I repositioned the bag, unzipped it, and folded back the top. "Could one of you guys give me a hand?"

They looked at one another, no one moving. Finally Sheriff Dixon said, "Jim, get over there and help the perfessor." Cotterell grimaced but complied.

"There's another pair of gloves sticking out of my back pocket," I said. "You're gonna want those, I'm thinking." He tugged them free and pulled them on. "Let's lift her legs and swing those over first," I said, "then her upper body." He nodded and took hold of the left shin, while I grasped the right, wishing the feet were still there to help keep my grip from slipping loose. "Okay, on three, we lift and swing. One, two, *three.*"

With a lift, accompanied by a grunt from the stocky deputy, we got her legs and pelvis onto the rubberized fabric.

"Okay, same thing with the arms." He nodded, and we hoisted and swung the upper body onto the bag, then I folded the flap across the body and tugged the C-shaped zipper closed. Then, with the added help of the sheriff and the TBI agent, we lugged the bag up the slope and slid it into the back of my truck.

I took my leave of the sheriff, his deputy, and Special Agent Bubba, promising to fax a preliminary report by Tuesday. Meffert raised his eyebrows. "You know that's Christmas Day, right?"

"Crap," I said. "No, I forgot. How about Wednesday, the twenty-sixth?"

Meffert shrugged; the sheriff nodded, allowing as how he reckoned that would be all right. I removed the gloves and tossed them in the back of the truck, and motioned for Cotterell to do likewise, then closed the tailgate and the shell.

I drove slowly down the park's narrow road and rumbled across Jordan Branch, then sped up as the road straightened and widened near the prison. Ten minutes after I turned onto the highway toward Knoxville, I noticed another two-lane road, state route 116, T-ing in from the left. PETROS 2 said a sign pointing up 116. BRUSHY MOUNTAIN STATE PRISON 3. On a whim, I slowed and took the turn.

Petros was a cluster of modest homes—a few dozen or so—plus a handful of small churches, several dilapidated repair shops, a cinder-block grocery store, and a volunteer fire department. A mile beyond what passed for downtown—just before the highway made a hairpin turn and started angling up a mountainside—I came to the turnoff for Brushy Mountain.

The prison occupied the back end of a small, deep valley—a hollow, or "holler," in East Tennessee dialect—and even from a quarter mile away, the façade was forbidding: a huge, brooding fortress of stone, topped by castlelike crenellations and flanked on three sides by steep forested mountains, as if the prison itself had taken up a defensive position and were making its last stand. And in a way, perhaps it was, for Agent Meffert had said that the state was planning to close the facility, as soon as the Morgan County Correctional Complex could be expanded to accommodate Brushy's hard-core convicts.

Idling toward the grim stone fortress, I imagined James Earl Ray and six other desperate men scaling the fence, then scrambling up the steep, rocky slopes toward Frozen Head. Was that the same route this latest fugitive had taken—the sack-of-excrement "boy" Sheriff Dixon was intent on capturing? Had he gotten farther than Ray? And had his path crossed with that of an unlucky hiker—a woman who happened to be in a terribly wrong place at a fatally wrong time?

As I crept forward, I noticed a patrol car leave the prison's gate and head in my direction. Then—imagining the scene that might ensue if I were stopped and the back of my truck searched—I made a hasty U-turn and headed back toward the highway, and the comforts of UT.

By most measures, Stadium Hall was a shithole. But compared to Brushy Mountain, it was the lap of luxury. A lavish, lustrous ivory tower.

5

"NO WAY. I CAN'T bring that inside," said Dr. Kimbrough, wrinkling his nose as he peered down at the body bag. My truck was backed up to the loading dock at UT Medical Center, and I'd slid the body bag onto the dock and unzipped it just enough to show the skull to Kimbrough, the young radiology resident unlucky enough to be spending Saturday evening on call. "No way," he repeated. "The attending would have my head on a platter."

"He won't even know," I pleaded. "It's the weekend, the E.R.'s quiet right now—the drunk-driving accidents and bar fights don't rev up till midnight—and I really, really need to know if there's a bullet somewhere in her."

"Won't even *know*? Are you kidding?" He gave a barkish laugh. "We'd have patients and hospital staff running for the exits, puking as they ran." I had to admit, he might have a point there. "Isn't there some other way to tell if there's a bullet in her?"

There was a way, actually—sift through all the liquid and goo I'd get when I simmered the soft tissue off the bones—but I didn't want to wait that long or work that hard, so I hedged. "Look, this is life-and-death stuff. Somebody's killed this woman, and I'm desperately trying to figure out who, and how. I've got a county sheriff and a TBI agent breathing down my neck so hard my wife's starting to get jealous."

He smiled, but the smile was followed by a head shake. "We cannot take that inside. Not negotiable. What I *can* do, though, is bring the portable X-ray machine down here and shoot some films here on the dock. We don't even have to take her out of the bag."

"How's the quality?"

"Not great. Best you're gonna get, though—from me at least—so take it or leave it." He saw the doubt on my face. "Look, if there's a lump of lead in there, it'll light up that film like a full moon at midnight."

IT WAS A dark and moonless night, figuratively and forensically speaking: The woman's corpse did not contain a bright round bullet, I saw when I reviewed the films with Kimbrough. That didn't surprise me, as I'd noticed no entry or exit wound in the intact regions of the body.

What *did* surprise me—what stunned me, in fact, when I saw the X ray of the head—was the brilliant latticework of metal in the woman's skull: four flat, L-shaped brackets of metal, screwed to the upper jaw. At some point the woman's face had been bolted back together. "Holy crap," I said to the radiologist. "She must've taken one hell of a blow to the teeth."

He nodded. "That's a classic LeFort fracture," he said. "Car wreck? She take a steering wheel in the face?"

"I have no idea. All I know is, that's not what killed her."

"Type One," he went on, as if we were making medical rounds. "Horizontal fracture plane in the maxilla, just below the nose, detaching the teeth and palate. Could've been worse," he added, his index finger tracing an arc above the woman's nose. "A LeFort Type Two breaks off the entire maxilla and the nasal bone—wiggle the teeth, and the whole nose wiggles. A Type Three breaks off the zygomatic bones, too, so the whole face hangs down. This lady was lucky."

"Tell her, not me," I said. "Oh, you can't—she's dead." He flushed, and I felt bad for him. But not as bad as I felt for her. "Sorry. Thanks for the help—I do appreciate it." I tugged the bag off the loading dock and into the truck, then headed back toward the stadium. Crossing the river, I glanced upstream at the black, cold waters of the Tennessee spooling past Knoxville and the university, wondering what dark currents had swept this woman to her fate. I still didn't know who she was or how she'd died, but I now felt confident of identifying her. Whoever had done the dental and facial surgery would surely remember it. All I had to do was find that person.

I parked a hundred yards from Stadium Hall, the truck backed up to a corrugated metal building labeled ANTHROPOLOGY ANNEX. The Annex, like the sow barn, had been conferred on me by the dean in the wake of what was now widely known as "the Shower Incident," when the janitor had found the rotting corpse I'd stashed overnight. On a scale of one to ten, the Annex rated a minus three; the uninsulated metal structure was an oven in summer and in icebox in winter. Still, it had plumbing and electricity. More to the point, it had no other tenants . . . and it had a steam-jacketed kettle, an immense cauldron that—over the course of twenty-four simmering hours—could transform a decomposing body into a clean skeleton.

I opened the back of the truck, then wheeled a gurney from the Annex and slid the body bag onto it. I rolled it across the concrete floor and into the processing room, which contained a long counter, a bathtub-sized sink, and the steam-jacketed kettle. Opening a tap, I began filling the kettle with hot water; as it filled, I dumped in a half cup of Adolph's Meat Tenderizer and a cup of Biz laundry powder—my secret ingredients, to help soften the tissue and sweeten the smell. Once the kettle was full and the tap was off, I noticed a faint noise coming from direction of the body bag. *Crap*, I thought, warily unzipping the bag to reveal teeming masses of maggots, which had emerged from the torso's interior during the long, dark ride back from Morgan County. In the quiet of the Annex, I could hear them, and the sound of their moist wriggling and chewing bore a striking, unsettling similarity to the *snap crackle pop* of Rice Krispies—a breakfast I vowed, then and there, never to eat again.

I glanced up at the clock on the wall: 6:43 P.M. *Crap*, I thought again, *I'm late for supper, and where the hell is Bohanan?* Art Bohanan was a forensic specialist with the Knoxville Police Department, and his area of particular expertise was fingerprints. I'd worked on a case with Art several months before, and I'd watched, astonished, as he took a shriveled husk of skin that had sloughed off from a dead man's hand, moistened it, and then lifted a perfect set of prints. The Morgan County sheriff had scoffed at my suggestion that we try to get prints from the Jordan Branch corpse, and even the TBI agent, Meffert, had shaken his head dismissively. But I wasn't willing to give up without trying, so on the way back to Knoxville I'd stopped at a gas station and phoned Art to ask for help. He'd agreed to meet me at six-thirty. So why wasn't he here?

Just as I was headed for the phone to send a nagging page, the building's corrugated wall boomed like thunder, and then the door screeched open. "Shoo-*eee*," came Art's folksy drawl. "Either there's a really ripe one in here, or you are wearing the world's nastiest aftershave."

I grinned. "I don't particularly care for it, but it's my wife's favorite, and I do try to please her."

"She's one lucky woman."

"Thanks for coming. You're my only hope for fingerprints. Even the TBI agent threw up his hands."

"But why was a TBI agent eatin' his hands in the first place?"

"Man," I groaned, "and people say *my* puns are bad." I folded back the flap of the body bag to expose both arms, then lifted the left one by the wrist, palm up. "What do you think—can you get usable prints?"

"I believe so," he said, leaning down to study the fingers. "Can you give me a hand?"

"Sure. How can I help?"

"Give. Me. A hand." I stared at him, puzzled; he stared back with an expression of weary patience on his face, as if waiting for a slow-witted child to grasp the simplest of instructions. Finally he rolled his eyes and, with the blade of his hand, pantomimed a sawing motion in the air above the woman's wrist. "Give me a hand. Be easier to work with if I can take it back to the KPD lab with me."

"Ah" was the only syllable that came out of my startled mouth. This was a first for me, but Art was the expert, so—taking a scalpel from a tray of tools on the long counter, I cut through the tendons and ligaments of the left wrist, taking care not to nick any of the bones. I wrapped the severed hand in a paper towel and then zipped it into a plastic bag.

Art tucked it into the outside pocket of his jacket as casually as he might have deposited his car keys or a candy bar. "I'll let you know what I get," he said. "You about to start cooking?" I nodded. "Want me to help you get her into the pot?" I shook my head. "Darn," he said. "You never let me have any fun." With that and a wave, he was gone.

Ten minutes later so was I, leaving the corpse curled up in the kettle and the thermostat set at 150 degrees.

"GAG," SQUAWKED KATHLEEN when I dashed up the basement stairs and into the kitchen. "You *reek*." I headed toward her, my arms opened wide, as if to enfold her in a bear hug. "*Away*, vile one," she squealed, swatting at me with a dish towel. "Go back downstairs and take a long shower. Then take another one." I nodded obediently. "But first, go out to the garage and take off those clothes."

"Oh, baby," I said. "I do love it when you tell me to take off my clothes."

"In your dreams, stinky. Put them in the washing machine on *hot*." As I started down the stairs, I heard her calling after me, "The *old* machine. Don't you *dare* put those in the new one."

6

December 24

I CHECKED A THIRD time, and for the third time I came up one bone short. Actually, technically, I was forty-five bones short; the adult human skeleton contains 206 bones, and the skeleton I'd laid out on the counter had just 161. But the feet and ankles accounted for forty-four of the absent forty-five bones, so I'd already mentally subtracted those from the total. The unexpectedly missing bone—the maddeningly missing bone—was the one I'd been banking on to tell me how the woman was killed. "Where the hell's the hyoid?" I muttered.

As soon as I'd seen the woman's body in the woods, I suspected severe trauma to her neck—a slashed throat or, more likely, strangulation. When blowflies find a corpse, they seek moist orifices in which to lay their eggs: eyes, nose, mouth, ears, genitals, and, above all, bloody wounds. In this case, the soft tissues of the woman's neck had been completely consumed, exposing the cervical vertebrae. That told me her neck was particularly attractive to the flies—evidence that it had been bleeding or badly bruised. I'd seen no blood on the ground—and no knife marks on the vertebrae as I'd fished them from the steam kettle just now and laid them on the counter—so I felt fairly sure she'd been strangled rather than slashed. Trouble was, to confirm my hypothesis, I needed a hyoid—specifically, a hyoid crushed by a killer's lethal grip. And the hyoid was not to be found, no matter how carefully I sifted and squeezed the gooey residue remaining in the bottom of the kettle.

"Damned dogs," I muttered. The ends of the woman's legs were covered with gnaw marks, which indicated that her feet had been chewed off by canids—wild dogs or, more likely, coyotes roaming the hills of Morgan County. Had they also gnawed at the woman's neck? I studied the vertebrae again, this time looking for tooth marks rather than cut marks. There were none. Was it possible that some especially dexterous dog or coyote—seeking a particular delicacy—had managed to pluck the hyoid from the throat without doing damage to any of the adjacent bones? *No way*, I thought, then said again, "So where the hell is the hyoid?" Had I been so sloppy and careless, in my haste to get the corpse into the body bag, that I'd failed to notice a stray bone lying on the ground, right beside the exposed cervical vertebrae?

Frowning, I laid down the last of the vertebrae, shucked off my gloves, and opened the large envelope resting on the counter. I'd picked up the envelope at Thompson Photo on my way to campus. Inside, tucked snugly into slots in a sheet of clear plastic, were the thirty-six color slides I'd shot two days before, at the death scene in the mountains. As I'd spiraled in toward the corpse, I took half a dozen close-ups of the neck, including two from each side. Now, as I laid the slides on a light box and picked up a magnifying glass, I both hoped and feared what those close-ups might reveal: the woman's hyoid, and my carelessness.

In fact, the close-ups revealed nothing except what I remembered seeing: exposed cervical vertebrae, resting on a layer of dead, dry leaves. "Where the hell is the *hyoid*?" I was sounding like a broken record. I snapped off the light box, then, an instant later, I snapped it back on, realizing that something in one of the other slides seemed odd. It was the first photo I'd taken—the one with my zoom lens at its widest setting—and it was the last photo I'd have expected to reveal an important forensic detail. I stared at it, and as I realized what I was seeing, my understanding of the crime scene—and even the crime—was transformed.

In the upper corner of the photo, barely within the frame, was something I'd completely overlooked two days before: a dark, greasy-looking circle, a foot or so in diameter, located eight or ten feet up the slope from where the woman's body lay splayed against the tree. I heard myself say once more, "Damned dogs!" This time I said it with a laugh.

The body, I now realized, had not been posed by the killer in a shocking sexual display; the body hadn't been posed at all, in fact. The dark, circular stain marked the spot where the body had originally lain, the spot where it first began to decompose. The stain was a slick layer of volatile fatty acids, released as the body had begun to decay. The body's final resting place, against the tree—although perhaps "resting" was the wrong word—marked the spot where the dogs or coyotes had dragged it, en route to their den or some other sheltered spot, before the legs parted around the tree and the trunk stopped her downward slide. Picturing the scene in my mind, I imagined the confusion and frustration of the two coyotes on either side of the sapling as the corpse yanked to a halt; I imagined their disappointment as they were forced to settle for only the feet, their meager consolation prizes. "Poor doggies," I said, snatching up a small paper evidence bag and tucking it into my shirt pocket. Snapping off the light box again, I headed for the door of the Annex.

I stepped out into the cold, gray light of the late December morning, the sky swirling with low, ominous clouds. Then, on an impulse, I stepped back inside. As long as I was making the drive to Morgan County, I might as well get as much mileage from the trip as possible. No point showing up empty-handed.

7

Perimortem Revisited

THE COURTHOUSE CLOCK READ 9:05 as I got out of my truck and headed for the door of the sheriff's office. My wristwatch, on the other hand, read 11:45—the drive had taken an hour, and I'd made a thirty-minute stop on my way into Wartburg. I smiled when I realized that the clock's hands hadn't moved since my prior visit. *Come to Morgan County,* I thought, composing an imaginary slogan for the Chamber of Commerce. *A place where time stands still.*

"He's not here," the sheriff's dispatcher told me.

"How about Deputy Cotterell?"

"Him neither. Nobody's here but me. They're all out with the posse."

"Posse?" Had the dispatcher actually said "posse"? "What posse?"

"They're after an escaped convict. They was out all night. A whole big bunch of 'em—a hunnerd volunteers, come from all over the place. Somebody called yesterday, sayin' they seen the guy down toward Coalfield. So the sheriff 'n' ever'body's down yonder." She looked me up and down, sizing me up, then asked, "Was you wantin' to join up with the posse?" Her tone was dubious; evidently I did not look like posse material.

"Heavens no," I said. "I've been looking at the bones of the dead woman—the woman whose body was found in the park on Friday. I've just found another bone out at the scene, and I need to show it to the sheriff."

She looked startled, then puzzled, then a glimmer of understanding dawned in her eyes. "Oh, you're that bone detective from UT," she said, and I nodded. "Was you needin' something? Anything I can do for you?"

I shook my head, but then I thought of something. "Actually, yes, maybe you can help me. Who's the best dentist in town?"

"Ha! That's easy. Ain't but one, anymore, now that Doc Peterson's passed on. Dr. Hartley. He's a lot smarter'n Doc Peterson was. Younger 'n' better lookin', too." She pointed. "Two blocks thataway, down Main Street. Big old house on the left. If the door's locked, try ringing the bell. He lives right upstairs."

CLOSED UNTIL JANUARY 2, read a hand-lettered sign in the leaded-glass door of Dr. Hartley's office, which occupied the ground floor of a two-story

Victorian. Recrossing the wide front porch and descending the steps, I looked up at the second-story windows. The sky was surprisingly dark for midday; the swirling clouds seemed to be pressing down upon the house. Through wavy glass, I saw lights burning in two upstairs rooms, so I returned to the door and rang the bell. There was no response, and after a while I tried it again. Still no answer. *Third time's the charm*, I hoped, and pressed the button once more, holding it down long enough to show I meant business.

This time I heard rapid footsteps on a staircase, and then a light flicked on and an unhappy face appeared, fractured into odd angles and planes of anger by the beveled glass. A dead bolt snicked back and the door opened, the face unfractured now, but unhappy still. "The clinic's closed until next Wednesday." He tapped the sign for emphasis, and the panes rattled slightly within their channels of lead.

"I know," I said, "and I'm sorry to intrude, Dr. Hartley, but it's important. I'm investigating a murder, and I'm hoping you might be able to help me identify the victim."

The annoyance on his face gave way to a mixture of puzzlement and curiosity. "Are you with the sheriff's office?"

"No sir. My name's Bill Brockton; I'm a forensic anthropologist at the University of Tennessee. The sheriff brought me in to help ID the victim and determine the manner of death. I'm hoping you might recognize this dental work."

"Well, I'll be glad to help if I can. Do you have

X rays of the teeth? Or dental charts?" His eyes narrowed as they took in the hatbox under my arm.

"Better than that," I said. "I've got the teeth themselves. The jaws, too. The whole skull, in fact. The dental work is quite distinctive."

His gaze shifted from my face to the box and back again. "Well," he said finally, his startled expression giving way gradually to one of mild amusement. "I must say, this is a first. Come in, have a seat, and let's have a look."

He sat behind a large wooden desk in an oak swivel chair, one that might have been as old as the house itself; I sat facing him in a high-backed wing chair, also an antique, the box on my lap. "I reckon I should ask if you're squeamish."

"Me? Lord no. Squeamish people don't make it through dental school—or didn't twenty years ago, when I was a student. Back then, they started us off dissecting cadavers. They don't do that anymore, but they should. Weeds out the weak, and teaches you the anatomy, inside and out. So no, a skull won't faze me in the least."

I nodded. "Just checking." I removed the box lid and set it on the floor, then lifted the skull from the nest of paper towels with which I'd cushioned it. I leaned forward, my elbows on the desk, and turned the face of the skull toward him, hoping for a flicker of recognition in his eyes.

Instead of a flicker, I saw a seismic shock. Hartley gasped, shoving his chair back from the desk so hard that his head hit the wall. He blanched, and a moment later he bent forward and scrabbled beneath his desk. I heard the clatter of a metal trashcan, and then I heard violent retching. It continued, off and on, for a minute or more, and when he finally sat up, the retching had given way to weeping.

"SHE SAID HER horse had kicked her in the mouth," he whispered, "but I knew better. I knew that sonofabitch did it. A baseball bat, a two-by-four, a candlestick—I don't know what he hit her with, but whatever it was, it could've killed her." He shook his head angrily. "She always stuck to the script—she was too scared to tell the truth—but I knew. And she knew that I knew."

"Who is 'she,' Dr. Hartley? And who's the sonofabitch?"

"Denise Donnelly," he said. "The wife—the possession—of Patrick Donnelly." He said both names as if I should know them. He said the man's name as if I should loathe it.

"Sorry, I'm not from here," I said. "Who are they?"

"The richest people in Wartburg. Not that there's many of those. He's got mineral rights to half the county. Owns two or three strip mines—legal ones—and probably half a dozen wildcats." Seeing the puzzled expression on my face, he translated. "Wildcat mines are illegal, fly-by-night mines—no permits, no health and safety procedures, no environmental protection. Cheap, quick guerrilla raids on shallow seams of coal. Get in and get out, rape and pillage, before the regulators know you're there." He looked down, twisting a ring on his right hand, a haunted expression on his face. "I knew he'd kill her someday if she didn't get out. I begged her to leave him." Suddenly he shuddered and buried his face in his hands, and his body shook with the force of his sobs.

When he finally looked up at me again, the light in his eyes had gone out, and he seemed twenty years older than when he'd answered the door. And in that moment I understood. "I'm so sorry, Dr. Hartley," I said. "You're obviously shocked. And . . ." I wasn't sure if I should go on, but I did. "It's none of my business, but I gather that you and Mrs. Donnelly were . . . close, so I truly apologize for springing this on you." He nodded bleakly. "When did you hear she was missing?"

He blinked, startled. "I didn't. I don't think *any-body* did—a town this size, word gets around, you know? But I should have guessed." He looked away, and when he looked back at me, it was as if he'd decided something. "At first she was just a patient whose teeth I cleaned twice a year. Then, after . . . *this*"—he pointed at the skull—"she needed a lot of post-op care. I saw her every week for six months. And eventually . . ." He didn't need to finish the sentence. "She called me two weeks ago. Patrick had bugged the phone; he knew everything. She said she was going to California, to stay with her sister for a while, to sort things out. Told me not to try to contact her. Said it would just make things more painful for everyone." He drew a deep breath, and as he exhaled, his face seemed to harden. "Then Patrick took the phone from her. He said that if I ever called or spoke to her again, Denise and I would wish we'd never been born. Then he hung up. I hoped she'd find a way to call me again, but she didn't." He looked at the skull and gave a bitter semblance of a laugh. "Now I know why."

We sat in silence, the only sound the ticking of an antique clock. Then, in the distance, I heard the sound of car horns—faintly at first, then louder and louder, so numerous they blended together into one cacophonous clamor. A moment later a jubilant procession—or was it a riot on wheels?—roared past the dentist's house and up Main Street toward the courthouse.

"What on earth is that?" I said. And then—with a sudden, sickening feeling—I knew what it was.

I FELT LIKE a football running back, fighting my way through a hundred defensive linemen, as I forced my way through the whooping crowd surrounding the courthouse. Thunder rumbled overhead, as if the storm gathering on the ground were mirrored in the purple-black sky.

Two deputies, both armed with pump shotguns, stood on the steps and blocked the entrance. "I have to see the sheriff," I said.

"The sheriff's busy," said one.

"Interrogating a prisoner," smirked the other.

"That's why I need to see him," I said. "I'm with the state medical examiner's staff." I pulled my ID badge from my wallet and held it out, but the deputies seemed uninterested. "I know who the dead woman is," I went on. Now, for the first time, I had their attention. "I've just identified her."

"What's her name?" the first deputy asked.

"Take me to the sheriff," I insisted. "That information's for his ears only."

It was a spur-of-the-moment fib, but it was effective. The two deputies exchanged glances, and the first one—who seemed to outrank the second one—disappeared through the door. Several moments later the door opened and the deputy leaned out, beckoning me inside. He led me up to the third floor, into the jail, and down a row of cells. Deputy Jim Cotterell was standing at the end of the hall, just outside a cell door, his expression grim. As I approached, I heard a dull thud inside the cell, followed by a quick grunt and a slow groan.

"Sheriff? Here's the bone doc," said Cotterell. Peering through the bars into the cell's dim interior, I saw the sheriff step away from a hunched figure—a black man, bent nearly double, who slowly straightened. Blood trickled from his lips and nose and from a laceration on his right cheekbone. The man's left arm ended at the wrist—a broad, blunt stump—and his right wrist was encased in a filthy cast.

"I hear you got something to tell me." Sheriff Dixon stepped from the cell, his face glistening and his eyes glittering, and walked toward the far end of the cells.

"Two things, actually," I said. "The woman was named Denise Donnelly." His eyes flickered, but he didn't react as strongly as I'd suspected. "I gather she's a prominent citizen?"

"You might say that."

"But she hadn't been reported missing?"

"Not to me." His eyes bored into mine. "You sure it's her?"

"I am," I said.

"How sure? Ninety-five percent sure?"

"No. This time I'm a hundred percent sure. I showed her teeth—her skull—to her dentist." An expression I couldn't quite decipher flitted across the sheriff's face, and I wondered if the sheriff, too, knew about their affair. "She'd had extensive dental surgery—reconstructive surgery, to repair an injury. The dentist recognized the work instantly."

"Yates!" The sheriff's shout boomed across my ear. Down the hall, the deputy who'd brought me upstairs turned from the prisoner's cell and trotted toward us. "Pat Donnelly's outside," the sheriff told him. "Go get him. Tell him I need to see him." He looked at me again. "What else? You said you had two things to tell me."

"She was strangled," I said. "Her hyoid—a bone in the throat—was crushed." Reaching into my shirt pocket, I removed the evidence bag and carefully extricated the bone.

Three hours before, on my way into town, I'd stopped at the scene and, on hands and knees, sifted through the leaves on the hillside, at the stained spot a dozen feet above the body's final resting place. "Eureka," I'd proclaimed when I plucked the bone from the ground and saw the fractures: saw what had killed the woman.

But the sheriff gave the bone only a glance before turning away. I grabbed his sleeve, forcing him to look and listen. "Sheriff, I don't think the man you've got back there would be physically capable of strangling someone." I remembered a third thing—a phone call I'd gotten from Art Bohanan just before I left. Art hadn't yet found a match to the prints, but he did find something else interesting. "A forensic expert with the Knoxville Police Department took a set of prints from her left hand. She fought, Sheriff. She had skin under her fingernails. White skin. And one red whisker." He didn't respond, so I plowed ahead. "From what I hear, the Donnellys' marriage had some serious problems." For the first time, I seemed to have his full attention. "You might want to consider the possibility that Patrick Donnelly killed his wife."

I saw his jaw tighten. "I might want to *consider* the *possibility*?" His eyes narrowed and his chin lifted slightly. "I tell you what. *You* might want to *consider* the *possibility* of knowing where your job stops and my job starts. Now, is that ever'thing you had to tell me? 'Cause if it is, I've got an interrogation to get back to."

He turned to go. "Sheriff?" I said to his broad, sweaty back. He stopped and looked over his shoulder. "How'd she get there?" He held my gaze but didn't speak. "Where's her car?"

He shook his head. "No telling," he said. "Bottom of a quarry. Bottom of a river. In a chop shop, gettin' parted out. In a scrap yard gettin' shredded. I don't know, and it don't matter. But when I find out, I'll send you a memo. That make you happy?"

"You're saying this guy disposed of the car and then walked back into the mountains?"

"I'm saying it don't make a bit of damn difference where the car is," the sheriff spat. "The damn *car* didn't kill the damn woman, did it? This nigrah *pervert* killed the woman."

"I don't think so," I said. "I think she was killed somewhere else—maybe at her own house—and taken out there and dumped. That's why there was no car—no nothing—at the scene. Her body had been out on that hillside long enough to decompose. At least a week, I bet. Maybe two. Ask around, Sheriff—see if anybody saw her or talked to her in the past ten days. This guy escaped, what, forty-eight hours before she was found? The timing doesn't fit."

"Cotterell!" he roared. The deputy, who I felt sure had overheard our exchange, jogged heavily in our direction. "Get this man out of here and on his way back to Knoxville."

"Yessir." Cotterell took my elbow and steered me into the stairwell.

We were only halfway down the first flight of stairs when the sheriff bellowed the deputy's name again. "Get back up here," he shouted. "He's so fuckin' smart. Let him find his own damn way out."

Cotterell squeezed my elbow, then I felt him slip something into my hand. It was a business card embossed with the blue-and-gold logo of the Tennessee Bureau of Investigation, and below that, the words SPECIAL AGENT WELLINGTON H. MEFFERT II. "Get to a phone and call Bubba, quick," he hissed. "They're fixin' to lynch this fella."

"Did you say 'lynch'?" I stared at him. "You can't be serious. This is 1990."

He shook his head. "Not in their minds it ain't. Dixon don't speak for everybody—he sure don't speak for me. But them people milling around? They're Klan. Outsiders, mostly—Carolina, Virginia, Alabama. Dixon called 'em in for his posse. His posse, their party. I'm tellin' you, this is a done deal. They're fixin' to string this man up right here, right now."

"Cotterell!" boomed the sheriff. "You get your fat ass up here!"

"*Call Bubba*," the deputy hissed, and hurried up the stairs.

Just as I reached the ground floor, the outside door opened and Deputy Number One—Yates?—entered. He was accompanied by a tall, barrel-chested man. He had red hair and a red beard. He also had red scratches on his face.

I ducked down a darkened hallway and found a vacant office. Switching on a desk lamp, I laid down the card and picked up the phone. It took several tries to get through—I had to push down one of the clear buttons on the base of the phone and then dial 9 for an outside line, and my trembling fingers misdialed twice. Finally, miraculously, I heard Meffert's voice.

My voice shaking, I recounted what I'd learned, what the sheriff had said and done, and what Cotterell predicted.

"Shit," said Meffert. "Shit shit *shit*."

"You really think they might lynch this man?"

"You remember what happened in Greensboro? Bunch of Klansmen shot up a crowd of black protesters. Killed six people, including a pediatrician and a nurse. That was in 1979. Two years later, in Mobile, they hung a black man from a tree, just to show they could. Sheriff Dixon's telling them a black sex offender has raped and murdered the most prominent white woman in Morgan County, Tennessee? Do I think it might happen? No—I *know* it'll happen. Take a miracle to stop it."

I was just putting the phone back in the cradle

when I glimpsed movement in the darkness beyond me. An instant later a pistol entered my small circle of light. A hand aimed the pistol at my chest, and a voice—the sheriff's gravelly voice—said, "What do you think you're doing?"

"I was just calling my wife," I said. "I told her I'd be home by mid-afternoon. I didn't want her to worry."

"Now ain't that sweet," he said. "Let me call her, too, and tell her how much we 'preciate your help." With his free hand, he lifted the handset and pressed Redial. He angled the earpiece so that both of us could hear it ringing.

Don't answer, Bubba, I prayed.

"Meffert," I heard the TBI agent say, and my heart and my hopes sank.

"YOU GET IN there," the sheriff snarled, prodding me with the pistol, "and don't make me tell you twice."

Cotterell was in the corridor, a plastic cup in one hand, a blank look on his face. "Here, let me help you, Sheriff," he said, opening the cell door wider. "How about we cuff him, too? Here, hold my coffee for just one second?" Without waiting for an answer, the deputy handed Dixon the cup, then—to the astonishment of both me and the sheriff—he snapped one handcuff on his boss's outstretched wrist and, with a quick yank, clicked the other cuff to the cell door. As Dixon stared in bewilderment, Cotterell twisted the pistol from the sheriff's other hand and shoved him into the cell, the sheriff's movement pulling the door shut behind him.

"What the *fuck* are you doing?"

"I'm placing you under arrest, Sheriff."

"Bull-*shit*. What are you talking about?"

"I'm talking about assault. I'm talking about obstruction of justice. I'm talking about evidence-tampering, and conspiracy, and corruption, and probably civil-rights violations, too, though I reckon the D.A. or the U.S. Attorney will know more about that than I do."

"You're fired, Cotterell. And that's the least of your troubles. You unlock this cell and unlock these cuffs, and I mean *right* now, or I will *bury* you under this goddamn courthouse."

"I can't do that, Sheriff. I'm sworn to uphold the law, same as you. Difference is, I really aim to do it."

A CHEER WENT up from the crowd when Cotterell and I emerged onto the courthouse steps, where one of the shotgun-wielding deputies still stood sentinel, but it quickly faded when the door closed behind us.

"Where is he?" shouted the big red-haired man I'd seen going inside earlier. *Donnelly*. "Where's that sick sumbitch that killed my wife?"

"Where is he?" echoed a jumble of other voices. "Bring him out!"

"Hang on, *hang* on," Cotterell called. "Y'all just hold your horses. Sheriff Dixon's still interrogatin' him."

"We already know ever'thing we need to know," shouted Donnelly.

"Yeah." I heard. "*Yeah!* Let's get it on!"

Suddenly there was a commotion to one side, and the crowd there parted, revealing a six-foot cross, its frame wrapped in layers of cloth—*wrapped in swaddling clothes*, I thought, in an absurd echo of the Christmas story—and a tongue of flame climbing up from its base and spreading to the outstretched arms. The crowd roared its approval.

"Come on!" yelled Donnelly. Someone thrust something into his hands, and I felt my stomach lurch when I recognized the distinctive shape of a rope noose.

Cotterell held up both hands in an attempt to quiet the crowd. "Not so fast," he yelled. "We might be gettin' ahead of ourselves. We ain't sure we got the right man."

"Hell *yeah* we got the right man," Donnelly jeered. "No doubt about it. Now shut up, Jim. Get with us or get outta the damn way."

To my surprise—to my deep dismay—I felt myself take a step forward. "Listen to me," I shouted. "You all are making a mistake."

"Who the hell are you," Donnelly bristled, "and what business is this of yours?"

"I'm a forensic scientist," I said. "I'm the one who identified your wife's body. The man inside didn't kill her." A wave of discontent rippled through the crowd. "Denise Donnelly was strangled. Her throat crushed. That man's a cripple—he couldn't have done it."

"He's full of shit," yelled Donnelly. "That nigger is a rapist and a killer, and he's got to hang." His words prompted a raw, enraged chorus of agreement.

"That man was behind bars in Brushy Mountain while she was being killed," I shouted. "She was already dead—long since dead—by the time he escaped." I fumbled at my shirt pocket, my shaky hand reaching for the small, folded paper bag—the bag containing the hyoid bone I'd plucked from the stained leaves on the hillside a few hours before. But before I could extract it, I was interrupted by a shout from the crowd.

"Nigger-lover," yelled someone deep in the pack, and the insult was taken up by dozens of voices. "Nigger-lover! Nigger-lover! Nigger-lover!"

Donnelly held up a hand for quiet, and the taunts died away. "We don't need some liberal, egghead *scientist*"—I saw spittle spray from his mouth when he spat out the word—"coming in here acting like he's better and smarter than we are. Go back to your library, professor, and stay the hell out of our business."

"I'm on the staff of the Tennessee State Medical Examiner," I said, reaching for my belt and grabbing my badge.

"I don't give a good goddamn about that," he shouted. "We got plenty of rope. It wouldn't take two minutes to cut another piece for you. And that oak limb is plenty strong enough for two men to swing from."

"Denise Donnelly fought for her life," I yelled to the crowd. "She had her killer's skin under her fingernails. A *white man's* skin, and a red hair, too." I pointed at Donnelly. "Y'all ought to be asking Mr. Donnelly here how he got those scratches on his hands and face."

Finally, my words seemed to be having some effect. The mob quieted, and I saw heads craning to peer at Donnelly.

"I got these scratches clearing a briar patch last week," Donnelly shouted. "Anybody wants to come see the brush pile tomorrow, you're more'n welcome. But anybody calls me a liar to my face, you've got a fight on your hands."

I played the last card I had to play. "She'd been unfaithful to him. He had a motive to kill her."

There were mutterings in the crowd—the sounds of doubt—and I felt a surge of hope. Suddenly, from high overhead, came the sharp sound of glass shattering, followed by a shout from a second story window of the courthouse. "Hey! *Hey!*" The heads of the mob swiveled upward. Deputy Yates leaned out the broken window. "It's the sheriff! They've got him handcuffed and locked in a cell up here!"

"The sheriff was breaking the law," shouted Cotterell. "Just like y'all are talking about doing. I couldn't let him do that. I can't let y'all do it, either."

"Get out of the way, Jim, before you get hurt," warned Donnelly. "Come on, let's get the sheriff out and give that nigger what he deserves."

The crowd surged forward. Cotterell snatched the shotgun from the deputy beside him. He fired it into the air, and they hesitated, but only briefly, then surged again. He racked the slide and fired once more, but by this time the mob was already swarming up the steps. Half a dozen hands laid hold of my arms; another half dozen began pummeling my head and shoulders. Beside me, I sensed the same thing happening to Cotterell.

Suddenly my attackers hesitated, then froze, and over the shrieks of the mob, I heard the whine of sirens—many sirens, growing louder as they approached the courthouse. Then I heard the squawk of a loudspeaker. "This is the FBI. Put up your weapons and disperse immediately, or you will be arrested. Put up your weapons and disperse immediately, or you will be arrested on federal charges."

The hands clutching my arms let go, the rain of blows ceased, and I felt myself sag against the door as I was released and my attackers began backing away. I heard a commotion—a din of voices shouting "FBI! Make way! Make way!"—and the crowd parted and fell back, their faces scowling and cringing, like dogs who've attacked in a pack then were routed and set fleeing, tails between their legs. A wedge of federal agents—a dozen or more, all wearing body armor emblazoned FBI, all carrying short-barreled shotguns that they looked ready, willing, and able to use—forced their way to the courthouse steps. A man in civilian clothes stepped from the crowd and huddled with one of the agents. He pointed at Donnelly and at three others in the front ranks, and four agents spun from the wedge and put the men facedown on the ground, cuffing them in the blink of an eye.

I heard angry mutterings and wondered if the mob might turn on the FBI agents, but over the mutterings there were more sirens and more commotion at the back of the square. Moments later a phalanx of uniformed Tennessee state troopers, led by Special Agent Meffert, mounted the courthouse steps and stood shoulder-to-shoulder facing the crowd.

Meffert conferred briefly with the ranking FBI agent, then from the top step called out, in a voice that might well have carried halfway to Knoxville, "You have two minutes to disperse. It is now 8:03. Anyone still on the courthouse grounds at 8:05 will be arrested. You'll be charged with engaging in a hate crime, and you will be cuffed and transported to arraignment in a United States criminal court. Make your choice, and make it fast. The man in that jail is not an innocent man, but he didn't kill that woman. Anybody wants to go to prison for trying to lynch him, step right up—your future beckons."

The crowd had fallen back, but it had not scattered. Meffert made a show of checking his watch. "Y'all got one minute," he called, then added, as if it were an afterthought, "Now, I don't know from personal experience, but I hear there's a lot of big black men in federal prison be glad to add a little white meat to their diet, if you catch my drift. Variety bein' the spice of life and all. Who wants to be first in line for that? Step right up, *step* right up, you cowardly sons of bitches. I'll drive you there myself. I'll even hand you the soap and point you toward the showers. Come on, by God!"

As his challenge hung in the air, the flaming cross flickered and went dark, the fire went out of the mob's eyes, and the men slunk away, by twos and threes and tens, their tails tucked between their legs.

When the square stood empty—except for the law enforcement officers and the cuffed men and the undercover agent who'd pointed out the ringleaders—Meffert turned to Cotterell and me. "Well *that* was fun," he said, shaking his head. "Jim, you interested in running for sheriff again? I'm thinking you might win this time around."

"I'll give it some thought," muttered Cotterell. "First, though, I got to go change my britches."

Meffert smiled, then clapped me on the shoulder. "Welcome to the Volunteer State, Doc. How you likin' it so far?"

I stared at him, then heard myself chuckle. Within moments the three of us were howling with laughter—laughter of relief and disbelief and, above all, gratitude for our unlikely deliverance—there on the courthouse steps.

Can't get enough of Dr. Bill Brockton's forensic cases?

A decade after creating the Body Farm, Dr. Bill Brockton is at the peak of his career. The latest case: Brockton is asked by the FBI to identify the charred remains of a wealthy and adventurous philanthropist, killed in a fiery plane crash.

But even as Brockton is basking in success, storm clouds are massing. The FBI case takes a baffling turn when disturbing allegations about the dead man come to light; another, deeply damaging turn occurs when Brockton's identification of the crash victim is called into question. Even more disturbing, Brockton is visited by a ghost from a prior case: serial killer Nick Satterfield. And from Brockton's beloved wife Kathleen—his lodestone and his source of security—comes the most shocking news of all.

Keep reading for a sneak peek at

THE BREAKING POINT

in stores September 2014 from William Morrow.

CHAPTER 1

Knoxville, Tennessee

McCREADY—SPECIAL SUPERVISORY AGENT Clint McCready—stopped beside a rut in the dirt road, holding up one hand to halt the group of agents trailing him. The road, if the pair of faint tracks through grass, weeds, and leaves could be called a road, meandered down a hillside of oaks and maples, their trunks girdled with vines. The June air was perfumed with honeysuckle blossoms, but underneath the wafting sweetness hung something malodorous and malevolent.

McCready knelt to study the rut, which was deeply imprinted with tire tracks. He pulled two evidence flags from a back pocket and marked the ends of the rut, then took a series of digital photographs—wide shots at first, followed by tighter and tighter shots. As he snapped the final, frame-filling close-ups of the tracks, he said, "It rained, what, couple days ago?"

"Night before last." The answer came from behind him—from Kirby Kimball, the youngest, newest, and therefore most eager member of McCready's Evidence Recovery Team. "The front passed through about thirty-six hours ago. Rain stopped shortly after midnight, according to the National Weather Service."

McCready nodded, smiling slightly at Kimball's zeal, and lowered the camera, pointing at the rut with one hand. "These tracks look like they've been *machined*. What does that tell us?"

"New tires," said Kimball. "Deep tread blocks. No wear."

"What else?"

"Off-road tires," Kimball added. "SUV or a four-by-four."

"Christ, somebody besides Kirbo say something. What else can we tell from these? Somebody. *Any*body."

"The vehicle passed through after the rain stopped." This from Anderson, a 30-something agent who generally noticed quite a lot but said very little.

"Right, but can you be more precise than that?"

Anderson stepped forward and crouched beside the rut, his brow furrowing, his gaze shifting from the tracks to the grass and weeds beside them. "Quite awhile after the rain stopped. Hours later; maybe even a day later."

"Because?"

"If there'd been still standing water at the time," Anderson said, "the impressions wouldn't be so crisp. Plus there'd be mud spatters on the vegetation. And there aren't."

"Good." McCready glanced over his shoulder, looking for Kimball; finding him. "Kirbo, you're an eager beaver this morning; you wanna cast these?" It wasn't actually a question.

"Yessir. On it." Kimball jogged back to the truck, with the Justice Department logo on the side and the foot-high letters reading FBI EVIDENCE RECOVERY TEAM. Opening a hatch on the side of the vehicle, Kimball hauled out a large tackle box and lugged it to the tracks. He unlatched the lid and took out a gallon-sized ziplock bag, half-filled with beige powder—gypsum crystals, or "dental stone"—and a graduated squeeze bottle; squirting ten ounces of water into the bag, he resealed it and began kneading, creating a slurry the consistency of thin pancake batter: runny enough to flow into even the finest features of the tire tracks, thick enough not to seep down into the soil.

McCready had already moved on, following the tracks. "Looks like they parked here," he said, stopping to study the ground again. The soil was covered with leaves, and McCready frowned at the lack of castable shoe impressions. A trail of scuffed leaves led toward the trees at the edge of the clearing, but the undergrowth beyond the treeline appeared to be undisturbed; indeed, the scuff marks led only as far as a large, convex oval of mussed leaves situated just short of the tree line. McCready began circling the oval, pausing occasionally to take photos. "This fits the description," he said, to no one and to everyone. "Let's get some rakes and probes, remove this layer of leaf litter." Three of his subordinates fetched rakes from the evidence truck, and they uncovered a low mound of red-brown clay, roughly four feet by six feet. The clay was broken and infused with pale, shredded roots, freshly torn from the soil.

He sat back on his heels. "Screen everything—dirt, leaves, twigs, air. Everything. Could be bullet casings in here; maybe cigarette butts, too, if they were careless or stupid. If we're lucky, maybe the shooters left us some DNA."

"Maybe a signed confession, too," joked one of the agents. McCready did not laugh, so no one else did, either.

"All right," he said. "Fun's over. Let's start digging. Easy does it. Our informant says we'll find three in here—the two buyers and our undercover guy. Way the C.I. tells it, the traffickers never intended to sell—their plan all along was to kill the buyers, keep the coke, and move their own distributors into the turf of the dead buyers."

"Nice guys," muttered someone.

"Aren't they all?" someone else responded.

THEY BEGAN BY defining the margins of the grave with T-shaped probes—four-foot rods of stainless steel. Pressed into the soft earth of a fresh grave, the slender shafts sank easily; pushed into undisturbed soil, they resisted. The probes were largely unnecessary with the edges of the grave clearly visible. Still, the Bureau prided itself on thoroughness, and McCready was a Bureau man all the way.

Once the grave's perimeter was flagged and photographed, three of the agents—now wearing baggy white biohazard suits—began digging. They started with shovels, working at the margins, digging down a foot all the way around before inching their way toward the center. After a grim twenty minutes, Starnes, a young agent, paused and leaned in for a closer look. "Sir? I see fabric. Looks like a shirt sleeve."

McCready knelt beside her. With the triangular tip of a thin trowel, he flicked away crumbs of clay. "Yeah. It's an arm. Lose the shovels. Switch to trowels."

Two hours later, they'd uncovered a tangle of limbs, torsos, and heads. "All right," he said finally. "I need three bags over on this patch of grass. Let's lift them out one at a time. Give me a minute for pictures after each one."

It took another half hour to lay out the three corpses, face-up, on the open body bags. The second of the three dead men—his eyes gone to mush, his cheeks puffed out—was recognizable, barely, as the man whose photograph McCready passed around. "This is Haskell, our undercover agent," he said grimly.

"So your C.I. was telling us true," said Kimball.

"Looks like it," said McCready. "Let's ask him." He turned, looking over one shoulder into the trees beyond the clearing.

"You," he called out. "Behind the oak tree. Step out with your hands where I can see them."

CHAPTER 2

Brockton

"I'M UNARMED," I YELLED in response. "But I've got a Ph.D., and I'm not afraid to use it. Holster your weapons, or I'll talk you to death." I heard laughter as I stepped into the clearing and approached the grave. The three corpses had attracted a cloud of blowflies, some of which strayed—at random or in an excess of eagerness—from the faces of the dead to the faces of the quick. Off to one side lay the wire screen and—atop the mesh—three cartridge casings, two cigarette butts, one wad of chewing gum, and a gum wrapper.

I scrutinized the screen, then the bodies, then the hole in the ground, taking my time before turning to face the assembled agents. "That's it? That's all you got?" Their expressions, which had been confident and proud a moment before, turned panicky. "I can't believe you didn't dig deep enough to find the fourth body." Stunned and mortified, they rushed to the edge of the grave. I chuckled. "Kidding," I said, and a chorus of good-natured groans ensued.

"So, tell me what you've learned from the scene."

Kimball, the eager young agent who'd cast the tire impressions, spoke first. "They all came together," he said. "Just one vehicle."

"The cartridge casings are from two different weapons," said one of the dirt-sifters. "They're all nine millimeter, but the firing-pin impression on one of the headstamps is different." I nodded approvingly; when I'd asked a friend on the campus police force for spent shells, I'd specifically requested shells from two different handguns, so I was pleased that the difference had been noticed. "Also," he went on, "one of the shooters was a woman. There was a trace of lipstick on one of the cigarette butts."

"Good," I said. "So you might get DNA from the butts; maybe from the gum, too. What did you learn from the bodies and the grave?"

"All three were killed with a single shot to the back of the head," said McCready. "Execution-style killings." The "shot to the head" was the least realistic thing about the exercise: It had struck me as both disrespectful and unnecessary to fire bullets into donated bodies simply for the sake of added authenticity, so instead, I'd daubed a circle of red food dye onto the back of each head.

"What else?" A long silence ensued. "Did you find blood in the grave? Did you find blood *anywhere*?" Heads began to shake. "So what does that suggest to you?"

"They were killed somewhere else," said the blond woman. "And brought here."

"Which would explain why there was only one

vehicle," I pointed out. "How often do drug traffickers and drug buyers carpool to the site of the deal?" I noticed a rueful smile on the face of Kimball, the tread-caster; he, of all people, should have given more thought to the absence of a second vehicle. "Also, how likely is it that only three bullets would be fired during a drug-deal shootout? All of them to the back of the victims' heads?" I could see them rethinking the scenario. "Anything else?" The agents looked from the grave to the bodies and back to the grave, then at one another, then at me. I decided they could use a hint. "Look closely at the three faces," I said. "See any differences?"

"Ah," said the blond woman. "The two buyers look fresher than the undercover agent."

"Bingo," I said. "They've got virtually no trace of decomposition—and no maggots—but your guy is beginning to bloat, and he's got a lot of dead maggots on him. See how puffy his cheeks are? His mouth is full of dead maggots. Did anybody look in there?" Faces grimaced; heads shook sheepishly. "So what does the differential decay tell you?"

"He must've been killed before the other two," she replied.

"Exactly," I said. "And he was probably killed somewhere outdoors, where blowflies could get to him and lay their eggs in his eyes and nose and mouth. In fact, judging by the number and the size of the maggots, the flies had access to him for quite awhile. Next time, check for maggots. And collect samples of the biggest ones." I bent down and plucked one from an eye socket, holding it in my palm for them to inspect. "A good forensic entomologist could tell you these maggots were three days old," I said. "These two bodies, on the other hand, don't have any maggots." I pointed to a grainy, grayish-white dab on the neck of the dead agent. "See that smear? Those are blowfly eggs that haven't hatched yet. See any of those on the two fresh bodies?" They didn't. "So knowing that these guys were killed several days after your undercover man—and were probably killed indoors, away from the flies, and buried almost immediately—what does that tell you about your confidential informant?"

"It tells us that he's a lying sack of shit," said McCready. "It calls his whole story into question. And it might mean that *he's* the one who set up our guy and ratted him out to the traffickers."

I nodded. "So be careful who you trust," I said. "Bad guys will lie through their teeth. Bugs, on the other hand?" I pointed to the middle body. "You can always trust what they're telling you."

CHAPTER 3

Brown Field Municipal Airport

San Diego, CA

TWIN SHAFTS OF LIGHT, one green, the other white, cut the ground fog like luminous blades as their source, a rotating airport beacon, turned with blind, unblinking constancy.

Poised at the western end of the runway was a twin-engine business jet, its airframe quivering like a racehorse trembling within the starting gate.

The pilot—his face ghostly in the glow of gauges and screens—worked his way down the takeoff checklist, item by item: Engine instruments, check; fuel, full; altimeter, set; avionics, checked and set; flaps, set for 10 degrees; flight controls—rudder, ailerons, elevator—all moving freely. Satisfied, he throttled back the engines. He did not hurry; he could take all the time he needed or wanted, with no risk of being disturbed. The control tower had closed at seven p.m., and at the moment—a moment shortly after 3 a.m.—the dawn's early light, and the first stirrings of human and aircraft activity, were still hours away. And by then he would be long gone.

The checklist completed, he sighted down the runway, an 8,000 foot ribbon of darkness, defined by jewellike orange lights that seemed to converge at the far end. It was pure coincidence, but it was nonetheless an interesting and apt coincidence, that Mexico, too, lay almost exactly 8,000 feet away as well: a mile and a half due south of him; less than 30 seconds away, if he banked hard right immediately after takeoff.

He folded the paper copy of the flight plan he'd phoned in an hour before—"visual flight direct to Las Vegas"—then took one last look at the sectional chart, the detailed aviation map for Southern California. The map's green and tan landforms were splashed with yellow splotches denoting cities, and the entire area around San Diego was overlaid with a crazed crosshatching of blue lines that represented a multitude of borders and boundaries that made San Diego's airspace the most complex in the nation. Brown Field, a sleepy municipal airport that had no commercial air traffic—mostly single-engine private planes, plus a few corporate jets and charter aircraft—lay just outside the navigational nightmare. As a result, it was possible to get in and out of Brown with minimal hassle and red tape: no queue, no clearances, and no controllers in the tower, at least not at night or on weekends.

It was time. "Brown traffic," he radioed to the empty night sky around him, "Citation 666 rolling on runway Eight Left. Departing the pattern to the northeast." He unleashed the shuddering craft, and it sprang forward, with single-minded purpose and gathering speed and full-throated joy.

Southern California Air Traffic Control Center

San Diego, CA

WILSON RUBBED HIS eyes and reached for his coffee mug. The night was quiet—damnably quiet; the inactivity made it hard to stay awake and alert. The radar screen showed only two aircraft—a Marine Corps F-18 inbound for Miramar, and a civilian Citation twenty miles southeast, just off Brown and climbing.

Wilson's mug was empty. "Shit," he muttered. Spinning in his chair, he snagged the handle of the coffee pot and poured himself a refill, then took a swig and grimaced. By now the coffee had been cooking for three hours; it was no longer a liquid but a sludge, something suitable for treating fenceposts against insects and rot, perhaps, but utterly undrinkable. Wilson took another glance at the screen, reassured himself that his two targets posed no risk to one another, and headed to the sink to dump the coffee, rinse the pot, and put a new packet of grinds into the brew basket. It took him less than 90 seconds.

When he returned to his seat, the F-18 was already on the ground at Miramar; the Citation had leveled off at 2,700 feet and changed course by 90 degrees. "What the hell?" said Wilson aloud, though no one else was there to hear it. The jet was heading southeast now, streaking toward the border; it would enter Mexico's airspace in less than a minute, due south of Otay Mountain. As Wilson stared, the airplane icon began to blink hypnotically, and two words appeared on the screen, flashing in sync with a harsh electronic buzz: LOW ALTITUDE ALERT.

CHAPTER 4

Brockton

I WAS HALFWAY THROUGH my morning shower when Kathleen flung open the bathroom door. "Bill, come quick," she said, then turned and ran. "Hurry. *Hurry!*"

I flipped off the water and grabbed my towel, calling after her, "What's wrong? Kathleen? *Kathleen!* Are you hurt?"

"No, I'm fine," she yelled from the kitchen. "But there's something on the news you need to see."

I mopped the suds from my head and chest and wrapped the towel around my waist. Still dripping, I hurried to the kitchen, where Kathleen watched the Today show every morning over breakfast and coffee.

She tapped the television, where the Today show's news anchor, Ann Curry, was on screen and commencing her 7 a.m. rundown of the morning's top stories. "They teased this story right before the commercial break."

Curry's face was solemn. "Authorities are investigating a fiery plane crash outside San Diego last night," she began. "The crash is believed to have claimed the life of pilot and humanitarian Richard Janus, founder of the nonprofit organization Airlift Relief." The image cut to aerial footage of a steep, rocky hillside, lit by an immense fire blazing high into the sky. "Janus, an investment banker-turned-philanthropist, was reportedly on a solo night flight from San Diego to Las Vegas in his twin-engine jet. Just minutes after takeoff, the plane slammed into a dark mountainside and exploded." The aerial footage was followed by ground shots showing emergency vehicles and firefighters gathering on a ridge above the blaze. "Darkness and rough terrain are hindering search-and-rescue efforts," Curry went on. "And with high winds, wooded terrain, and hundreds of gallons of jet fuel feeding the fire, authorities say the blaze could continue to burn for hours."

The newscast moved on to the next story—the latest psychic meltdown by pop singer Britney Spears—and I turned down the sound. "That's awful," I said. "Poor Richard." Kathleen nodded. I didn't actually know Richard Janus, but Kathleen and I had admired his humanitarian work for years, and we were regular contributors to Airlift Relief, which delivered food and medical supplies to areas devastated by natural disasters and human violence. "The one silver lining," I added, "if you can call it that, is that he probably died instantly. It's possible he never even saw it coming." I had worked a few plane-crash deaths, including the crash of an Air Force transport in the Great Smoky Mountains, and I was familiar with the swiftness and force with which airplanes and bodies could disintegrate.

Kathleen laid a hand on my arm. "Let's send them a check."

"But we send them money every December."

"I know. But this is a huge blow to the organization. Don't you think it would be a nice way to express our sympathy?" There were many things I loved about Kathleen, but her instinctive compassion and reflexive generosity—qualities I myself had benefited from time and again—ranked high on the list.

I smiled and kissed her forehead. "You're a good woman, Kathleen Brockton."

She responded by wrapping her arms around me and giving me a full-body hug. "You're an observant man, Bill Brockton." After a moment, she reached down and gave a quick tug on the towel I was wearing. When it came free she let it fall to the floor, then she slid a hand between us and untied her bathrobe, opening the front to press against me, skin to skin.

"Oh my," I said, surprised at the sudden catch in my breath. "A lucky man, too." After three decades of marriage, Kathleen still retained the capacity to surprise me and even, to take my breath away. I gasped as she reached down and touched me. "To what," I managed to say, "do I owe this stroke of good fortune."

"I was just thinking about Richard Janus's wife," she murmured, "and thinking how devastated I'd be if I lost *you* suddenly. So *carpe diem*, I guess."

"*Carpe me-um*," I murmured back.

She gave me a squeeze hard enough to make me yelp. “One more bad pun,” she whispered in my ear, “and I might just change my mind.”

“My lips are sealed,” I breathed back. I began kissing and nibbling the side of her neck, seeking what I liked to think of as the magic spot. When she groaned, I thought I’d found it. Then I realized that the telephone was ringing, and I echoed her groan.

“Let it ring,” I pleaded. “Don’t answer.” But it was too late; she was already pulling away. “Dammit,” I said.

“Hello?” She sounded as if she’d run to the phone; her eyes were shining, the pupils dilated wide. “Yes. May I tell him who’s calling?” Her gaze grew focused and serious, and she held the receiver toward me.

AN HOUR AFTER the phone call, I was standing on the tarmac with my “go” bag in hand, watching as a white Gulfstream V—its only markings an aircraft registration number stenciled on each of its two engines—touched down at McGhee-Tyson Airport and taxied toward the general-aviation terminal. Taxied toward me.

The jet stopped, but its engines didn’t. The cabin door flipped down and I climbed the stairs that were notched into the door’s inner surface. Clint McCready gave me a hand up—a gesture that continued into a quick handshake—then he pulled the door up and latched it. “Thanks,” he said, motioning me to one of the posh leather seats. “Glad you can help us.”

The engines spooled up, and we began moving as I was taking my seat. Within moments, the acceleration was pressing me into the leather as if I were on a theme-park ride. "This thing has a bit more giddyup than a 737," I remarked.

"Beats the hell out of a Crown Vic, too," he joked. "We're climbing at 4,000 feet a minute. This baby has a range of over 6,000 miles, and a cruise speed of nearly 500 knots—575 miles an hour."

"No offense," I said, "but does the FBI really have such a need for speed?"

"Sure," he said. I couldn't be certain, but I might have heard a trace of irony in his answer. "We got this baby after 9/11. So the Bureau could respond quickly, to terrorist threats anywhere in the world."

I turned toward him, staring, all seriousness now. "Wait. Are you saying Richard Janus's plane was brought down by terrorists?"

"No," he replied quickly, then added, "I'm not saying it *wasn't*, either. All I'm saying is, when the Gulfstream isn't needed for a national security mission, it's an asset we can deploy for other missions. Like high-profile, high-priority investigations."

"And a private plane crash is a high-priority investigation because . . . ?"

He didn't answer, so I completed the question: " . . . because the accident wasn't actually an accident?"

He shrugged. "Too soon to know."

"But you have reason to think Janus was murdered?"

He shrugged again.

I'd worked on enough FBI cases over the years

to know that the Bureau liked to hold its investigative cards close to the vest. So I wasn't surprised, a moment later, when McCready gave me a polite, apologetic smile, pulled his laptop computer from the briefcase beneath his seat, and buried himself in his work.

He did not look up until four hours had passed; not until the Gulfstream had descended to a few thousand feet and the pilot had put us into a steep bank around a rocky peak, one that appeared at first glance to be an active volcano, a plume of thick smoke roiling skyward from it. It was only when I saw the emergency vehicles clustered on a nearby ridge that I realized what I was seeing: I was looking down at the burning remains of Richard Janus's crashed jet, and at the burning remains of Richard Janus himself.

Or was I?

THE FINEST IN FORENSIC SUSPENSE

JEFFERSON BASS's

THE BODY FARM NOVELS

THE BONE YARD

978-0-06-227741-1

Dr. Bill Brockton has spent his career surrounded by death at the Body Farm—the scientific compound where human remains lie exposed to be studied for their secrets. On a trip through Florida's panhandle Brockton's team makes a grisly discovery: a cluster of shallow graves containing the bones of teenage boys, all of whom suffered violent deaths.

THE BONE THIEF

978-0-06-227740-4

A routine case for Dr. Bill Brockton, the exhumation of a body to obtain a bone sample for a DNA paternity test, leads to a shocking discovery when the coffin is opened: the corpse inside has been horribly violated. The grisly find embroils Brockton in a dangerous investigation into a flourishing black market in body parts.

BONES OF BETRAYAL

978-0-06-227739-8

Bill Brockton is shocked when an autopsy reveals the cause of Dr. Leonard Novak's death: a radioactive pellet inside the elderly scientist's body. Is the horrific crime related to Novak's role in the Manhattan Project, the secret World War II program that helped create America's deadliest weapon?